A
Daughter's
Hope

Donna Douglas lives in York with her family. When she is not writing, she enjoys running, reading, watching movies, cooking, drinking cocktails with friends and building Duplo with her grandchildren.

Also by Donna Douglas

A Sister's Wish
A Mother's Journey

A Daughter's Hope

Donna DOUGLAS

ORION

First published in Great Britain in 2022 by Orion Fiction
an imprint of The Orion Publishing Group Ltd
Carmelite House, 50 Victoria Embankment
London EC4Y 0DZ

An Hachette UK Company

1 3 5 7 9 10 8 6 4 2

A CIP catalogue record for this book is
available from the British Library.

ISBN (Mass Market Paperback) 978 1 4091 9095 0
ISBN (eBook) 978 1 4091 9096 7

Typeset by Input Data Services Ltd, Somerset

Printed and bound in Great Britain by Clays Ltd, Elcograf S.p.A.

www.orionbooks.co.uk

To my wonderful granddaughter
Marjorie Ellen Glenda Smith

Chapter 1

July 1942

'Say that again, Beattie Scuttle, and I'll flatten you!'

Big May Maguire glared at the scrawny little woman sitting beside her. Beattie Scuttle was her oldest friend. They had known each other nearly all their sixty-odd years. They had grown up together, gone to school together, worked side by side in the netting lofts and brought up their families together. They had laughed, bickered, cried on each other's shoulders and even had a couple of catfights in the middle of the street. Beattie was closer to Big May than her own sisters.

But she was pushing her luck with what she'd just said.

'I'm only speaking the truth,' Beattie repeated. 'Your Iris is married to my Sam now. That makes her a Scuttle.'

Big May's palms itched to slap the smirk off her face. 'In name only,' she muttered. 'She's still my daughter.'

'And mine too now.' Beattie looked pleased with herself. 'I've always wanted a girl, what with having two boys.'

Be careful what you wish for, Big May thought. She had two daughters, and between them they had both brought her more worry and heartache than her three sons put together.

'I'm glad Iris and Sam are wed at last, anyway,' Beattie said. 'I was beginning to think they'd never get married!'

Now that was something Big May could agree with. Her daughter Iris had kept them all waiting for a long time before she finally agreed to marry Sam Scuttle. Big May sometimes wondered how the poor lad had kept his patience for so long. Any other man would have given up waiting.

But then, Sam was devoted to Iris. He always had been, even when they were bains growing up together. But it had taken Iris many more years before she realised she felt the same.

And even then, she'd dithered about it for a good while before she accepted his proposal. Not that Big May blamed her for that. The poor lass had been through a lot of heartache in her life, losing her first husband and then her little daughter. She had been wretched for so long, it was little wonder she didn't trust happiness when she found it.

But at least she was happy now. Even the steady rain that had sheeted down all day couldn't dampen her daughter's spirits. Big May could hear her from the parlour, laughing and joking with their family and friends. It was lovely to see her so happy at last.

Everyone was enjoying themselves. Beattie, Big May and her daughter-in-law Ruby had worked hard to put on a good spread for Iris and Sam. Now everyone was crowded into their little terraced house at the end of Jubilee Row, enjoying the party. Harry Pearce from the corner shop was already on the piano in the parlour, thumping out some good old tunes, while people sang along and danced around, spilling out into the passageway. The sounds of singing and laughter drifted down to the kitchen where Beattie and Big May sat facing each other across the fireplace. May's grandchildren played around them, running to and fro, dressed in their Sunday best. The youngest, three-year-old Kitty, kept tripping over the hem of her frilly frock as she ran to keep up with her ten-year-old brother and their cousins.

'It's good to have something to celebrate for once,' Beattie said, sipping on her sherry.

'I know what you mean,' Big May agreed. 'Life's been hard on us. Especially this past year.'

She sometimes wondered how they had made it through the past twelve months. Hull had suffered night upon night of relentless air raids that left most of the city in ruins. So many people had died, including Big May's daughter-in-law Dolly and her own granddaughter, Iris's daughter Lucy. Her other daughter-in-law Ruby's house had been nearly destroyed by an incendiary, wiping out most of her belongings and many precious memories.

But May knew she could not complain. There were too many bains without families, too many people without a roof over their heads, for her to shed any tears over what she had lost.

'At least you've still got your family around you,' Beattie said. 'And they're all here for once.'

'Aye.' It was an unexpected blessing that they could all come home for Iris and Sam's wedding. Her eldest, Jimmy, was on leave from the minesweepers, and John, the youngest, had come home from the Merchant Navy for a few days.

And by some good fortune, her twin granddaughters, Sybil and Maudie, were at home for a few days between finishing their basic training and getting their first WAAF posting. It couldn't have worked out better if May had planned it herself.

But having them all around her was bittersweet because it made her realise how empty the place was when they were gone.

'It's just a shame they'll all be gone again soon,' she sighed.

'At least you've still got your Florence.'

May flashed a look at her friend. Beattie was straight-faced, but there was a mischievous gleam in her eye.

As if she had somehow heard her name, at that moment May's eldest daughter flew into the kitchen with an expression like thunder. She stormed past them and headed straight for the back door, pulling her coat off the hook. The children stopped playing and stared at her, agog.

'Where are you going?' Big May asked.

'Out.'

'But it's pouring with rain!'

'I don't care. I know where I'm not wanted.'

Big May and Beattie exchanged looks.

'What's happened now?' May sighed.

Just then, Iris stomped in, her wedding dress bunched up in her fists, the delicate lace a contrast to her flushed, angry face. 'Are you trying to ruin my wedding day?' she demanded.

Florence glared at her, then turned away to shrug on her coat.

Big May looked from one to the other. 'Would someone mind telling me what's going on?'

'Iris told me I wasn't welcome,' Florence said.

'I said you didn't have to stay if you didn't want to.'

'Fine. Then I won't.'

Big May looked at her eldest daughter. Florence towered over her, as tall as her brothers. She had the same dark good looks as the rest of the Maguire children, but in Florence they always seemed marred by a sullen or angry expression. May couldn't remember the last time she'd seen her daughter smile.

'What did you say to your sister?' she asked.

Florence turned on her, brows drawn low over snapping dark eyes. 'That's right. It has to be me, doesn't it? It couldn't be our Iris's fault.'

'It *was* your fault,' Iris protested. 'Just because you're jealous.'

'Jealous? Of you marrying Sam Scuttle?'

'Now then. That's my lad you're talking about!' Beattie piped up.

4

Big May turned to Iris. 'Well? What's been said?'

'She said my wedding was a waste of time and money.' Iris glared at her sister.

'I only said it was a lot of fuss over nothing,' Florence shrugged. 'I don't know why you couldn't have just gone to the register office and got it done. After all, it's not like it's your first time, is it?'

'You see?' Iris said to May. 'She's jealous.'

'Of course I am!' Florence shot back. 'Having a husband is the be-all and end-all of everything, isn't it?'

'You never managed it,' Iris said in a low voice.

Big May saw her eldest daughter's face flush and stepped in quickly. 'Take no notice of Iris, she's only joking,' she said.

'No, I'm not,' Iris snapped. 'I'm speaking the truth. Talk about always the bridesmaid, never the bride!'

'I didn't ask to be your bridesmaid!'

'And I didn't want you!' Iris flashed back. 'I only asked you because Ma said I had to.'

'Iris!' Big May put in.

'As if I'd want you looking miserable in my wedding pictures,' Iris muttered.

Big May glanced at Beattie. She was looking down, trying not to laugh. Big May pressed her lips together to hide her own smile, but not quick enough for Florence.

'I might have known you'd take her side,' she snapped.

'I'm not taking anyone's side.'

'No? I can see you think she's funny.'

'We're only having a laugh. You should try it, it might crack that sour old face of yours!' Iris put in.

'That's enough, Iris.' May turned to rebuke her daughter, but Florence had already slammed out of the house, banging the back door behind her. 'You'd best go and apologise,' May said.

5

'I'll do no such thing!' Iris replied. 'Let her sulk if she wants to. She'll come back in when she's calmed down, I daresay.'

And how long will that be? Big May peered out of the kitchen window through the rain that streamed down the steamy glass. Florence's prickly pride meant she would rather catch her death than climb down off her high horse. 'She'll get soaked out there.'

'I don't care. I'm going back to my wedding.'

Iris gathered up her dress and flounced off, leaving Big May and Beattie alone in the kitchen.

Beattie chuckled. 'Never a dull moment with your girls, is there?'

'No,' Big May said. 'No, there in't.'

She looked towards the back door, wondering whether to go out and talk to Florence, then decided against it. Iris was right – it was better to let her calm down.

Florence was her own worst enemy, she thought. She managed to rub everyone up the wrong way.

Big May Maguire loved all her children, but she could never get close to Florence. She wasn't like the others. She had always been so clever and complicated, even as a child. And sharp, too – she had a tongue like a knife blade.

Perhaps she would have been different if she'd had a home and family of her own, like Iris and the lads. May might have felt closer to her then; she would have been able to offer her help and advice. But Florence had gone her own way. She had a good job with the Corporation, she made her own money and depended on no one. She didn't need anyone, least of all her mother.

Big May sometimes felt her eldest daughter looked down on the rest of the family, in their humble terrace, scraping together their living on the trawlers and down at the fish docks.

'As I was saying,' Beattie chuckled. 'At least you've still got your Florence.'

'Aye,' Big May said grimly. 'So I have.'

God help me, she thought.

Chapter 2

Florence could hear the sounds of laughter and singing drift-ing from the house as she stood shivering in the rain. No one bothered to come after her or make sure she was all right. They'd already forgotten all about her.

She had been too hasty in storming out, she decided. There was nowhere to shelter in the back yard, and her coat was no match for the steadily falling rain. Her best shoes were already soaked through, and her carefully styled hair clung in miserable tendrils around her face. And it had taken her ages with a curling iron, too. Florence hated wasted effort.

She didn't even want to be at the wretched wedding. She had only taken the day off work because her mother had in-sisted she should be there.

'You've got to do it for your sister,' Big May had said. As if Iris cared whether Florence was there or not. She had already made that very clear. Besides, she was too busy showing off to everyone in Jubilee Row, grinning like the Cheshire cat, just because she'd snagged herself another husband.

You never managed it.

Her sister's cruel taunt came back to her.

It wasn't what Iris had said that had upset Florence. It was the way her mother had just stood there and let her say it. Oh, she'd made a half-hearted attempt to step in, but Florence had caught the smirk on her face, even though she'd tried to hide it. She thought Iris was so funny, with her cruel wise-cracks and taunts.

But the minute Florence bit back – well, that was another story, wasn't it? God forbid she should ever say anything to upset her precious sister.

Talk about the odd one out, Florence thought. Her mother couldn't have made her feelings more plain if she'd tried. Iris was the favoured one, all right. She was like their mother in every way. They went shopping together, cooked meals together, looked after the children between them; they even worked together down at the netting loft.

And then there was Florence, forty-two years old, no husband, no children and still living at home with her parents.

No wonder her mother couldn't be doing with her.

The back door opened behind her.

'If you've come to tell me to make it up to Iris, you can forget it,' Florence said, not turning round. 'I'll apologise to her when she does the same to me . . .'

'Florence?'

She looked over her shoulder to see her friend Joyce Shelby standing behind her, sheltering under an umbrella.

'I thought you were Ma,' she mumbled, turning away.

'She's still in the kitchen, putting the world to rights with Beattie Scuttle.' Joyce picked her way across the yard to stand next to her, putting the umbrella over her head. 'I saw you having words with your Iris and came looking for you.'

'It's nice to know someone cares. No one else has even noticed I've gone.' As if to prove her point, a roar of laughter went up from inside the house.

'Don't be like that,' Joyce said mildly. She was the same age as Florence, a slender, quietly spoken woman, with brown hair and kind blue eyes. They had been friends since they were at elementary school together. They had both grown up on Jubilee Row, and played together on the cobbled streets where her own nieces and nephews now played.

'It's true. They're all too busy congratulating my sister on finding herself a husband.'

She hated the bitterness in her voice. Perhaps Iris was right, she thought. Perhaps she was jealous?

But deep down she knew she wasn't. She was pleased for Iris. God knows, her poor sister had been through an awful time, and she deserved some happiness.

'Do you wish it was you?' Joyce asked.

'Marrying Sam Scuttle? No, thank you!' Florence laughed. 'Don't get me wrong, he's nice enough. But he's hardly my type!'

'I don't mean Sam! I mean, do you wish it was you getting married?'

Florence thought about the question. No, if she was jealous of Iris it wasn't because of her new husband. It was because her sister belonged in a way that Florence never could.

All those weeks leading up to the wedding, Florence had watched enviously as her mother and sisters-in-law had rallied around Iris, planning and organising her big day, preparing food, even offering her their clothing coupons so she could get herself something special to wear.

Florence had tried to join in with the preparations. But when she had offered to help, they had rebuffed her.

'Oh no, we can manage. It in't your sort of thing, is it?' her mother had said. So Florence had been made an unwanted bridesmaid, as much to keep her quiet as anything else, while the rest of the Maguire women closed ranks around the bride, like a secret club that only wives and mothers could join.

'I think my mother wishes it were me,' she said. 'She's never forgiven me for not finding a husband.'

'That was hardly your fault, was it? You might have been married to Donald by now, if he'd come home . . .'

Florence stared at her friend, startled to hear the name after so long. Donald Davis had been her sweetheart once, but twenty-five years on, she could barely remember what he looked like.

Donald had worked with her older brother Jimmy on the trawlers, but when the Great War began, they had all signed up and gone marching off to France. Florence remembered them all going off together, their faces bright and full of hope, laughing about how they would come home once they'd seen off the Germans. Donald had taken Florence in his arms and kissed her in full view of everyone, much to her embarrassment, and made her promise to wait for him.

It had been her first and her last kiss.

Many of the local lads had eventually come home when the war ended, and Florence had watched as her friends got married one by one. Iris married her sweetheart, and her brothers all wed their girls too. But Florence was one of the unlucky ones, and she was painfully aware of the pity in everyone's eyes.

'You'll find someone else, I'm sure,' her mother had tried to console her.

But the reality was there simply hadn't been enough young men to go round, and Florence had already made up her mind that she wasn't going to be one of those girls, desperately pining and seeking a man. Like so many other young women, she was going to make her own way in the world and fend for herself. She stayed on at school and gained her qualifications, then found a good job in the Accounts department at the Corporation, supervising the typing pool.

But no matter how well she did and how much she had achieved, she always felt as if it wasn't enough for her family.

She could see her own failure reflected in the disappointment in her mother's eyes.

'Anyway, finding a husband isn't the be-all and end-all,' Joyce said, interrupting her thoughts. 'I mean, look at me!'

Joyce was a cautionary tale, all right, Florence thought. Unlike her own family, Joyce's parents had wanted her to stay on at school. But instead Joyce had shocked everyone by eloping with a local tinker called Reg Shelby. Their marriage had quickly turned sour, and poor Joyce had suffered years of unhappiness and abuse before she had found the courage to divorce him.

Now she was perfectly happy living on her own, running the ironmonger's shop on Anlaby Road, assisted by Beattie Scuttle's eldest son Charlie.

'Have you heard from Reg lately?' Florence asked.

'No, thank God.' Joyce suppressed a shudder. 'Last time I heard from him, he was making some other poor woman's life a misery over in Grimsby. But I don't care what he does as long as he stays well away from me!' She smiled at Florence. 'If you'd been through the same unhappiness I've had, you'd know there are a lot worse things than being on your own.'

Just at that moment, the back door flew open and Florence heard her mother's voice coming through the darkness, rising over the sound of the falling rain.

'You've made your point. Now are you coming back in or what?'

Joyce raised her eyebrows. 'Looks like you've been summoned.'

'You go. I'll be there in a minute.'

'Here, you'd best take this.' Joyce handed her the umbrella. Then, as she turned to go, she added, 'Remember what I said, Florence. It's far better to be on your own than married to the wrong person.'

Florence glanced past her towards the house. She could hardly see anything through the dense blackout and the driving rain, but she could feel Big May's beady eyes on her all the same.

'Try telling that to my mother,' she murmured.

Chapter 3

'Where's your sister? Surely she should be home by now?'

Maudie Maguire watched her mother peering anxiously out of the kitchen window into the rainy back yard. She had been doing the same thing on and off for the past hour.

'You know what Syb's like,' Maudie said. 'She's probably lost track of time again.'

'As long as she doesn't make you miss your train.' Her mother turned back to the bread she was spreading with dripping. She had been trying to keep busy all day, and Maudie knew it was so she didn't have to think about them leaving. 'Where is she, anyway?'

'She went into town to meet some of the girls from Hammonds. Peggy and Cath are on leave from the ATS, so they wanted to catch up before we go.'

'Didn't you want to meet them too?'

Maudie shook her head. 'They're more Syb's friends than mine. Besides, I'd rather stay here.'

Maudie was secretly annoyed at her sister for going out. Anyone could see Ruby was struggling, and it would have meant so much to her if she could have spent one last day with both her girls.

Poor Mum, Maudie thought. Her family was her whole life, and now they had all left her. Their eldest sister Ada was married with a home of her own, and their father was away at sea for months on the minesweepers.

At least she and Sybil had managed to get a few days at home on leave between finishing their training in London and starting their first official posting. But she wasn't sure now if it had been a wise thing to do, since it meant going through the wrench of saying goodbye to the family all over again.

'It's lucky we've been posted local,' she said, desperate to cheer her mother up.

'Aye,' Ruby agreed. 'I s'pose they could have sent you anywhere, couldn't they?'

'We could have ended up on the south coast, or down in the West Country.' It had been nothing more than sheer good luck that they had ended up at RAF Holme, a bomber station about twenty miles outside Hull.

'It still feels a long way away, though,' her mother sighed. 'The house is so quiet without you two.'

'Without Sybil, you mean!'

Ruby smiled sadly. 'I suppose so.' She looked at Maudie. 'You will look after your sister, won't you?'

'Don't I always?'

'I know,' Ruby smiled fondly. 'You're a good lass. And it was so kind of you to give up your chance to—'

'Don't,' Maudie cut her off before she could finish her sentence. 'You know I wouldn't have gone anywhere without Syb.'

'Talk of the devil . . .' Ruby turned as the back door flew open and Sybil breezed in, her coat flapping.

'What time do you call this?' Maudie glanced at the clock. 'You promised you'd be back by half past.'

'Keep your hair on, I'm here now.' Sybil threw her hat down on the kitchen table and helped herself to a sandwich.

Ruby slapped her hand away. 'Don't touch them. They're for the journey.'

'What difference does it make whether I eat them now or later?'

'Because you'll be hungry again by the time we get on the train and you'll end up wanting to share mine,' Maudie said.

Sybil grinned at her. 'We're twins. We're supposed to share everything,' she said through a mouthful of sandwich.

'Don't I know it?' Maudie sighed. She and Sybil had been inseparable since they'd come into the world twenty-two years earlier. Sybil, typically, had shouldered her way out first, never being one to miss anything.

'Listen.' Ruby lifted her hand. 'Is that Pop I can hear?'

Maudie cocked her head. From out in the street came the faint clip-clop of hooves on the cobbles. She hurried up the passageway and opened the front door.

There was her grandfather, known to all as Pop Maguire, sitting on top of his wooden rully, his cap pulled down low over his eyes, the collar of his battered coat turned up against the rain. Bertha, his faithful old horse, stood still, her heavy head nodding.

'All right, lass?' Pop caught sight of her and pushed the peak of his cap back to get a better look. 'My, you're a fine sight.'

Maudie glanced down at herself. She had forgotten she was in her WAAF uniform. She had taken a lot of trouble with it as it was their first posting. Her blue skirt and tunic were neatly pressed, the brass buttons gleaming thanks to a lavish amount of Duraglit and elbow grease.

Pop twisted round in his seat. 'May?' he called out, his voice ringing down the street. 'Have you seen our Maudie?'

Almost immediately, the front door opened and her grandmother's bulky form appeared, arms folded across the chest of her flowered pinny. Maudie knew full well she had been lurking behind the lace parlour curtains, watching out for them. Very little happened on Jubilee Row without Big May Maguire knowing about it.

'Will I do, Grandma?' Maudie turned to face her, suddenly shy. She could feel herself blushing as her grandmother's appraising gaze moved up and down. Big May was a tough woman to please.

'I reckon you will, lass.' Her grandmother's voice sounded gruff with emotion. Maudie could have sworn she saw a tear in her eye. But that wasn't possible because everyone knew Big May never cried.

'What about me? Will I do?'

Sybil appeared behind her, still fumbling with the buttons of her tunic. Her tie was crooked and her cap sat askew on her head. But typical Sybil, she somehow managed to carry all her faults with aplomb.

Maudie looked at her sister and saw herself mirrored in her slim figure, dark hair and brown eyes. People often asked her what it was like to see her face on someone else, but Maudie had never known any different. She and Sybil had always been two halves of a whole.

'Look at them,' Ruby said fondly. 'My babies.'

'They in't babies any more,' Big May said. 'They're young women, off to do their duty for their country.'

She pressed the heel of her hand into her eye, and this time Maudie was certain she was dashing away a tear.

By the time Pop had hoisted their kitbags into the back of the cart and covered them with canvas to keep the rain off, most of the street had turned out to see them off. Seeing all their friends and neighbours standing on their doorsteps made Maudie feel emotional all over again.

For the first time, it began to dawn on her that they were going away for good. Even when they were in London, Jubilee Row had been her whole life for the past twenty-two years. Her whole family lived on the narrow little terrace, bordered by the fish docks of Hull's Hessle Road. It suddenly hit her like a blow that she would no longer be able to nip in for a gossip with her grandmother or her aunties every day, or hear the laughter of her niece and nephews ringing out as they played on the street.

Their mother hugged them both fiercely.

'You will let me know when you've arrived safely, won't you?' she said.

'We're only going down the road!' Sybil scoffed, wriggling from her mother's embrace to scramble up onto the bench seat beside Pop.

'We'll write as soon as we can,' Maudie promised. 'And we'll come and see you the minute we get leave.'

'What did you have to say that for?' Sybil hissed, as Pop jingled the reins and the rully lurched off. 'We can't keep coming back here every five minutes, you know. We might have better things to do with our time.'

Maudie looked sideways at her sister. 'You mean boys?'

'Why not? Just think of it, all those handsome pilots!'

Maudie sighed. Sybil's lively social life took up most of her time. She usually had at least one boyfriend on the go, often more.

While Maudie had been learning cloud formations and memorising weather charts in London, Sybil had spent most of her time chasing around the West End with a dashing Frenchman who had come over to England with De Gaulle and his Free French army.

'What about Jacques?' she asked.

Sybil blinked at her. 'Who?'

'The man who declared his undying love to you at King's Cross Station two days ago?' He had caused quite a stir, running along the platform beside the train, gabbling away in French.

'Oh, him.' Sybil smiled at the memory. 'He was fun while he lasted. But it doesn't do to go round getting too serious, you know. The war's put paid to all that. No, we've just got to have our fun while we can.'

'I reckon you're having enough fun for both of us.'

Sybil nudged her in the ribs. 'This is our chance to change all that. You'll see, Maud. We'll have our pick of men at Holme.'

Maudie didn't reply. She was too preoccupied staring at her sister's silk-clad legs, so elegant next to the thick lisle she wore.

'You do know silk stockings are for officers only?' she reminded her.

'So?' Sybil was already delving into the sandwiches their mother had made for them.

'So you'll be in trouble if you're caught.'

Sybil grinned mischievously. 'They'll have to catch me first!'

'I wish you'd take this seriously, Syb. You were bad enough in training, but we're proper WAAFs now. They're not going to put up with any nonsense from you. You can't go round breaking the rules.'

'Honestly, Maudie, you and your rules!' She proffered the bag. 'Want one?'

'No thanks.' Maudie turned away. There was no point in telling her to save the food. There was no point in telling her sister anything.

She was going to have her work cut out keeping her promise to their mother, Maudie thought as they lurched down Hessle Road, heading for the station.

Chapter 4

They reached Paragon Station just as the guard was blow-ing his whistle. Sybil and Maudie ran towards the platform, shouting and dragging their kitbags, but the train was al-ready pulling away slowly, disappearing in a belch of dirty steam.

Maudie stood and watched it go in despair.

'Now what do we do?'

Sybil shrugged. 'Wait for the next one, I suppose.'

'But they're expecting us at Holme by four o'clock.'

'Then they'll just have to wait, won't they?'

Maudie looked back down the empty train track. 'That won't make a very good impression.'

Sybil sat down on her kitbag and took out her cigarettes. Maudie stared at her in frustration.

'This is all your fault,' she accused.

'Me?'

'If you hadn't come back so late from meeting Peggy and Cath . . .'

'Oh, give it a rest, Maud,' Sybil said irritably. 'You've been moaning about it since I got back. I was enjoying myself and lost track of time, all right? You should try it sometime,' she muttered under her breath.

'And where would we be if we were both as irresponsible as you?' Maudie turned away in disgust and noticed a sandy-haired young man in an RAF uniform standing a few yards away, watching them with interest. Maudie glared back at him until he turned away.

'I'm going to find out when the next train is due,' she said.

'Bring us back some matches, if you can find any. I've forgotten mine,' Sybil called after her.

'Get them yourself,' Maudie muttered under her breath. As she stomped past him, the young man turned his head to watch her. Maudie ignored him.

It took her a few minutes to find out the time of the next train. Paragon Station was crowded with service personnel, a hubbub of kitbags and khaki and blue. Many had gathered around the WVS tea wagon. Seeing the woman at the hatch, so proud in her green uniform, gave Maudie a pang. Her mother was a stalwart of the Women's Voluntary Service and often spent her days manning such a wagon, handing out tea and sandwiches.

Maudie queued up with the others to buy a box of matches for Sybil. As she waited to be served, her gaze went to a group of young girls, saying tearful goodbyes to their families. She felt tears sting her own eyes as she remembered her mother and father seeing them off three months earlier, when they set off for their basic training. It seemed like a lifetime ago now.

When she returned, Sybil was not alone. Maudie's heart sank when she saw the young man leaning down beside her, talking to her. She suspected he had been waiting for his moment to pounce.

Sybil turned to smile at Maudie as she approached. 'Here she is now,' she said. 'You took your time.'

'I queued up to get these for you.'

Maudie held the matchbox out to her, but Sybil held up her lighted cigarette and said, 'I don't need them now; Mike gave me a light.'

The young man straightened up, brushing down his trousers. 'I'm Mike Mitchell,' he said.

'Pleased to meet you. Sybil, our next train isn't for another hour.'

'Oh, that's all right,' Sybil said breezily. 'Mike says he'll take us.'

'I couldn't help overhearing you saying you were on your way to Holme?' Mike said. He was well spoken, Maudie noticed, but with the faintest hint of a local accent. 'I'm stationed there myself – I'm just waiting for the lorry to pick me up. You're welcome to have a lift if you don't mind roughing it a bit?'

'Of course we don't,' Sybil answered for them. 'That's very kind of you. In't it, Maudie?'

Maudie looked up and down the station platform, thinking about it. It was a long wait for the next train, and she didn't want them to be late on their first day.

Besides, she could see the gleam in Sybil's eye and knew she had already taken a fancy to Mike, though he wasn't her usual type. He was tall and sort of gawky-looking; his sandy hair was cut too high over his ears, and there was a gap between his front teeth. But his freckled face wasn't bad to look at, and his eyes were a nice shade of somewhere between amber and green. They reminded Maudie of Beattie Scuttle's cat.

'Thank you,' she said. 'A lift would be very nice.'

No sooner had she said the words than a voice roared across the station.

'Mitch! Put those WAAFs down immediately. You don't know where they've been!'

Everyone on the platform turned to look their way, and Mike blushed, the tips of his ears turning red.

'I'm sorry,' he mumbled. 'Take no notice of Ackroyd.'

22

He slung his kitbag over his shoulder and picked up theirs, one in each hand, and carried them towards the station entrance, where a fair-haired young man lounged against the wall. He was tall and angular, with sharp cheekbones and a long thin nose. He looked amused to see Sybil and Maudie.

'And what have we here?' he drawled, pushing his cap back to get a better look. 'Picked up two girls, Mitch? And I thought you were such a shy boy.'

'Two new recruits for Holme. I said we'd give them a lift.'

'Delightful. I'm all for a bit of female company.' The young man winked at Maudie. She blushed furiously and looked away, which only seemed to amuse him more.

'This is Pilot Officer Ackroyd,' Mike introduced them. 'Be warned, he has a reputation.'

'And thoroughly deserved, I assure you. Well, come along, ladies,' he swept his arm to usher them through the door. 'Your carriage awaits.'

Their 'carriage' was a battered old lorry, with an impatient LAC at the wheel. He glared at Maudie and Sybil in the wing mirror as Mike and Ackroyd tossed their kitbags into the back of the truck, then gave each of the girls a leg-up.

Ackroyd launched Maudie over the tailgate into the back of the truck, straight into the lap of a grinning pilot officer.

'Excuse me,' she muttered.

'No harm done, I assure you.' He looked from Sybil to Maudie and back again. 'Good gracious, am I seeing double?'

'Double trouble, you mean!' a gruff Scotsman at the back of the truck muttered.

There were at least a dozen young men, crammed in two rows on either side of the lorry. Maudie was embarrassed to find herself the focus of so much attention, but Sybil seemed to be taking it all in her stride as she sat opposite, wedged in between Ackroyd and a burly Welshman.

'First posting, is it?' the pilot officer asked Maudie. He was breathtakingly handsome, with dark hair and intense blue eyes.

She smiled back nervously. 'Yes.'

'Thought so. You can always tell the rookie WAAFs by the duff knots in their ties!' he grinned.

'And those long flapping greatcoats!' the Welshman joined in.

They all laughed, and Maudie stared down at her lisle-clad knees in dismay.

'Pay no attention, I'm only teasing you,' the pilot officer said. 'I'm Tom, by the way. Tom Davenport.'

'Maudie Maguire.' She bent down to shuffle her kitbag under her seat.

'Here, let me.' Tom reached down to help her and let out a groan. 'Christ, that's heavy,' he said. 'Don't tell me you've smuggled your boyfriend in?'

'We had to,' Sybil spoke up. 'We heard there were no decent men at Holme.'

Tom laughed. 'And what do you think now you've met us?'

Sybil looked him up and down. 'I'll let you know,' she said finally.

'Let me know if I can do anything to improve your opinion.'

'Oh, I will.'

Maudie saw the flirtatious glance that passed between Tom Davenport and her sister. Poor Mitch, she thought. He wasn't going to get a look-in.

Not that he seemed too troubled as he sat wedged in beside Maudie, their shoulders touching as the lorry lurched along. Maudie ducked her head to try to catch one last glimpse of the city as it disappeared behind them.

'Not much to see, is there?' Mitch seemed to read her thoughts. 'The Luftwaffe saw to that.'

He was right, Maudie thought. A year ago, German bombers had laid waste to the centre of Hull, reducing it to little more than a heap of smoking rubble. So many of the city's familiar buildings and landmarks had been destroyed that Maudie scarcely recognised it any more.

Among the buildings that had gone was Hammonds, the department store where Maudie and Sybil had worked selling hats. They'd managed to reopen again in West Street, where the staff air-raid shelter had been. But it wasn't the same. It was almost a relief when they were called up to register for war work.

'Are you local?' she asked.

'My family lives in Kirk Ella.'

That explained the well-to-do accent, Maudie thought. Anyone who spoke so nicely would have to come from a smart suburb like that. She imagined his father must be a solicitor, or a bank manager.

'How about you?' Mitch asked.

'Hessle Road.' She braced herself, waiting for him to lose interest or turn his nose up at her. But his expression didn't even flicker.

'Where will you be working at Holme?' he asked.

'The Met Office.'

'Met girls, eh?' Ackroyd spoke up. 'So you'll be the one deciding if it's safe for us to fly or not?'

'I hope not!' Maudie thought about all the instruments she had learned about over the past month: the barometers and barographs, thermographs and hygrometers, wind anemometers and rain gauges. She had barely got to grips with what they all meant.

'Shut up, Ackroyd. Can't you see you're terrifying the poor wee girl?' the Scotsman, whose name was Ferguson, said. He was an older man, in his thirties, with a weather-beaten face and bright green eyes. 'Take no notice of him, lassie,' he said to Maudie. 'It's not all in your hands.'

'Although a few prayers never go amiss,' Mitch said, and the other men muttered in grim agreement.

Maudie looked around at them all. They seemed like nice lads. A couple were very young, barely more than boys, and a couple, like the Scotsman, were a few years older. Most of them were around her age, full of fun and laughter.

Maudie discovered that they were all air crew, returning to RAF Holme after a couple of weeks away at a bomber station in Lincolnshire, where they had been learning to fly Avro Lancaster planes, a replacement for the Halifaxes they had been using.

'Except Mitch, he's been on leave. Lucky blighter!' Ackroyd reached across and ruffled his friend's hair.

'I had a broken arm!' Mitch protested.

'You know what's going to happen, don't you?' the Welshman, Owen, piped up beside Maudie. 'We're going to be up there, flying over the target, and he'll be fumbling around, trying to find the right button to get the bomb bay open!'

'I'm sure I can pick it up quickly enough,' Mitch said. 'I mean, how hard can it be if they can teach you lot?'

'And now we're going back to Holme,' Tom said, pulling a face.

'What's it like there?' Sybil leaned forward.

'It's a dump!' Ferguson grumbled.

'It's not that bad,' Tom said. 'Just a bit small, that's all.'

'A small dump, then!' Ferguson said.

'Anyway, you'll find out soon enough.' Tom lifted the canvas flap and peered out as the truck turned off the road and began to bump along a rough track. Maudie had to cling onto the edge of the bench seat to stop herself tipping off. 'Looks like we're nearly here.'

'Aye, I can tell by the smell.' Ferguson inhaled a deep breath, then turned to Sybil and Maudie. 'Well, here we are, lasses. Holme, sweet Holme!'

Chapter 5

Their first sight of RAF Holme was not promising.

The station consisted of a huddle of rounded Nissen huts with cinder paths leading here and there, all looking dismal under the darkening canopy of sky. A few grey-blue-clad figures could be seen trooping from one hut to another.

At the end of the track was a two-storeyed building, and beyond that a vast empty space. As they watched, an aircraft lumbered across it on its way to the runway. Sybil looked at Maudie and could tell immediately she was thinking the same thing.

This was it. After weeks of training, poring over books, going to lectures and enduring hours of drill practice, they were finally fully fledged WAAFs with a real job to do.

They booked in at the Guard Room and were told to make their way to the Control Tower to report for duty.

The Met Office was on the ground floor. It was a large room, with windows on two sides looking across the airfield. A long plotting bench dominated the centre of the room, where a WAAF sat feverishly scribbling on a chart while another reeled off figures aloud from a long scroll of white paper. They were watched closely by the Met officer, a middle-aged, bespectacled man in plain clothes, and a pair of senior air-crew officers. No one looked very happy, Maudie noticed.

A moment later, the officers left and the man noticed them for the first time. 'Good lord, who are you?' he asked, peering at them over his spectacles.

Sybil found her voice first. Straightening her shoulders, she announced, 'We're the new Met assistants, sir.'

'New girls?' The man turned to the WAAFs poring over the chart. 'Did you know we were getting new girls?'

The WAAFs looked blank. 'No, sir,' they chorused.

'That's just what we need. As if we weren't busy enough already!' the Met officer groaned. 'Oh well, you'd better show them round,' he said to one of the WAAFs. 'Give them a quick tour, then send them up to the Waafery. Let them deal with them up there. And mind you get back here as soon as you can,' he called after her.

'Don't mind him. He's always tetchy on ops night,' the girl said as she closed the door quietly behind them. 'I'm Rose, by the way.'

'I'm Maudie, and this is Sybil.'

'Twins, eh?' She was about the same age as them, tall and slender with sleek chestnut hair tucked neatly into her cap. Every one of her buttons gleamed. 'That must be fun. You're lucky you ended up posted to the same place.'

Maudie looked at Sybil and saw her own horror dawning on her sister's face. It hadn't even occurred to either of them that they might be separated. Much as she moaned about her sister, the idea of them not being together filled her with panic.

Rose took them around the Control Tower, pointing out the Flying Control Office, which took up the entire upper floor, and the Signals Office and the Telephone Exchange on either side of the Met Office. At the far end of the corridor was a door mysteriously called 'Intelligence'.

'Don't worry about that. We lesser mortals aren't allowed to go in there,' Rose told them. 'The girls keep themselves to themselves.'

Outside, she pointed out the Navigation Office and the air crews' Briefing Room on the other side of the main cinder road.

'They're always coming over to the Met Office after debriefing to let us know how right or wrong our forecast has been,' she grimaced. 'A lot of the pilots take our reports seriously, but some think it's all mumbo jumbo.'

Maudie thought about Ackroyd's mocking smile in the back of the truck. It was hard to believe he took anything seriously.

When the tour was over, Rose summoned a passing truck and asked the LAC to take them up to the WAAFs' living quarters – the Waafery, as everyone called it. This turned out to be a dismal semicircle of about ten Nissen huts at the furthest reach of the station, beyond the perimeter of the airfield, the hangars and the runways, a no man's land on the fringe of woodland and fields.

Maudie looked back down the track as she clambered out of the truck. She could barely make out the main buildings in the distance.

'You might have to beg or borrow a bicycle if you don't want a long walk every day,' the LAC said cheerfully, reading her thoughts. 'Either that or hope you can flag down a car coming from one of the hangars.'

Miss Leech, the section officer, was waiting for them in the WAAF Guard Room. She was a motherly woman in her forties, with a soft, round, smiling face and pink cheeks. Maudie and Sybil offered their papers and were issued with towels, sheets and pillowcases and instructed to go to Hut Number Nine.

The huts were long and low, with ten beds arranged down each side at right angles to the walls. Each bed had a small chest of drawers beside it and a couple of hooks above.

There were several girls there already, gathered around the coke stove at one end. A lanky redhead was ironing a shirt, her iron precariously plugged to the light fitting above her head. She froze as Maudie and Sybil walked in.

'Thank God for that,' she breathed out, her hand to her chest. 'I thought you were the section officer, come to do an inspection.'

A long-limbed blonde, with corporal's stripes on her sleeves, got up and approached them.

'You're the new girls?' She looked from one to the other. Thankfully she didn't comment on them being twins; Maudie had heard it so many times that day, she thought she might scream. 'I'm Corporal Banks. There are spare beds there, if you'd like to unpack?'

She pointed to two empty bed frames on opposite sides of the hut. Maudie immediately started to drag her kitbag towards one of them, but Sybil hesitated.

'Is something wrong?' Corporal Banks asked.

Maudie knew what her sister was going to say before the words came out of her mouth.

'Can't we be next to each other?' she asked.

'I beg your pardon?' Corporal Banks blinked at her.

'We'd like to be next to each other. We're not used to being apart, you see.'

'You're only opposite each other,' the corporal pointed out.

'Yes, but we'd rather be next to each other. If it's all the same to you?' Sybil gave the corporal her most winning smile. It usually worked well, but Corporal Banks was unmoved.

'Those are the only beds we have spare,' she said coldly.

Maudie cringed. 'It really doesn't matter—' she started to say, but Sybil interrupted her.

'Perhaps someone would like to move?'

She looked around hopefully at the other girls. They looked back at her with stony faces. Talk about making an impression!

'It's all right, really,' Maudie stepped in quickly. 'We're happy where we are. In't that right, Sybil?' She sent her sister a pleading look.

'I'm relieved to hear it,' Corporal Banks replied. 'Get unpacked quickly, we'll take you down to the Airmen's Mess for something to eat at seven.'

With a last long look at Sybil, she turned and went back to her place beside the stove. One of the other girls leaned over and whispered to her, and then a couple of them started giggling.

'What did you have to say that for?' Maudie hissed at Sybil.

Sybil shrugged. 'It never hurts to ask, does it?' she said.

Maudie stared at her sister. Sybil had the cheek of the devil, their grandmother always said. With that, and a big dose of charm, she usually managed to get her own way.

But Maudie had a feeling these girls would not be pushed around so easily. Especially Corporal Banks. The way she was looking at Sybil, she clearly already had her card marked.

Chapter 6

They dumped their kitbags and then unstacked and made up their beds.

Learning to make a bed to Air Force standards had been a big challenge for both of them. The mattress came in three hard, flat sections, called 'biscuits', which had to be laid out every night and then stacked in a neat pile again every morning.

Maudie was trying to tuck in the sheet, starched as stiff as cardboard, when one of the girls came over. She was mousey-haired, with a slight build and pale, watery eyes.

'I've left the top two drawers empty,' she said, nodding to the chest of drawers that separated two beds.

'Thanks.'

The girl sat down on the bed next to Maudie's. 'I'm Joan,' she said. 'Joan Mason.'

'Maudie Maguire.'

Maudie tucked the sheet untidily under one corner. It wouldn't pass inspection, but it was the best she could do. She glanced over at Sybil, who seemed to have given up even trying to tuck hers in.

'I don't mind moving?' The girl, Joan, spoke up again. She had a clear, well-spoken voice with a southern accent. 'If you want to be next to your sister?'

'Thank you, but we're fine.'

'Are you sure? She seemed very insistent . . .'

Maudie glanced across at Sybil, who was now struggling to spread out her grey official-issue blanket over the bumpy mattress. 'She'll be all right. But thank you for the offer.' She flashed the girl a quick smile.

She started to unpack her belongings, hanging up her gas cape on the peg beside the bed and her greatcoat and best blue uniform on hangers underneath it. All the while, she could feel Joan watching her.

'Have you come far?' she asked.

'Only from Hull.'

'That's not far at all. Lucky you. My family are all down in Sussex. Heaven knows when I'll see them again.'

Maudie had no idea where that was, but from Joan's doleful expression, she guessed it was a long way.

'Have you been here long?' she asked.

'A month, I think. Although it seems like a lifetime!' she smiled. Her smile transformed her little face, lighting up her pale eyes. 'Are you an R/T operator too? They didn't mention anyone new coming.'

Maudie shook her head. 'We're Met assistants.'

'So you'll be working with Libby and Alice?' Joan nodded towards the redhead with the iron and a plump, brown-haired woman a few years older than them, who was knitting furiously beside the coke stove. 'And Corporal Banks, of course,' she added. 'They're a nice group of girls,' she went on. 'You'll like them. Even Imogen – Corporal Banks – is one of us.'

But will they like us? Maudie looked at the cool blonde, writing a letter by the stove. She hoped she wouldn't hold Sybil's cheekiness against them. They hadn't exactly made a good first impression.

'Come and say hello,' Joan said, standing up.

Maudie was slightly apprehensive, meeting her new roommates for the first time. She was glad to have her sister beside her. Sybil was usually the one who did all the talking – a bit too much, sometimes! But Maudie was usually grateful for her sister's outgoing nature, especially as she was generally so shy herself.

Anyway, she needn't have worried. The other girls were all very friendly and welcoming. Even Corporal Imogen forgot her cool reserve as they chatted. They moved round to make room for Maudie and Sybil around the stove, and one of the girls – Diana – brewed up some cocoa and offered them each a slab of home-made cake.

Maudie found out that Alice was newly married, and that her husband had been transferred from Holme to another bomber station in Lincolnshire shortly after they were wed.

'We barely even got a wedding night,' she said sadly. 'Now all I can do is knit socks for him.' She held up the needles.

'Do you have boyfriends?' Libby asked Maudie and Sybil. They both shook their heads.

'You could have a different boyfriend every week here, if you wanted to,' Diana said.

'I daresay my sister will!' Maudie replied.

Sybil glared at her. 'And why not? You'd have to be an idiot to get yourself involved with everything that's going on. What's the point of falling for someone when they could be here one minute and gone the next!'

Maudie glanced at new bride Alice's head, bent over her knitting. Her hands were shaking, she noticed. She really wished her sister would think before she spoke sometimes.

'Try telling that to Corporal Banks,' Libby said. 'She's fallen head over heels for her man. Isn't that right?'

'Stop it, or I'll put you on a charge.' Imogen was smiling as she said it.

'It took her long enough to get him!' Alice laughed.

'She'd been chasing him for ages,' Libby confided to Maudie. 'Honestly, we were all starting to despair!'

'Yes, well, he was worth waiting for.' Imogen stood up. 'Anyway, come on, you lot. Time to go down to supper. I don't know about you, but I'm absolutely famished.'

The Airmen's Mess was a large, hangar-like building with a counter at one end and long trestle tables across the width of the room. The WAAFs' table was at one end of the hall. Maudie, Sybil and the other girls collected their cutlery – or 'irons', as the others called them – then joined the queue that stretched to the door. They were joined by Rose, the Met WAAF who had shown them around.

But no sooner had they joined the queue than Imogen said, 'I won't be a minute,' and slipped back out of the door.

The other girls exchanged knowing looks. 'No prizes for guessing where she's going!' Libby grinned.

'I thought she said she was ravenous?' Joan said innocently.

'She's ravenous, all right. But it's not for anything they're dishing up in here!'

'Her boyfriend has been away for two weeks,' Alice explained to Maudie and Sybil. 'He only came home this afternoon, and poor Imogen's been desperate to see him.'

'Where is he?' Sybil asked, looking around.

'Oh, he's not here. He's a pilot officer,' Diana said. 'He eats in the Officers' Mess.'

'Officially he's not supposed to fraternise with other ranks,' Libby said. 'Except everyone does it.'

'My husband is a flight lieutenant,' Alice said. 'No one really cares, as long as you're a bit discreet about it, and you're not seen together in public while you're in uniform.'

'No wonder Tom's always trying to get Imogen out of her uniform!' Libby cackled.

'I imagine he won't have any trouble getting her out of it tonight,' Alice said. 'You know what they say. Absence makes the heart grow fonder. And I should know,' she sighed.

'Tom?' Sybil said.

'Flight Lieutenant Tom Davenport,' Libby replied. 'I daresay you'll meet him later. He always likes to size up the new girls.'

Maudie looked at her sister. She knew exactly what she was thinking.

He already has, she thought.

They left the Mess just as the aircraft were taking off on their ops. Maudie and Sybil clutched each other in fear at the deafening row of the heavy bombers over their heads. They seemed so huge, it was a wonder that they could get off the ground.

'Don't worry, you'll get used to it,' Alice grinned. 'Quite a sight, isn't it?'

'Wait until they pass right over the hut in the middle of the night!' Libby said.

They headed back to their hut and someone coaxed the old cast-iron stove back into life. They spent the rest of the evening knitting, writing letters or just chatting quietly together. But Maudie noticed that the other girls all seemed more subdued this evening. There was none of the laughter there had been earlier.

'It's because there are ops tonight,' Joan explained quietly. 'Everyone's always nervous until the boys come home.'

At half past ten, Imogen declared it was time for lights out, and they all settled down to sleep. Maudie turned over, pulled the scratchy grey blanket up to her chin and prepared herself for a sleepless night.

All she could think about was her cosy bed back in Jubilee Row. Her mother would be all alone in the house now their father had returned to sea. Maudie wondered how she would be coping. She hoped she had sought some company over at Granny May's.

She must have finally dropped off because she was suddenly shocked awake by what sounded like thunder overhead.

'What was that?' She sat bolt upright in the darkness. Looking around her, she saw the other girls were all sitting up too, their faces turned towards the corrugated-iron ceiling.

'They're coming home,' Alice whispered in the darkness. 'Listen . . .'

Plane engines throbbed overhead. Suddenly the atmosphere in the hut seemed to be charged with a tension she did not understand. In the bed beside her, she could hear Joan counting softly under her breath.

'Six . . . seven . . . eight . . .'

As the last engine passed over and silence fell, a collective sigh went up around the hut.

'That's the lot,' Libby's voice came out of the darkness. 'All home, thank God.'

The girls immediately settled down, pulled their blankets over them and went back to sleep. All except for Maudie, who lay awake, staring into the darkness.

Alice was wrong, she thought. She didn't think she would ever get used to it.

Chapter 7

August 1942

Most of the girls in the typing pool were already at their desks and tapping away busily at their typewriters by the time Florence Maguire arrived for work at the Guildhall on Monday morning. She swept a critical eye over them as she slipped off her coat and hung it on the stand by the door.

'Is that nail varnish I can see, Deirdre Taylor?' The girl blushed and hid her hands under the desk. 'What have I told you?' Florence said. 'Nail varnish is for the dance hall, not the office.'

'Yes, Miss Maguire. Sorry, Miss Maguire.'

'And the same goes for all that rouge,' Florence eyed Gillian Munroe in the far corner.

The other girls all ducked their heads and showed a sudden interest in their work, hoping they would not catch Florence's attention. But it was her job as typing-pool supervisor to keep up standards, and her stern gaze never missed anything. She prided herself that she could spot a grubby collar or a smudge of lipstick as easily as she could spot a typing error in an invoice.

One desk in the middle row was still empty. No prizes for guessing who was missing, Florence thought.

'Has anyone seen Mabel Burrows this morning?'

'No, Miss Maguire.'

'Not yet, Miss Maguire.'

'Happen she's poorly, Miss Maguire.'

Or happen she just couldn't be bothered to get to work on time, Florence thought. Mabel Burrows was a sullen, slovenly girl, as sloppy in her work as she was her punctuality. Florence was forever taking her to task over something or other.

She was sitting at her desk on the raised dais, checking over a late payment reminder that one of the girls had typed when the administration manager, Clement Saunders, came in.

'Good morning, ladies,' he greeted them all brightly. 'How are we all today?'

'Good morning, Mr Saunders,' the girls chorused.

Florence kept her head down, her teeth gritted. Just seeing his grinning face irritated her beyond belief.

He was in his mid-forties, a tall, lanky man with thick, curly brown hair, hazel eyes and a pronounced limp – the result of a war injury twenty-five years earlier, so Florence had been told. In spite of his disability, he came in like a whirlwind, a flurry of disjointed, clumsy limbs and walking stick, disturbing everything and everyone around him.

Florence lowered her gaze to her work so she didn't have to look at him. There was a general air of untidiness about him that grated on her.

She hoped he might leave, but he made his way down the rows between the desks, leaning heavily on his stick, scattering compliments like confetti as he went.

'Is that a new blouse you're wearing, Miss Grey? It's very fetching.'

'Thank you, Mr Saunders,' Ivy Grey simpered.

'And you've done something new to your hair, haven't you, Miss Munroe?'

'It's a permanent wave, Mr Saunders. My sister did it for me.'

'Did she, indeed? Splendid. Perhaps she could do mine?' He touched his springy hair, which of course set all the girls off giggling.

It was pathetic, Florence thought. He was supposed to be the manager, a person of authority. She glanced towards the frosted-glass door that led to his office. Why couldn't he stay in there where he belonged, instead of coming out here disturbing everyone's work?

It would never happen if I was the administration manager.

And she might have been, if it hadn't been for Clement Saunders. Florence had worked diligently as the typing-pool supervisor for years, never putting a foot wrong, never a day late or off sick, just waiting for her chance. Mr Casey, the former administration manager, had been about to retire, and she had as good as been promised that that job would be hers.

And then Clement Saunders had arrived. Florence didn't know much about him, apart from the fact that his wife's uncle happened to be a close friend of Mr Tarran, the city's sheriff. Two weeks before Mr Casey was due to retire, it was suddenly announced that Clement Saunders would be taking over as administration manager. So here he was, two years later, happily ensconced in the office that should by rights have been hers.

Florence wouldn't have resented him so much if she had felt he deserved the job. But he had no administrative experience as far as she could tell. Most of the time, he didn't even pretend to know what he was doing.

He didn't seem to care, either. Once, Florence had walked into his office and found him idly flicking rubber bands at a portrait of the mayor hanging over the fireplace.

'And how about you, Miss Maguire?' She cringed as Clement Saunders turned his attention to her. 'Did you have a good weekend?'

'Yes, thank you.' Florence kept her head down, making it as clear as she could that she didn't wish to speak to him.

'Busy with your red pen as usual, I see?' He looked over her shoulder and pulled a face. 'Oh dear, that looks rather alarming.'

A couple of the girls giggled. Florence glared at them.

'I don't like mistakes, Mr Saunders,' she said tightly.

'Indeed, Miss Maguire. Nothing escapes your eagle eye.'

'I take my responsibilities seriously, if that's what you mean.'

One of us has to, she added silently.

Before he could reply, the door at the far end of the typing pool opened and Mabel Burrows crept in.

'And what time do you call this?' Florence turned her suppressed fury on the girl.

'I'm sorry, Miss Maguire,' she said. 'My bus didn't stop in the usual place. I had to walk all the way from Ferensway.'

'Everyone else managed to get here on time.'

'Happen they didn't come the same way as me.'

Florence stiffened at the girl's insolence. 'I beg your pardon?'

'To be fair, the buses are dreadful,' Mr Saunders said quickly. 'They're going all over the place to avoid the bomb damage.'

'Most of the bomb damage happened months ago,' Florence snapped. 'You would have to be very stupid indeed not to understand the routes by now.' She looked at Mabel Burrows, who had crept to her desk. 'What's the real reason you're late?'

'I already said—'

'You've given me a feeble excuse. I'd like the truth, please.'

Mabel Burrows stared back at her in obstinate silence. If she hadn't been so insolent, Florence might have let the matter slide, but she was aware of the other girls watching her closely, and she knew she had to make an example of the girl, or lose any authority she had.

She straightened up. 'Very well, if you can't tell the truth you can stay an extra hour after work tonight to make up for it.'

Mabel looked panicked. 'I can't.'

'I suppose you've got a date, have you? Well, you'll just have to tell your young man you can't make it.'

'There's no need for that,' Mr Saunders said quietly.

Florence turned on him. 'I beg your pardon?'

Mr Saunders ignored her, looking past her shoulder to where Mabel sat. 'It's all right, Miss Burrows. You don't have to stay late tonight. Just do your best to catch up.'

'But—' Florence started to speak, but Mr Saunders held up his hand, silencing her.

'Get on with your work and we'll say no more about it,' he said.

'Yes, sir. Thank you, sir.' Mabel took a sheet of paper from the tray and fed it between the rollers of her typewriter.

Florence looked around at the other girls. They all stared back at her. At the back, a couple were whispering behind their hands.

Her authority and her reputation depended on what she did next, she realised.

'A word, please,' she said to Mr Saunders. 'In your office.'

Chapter 8

Florence followed Clement Saunders into his office. As soon as she closed the door behind her, she heard the typing pool erupt with eager chatter.

'What do you think you're playing at?' she demanded.

Clement Saunders propped his stick beside his big, carved desk and sank into the leather chair. Behind him, the tall window gave a commanding view over Alfred Gelder Street, bathed in summer sunshine. The desk was completely covered with bits of paper, scribbled notes and discarded reports. Florence turned away with a shudder. How he ever got anything done was completely beyond her.

Clement leaned back in his chair and faced her. 'I suppose you're talking about Miss Burrows?'

'How could you?' Florence said. 'How could you undermine me like that in front of my staff?'

'I wasn't trying to undermine you. I was only doing what I thought was best.'

Florence felt her anger rising, burning her throat. 'How am I supposed to run the department? It's hard enough trying to keep any authority with you wandering about, laughing and joking all the time.'

'I'm only trying to keep their spirits up.'

'They come here to work, not to have fun!'

'Surely they can do both?'

'Not in my typing pool!' Florence faced him across the desk. 'I'm trying to do a job here, Mr Saunders. Those girls are very young and giddy, and I need to keep order. You should be helping me. You are supposed to be in charge of this department, after all.'

Mr Saunders' smile faded. 'You don't have to remind me of that,' he said quietly.

Florence looked down at the desk. Among the mountain of discarded papers, she spotted a pile of rates bills she had passed to him the previous Friday, sitting under a framed photograph of Mr Saunders and his wife on their wedding day.

You could get away with anything if you were a man and related to the right people, she thought.

'You should have let me deal with Mabel Burrows in my own way,' she said.

'You were being too harsh to her.'

'Why? Because she's young and pretty, I suppose?' She looked scornful. 'You think I should allow her to get away with anything?'

'It's not that—'

'You don't know what she's like, Mr Saunders. I've had trouble with her before. I've had cause to speak to her several times about her work and her attitude. She's lazy, she's slovenly, she needs discipline—'

'What she needs is a bit of understanding!'

His hand came down on the desk with a crash, making her jump.

Florence blinked at him. 'I beg your pardon?'

'Do you know anything about Mabel Burrows, Miss Maguire? Do you? Do you know she lost her mother during the Blitz last year? That she's been caring for her crippled father and her four younger brothers and sisters ever since?

She has to get them all fed and dressed before she comes to work, and find the time to cook and shop and clean, too. No wonder she's late every morning and can't keep her mind on her work. She's probably worried sick about what's going on at home.'

Florence faltered. 'I had no idea—'

'No, you didn't. Because you never bother to talk to them or get to know them. You're not interested in what their lives are like, as long as they're sitting at their desks from nine o'clock until five, hammering out bills and final demands.'

Florence looked back towards the frosted-glass door. From the other side came the rapid, rhythmic clacking of type-writer keys as the girls settled back to work.

Clement Saunders was right, she knew very little about the girls. Nor did she ever spare a thought for them once they'd put on their coats and left the office. But surely that was the way it should be? 'I feel sorry for Mabel Burrows, of course,' she said stiffly. 'But we're here to do a job. And feeling sorry for ourselves won't get us through this war, either. We need discipline and order.'

'We also need friendship and understanding.'

There was something about the way he said it that rankled with her. 'I don't come to work to make friends.'

'Oh, I know that, Miss Maguire, believe me.'

He was smiling now, that infuriating grin that made Florence want to reach across the desk and throttle him.

She looked back at the photograph on his desk. A much younger Clement Saunders, his beautiful blonde bride on his arm. She had never bothered to find out anything about him, either. Nor did she really want to know.

Before she could reply, the door opened and Councillor Willis from the Recreation and Amenities Committee

46

strolled in. He was a florid-faced man with a shock of white hair and a sense of his own importance.

'Oh, I'm sorry. Am I interrupting something?' he said, looking from one to the other.

'Miss Maguire and I were just discussing staff morale, Councillor,' Clement Saunders said, glancing at Florence.

'Really? What a coincidence. That's what I've come to talk to you about.'

'Oh, really?'

'I'll go . . .' Florence started for the door.

'No, Miss Maguire, I'd like you to stay. This concerns you, too.' The councillor plonked himself into the chair opposite. 'You'll have heard the Americans have taken over Goxhill?'

'I read something about it in the newspaper,' Clement Saunders said.

It was hard to miss the story. The US Air Force had moved into the base at RAF Goxhill, on the other side of the Humber. Florence had already spotted a few American uniforms around the city.

'They're having a dance next week and they've asked if we can send some of our lasses over. Single, pretty ones, of course!' Councillor Willis chortled.

'I'm sure they'd love—' Clement Saunders started to say, but Florence interrupted him.

'I'm sorry, Councillor, but this is a typing pool, not a cattle market,' she said. 'I have no intention of procuring girls for our American friends. Especially when I've heard such bad things about them.'

The councillor looked taken aback. 'I'm inviting them to a dance, Miss Maguire, not selling them into slavery! I just thought they might enjoy a night out.' He glared at Florence.

'Besides, we all have to do our bit to keep the Yanks sweet, since they're helping us win this war.'

'Are you suggesting that our Allies' co-operation depends on whether the girls in our typing pool go dancing with them?' Florence said.

Councillor Willis looked nonplussed for a moment, then turned to Clement Saunders. 'What say you about it, Saunders?'

'I say we should ask the girls and let them decide. As you say, they might enjoy a night out. And if Miss Maguire is concerned about their welfare, perhaps she would like to act as a chaperone?'

'I don't think—'

'That's a capital idea.' Councillor Willis heaved himself out of the chair. 'I'm sure no one would dare try any hanky-panky with you keeping watch, eh, Miss Maguire?' he roared with laughter.

'I only wish I could be there to see it,' Clement Saunders smirked.

'Oh, I expect you to come too, Saunders.'

'Me?' Clement Saunders looked flustered. 'I'm afraid I'm not really one for dancing . . .' He pointed to the stick propped against his desk.

'You heard what the councillor said, Mr Saunders.' Now it was Florence's turn to smirk. 'We all have to do our bit to keep the Yanks sweet.'

'Indeed, Miss Maguire. Anyway, I doubt if the Americans would want to dance with you, Saunders. Your wife, on the other hand . . .' Councillor Willis picked up the photograph on the desk. 'What's her name again?'

'Gwendoline, sir.'

'Gwendoline. A charming name for a charming lady.' He handed the photograph back to Clement. 'I daresay she'll know exactly how to charm our American friends.'

'I don't know about that, sir.'

'Nonsense, I'm sure a night out will do you both good.' Councillor Willis slapped him on the shoulder. 'From what I've heard, those Yanks don't skimp on their hospitality. Might as well make use of it, eh?'

'Yes, sir.'

Clement Saunders gave the photograph a last long look before he placed it back down on the desk. For once, he wasn't smiling, Florence noticed.

Chapter 9

It was a blustery morning, and the iron ladder to the top of the Flying Control building swayed precariously as Sybil clung to the top rung, struggling to haul herself up onto the flat roof while the wind wrenched at her.

She shouldn't have even been there. It was supposed to be Imogen's turn to check the instruments, but she had pulled rank on Sybil and sent her instead.

'It's best if I do the chart, since I have more experience,' she had said. 'We don't need any more mistakes.'

Just because Sybil had got flustered and given HQ the wrong barometric pressure reading the previous day. It wasn't her fault she had scribbled down the numbers too quickly and couldn't read her own writing. She couldn't even see how it mattered, although that didn't stop the duty Met officer flying into yet another apoplectic rage.

Sybil hauled herself onto the roof and straightened up, still gripping the cold metal handrail of the ladder for support as she braced herself against a powerful gust of wind that nearly knocked her off her feet. It was all a bit much, really. In London, where they had trained, they'd had anemometers to take wind speed readings. Here there was no such luxury, and instead, every hour, one of the Met girls had to scramble up onto the roof of the Flying Control building and check the wind speed and visibility by peering at the windsock fluttering on the distant airfield.

This afternoon it wasn't so much fluttering as being nearly ripped from its pole. Sybil could hardly stand straight with the force of the buffeting wind. She pushed her hair back from her eyes and looked around her. Aircraft stood at various dispersal points like great grey grounded beasts.

Having made her hasty assessment, Sybil carefully tried to manoeuvre herself back down the ladder. All the while, the wind tugged at her and her hair flew about her face, making it difficult for her to see.

She was just a few rungs from the bottom when a cheery voice called out, 'Go on, jump. I'll catch you.'

She glanced down to see Tom Davenport standing at the foot of the ladder looking up at her. Pilot Stuart Ackroyd was with him. They made a dashing pair, one darkly handsome, the other silvery fair.

For once, Sybil was glad she was wearing battledress. The blue serge top and trousers might be ugly, but at least there was no risk of flashing her official-issue knickers, or blackouts, as they were nicknamed. But even so, she was conscious of the two pilots watching her as she made her way slowly and carefully to the ground.

'You should have let me catch you,' Tom said.

'I wouldn't trust you.'

'Sounds like she's got the measure of you, old man!' Ackroyd hooted with laughter.

'What's the weather like up there, anyway?' Tom asked.

'Can't you tell?' Ackroyd chuckled. 'Look at her, man. Who needs a windsock when you've got LACW Maguire's hair?'

Sybil put her hand up to her hair, now a tangled mess around her face.

'Allow me.' Tom reached out and tucked a stray lock behind her ear. 'That's better. We can see those beautiful green eyes now.'

'They're brown.'

'Are they? Let me see . . .'

He leaned closer, until Sybil was looking into his deep blue gaze. He smelt of soap and brilliantine. She was surprised to find she was blushing.

Tom's mouth curved, as if he knew the effect he was having on her. 'So they are,' he said softly. His gaze held hers a moment longer, then he looked away.

'One thing's for sure,' Ackroyd said, breaking the tension, 'we won't be going up in this weather.'

'You never know.'

Sybil could have bitten her tongue as soon as she had uttered the words. Tom and Stuart Ackroyd both turned to her avidly.

'What do you mean?' Tom asked.

'Nothing. I mean, I can't say . . .'

'You know something, though? About tonight's ops?'

'Are they on or off?'

'I-I can't . . .'

'Go on,' Ackroyd urged. 'Be a sport and tell us. We won't let on to anyone, honestly.'

Sybil looked from one to the other. She'd already said too much. But then, what harm would it do? The duty Met officer was already briefing the top brass. They'd know all about it in the briefing soon enough.

'The wind's set to drop this evening,' she said.

'Is it? Oh, thank the lord for that,' Ackroyd said. 'I hate it when ops are cancelled, don't you, Davenport?'

'Absolutely. Talk about an anticlimax.'

'Don't say anything, will you?' Sybil begged.

'Mum's the word,' Ackroyd promised solemnly.

Back in the Met Office, Imogen was waiting for her. Sybil had hardly got through the door before she pounced.

'You took your time. They're waiting for those figures at HQ. The bell's gone off three times.'

'Happen you should try going up that ladder yourself in a force seven and see how long you take,' Sybil snapped back.

'Don't talk to a corporal like that!' Imogen bristled. 'Anyway, it's never a force seven,' she added. 'Five or six at the most, I'd say. Really, Maguire, no wonder your readings are always so sloppy. Don't you know anything?'

'I know I was nearly blown off the roof just now!'

'Yes, well, you'd better get on with sending those figures,' Imogen said. 'And do something about your hair,' she added. 'It looks like a bird's nest.'

Sybil thought about the brush of Tom's fingers as he tucked her hair behind her ear, and found herself blushing again.

'Maguire?' Imogen's voice shattered her daydream. 'What are you still standing there for? Get a move on!'

Sybil went to the teletype machine to type in the figures. Every hour without fail, each station had to transmit their readings to Bomber Command in High Wycombe. If they were ever late, the Met assistant at Group HQ would be ringing and sending terse little messages, urging them to hurry up and accusing them of jeopardising the war effort.

As Sybil typed in the figures, she was aware of Imogen watching her from the plotting table, where she was supposed to be making up the latest weather chart. She could sense the corporal had something she wanted to say.

Finally, she spoke up. 'Did I see you talking to Tom just now?'

Her tone was casual, but Sybil wasn't fooled. She had a feeling Imogen had been watching them from the window.

'That's right. He was passing on his way to the Briefing Room with Ackroyd.'

'What were you talking about?'

'Nothing in particular.'

'Did he mention me?'

'No. Any reason why he should?'

Sybil smiled to herself as she typed the figures into the teletype machine. She could almost feel Imogen glowering behind her, her eyes burning into her back.

She might not have enjoyed teasing the corporal so much if she'd been a bit nicer to her. But in the month she and Maudie had been at the station, Sybil had become the focus of Imogen's attention. Nothing Sybil did was ever right, from the way she stacked her bed to the way she wore her hair. Not a day had gone by without Sybil finding herself on yet another charge.

No prizes for guessing why, either. Imogen's jealousy was as plain as day.

'He's not interested in you, you know,' the corporal blurted out suddenly.

'I beg your pardon?' Sybil feigned innocence as she carried on typing in the figures.

'Tom. I know he likes to flirt, but it doesn't mean anything. He's mine.'

'So you keep telling everyone,' Sybil murmured, over the hum of the machine.

'What's that supposed to mean?'

'I mean you can't be very sure of him, if you have to keep warning people off.'

'Of course I'm sure of him,' Imogen snapped. 'Tom and I are in love.'

'If you say so.'

'I'm just telling you, that's all. So you don't get the wrong idea about him.'

'What makes you think I have any ideas about him?'

'I've seen the way you look at him.'

What about the way he looks at me? Sybil thought about his deep blue gaze, meeting hers. Just the memory made her blush.

'I think you should be talking to Tom about this, not me,' she said over her shoulder.

Before Imogen could reply, the door flew open and Flight Lieutenant Ormerod, the duty Met officer, stormed in.

'What's all this I hear about you giving weather forecasts now?' he demanded. He was in his forties, a small, bespectacled man who, in spite of his title, had never been up in a plane in his life.

'I'm sorry?' Sybil looked at him blankly.

'I've just had two pilot officers informing me that ops are definitely on for tonight, because apparently one of the Met girls told them.'

Sybil fumed silently. So much for Tom and Ackroyd keeping their promise!

'I was only making conversation, sir,' she said.

'Well, don't. If you're going to flirt with the pilots, then find something else to talk about. Or better still, don't talk at all!' Flight Lieutenant Ormerod's face puckered with rage. 'It's bad enough that we have airmen coming in and out of here all day when you're on duty, distracting you and disturbing everyone's work. From now on, you're to conduct your love life away from this office. Is that clear?'

'Yes, sir.'

'And you can stop trying to do my job, too. At least until you can do your own properly!'

'Yes, sir.' Sybil couldn't bring herself to look at Imogen. She could only imagine the corporal's smug expression.

*   *   *

It was a relief when her shift ended an hour later and she was finally able to escape the tense atmosphere of the Met Office. She hurried straight back to the hut to find Maudie.

She was annoyed to find her sister with Joan Mason again. The two of them had become quite thick with each other in the month the twins had been at Holme. Whenever Sybil wanted to spend time with her sister, Joan Mason always seemed to be hanging around, her thin little rabbit face peering out from under the low peak of her cap. Sybil wished Maudie would tell Joan to go away, but her sister was far too soft-hearted for that.

'I wish you'd try to be friends,' Maudie had urged Sybil. 'She's really quite nice once you get to know her.'

Sybil had made a half-hearted attempt for her sister's sake, but she soon found Joan too tedious. Joan was more interested in being friends with Maudie anyway, which irritated Sybil even further.

They were sitting side by side in front of the cast-iron stove. Maudie was darning her stocking, while Joan was reading aloud yet another endless letter from her RAF mechanic boyfriend, who was stationed somewhere near Cambridge. How on earth did he find time to write so many pages? Sybil wondered. Life in Cambridge must be very dull indeed.

She admired her sister's patience, putting up with it. But Maudie seemed happy enough as she listened to Joan reading out the relative merits of a Halifax and an Avro Lancaster.

She put down the letter when Sybil came in.

'Oh, don't let me stop you,' Sybil said. 'It sounds like riveting stuff.'

Joan's face reddened, and Maudie shot Sybil a warning look.

'Good shift?' she said.

'Not particularly.'

Maudie set down her sewing. 'What happened?'

'Our beloved Corporal Banks.' Sybil took off her cap and examined her hair in the mirror. The corporal was right about something – it did look like a bird's nest.

'What about her?'

Sybil picked up a brush and set about tugging it through her tangled locks. 'She's convinced I'm after her wretched boyfriend, and she's making my life a misery about it.'

Sybil caught the look Maudie and Joan exchanged in the mirror behind her.

'What?' she said.

Maudie looked uncomfortable. 'You do flirt with him a bit,' she said.

'It's only a bit of fun.'

'Happen Corporal Banks doesn't see it that way.'

'That's her lookout then, in't it?' Sybil teased at a knot. 'Anyway, it's not all my fault. Half the time he's the one flirting with me.'

'Then happen you should stay away from him?' Maudie suggested.

'And let Banks think she actually can tell me what to do? Not likely!' Sybil lost her patience and wrenched the brush through the troublesome knot.

'She is a corporal,' Joan pointed out quietly. 'That means she can tell you what to do . . .'

Sybil shot her a look and she fell silent, her gaze dropping to the letter in her lap.

'Joan's got a point,' Maudie said. 'You want to watch yourself, Syb. Imogen could really make trouble for you if she set her mind to it.'

Imogen looked back at herself in the mirror.

And I could make trouble for her, too, she thought, smiling at her reflection.

Chapter 10

'I don't even know why I have to go to this dance anyway, let alone dress up for the wretched thing!'

Florence shifted impatiently from foot to foot as Joyce Shelby knelt at her feet, pinning the dress she wore. She had already been fiddling with it for far too long in Florence's opinion, a dart here and a seam there, then sitting back to scrutinise her handiwork. As if it really mattered whether it fitted her or not.

'Stop moaning and keep still,' Joyce threatened through a mouth full of pins. 'Honest to God, Florence, you're worse than a bain!'

'You didn't need to go to so much trouble, honestly,' Florence said. 'I'm sure I could have just worn one of my old skirts and blouses.'

'You'll do no such thing!' Joyce looked up at her, scandalised. 'I'm your friend and I'm not letting you go to this dance wearing an old blouse and skirt. You never know who'll be there.'

Florence looked down at her, bewildered. 'I know exactly who'll be there. A handful of councillors and their wives, a lot of overexcited girls from the typing pool, and Clement Saunders. And I certainly have no interest in impressing *him*!'

Joyce gave a slightly exasperated look, which Florence did not understand.

Poor Joyce, she thought. She must be regretting ever offering to help her find something to wear. She wished she knew how to fuss over her appearance like Iris or the other women, but it was so long since she'd bothered, she had almost forgotten how.

'Thank you for offering to lend me something,' she said, to make Joyce feel better.

'Oh, that's all right. I've got a wardrobe of dresses that never get used.' Joyce finished pinning and sat back on her heels. 'I think I'm going to have to take down the hem a couple more inches, since you're so much taller than I am.'

'A beanpole, you mean!' Florence grimaced. She had always been self-conscious that she was nearly the same height as her brothers.

'You're tall and elegant,' Joyce corrected her. 'You should be proud of yourself.'

'I don't know about that,' Florence mumbled, embarrassed. 'It's all a lot of fuss over nothing, if you ask me. I just wish I could find an excuse not to go.'

'Why? I'd jump at the chance of a night out. Aren't you curious to get a look at the Americans?'

Florence frowned. 'I've seen enough of them around town, thanks very much.' And what she had seen had not impressed her. 'They all seem rather loud and obnoxious to me.'

'I think they're quite glamorous,' Joyce said. 'And I love their accents. They sound like film stars!'

Florence stared down at Joyce, snipping merrily away at the hem of the dress. She seemed to be getting very giddy in her old age.

Joyce finished the hem and sat back on her heels again. 'There,' she said. 'That's better. Taking the hem down has made all the difference. What do you think?'

'Lovely,' Florence replied absently.

'You haven't even looked at yourself yet!'

'I don't need to. I'm sure it will be fine.'

'Florence!'

'What?'

'Have a look at yourself and tell me what you think.'

Florence turned reluctantly to face her reflection in the full-length mirror.

'You see?' Joyce said behind her. 'You look beautiful.'

It was certainly a lovely frock, Florence thought. A soft, rustling silk with a beautiful pattern of crimson roses. It was somehow modest and eye-catching at the same time, with its fitted bodice and wide neckline that showed off just a glimpse of collarbone. The shape of the three-quarter-length sleeves made her wrists and hands look almost dainty.

Florence was almost embarrassed at how nice it looked. She felt she was letting it down with her drab face and sensible bun.

As if she knew what she was thinking, Joyce said, 'You'll need some heels to go with it. And you'll have to take your hair down ...'

'Don't.' Florence stopped her as she went to remove the pins from her hair. 'I always have it like this.'

'Then it's time for a change, isn't it?'

'It's too late for that, I reckon.'

'It's never too late,' Joyce said quietly.

Florence looked back at her reflection in the mirror. Joyce might be feeling fanciful, but Florence had her feet planted firmly on the ground. She saw herself for who she really was: a drab forty-odd-year-old woman in a pretty dress. Why pretend to be something she wasn't?

Joyce finished her pinning and they made their way downstairs. In the hall, they met Charlie Scuttle, bearing a jug of tall pink flowers. He smiled sheepishly when he saw Joyce and Florence.

'Oh, what lovely flowers,' Joyce exclaimed. 'Did you pick them for me?'

Charlie nodded, his gaze sliding towards the floor. Florence noticed a blush rising from his shirt collar.

'Well, it was a very nice thought,' Joyce said. 'Happen you'd like to stop for a cup of tea before you go home? I was just about to put the kettle on for us.'

Charlie shot Florence a quick look from under his sandy fringe, then shook his head.

'You won't be intruding,' Joyce seemed to read his thoughts. 'Florence won't mind if you stay.'

'Of course not,' Florence smiled encouragingly. 'The more the merrier.'

Charlie sent her another look, then shook his head again. He set the jug down on the hall table, gave them both a nod of goodbye, then left.

'Well, that's strange,' Joyce said as they watched him go. 'He generally stops for a cup of tea after he's closed up the shop. I wonder what's got into him today?'

'Perhaps he's shy of me?' Florence said.

'Hardly! You two grew up together.' Joyce shook her head. 'Oh well, you never know with Charlie, do you? I've learned it's better not to push him if he doesn't want to do something.'

'You certainly seem to understand him better than most.'

'I'm not surprised, all the time we spend together!' Joyce smiled. 'He's been such a help to me, running this place after Reg left. I suppose we've just got used to reading each other's minds.'

You'd have to read Charlie Scuttle's mind, Florence thought; there was no other way to communicate with him, since he hadn't uttered a word in nearly twenty-five years, not since he'd returned from the war a shattered wreck of the handsome young man he had once been.

It wasn't that he couldn't talk. Beattie Scuttle had taken her son to all kinds of doctors, and they'd all said the same thing. He would speak when he was ready, they told her. But more than twenty years on, he still hadn't found his voice. The scars were still there, plain to see in the anxious eyes that peered out from under a shock of red-brown hair. He looked more like a frightened boy than a grown man.

Florence turned her gaze to the jug of flowers. 'Why on earth has he filled a vase with fireweed, I wonder?'

'Their proper name is rosebay willowherb,' Joyce said. 'That sounds much nicer, don't you think?'

'A weed is still a weed, whatever you call it.'

'I like them.'

'I can't think why.' The tall, spiky pink blooms sprang up everywhere over the ruined city, mostly from the ashes of burned-out bomb sites. Florence found the sight of them utterly depressing.

'Because they give me hope,' Joyce said. 'You know, something wonderful growing out of something everyone believed was long dead?'

Florence stared at her friend's dreamy expression. Joyce really was getting very fanciful in her old age.

Chapter 11

Miss Leech, the section officer, might have looked like a maternal sort, with her soft pink cheeks and warm smile, but she could be anything but motherly when she wanted to be.

During kit inspections, for instance. All the girls dreaded being summoned to stand by their beds, their kit neatly piled at the foot, waiting for judgement to be passed on them.

Maudie was especially worried as she watched the section officer making her way down the row of beds opposite, followed by Corporal Banks. Not for herself, but for her sister.

Sybil was never properly prepared for kit inspection, no matter how often Maudie nagged her about it. She was always warning her to keep her belongings neat, her shirts pressed and her shoes polished just in case, but Sybil left everything to the last minute, and the inspections always caught her out.

Maudie watched her sister's tense face across the hut. Poor Syb, the last thing she needed was another charge.

Finally, the section officer reached Sybil's bunk.

Maudie could hardly bear to watch as her sister's hand started to rise in salute.

Please do it properly, she prayed silently. *Palm of the right hand facing forwards, fingers straight and thumb together so no light shows between them. Longest finger to be placed exactly one inch behind the side of the right eye over the temple . . .*

Every time Sybil tried it, she somehow managed to dislodge her cap over one eye, much to the amusement of the other WAAFs and the fury of whichever officer happened to be on the receiving end.

But this time there was no stifled laughter. Maudie dared to open her eyes, to see Miss Leech rummaging through her belongings. Sybil stood as stiff and straight as a ramrod, staring straight ahead of her. Maudie caught her eye and tried to give her an encouraging smile.

It'll be all right, she mouthed across the hut. But no sooner had she said the words than Corporal Banks picked up Sybil's best blue tunic and held it out for Miss Leech's inspection. The section officer examined it for a moment, then declared, 'Aircraftwoman Maguire, these buttons are a disgrace.'

Don't answer back, please don't answer back. Oh God. Maudie stared at Sybil, silently beseeching her to keep quiet, and for once she did.

'Make sure they're properly polished before you set foot outside this hut, if you please.' Miss Leech turned to Corporal Banks. 'Put this WAAF on a charge, Corporal.'

'Yes, ma'am.'

There was no mistaking the gleam in the corporal's eyes. Imogen Banks truly had it in for Sybil, Maudie thought. And her sister really only had herself to blame for it, too. She certainly didn't do herself any favours as far as the corporal was concerned.

'I hope they don't throw the book at her,' she fretted to Joan when inspection was over. Sybil had gone off with Corporal Banks to find out what her punishment was to be. 'I warned her over and over again about those buttons. I even offered to do them for her . . .'

'I don't know why you're worrying so much,' Joan said. 'It's nothing to do with you.'

Maudie glanced sideways at her friend. Even after all her efforts, there was little love lost between Sybil and Joan. Sybil was jealous of the time Maudie spent with Joan, and Joan thought Sybil was too silly and selfish for words.

Maudie had given up trying to make them like each other.

'You're right,' she said. 'But I did promise our mother I wouldn't let her get into any trouble.'

Although she might as well try to stop the sun from shining. Sybil seemed to attract trouble wherever she went. It wasn't that she was mean or malicious; she just didn't stop to think before she did anything.

And the more someone tried to stand in her way, the more determined she became.

'That girl would do anything for devilment,' Granny May used to say.

Sybil returned, looking mutinous.

'Well?' Maudie asked. 'What did she say?'

'I've got to clean the NAAFI kitchen.' Sybil plonked herself down on the end of her bed. 'Honestly, a couple of unpolished buttons, and she's got me scrubbing floors and washing pots all afternoon. It hardly seems fair to me.'

'I'm sorry, Syb.'

'And you know why she's making me clean the NAAFI, don't you? So all the boys will see me. She wants to humiliate me.'

Maudie exchanged a look with Joan. Her friend's face was devoid of all sympathy.

'You won't be humiliated, I promise,' she said. 'I'm sure no one will think any less of you—'

'Will you help me?' Sybil interrupted her.

'Me?'

'You're not on duty this afternoon, are you? You could give me a hand, then we'd get it done a lot quicker.'

'Well . . .'

'Or at least keep me company? Please, Maudie?' she begged. 'I wouldn't feel so bad if you were there with me.'

'I—'

'She can't,' Joan interrupted bluntly. 'Maudie's coming out for a cycle ride with me and the other girls this afternoon. Isn't that right?'

'A cycle ride?' Sybil looked at Maudie. 'I wasn't invited.'

'You might have been if you bothered to make friends with anyone,' Joan muttered.

Maudie saw her sister's face fall and stepped in quickly. 'I don't mind staying behind to help you,' she offered.

'It's all right,' Sybil said in a small voice. 'I'd hate to spoil your afternoon with your friends . . .' She glared at Joan as she said it.

'I don't mind, honestly. Like you said, we'll get it done quicker if we work together.'

Sybil's face brightened. 'If you're sure? Thanks, Maud, you're a real pal!'

She sauntered off, leaving Maudie and Joan in the hut. Maudie could scarcely look at her friend; she knew what she would be thinking.

'What else could I do?' she pleaded for understanding. 'I couldn't leave her to struggle on her own.'

'Why not? She's the one who's supposed to be doing the punishment, not you.'

'I know, but . . .' Maudie shrugged helplessly. 'She'd do the same for me,' she said.

'Would she? I doubt it.'

'Of course she would. We're twins. We look after each other.'

'It seems to me like you're the one who does all the looking after. Perhaps it's time you stopped and let your sister stand on her own two feet?'

66

Maudie didn't reply. Joan meant well, but she didn't understand what it was like to have a twin. She and Sybil had come into the world together, and there was a bond between them that went beyond blood. Their mother said they used to cling to each other in their crib; when one was hungry or in pain, the other would cry.

It wasn't that Maudie really wanted to look after her sister; she just didn't know how to do anything else.

*   *   *

In spite of Maudie's reassurances, the flying boys were out in force to watch Maudie and Sybil as they set about their cleaning duties. They leaned against the wall, jeering and catcalling, thoroughly enjoying the entertainment.

'Keep at it, ladies. You're doing well!'

'You can come and scrub out our hut when you've finished!'

It was only harmless fun for them, but Maudie could see her sister's face flaming as she carried a bucket of dirty water out into the yard to empty down the drain. Maudie was glad she had decided to stay and help her; she had a feeling Sybil would have defied the corporal's orders and given up a long time ago.

'What's all this?' To Maudie's chagrin, the crew of P-Popeye sauntered towards them, led by their insufferable pilot, Stuart Ackroyd. Mike Mitchell, the crew's bomb aimer, brought up the rear with Wally Barnes, the flight engineer. Maudie kept her head down and prayed they would walk past, but, of course, Ackroyd had to stop and pass comment. 'What's all this?' he bellowed. 'I do believe it's that charwoman from off the radio. What's her name?'

'Mrs Mopp?' Owen Jones, the mid gunner, called out.

'That's the one.'

'"Can I do you now, sir?"' Wally Barnes mimicked the character's famous catchphrase.

'Bet that's not the first time she's said those words. Eh, Maguire?' Ackroyd guffawed.

Maudie saw the look of fury on her sister's face and knew exactly what she was going to do, seconds before she took aim with the bucket of dirty water.

'Syb, don't!' She launched herself forward, slipping on the wet ground, and just managed to grab the bucket from her sister's grasp before Sybil launched it at the unsuspecting pilot. Ackroyd, thankfully, was too busy laughing at his own joke to realise how close he came to a soaking.

'You should have let me drown him!' Syb muttered. 'The pig deserved it.'

'I know he did,' Maudie replied. 'But you can't go round chucking buckets of filthy water at an officer.'

'I don't care. I wish I had a bucket of slop to throw at him.'

'Here, let me take that for you . . .'

Suddenly there was Mitch, lifting the bucket from Maudie's grip. He gave her a knowing wink.

'She's right,' he whispered. 'He did deserve it.'

Maudie smiled back. 'I know. But she would have been on jankers for the rest of her life!'

The other men jeered even more as Mitch carried the bucket over to the drain and tipped it away.

'Got you well trained, haven't they, Mitchell?'

'Proper knight in shining armour you are!'

'I can't help being a gentleman, can I?' Mitch smiled easily at them.

'Gentleman, be damned!' Ackroyd hooted. 'I daresay he's after one of you two lovely ladies. But which one will it be?' He waggled his eyebrows suggestively at them.

'Does it matter, since they're exactly the same?' Wally Barnes laughed.

'I daresay Mitch can tell the difference. Eh, old boy?' Stuart Ackroyd said.

Maudie saw Mitch's face redden as he handed the bucket back to her.

'Take no notice of them,' she said. 'They're talking nonsense as usual.'

'How do you think I feel, shut in an aircraft with them for hours on end?' he smiled reluctantly.

'Well, don't just stand there, old man!' Ackroyd called out. 'Are you going to ask her or not?'

'Why don't you do us all a favour and shut up?' Mitch shouted back, his face turning even redder.

'What are they talking about?' Sybil asked.

'Mitch is trying to pluck up the courage to ask one of you lovely ladies to the dance at the Sergeants' Mess,' Owen Jones said. 'But the question is – which one?' He looked from Sybil to Maudie and back again.

'As if we didn't know!' Reg Thornley, the wireless operator, said.

'I told you, it doesn't matter. They're one and the same,' Wally Barnes laughed.

'Not to our Mitch! There's only one girl for him. Isn't that right, Mitchell?'

Mitch laughed sheepishly. Maudie caught the longing glance he sent towards Sybil and her heart sank.

'Excuse me . . .'

Maudie carried the bucket across the yard, nearly breaking into a run as she reached the kitchen.

She closed the door and leaned against it, her heart beating fast against her ribs. Mitch was going to ask Sybil to the dance. She was surprised at how much the thought upset her.

It hadn't occurred to her how much she liked Mitch until that moment. She'd always thought he was one of the nicest of the flying boys. He wasn't brash and loud like Ackroyd and Tom Davenport. He was more like her – quiet and unassuming, even a bit shy. He often called in at the Met Office to talk to her, and the other girls assured her he was interested. Maudie had shrugged it off at first, but gradually she had started to allow herself to think that perhaps he was interested in her.

Now, seeing the way he looked at Sybil, she realised she was wrong.

Of course he prefers Sybil, she told herself. He probably hadn't even really noticed Maudie at all. People seldom did when Sybil was around. She was so vivacious and full of life, while Maudie preferred to stay quietly in the background.

Usually it didn't bother her. It was the way it had always been, after all.

But for once, as she peered out of the door and saw them laughing together in the yard, she wished it could have been her that someone noticed.

Chapter 12

It was the day of the dance, and all the girls were wildly excited about it.

In spite of all Florence's misgivings and dire warnings, they had all welcomed the idea of going over to Goxhill and being entertained by American airmen. They had talked of nothing else for days, chattering about what they were going to wear, sharing out their meagre supplies of make-up and musing on what delights would await them over the river.

It was almost impossible for Florence to get them to concentrate on anything else. By the afternoon of the dance she had practically given up. She sat at her desk on the dais, listening to them twittering like birds as she tried to get on with checking through a list of recent library acquisitions for payment.

'I've heard they've got chocolate and ice creams and all sorts over there,' sighed Dulcie Allen.

'Never mind ice cream. It's a decent set of nylons I want to get my hands on,' Gillian Munroe replied.

'You'll have to let a Yank get his hands on you first!' Deirdre Taylor chuckled.

'We'll have none of that talk, thank you very much,' Florence warned. 'Don't forget you're representing the Corporation. I expect you to behave with modesty and dignity.'

That only made them giggle even more.

'You heard that, girls. Modesty and dignity,' Gillian mimicked at the back of the room. Florence shot her a sharp look. Gillian Munroe was a fast little piece who did not know the meaning of the word modesty, if her rouged cheeks and daring hemlines were anything to go by.

'Don't forget, I shall be there to make sure you behave,' she said.

The girls groaned. 'Spoil our fun, you mean,' Dulcie muttered.

'Yes, indeed I will be spoiling your fun, Dulcie Allen, if I don't consider it appropriate.'

'You in't spoiling my fun,' Gillian muttered.

'Gillian wants to marry a Yank, miss,' Deirdre called out.

Gillian reached across and gave her a sharp shove.

Florence regarded her curiously. 'Do you have one in mind?'

'Oh no, miss. She in't fussy!' another girl, Hilda Gornall, joined in.

'Shut up, you!' Gillian's blush deepened.

'She thinks they've all got money and big houses,' Deirdre said. 'She wants to go and live in America.'

Florence looked from one to the other, genuinely perplexed. Then she thought about her friend Joyce going starry-eyed over the thought of meeting Americans. Florence wondered if she was the only one unmoved by the prospect.

*   *   *

The dance was already in full swing by the time they arrived. Florence ushered the girls through the thickening twilight, picking their way carefully along the cinder path, following the sound of raucous laughter and music to the aircraft hangar at the far end.

For all their bravado, the girls clustered around her like chicks around a mother hen, looking apprehensively about them. Florence could well understand their nerves. The place seemed to burst with light and noise. The Americans were larger than life, looking glamorous in their blue uniforms with their slicked-back hair and gleaming white smiles.

The hangar was ablaze with coloured lights and crowded with people. At the far end, a band played lively music on a platform for the couples that swarmed the dance floor. Over to one side, there were tables groaning with more food and drink than Florence had seen in years.

Florence took charge and ushered the girls to the cloakroom.

As they took off their coats, she looked around her. There were a couple of American airmen hanging around, watching them like wolves eyeing up their prey, but there was no sign of Clement Saunders. He had promised to meet her there, to help her look after the girls, but as usual he had shirked his responsibilities.

'Ooh, Miss Maguire! You look lovely!' Hilda Gornall exclaimed as Florence took off her coat. Immediately, all the other girls turned round to admire her.

'That dress really suits you, miss,' Deirdre Taylor said.

'It sets off your colouring a treat,' Dulcie Allen joined in. 'I wish I had lovely dark hair like yours.' She twisted a limp tendril of her light brown hair around her finger.

'I reckon I might not be the only one looking for a nice American tonight!' Gillian Munroe laughed.

'There's no such thing as a nice American!' Embarrassment made Florence snap. 'You'd do well to remember that, Gillian. Keep your wits about you this evening—'

'Excuse me?'

Florence swung round, and found herself staring up at a very tall, very handsome man in an officer's uniform.

'I'm Colonel Forrest,' he introduced himself in a deep drawling voice. 'You must be the ladies from the council I was supposed to meet?' His warm grey gaze swept over them.

'That's right. I'm Florence Maguire, head of the accounts typing pool, and these are my girls.' Florence hardly knew what she was saying, she was so embarrassed. Had he heard what she'd said to Gillian? If he had, his polite smile gave nothing away.

'Thank you so much for coming, ma'am. I'm sure my men will really appreciate having such charming company . . .' He smiled at the girls, who all blushed and giggled like children. 'I hope you have a wonderful evening. And if there's anything I can do for you, please don't hesitate to come and find me.'

He bowed his head to Florence and then left, striding off towards the dance floor. Even as the crowd swallowed him up, Florence could still see his head and broad shoulders above everyone else.

'I wonder if they're all as handsome as him?' Dulcie sighed. That was enough to set them all off again.

'He looked like Gary Cooper, didn't he?'

'Do you think he's married?'

'How old do you think he was?'

'Too old for you,' Florence pulled herself together and turned to face them.

'But not for you, miss!' Gillian suggested archly. 'Did you see the way he was looking at you?'

'I did,' Deirdre joined in. 'He couldn't take his eyes off you.'

'Don't be ridiculous,' Florence snapped.

'I mean it, miss, he was very taken with you. I reckon—'

'I don't want to hear any more of this nonsense!' Florence cut them off. 'Now, remember, the last ferry home is at ten o'clock on the dot, all right? So I want you all back here to meet me by half past nine at the latest.'

Gillian groaned. 'That hardly gives us any time!'

'Can't we make it a bit later?' Hilda begged.

'Only if you fancy swimming back across the Humber!' Florence looked around at them all. 'Anyway, that's more than enough time to dance and fill your faces with food, but hopefully not enough time to get up to any mischief. Remember, girls, you're representing the Corporation, and I don't want you to—'

But they'd already gone, hurrying off towards the dance floor.

'Be careful,' Florence called after them, as a couple of the American airmen peeled themselves off the wall and sauntered towards them.

Florence felt a sudden twinge of maternal concern for them. They seemed so young and vulnerable, so full of hope . . .

She gave herself a mental shake. Good lord, she must be going soft in her old age! Better not let the girls see, they might start trying to take advantage.

She stared in the direction of the music and laughter. There was no getting away from it, she would have to go in there. It was her responsibility to keep an eye on those girls. God knows, Clement Saunders wasn't here to do it . . .

And then she saw him, limping into the hangar with a beautiful blonde woman on his arm, her slender shoulders wrapped in fur.

'Mr Saunders?'

He looked up sharply and did a dramatic double-take.

'Good lord!' he said. 'It's you.' He looked her up and down. 'You look . . . different.'

'Yes, well, I thought I'd make an effort.'

75

'I can see that.' His gaze trailed down to her feet and back up again, until Florence felt herself blushing.

'Do stop gawping, Clem! Can't you see you're embarrassing the poor woman?' the woman cut in with a smile. 'You must forgive my husband. Compliments are not his strong suit.'

'Nor mine,' Florence muttered.

The woman turned to Clement. 'Aren't you going to introduce us?' Then, without waiting for a reply, she held out her hand. 'I'm Gwendoline Saunders. But you can call me Gwen.'

She was very beautiful, with a small, pointed face and slanted green eyes like a cat's. Her blonde hair was twisted in an elegant chignon, showing off her long, slender neck. When she shrugged off her fur, her pale skin glowed like a pearl against the silvery fabric of her dress.

'Florence Maguire.' Florence was conscious that her hand seemed big and clumsy around the other woman's light, delicately boned fingers.

Gwendoline's eyes lit up. 'So you're the famous Miss Maguire, are you?'

Florence glanced at Clement Saunders. 'I'm not sure about famous . . .'

'Oh, you are. Clem never stops talking about you.'

'Gwen!' His face suffused with colour.

'You should hear him,' Gwendoline went on, ignoring her husband's protest. 'It's "Miss Maguire said this, and Miss Maguire did that." He makes you sound like an absolute paragon. The place couldn't run without you, so he says.'

'Steady on!' Clement Saunders looked mortified.

'Oh dear, am I embarrassing you, darling?' Gwendoline smiled. 'It's all right, I'm not going to tell Miss Maguire all the terrible things you say about her.'

'I can well imagine,' Florence said drily.

'How are the girls? Behaving themselves, I hope?' Clement changed the subject.

'They've only been here five minutes; I doubt if even that lot could get themselves into trouble in that time.' Florence looked at her watch. 'But I'm going to go and keep an eye on them, just in case.'

'Perhaps we could take it in turns?' Clement suggested.

But before Florence could reply, his wife interrupted with, 'For heaven's sake, they're trying to have some fun. They don't need you two watching over them all the time!'

'They're our responsibility,' Florence said primly.

'They're not in the typing pool now. Besides, no one likes to be watched like a hawk, do they?'

Florence noticed the look that passed between her and her husband. There was something going on, she thought.

The next moment, the band struck up with a lively tune, and Gwendoline was smiling again. 'I love this tune,' she said, tugging on her husband's arm. 'Come on, let's go inside.'

'Anything you say, darling.' Clement looked over his shoulder and gave Florence an apologetic smile as he shambled after his wife into the crowd.

Chapter 13

It was hard to keep track of all the girls on the dance floor. Florence flicked her gaze this way and that, watching the couples as they whirled around in front of her like a carousel of blue uniforms and colourful dresses.

Gillian ... Hilda ... Deirdre ... Ivy ... One minute they were there, before her eyes, and then they were gone again, spinning away from her. Turning around, she saw Dulcie Allen at the refreshments table, piling up her plate with food, but there was no sign of the other four girls.

Florence frowned, looking this way and that. She had already warned them about sneaking outside the hangar, or the perils of 'going for a walk' with a young man they hardly knew.

They're not in the typing pool now.

Gwendoline Saunders' words sprang into her mind. Perhaps she was right, Florence thought. They were young women, after all. Was there really any need for her to watch them so closely?

But she couldn't help feeling responsible for them. They were still very young, most of them barely eighteen. And the Americans seemed very predatory ...

Gwendoline foxtrotted past in the arms of an American lieutenant. She sent Florence a dazzling smile before the man whisked her away again, disappearing into the crowd.

'Wanna dance?'

The question took her by surprise. Florence looked down to see a stocky little warrant officer with Brylcreemed hair standing at least a head shorter than her.

'I beg your pardon?'

'Wanna dance?' he asked the question out of the side of his mouth. He was chewing gum with the other side, Florence noticed.

She pulled herself up to her full height. 'Do I look like I want to dance with you?' she said.

'I don't see anyone else offering,' he remarked.

Florence opened her mouth, but before she had a chance to reply, a voice behind her said, 'You're wasting your time, old man. You could be Fred Astaire and Miss Maguire would still turn you down.'

The man shrugged and wandered off, and Florence turned to face Clement Saunders. He was standing behind her, holding a plate piled high with sandwiches and cake.

'I'm quite capable of answering for myself, you know,' she said sharply.

'Oh, I'm sure you are,' he replied through a mouthful of sandwich. 'I'm sure you'd have taken great pleasure in putting him in his place, too. I was just sparing him one of your withering rebukes.'

Florence looked down at the plate of food, her lips pursed. 'I see you've wasted no time in availing yourself of our hosts' hospitality?' she commented.

'Why not? They've got plenty, as they're always reminding us. You should try some.'

'No, thank you.'

'Go on, enjoy yourself for once, Miss Maguire. Or may I call you Florence, since we're not in the office?'

'No,' Florence told him firmly. 'You may not.'

'I didn't think so.' He took another bite of his sandwich. He was wearing his best suit, but his lanky frame still managed to make it look messy and ill-fitting. 'Anyway, since we've been forced into spending our evening here, we might as well enjoy it.'

Florence nodded towards the dance floor. 'It looks as if your wife is enjoying herself?'

Clement looked up as Gwendoline swung past again, this time in the arms of a different man.

'She's always loved to dance,' he said. 'But I'm not much of a partner for her these days.' He tapped his stick against his injured leg.

The silence stretched between them, and Florence felt awkwardly aware of needing to fill it.

'How did it happen?' she asked, then immediately regretted it. Not all the men who came home wanted to remember their experiences. Her brother Jimmy never talked about his time in France. And as for Charlie Scuttle . . .

But Clement just nodded and said, 'A stray artillery shell at Mons. One of ours, would you believe? It was enough to get me sent home, even if I wasn't exactly covered in glory.' He sent her a sideways look. 'Not everyone was so lucky.'

'No.'

'You lost someone, I understand?'

Florence stared at him. 'How did you know that?'

'I suppose someone must have told me . . .'

'Who? Who told you?'

'Does it matter?'

'Yes, it does. I don't appreciate being gossiped about.'

'It's hardly gossip!' Clement frowned, as if he wasn't quite sure whether to take her seriously. 'I think I must have asked someone about you.'

'You've been asking about me?' Florence said sharply.

'No! I mean, yes, I suppose so. But only because I was interested in you.'

'If you were that interested then perhaps you should have asked me instead of going behind my back.'

'And would you have told me?'

'Of course not!' Florence bristled. 'I never bring my personal life into the office.'

'Of course, I forgot. You don't come to work to make friends, do you?' he parroted her own words back to her with a smile.

'Exactly,' she said, turning away. He was only trying to make conversation, she realised, but after so many years of being teased and judged, she sensed criticism everywhere. 'I'm going to get some food,' she excused herself before Clement could reply.

She had not seen anything like it in a very long time. The refreshments table groaned with platters piled high with sandwiches, sausage rolls, doughnuts, cakes and fruit and sweets and all kind of other treats Florence could scarcely remember.

Her mother would faint if she saw this, she thought. Big May Maguire prided herself on her ability to create a feast out of next to nothing, but even she could not have competed with this.

Florence was just debating whether she could slip a slice of ham and egg pie into a napkin to take home to Pop when a commotion behind her made her turn around.

'Get your hands off her!'

'I saw her first!'

'Stop it, both of you!'

The sound of a familiar voice made Florence set down her plate. She went to the edge of the crowd that now ringed the dance floor. Peering between the heads and shoulders, she could see two airmen squaring up to each other, chins jutting, fists drawn, while a squealing blonde girl in a blue frock tried to come between them.

'Gillian Munroe. I might have known,' Florence muttered. She started to shoulder her way through the onlookers, just as Gillian let out a scream.

Everything happened very fast after that. Suddenly, the airmen were fighting, fists and curses flying. As Florence pushed her way to the front of the crowd, she saw Clement making his way from the other side.

'Stop this at once!' He got to them first and waded in to separate them, but he must have been accidentally caught by a badly aimed punch, because the next moment he was sent sprawling on his back, his stick knocked away from him.

The shock made the airmen stop for a split second, long enough for Florence to dive in and pull Gillian out of the melee.

And then, suddenly, there was Colonel Forrest, striding into the fray, flanked by two corporals. The sight of him was enough to bring the young men to their senses. They parted immediately, standing to attention, blood dripping from their noses and lips.

'Deal with these two,' Colonel Forrest ordered the corporals tersely, then strode over to where Florence was standing with her arm around Gillian. 'Is everything all right, ma'am?'

'Does it look all right?' Florence snapped back. She turned to Clement, who was still on the ground. 'Are you hurt? Shall I fetch your wife?'

She looked around at the crowd and realised Gwendoline was nowhere in sight.

'Stop fussing, Miss Maguire, it really doesn't suit you.' Clement struggled to sit up and looked around. 'My stick . . .'

'Here.' Florence picked it up and handed it to him.

'Let me help you, sir.' Colonel Forrest reached out to haul him up, but Clement shook him off angrily.

'I can manage, damn it!' he muttered through gritted teeth. Florence watched as he clambered to his feet, leaning heavily on his stick.

'Are you sure you're not hurt?' she asked.

'I'll live.' He looked at Gillian. 'How about you, Miss Munroe?'

'A bit shaken, sir.'

She didn't look at all shaken, Florence thought. If anything, she looked quite pleased with herself.

She took charge of the situation. 'Right, gather the other girls together,' she said. 'We're leaving.'

'But we've only just got here, miss!' Gillian protested.

'I don't care. We're leaving before anyone else causes a fracas.'

'Miss Maguire is right,' Clement said, much to Florence's surprise. 'It's time we were leaving.' He looked around. 'I'll go and find my wife . . .'

'I think she's at the bar, sir,' Gillian put in helpfully. 'That's where she was last time I saw her.'

'Thank you.'

Florence watched him limp off the dance floor, his shoulders slumped. He must be mortified to have been knocked off his feet like that, she thought.

'There's no need for you to go, surely?' Colonel Forrest's deep drawl interrupted her thoughts.

'I think it's for the best, don't you?'

'Would you like a lift?' Colonel Forrest offered. 'I can have my men drive you, if you don't mind getting into the back of a lorry?'

'No, thank you,' Florence said, seeing Gillian's face light up. She looked a little too thrilled at the prospect of clambering into a lorry with an American. 'We're perfectly capable of finding our own way home. Hurry up and find the others, Gillian. The sooner we leave here, the better!'

Chapter 14

The day before the dance, at the Sergeants' Mess, Corporal Banks came down with a raging sore throat and a fever. By the following morning, she was so poorly she had to go to the sick bay. But before she was hauled off, she still managed one last act of spiteful revenge.

'You'll never guess what she's done now!' Maudie was confronted by her furious sister as she was coming out of the canteen after breakfast.

'Who?' she asked.

'That cow Imogen, who do you think? She's only gone and put me in her place on tonight's rota!'

Maudie stared at Sybil, realisation dawning. 'Oh no! So you won't be able to go to the dance?'

'She's done it on purpose. She's too ill to go so she wants to make sure I miss out, too. I hope her wretched cold turns to pneumonia!'

'Syb!'

'Well, I do.' Sybil looked mutinous. 'She spoils all my fun.'

'Happen she wouldn't if you'd been a bit nicer to her?' Maudie said, but Sybil ignored her.

She only had herself to blame, Maudie thought. She understood why Imogen Banks had made sure Sybil couldn't go to the dance. If Syb hadn't flirted so outrageously with Tom Davenport, then perhaps the corporal wouldn't have seen her as such a threat.

But, as usual, there was no point in trying to explain that to her sister. Sybil never listened to anything that didn't suit her.

'I'm sorry, Syb,' she said. 'I know how much you were looking forward to going to the dance.'

'Happen I still could,' Sybil said slowly.

'I don't see how . . .' Maudie looked at her sister's face and knew what she was thinking. 'No,' she said. 'We can't.'

'Why not? We used to do it all the time at school.'

'That was different.'

'How was it different?'

'We can't swap places, Syb. We'd get into terrible trouble.'

'Only if we were caught. And we've never been caught, have we? Even our own mother gets us mixed up sometimes.'

Not any more, Maudie thought. She had always thought that she and Sybil were the double of each other, but in the weeks they had been at the station, she had felt herself becoming different, more separate from her sister. Now, when she looked in the mirror, she did not see Sybil's face staring back at her, but her own.

'You don't really want to go to the dance anyway, do you?' Sybil urged her. 'There's no one you're interested in, is there?'

An image of Mike Mitchell came into her mind, but she dismissed it before the longing could set in.

'No,' she said. 'No, there isn't.'

'Well, then. Go on, Maud,' Sybil pleaded. 'You know how much I love dancing. I've been so bored here with nothing to do. I need a bit of fun, otherwise I think I'll go mad!'

Maudie sighed. What was the point of arguing? They both knew she was going to give in eventually. She always did.

'All right,' she agreed. 'But you've got to pretend to be me, otherwise we really will get caught.'

'I promise.'

'I mean it, Syb. No flirting and showing off.'

'I swear I'll sit like a little wallflower all night and not say a word,' Sybil said.

Maudie shook her head. *If only that were true*, she thought. But she knew her sister much better than that.

* * *

Maudie found herself on duty with a girl called Betty. She was from another hut and they had never done a shift together before, so fortunately Maudie didn't have to try too hard to pretend to be Sybil.

Betty was a friendly, chatty girl, with a round, sweet face and large blue eyes like a china doll. She was quite happy to miss the evening's entertainment, as she had already found the man of her dreams.

'I met my Gordon at an RAF dance the first week I joined up, and I swore then I'd never dance with anyone else,' she told Maudie with great pride.

She had brought a basket of mending with her. Maudie watched, astonished, as she pulled out a couple of shirts and what seemed like dozens of pairs of socks.

'I was a seamstress before I came here, and once word got around, all the crews started bringing me little stitching and mending jobs,' she explained. 'I don't mind helping out. I like to think someone's doing the same for my Gordon down at Waddington.'

'Here, pass some over,' Maudie said. 'I might as well give you a hand, since I've nothing else to do.'

And so the pair of them passed a pleasant evening, sewing on buttons and darning socks as they chatted about everything and nothing. Every hour, they would take it in turns to go outside and check the instruments. It was a welcome relief to step outside into the cold, fresh air after the fuggy warmth of the Met Office, with its open coke fire. The fumes made them so sleepy they could scarcely keep their eyes open.

It was always hard to stay awake during night duty. It was different on an ops night, when everyone was too tense to think about sleep. But on a night like this, when the skies were empty and silent, it was all too easy to drift off to sleep.

Sometimes one of the girls would get their hands on the caffeine tablets that were issued to the flying boys. But the rest of the time they had to make do with black coffee and sticking their head out of the window to gulp in the cool night air.

When eight o'clock struck, Betty put down her sewing and stood up, stretching her cramped limbs.

'My turn,' she said.

'I'll make some coffee for when you get back.'

'Good idea.'

Maudie was pouring the coffee into the cups when she heard the door to the Met Office creaking open.

'You're back just in time,' she said. 'I've made it nice and strong.'

'Just the way I like it.'

Maudie looked over her shoulder to see Mitch standing there, grinning.

'What are you doing here?'

'We arranged to meet, remember? When your rotas got switched, I promised I'd come and keep you company.' His smile faltered. 'You haven't forgotten?'

'No. No, of course not.' Maudie's heart sank inside her chest. Why hadn't Sybil warned her she had arranged to meet up with Mitch? She could have said something. Although knowing Sybil, she was so excited about getting to the dance she had probably forgotten. 'Would you like some coffee?'

'Thanks.'

Maudie was aware of him watching her as she poured another cup. She felt suddenly, absurdly nervous.

'You haven't been to the dance, then?' she asked.

'I stuck my head round the door. But it wasn't the same without you.'

Maudie's hand shook so much as she handed him the coffee cup, half of it slopped into the saucer.

Where was Betty? she wondered. She should be back by now.

Maudie sat down and picked up her mending. Mitch perched himself on the edge of the Met officer's desk and watched her.

'What's that you're doing?' he asked.

'Just darning some socks.'

'Who for?'

'I have no idea,' she admitted. 'Betty brought a basket of mending with her, and I thought I'd help out.'

'Really?' he frowned. 'You don't strike me as the sort to mend anyone's socks.'

He was right, Maudie thought. Sybil seldom sewed on her own buttons, let alone anyone else's. 'I had nothing else to do,' she muttered. She could hardly bring herself to look at him. She was sure if he looked into her eyes he would realise at once that she was not Sybil. 'Did you see my sister at the dance?' she asked.

He nodded. 'She seemed to be having a very good time. I don't think she left the dance floor once the whole time I was there.'

So much for being a wallflower, Maudie thought.

'I must say, I was rather surprised,' Mitch went on. 'I always thought she was so quiet.'

'Boring, you mean?'

'No, not at all. She seems like a lovely, caring girl to me.'

Maudie looked down so he wouldn't see her burning face. 'You talk as if you can tell us apart?'

'Of course I can.'

If only you knew, she thought.

She glanced towards the door. 'Hadn't you better be getting back to the dance?'

'I'd rather stay and talk to you.'

'We'll both be in trouble if the duty officer wakes up and catches you here.'

'Who's on tonight?'

'Flight Lieutenant Jarvis.'

'Oh, him. He'll be snoring for hours yet.' Mitch smiled mockingly. 'Anyway, you're not usually bothered about getting into trouble?'

'Yes, well, you haven't seen my charge sheet.'

'So you're turning over a new leaf?'

'That's right.' Maudie shifted away quickly as Mitch took a step towards her. But he moved past her, walked over to the window and lifted the blackout to peer out.

'What's it like in here when there are ops on?' he asked.

Maudie put down her mending and considered the question. 'Tense,' she said at last. 'The duty officer is always on edge, worried in case the forecast turns out to be wrong. It's such a responsibility, you see. And for the rest of us – well, it feels as if we're all holding our breath, waiting for you to come home.'

Mitch nodded, his expression thoughtful.

'What's it like for you?' Maudie asked.

'We don't really think about it,' he said. 'During the day leading up to it is worse. You wake up in the morning knowing that tonight's the night, and you try to just get on with it, but there's this sinking feeling, just here.' He pressed his fist into his abdomen, under his ribs. 'Then you sit through the briefing and try to take it all in, and you laugh and joke with your friends and try to pretend you're not all thinking that this is the night you don't come home.'

'Don't,' Maudie shuddered.

'It's true. Most of the flying boys don't last two weeks. I've been around more than three months, so I reckon I must be on borrowed time.' He smiled grimly.

Maudie felt the same sickness Mitch had just described, like a punch in her stomach. But he was right, she thought. Barely a week went by without them losing at least one of the crews.

'How do you live, knowing every day might be your last?' she whispered.

'You just make every day count.' He turned to face her. 'And you don't ever put off doing what you want to do.'

He was going to kiss her, Maudie realised. And she was going to let him, even though she knew the kiss wasn't really meant for her. She could feel the sensation rising, a tingle spreading up from the tips of her toes as she stared at him, the way his sandy hair fell over his smooth brow, his warm hazel eyes and the curve of his lips . . .

'I'm back!' Betty's sing-song voice broke the spell between them as she clattered through the door. 'Would you believe, I forgot my torch? I had to — Oh!' She stopped short when she saw Mitch. 'Hello! What are you doing here?'

'I just came for a chat.' He was already shifting towards the door with an air of studied nonchalance, but his blushing face gave him away.

'Don't let me interrupt you.'

'No, honestly, I'd best be on my way . . . I'll be seeing you . . .' With a quick nod at Maudie, he hurried out of the office.

'What was that all about?' Betty asked as she settled herself down again.

'I think he was bored.'

'The dance can't be much fun, if he'd rather come down here for entertainment!' Betty sent her an arch look. 'Unless he's got his eye on you?' she said.

Maudie shook her head. 'Not me.'

'Are you sure? I could have sworn I interrupted something—'

'I'll fetch your coffee,' Maudie cut her off. She didn't want to think about what might have happened if Betty hadn't walked in.

'Well, I think he likes you,' Betty called after her. 'Why else would he have come looking for you?'

Maudie smiled sadly to herself as she picked up the coffee cup.

Mitch had come looking, all right. Only it wasn't her he had come looking for.

Chapter 15

When Florence arrived at work the following morning, she found all the girls in the typing pool gathered around Gillian Munroe, who was eagerly recounting the lurid details of the previous evening.

'So I danced with Joe – that's the Italian one – and then he went to fetch me a drink. But he was gone such a long time, I thought he must have forgotten about me. So when Hank asked me to dance, of course I said yes. But then Joe came back, and he went mad. Him and Hank started shouting at each other, and the next thing I knew, they were fighting in the middle of the dance floor and everyone was watching.'

'Imagine having two men fighting over you,' Hilda said.

'I know, it was awful.' Gillian grinned with pride as she said it.

'You're quite right, Gillian, it was awful,' Florence interrupted them. 'It also ruined everyone else's evening. So I wouldn't brag about it, if I were you!'

Gillian fell sullenly silent and the other girls drifted back to their desks. As they passed, she heard Hilda mutter, 'I'll bet she's never had two men fighting over her!'

No sooner were they back at their desks than Clement Saunders came in.

Florence could immediately see there was something not quite right. He wasn't wearing his usual daft grin, nor did he stop to shower his usual compliments around.

93

'Good morning, Mr Saunders,' the girls chorused.

'Morning,' Clement Saunders grunted, then disappeared into his office, slamming the door behind him.

The girls exchanged curious looks.

'Someone got out of bed the wrong side this morning,' Hilda observed.

'What's up with him this morning, I wonder?' Mabel said.

'Did you see how tired he looked?' Gillian commented. 'He looked as if he'd hardly slept.'

'Whether Mr Saunders slept or not, it's none of our business,' Florence said briskly. 'Now, get back to work, all of you. We've already wasted far too much time gossiping this morning.'

The girls settled down to their work, and soon the typewriters were clacking away. Florence glanced over her shoulder at Clement Saunders' closed office door.

There was definitely something wrong with him, she thought. She noticed the way he had grimaced in pain when he walked in, leaning heavily on his stick. Perhaps he had hurt himself when he fell the previous night?

She dismissed the thought. It was no concern of hers, anyway, as long as it didn't interfere with her work.

Clement remained shut away in his office for the rest of the morning. He didn't even emerge when the tea trolley came round. When the tea lady knocked on his door, he waved her away irritably instead of engaging her in chit-chat about her bunions and her boys in the Royal Navy the way he usually did.

He finally came out just as Florence was getting ready to go to lunch. 'If anyone wants me, I'm in a meeting,' he said.

'What time will you be back?'

'I don't know.'

'Who are you meeting?' Florence called after him, but he had already gone.

She listened to his heavy, limping tread retreating down the passageway. There was no meeting, she thought. He was probably skulking off for the afternoon, as it was such a pleasant day. He had done it before, she was certain of it. Last year, on a hot, sunny August day like this, he had claimed he was going out for one of his meetings, only to return two hours later with a telltale stripe of sunburn across his nose.

She had a good mind to report him again, but she knew it would be no use. Clement Saunders had too many friends in high places within the council.

And meanwhile, I'm left doing all his work, she thought sourly.

She thought the same thing after lunch, when she went into his office to leave some reports in his in-tray. The desk was littered as usual, and the wire basket was overflowing. Florence placed the papers on top of the teetering pile. What had he been doing all morning, shut away in here? Whatever it was, he clearly wasn't concentrating on his work.

She looked around the empty office for a moment, then slid into the leather chair behind the desk. She settled back, surveying the room around her.

Now this was how it should be, she thought. She should be the one in charge, not Clement Saunders. At least there would be no sloping off for the afternoon whenever the fancy took her. And there would be no overflowing in-tray, either.

She looked at the papers. Her fingers itched to sort them out and put everything in order, even though it wasn't her job.

The door opened and she jumped guiltily.

'I-I was just . . .' Her words trailed away as she found herself looking up into the cool grey gaze of Colonel Forrest.

If anything, he looked even more dashing than he had the night before, in his immaculate uniform, his cap pulled low on his fair head. Unlike her, who had ditched her curly hair and beautiful silk dress for her old tweed skirt and sensible bun.

'Good day to you, Miss Maguire,' Colonel Forrest greeted her in his deep voice. 'I was told this was Mr Saunders' office?'

'It is, but he's in a meeting. I was just leaving some papers for him to sign ...' She blushed like a schoolgirl, thinking how it must have looked with her sitting in his chair.

'I see.' He smiled slightly.

'Is there anything I can help you with?' Florence offered.

'I just thought I ought to pay you a visit, to express my regret over what happened last night. You left in such a hurry, I didn't get the chance.' He glanced over his shoulder towards the door that led back to the typing pool. 'I hope your girls are OK after what happened?'

Florence thought of Gillian, regaling the others with every sordid detail of her story while they listened avidly. 'They're quite well, thank you,' she said. 'What about the young men in question?'

'Oh, they're being dealt with.' Colonel Forrest frowned. 'I'm sure they won't be brawling again after they've spent a week washing dishes and scrubbing out latrines!'

'I daresay they won't.' Florence smiled. 'Perhaps I should introduce a similar punishment in the typing pool?'

'It's very effective, believe me.'

'I'm sure it is.'

Colonel Forrest straightened his shoulders. 'I just want you to know I believe in discipline for my men, Miss Maguire. I wouldn't like you to think I'd let them get away with that kind of behaviour.'

'I'm glad to hear it, Colonel.'

The silence lengthened. Florence glanced towards the door.

'Speaking of discipline, my girls will be running riot if I don't get back to them soon. So if there's nothing else?'

'As a matter of fact, there is.' Colonel Forrest reached into the pocket of his tunic and pulled out a small box. 'I brought you these.'

Florence stared at it, scarcely able to believe what she was seeing. 'Chocolates?' She looked from him to the box and back again. 'What for?'

'Call it an apology. For last night.'

'That really isn't necessary.' She went to hand the box back to him, but Colonel Forrest shook his head.

'Please keep them,' he said with a smile. 'There's plenty more where they came from.'

Typical Americans, Florence thought. She looked down at the box in her hands. She was tempted to give them back, but it would be a shame to look a gift horse in the mouth.

'I'll make sure Gillian gets them,' she said. 'Unless you want to give them to her yourself?'

Colonel Forrest frowned. 'Gillian?'

'Gillian Munroe. The one that ended up in the middle of the fight? These are meant for her, aren't they?'

'I . . .' Colonel Forrest's face lost its look of handsome composure for a moment. 'I guess so,' he said slowly.

As Florence opened the office door, she could hear the flurry of feet and the scraping of chairs as the girls rushed back to their desks. By the time she walked into the typing pool, they were all back behind their typewriters, looking like butter wouldn't melt.

No one looked up from their work as Florence said goodbye to the colonel. But she could feel their eyes on her all the same.

She kept them waiting until she had taken her seat back on the dais. Then she summoned Gillian and handed her the box of chocolates.

'From Colonel Forrest,' she explained. 'By way of an apology.'

She expected Gillian to snatch them out of her hand, but instead the girl hesitated. 'Are you sure they're meant for me, miss?' she asked.

'Of course they're for you. Who else would the colonel be bringing chocolates for?'

'No idea, miss.'

Florence noticed the knowing grin Gillian gave the other girls as she returned to her desk. What was going on now? she wondered. They could be very perplexing with their little secrets.

But as long as it didn't interfere with her work, it was no concern of hers.

Chapter 16

The day after the dance, Sybil and Maudie were on duty together.

Her sister had been very quiet all morning, and Maudie knew that wasn't a good sign, as it usually meant she was hiding something.

'Well, come on,' Maudie prompted her at breakfast. 'Tell me all about last night.'

Sybil shrugged. 'There in't much to tell. I had a good time.'

'Is that it?'

'What else do you want to know?'

'Who was there? Who did you dance with? Was there any gossip?'

'If there is, I in't telling.'

'You *do* know something!'

'I told you, I in't telling.' Sybil gave her a maddening smile. 'Anyway, I daresay you'll find out soon enough.'

'That in't fair,' Maudie protested. 'I gave up my chance to go to the dance, so the least you could do is tell me all the details!'

'I told you, you'll find out soon enough. Anyway, how did you get on with boring Betty last night?'

'Don't talk about her like that. She's very nice.'

'If you don't mind listening to her droning on about her Gordon for hours on end! Did she bring a ton of mending with her? I hope you didn't help her?' Sybil eyed her accusingly. 'You did, didn't you? You're too soft for your own good, Maudie Maguire!'

'It helped to pass the time,' Maudie defended herself. 'Anyway, I've got a bone to pick with you,' she changed the subject. 'Why didn't you tell me you'd arranged to meet Mitch?'

'Did I?' Sybil looked vague. 'It must have slipped my mind.'

Maudie could have slapped her. She loved her twin sister, but she could be very careless of other people's feelings sometimes.

'Anyway, I'm sure it was fine,' Sybil went on. 'You and Mitch get on like a house on fire, don't you?'

'Not when I'm pretending to be you!' Maudie's face flamed at the memory. 'It was very awkward, if you must know.'

'I'm sure he didn't even notice,' Sybil shrugged carelessly.

'That's not the point. If you're not interested in him, you should tell him. It in't fair to keep him hanging on and hoping.'

'Why are you so concerned?' Sybil sent her a searching look. 'You're not interested in him yourself, are you?'

'No!' The denial escaped far too fast from her lips. But luckily the duty Met officer appeared before Sybil could say any more about it.

*　　*　　*

Sometime in the middle of the afternoon, Sybil went out to check the instruments while Maudie tried to fix the teleprinter machine. It was a temperamental beast at the best of times, and today it had decided to chew the figures from Group HQ into shreds.

Maudie was trying to coax the shredded paper from the guts of the machine when the door behind her opened. Thinking it was her sister, she said, 'This wretched thing's on the blink again. I suppose we're going to have to call a mechanic to unclog it.'

'Shall I have a go?'

She swung round to see Mitch standing in the doorway. She was so flustered she nearly lost her fingertips inside the mouth of the teleprinter.

'Don't sneak up like that!' Panic made her snap.

'Sorry.' He looked at the machine. 'Do you want me to take a look at it?'

'There's no need—' she started to say, but Mitch was already rolling up his sleeves.

'Let's have a look,' he said.

Maudie watched him as he probed inside the machine for a while. 'Can you fix it?' she asked.

'I'll have to take it apart first.' He grinned at her. 'Don't look so worried, I used to be a mechanic before I signed up. I know my way around machinery!'

He lifted the metal carapace from the machine and set it down. They both peered inside.

'There's your problem,' he said, pointing into the dark depths. 'The paper roll has got jammed.'

'Ah.'

'I'll soon have it sorted.'

Maudie watched him as he worked, her gaze fixed on his strong, sinewy forearms. The pale skin was covered with a light smattering of freckles, she noticed. There were freckles on the back of his neck, too, where his sandy hair curled slightly at the nape . . .

'Hello?'

She looked up sharply. Mitch was looking over his shoulder at her.

She dragged her gaze away, embarrassed at being caught staring. 'I'm sorry, did you say something?'

'I said, could you pass me that letter opener?' He held out his hand. 'I just need something to poke about with . . .'

'Here.' Maudie snatched it up and handed it to him, not meeting his eye.

'Thanks.'

She kept her gaze firmly fixed on her own feet as he went back to his work.

'I wonder that you didn't become a mechanic when you joined the RAF?' she said.

'That's what I planned to do. But they gave me all kinds of tests and then they told me they were putting me in an air crew instead. So I became a bomb aimer.'

I wish you could have stayed safe on the ground. The thought came out of nowhere, taking her by surprise.

'There. All sorted.' Mitch handed her a chewed-up scroll of paper. 'It's a bit of a mess, but I think you can still read most of the figures.'

'Thank you.'

For a while, neither of them spoke. Then Mitch suddenly said, 'I enjoyed last night. Perhaps we could do it again sometime?'

Maudie stared at him in panic. 'I can't,' she said.

Mitch laughed nervously. 'Oh lord, and there was me thinking I'd made a good impression!'

'It's not that. I just—'

'What?' he prompted her.

At that moment, Sybil burst in, brushing down her uniform and complaining bitterly at the weather.

'It was so wet, I nearly slipped off that ladder and broke my—Hello, what's all this?' She looked from Maudie to Mitch and back again. 'What are you doing here?'

'I was trying to ask your sister out,' Mitch said. 'But she doesn't seem to be too keen.'

Maudie stared at Sybil, willing her to say something. But her sister stayed stubbornly silent, staring back at her with a maddening smile.

In the end, she couldn't stand it any more. 'I'm sorry,' Maudie blurted out. 'I can't keep up this pretence any more, it really in't fair on you.' She turned to Mitch. 'I didn't mean to deceive you, honestly I didn't. I should have told you the truth when you turned up last night. Or Sybil should.' She glanced back at her sister, who still looked unconcerned.

Mitch frowned. 'So you're not Sybil?' he said slowly.

'No.' She shook her head miserably. 'Sybil asked me to do her duty for her so she could go to the dance. But she didn't mention that she had arranged to meet you here.'

'Why didn't you tell me last night?'

'I-I don't know.'

'I do,' Sybil said. 'It's because she likes you.'

'Syb!' Maudie turned on her, colour scalding her face.

'Well, it's true. You've always liked him, right from the moment you saw him at Paragon Station. But you're so shy you'd never do anything about it.'

'That makes two of us, doesn't it?' Mitch grinned.

'You're lucky to have a twin sister who knows you better than you know yourself, in't it?' Sybil said.

Maudie frowned, looking from one to the other. 'I don't see what's so funny . . .' she started. Then realisation dawned as the pieces began to fall into place. 'Oh! You mean to tell me you knew all along that it was me last night?'

'I told you I could tell you apart, didn't I?'

'Oh, Maudie!' Sybil laughed. 'I reckon you're the one who's been deceived!'

'But I don't understand,' she turned to Mitch. 'Why did you come if you knew I wasn't Sybil?'

'Because it's you he likes, you goose!' Sybil interrupted, before Mitch had a chance to answer. 'Only you were so wrapped up in your readings and your charts, you never noticed. And he was just as bad. He came in to ask you to the dance but he lost his nerve.'

'I did,' Mitch admitted, shamefaced.

'It was driving me mad, watching you both. That's why we decided to cook up our little plan. Eh, Mitch?'

'I saw you talking,' Maudie said. 'Outside the building last week . . .' Suddenly it all started to fall into place. 'Is that why you wanted to swap shifts with me, so I wouldn't go to the dance?'

'Oh no, I'm not that much of a saint!' Sybil laughed. 'I really wanted to go to the dance myself. But I thought since you were pretending to be me, you wouldn't have any choice but to play along when Mitch came to see you.'

'I'm sorry, Maudie,' Mitch said ruefully. 'But as your sister said, you would never have agreed to go out with me otherwise.'

Maudie stared at them both. She didn't know whether to be furious or delighted. 'I can't believe it,' she said. 'I don't think I'll trust either of you ever again!'

'So does that mean you won't go out with me?' Mitch looked crestfallen.

'Of course she'll go out with you,' Sybil cut in, before Maudie had time to reply.

'I don't see how I can refuse, as you've both gone to so much trouble,' Maudie grinned reluctantly.

At that point, the duty Met officer returned, and promptly sent Mitch packing. Under his watchful eye, Maudie and Sybil had to get on with their work, so it wasn't until the shift was over and they were getting ready to leave that Sybil said, 'You can thank me, if you like?'

'I feel like throttling you!' Maudie laughed. 'I really thought he liked you.'

'Sadly not,' Sybil sighed. 'For some mysterious reason, he only has eyes for you.'

'I'm sure you'll find someone else.'

'Happen I already have.'

'I knew it!' Maudie saw the telltale gleam in her sister's eyes. 'Who is it? Go on, tell me. Is it Owen Jones? I know he likes you.'

Sybil shook her head. 'It's a pilot.'

'An officer?' Maudie stared at her. 'Oh, Syb, you know that's not allowed—'

'Then I'll have to be careful, won't I?'

Maudie almost laughed. Careful wasn't a word she could ever use to describe her sister. 'It's not Ackroyd, is it?' she said. 'You know I can't stand him. He's so big-headed . . .'

'It in't Ackroyd. But it is a friend of his.'

There was something in her sister's smile, like the cat that got the cream. Maudie felt the hair on the back of her neck prickle.

'Oh no,' she whispered. 'Syb, you haven't? Please tell me you didn't? Not . . . not him?'

'I'm sure I don't know who you're talking about.' Sybil's face was the picture of innocence.

'Oh, Syb.' Maudie stared at her. 'You've gone too far this time, you really have. What have you done?'

Chapter 17

On Saturday afternoon, Florence took a trip to the Central Library on Albion Street to borrow some books.

When she returned to Jubilee Row, she found her nephews Freddie, George and Archie in a state of high excitement. They came running up the street to greet her.

'Auntie Florence! Guess what? There's a Yank in your house,' Jack's eldest, twelve-year-old George, announced breathlessly.

Florence frowned. 'Are you telling stories again, George? You know what your dad said—'

'It's true. He's come to see you,' George's brother Freddie said.

'He's a pilot,' Iris' son Archie put in.

'He's an officer,' George announced proudly. 'He had a silver eagle on his uniform, just here ...' He pointed to his shoulder. 'Who is he, Aunt Florence?' George asked.

'I have no idea.' There was only one American officer she knew, although why he would be sitting in her parents' house she had no idea. She looked past them towards the house. 'Is Granny May home yet?'

Archie shook his head. 'She's gone down to the Co-op. Mrs Scuttle said there might be onions.'

'Auntie Ruby's at yours, cooking tea,' Freddie said.

'She wouldn't let us stop and talk to him.' Archie looked put out. 'We wanted to ask him questions, but she said we had to go out and play.'

Florence started to walk briskly towards the house, and the boys trailed after her until she reached the doorstep. They went to follow her as she let herself in, but she said, 'You stay here.'

'But Aunt Flor—'

'You heard what your Auntie Ruby said.'

She closed the door on their wails of protest. She was putting her books down on the hallstand, just as her sister-in-law Ruby hurried up the passageway, carrying a tea tray.

'Is that you, Florence?' She looked surprisingly flustered for someone who prided herself on coping in a crisis. 'Oh, thank God. There's a man come to see you—'

'The boys told me.' Florence looked around as she took off her coat and hung it up. 'Where is he?'

'I put him in the parlour.'

'You left him on his own?'

'I couldn't very well bring him into the kitchen, could I? Anyway, he made me nervous.' Ruby shoved the tea tray at Florence. 'Here,' she said. 'You take this in to him. He's your visitor.'

Colonel Forrest was standing by the fireplace, looking at the photographs on the mantelpiece. He seemed to fill the parlour, his smart uniform out of place in the cramped little room.

He turned round and smiled when Florence walked in. There was a large cardboard box on the chenille-covered table, she noticed.

'Miss Maguire—' He began to speak, but Florence cut him off abruptly.

'What are you doing here? How did you find me?' Her voice came out louder than she had intended. Colonel Forrest looked taken aback.

'Pardon me. I took the liberty of telephoning the Corporation office—'

'And they told you where I lived?'

'I told them I was a friend of yours.' He looked shamefaced. 'A bit presumptuous of me, I know . . .'

'Yes, it was rather.'

His face coloured. 'If you'd sooner I left . . .?'

'And waste a perfectly good tea ration?' Florence set down the tray on the table. 'Besides, my mother would be furious if I turned a visitor away.'

Colonel Forrest smiled. 'Speaking of rations – I brought you something.' He nodded towards the box sitting on the table. 'Just a few treats from the Base Exchange. I know how tough it's been for you since the war started.'

Florence stared at the box, then back at him. 'That's very kind of you,' she said. 'But you really didn't have to.'

'I wanted to,' Colonel Forrest said. 'It's the least I could do, after your evening ended so abruptly.'

'Thank you.' Florence couldn't take her eyes off the box. She longed to rip it open and see what was inside, but she held herself back. 'I'm sure my mother will be very pleased.'

'And I hope you might visit the base again sometime?' Colonel Forrest went on. 'Just so we can prove we Yanks can be civilised when we try?'

'Oh, I'm not sure that's a good idea,' Florence said. 'Your men might be civilised, but I don't think I can say the same about for my girls—'

'I wasn't talking about your girls, Miss Maguire. The invitation was for you.'

Florence took her eyes from the box to stare at him. 'Me?'

Colonel Forrest nodded. 'I was hoping you would agree to come to the base as my guest one evening. Or, if not, perhaps you would allow me to take you out to dinner?'

'Whatever for?' The words were out before she could stop herself.

'Well . . .' The officer looked rueful. 'Why else would a man ask a woman out to dinner? I like you, Miss Maguire,' he explained, as Florence still stared at him blankly. 'And I'd like us to be friends.'

'Oh. Oh, I see.' Florence's gaze drifted back to the box. She could feel the heat crawling up her throat into her face.

'I'm sorry, have I offended you? Perhaps you're already spoken for?'

'I'm not.' She could have bitten off her tongue as soon as she'd said the words.

Colonel Forrest looked relieved. 'I'm mighty glad about that. So what do you say? You and me, having dinner together?'

The idea was so outlandish, she had no idea what to say. 'I'll think about it,' she replied.

'How about tonight?' he asked.

'I'm busy,' Florence said. 'I'm helping to train some new fire-watchers.'

'Tomorrow night, then?'

'I'm on ARP duty.'

'Next Friday?'

She shook her head. 'There's a full council meeting in the evening. I've volunteered to take the minutes.'

He smiled, his grey eyes crinkling. 'Are you playing hard to get, Miss Maguire?'

'Why on earth would I do that?' Florence stared at him, genuinely perplexed. 'I'm speaking the truth, Colonel. I have responsibilities, people are relying on me. I can't just drop everything on a whim. If I make a commitment, I like to stick to it.'

Colonel Forrest nodded. 'I respect you for that,' he said, then added, 'As long as you're not giving me the brush-off?'

'I told you I'd think about it.'

The officer looked at her thoughtfully for a moment, then he took a piece of paper from his inside pocket and handed it to her.

'Here's the telephone number for the base,' he said. 'Perhaps you'd like to call me when you've had time to think?'

Chapter 18

After she had seen Colonel Forrest out, Florence took the box of provisions into the kitchen.

She wasn't too surprised to see her sister Iris sitting at the kitchen table, talking to Ruby. News travelled fast in Jubilee Row, after all. And the arrival of a handsome American Air Force officer in the street was bound to set tongues wagging.

Florence moved past them to set the box down on the draining board.

'What are you two talking about, as if I couldn't guess?' she threw over her shoulder.

Ruby had the grace to blush to the roots of her red hair, but Iris was as brazen as usual.

'Who was that?' she demanded.

'Mind your own business. You're nosier than Beattie Scuttle.'

'Our Ruby says he's an American?' Iris said, ignoring her.

Florence looked back at them, briefly enjoying the moment. It was very rare that she caught her sister's interest.

'If you must know, I met him at the dance in Goxhill,' she said.

'Did you now?' Iris exchanged a meaningful look with Ruby across the table. 'You kept that quiet.'

'That's because there's nothing to tell.'

Iris nodded towards the box. 'What's that, then?'

'I don't know. He said they came from the base.'

'Let's have a look!' Iris and Ruby jumped from their seats, elbowing Florence aside in their rush to get to the box. She watched them tearing it open, as eager as bains on Christmas morning, oohing and ahhing over its contents.

'Look! There's coffee and rice and all sorts in here,' Ruby gasped. 'Ma will be pleased.'

'Never mind that – look at these!' Iris pulled out a packet of nylons. 'These are like gold dust.' She turned to Florence, her eyes shining. 'Blimey, what did you have to do to get your hands on these?'

'You must have made an impression on him,' Ruby said.

'More than an impression, I reckon!' Iris laughed. 'I hope you in't one of those girls, Florence? You know, the kind who'd do anything for a stick of bubblegum and a packet of Woodbines!'

'Certainly not!' Florence bristled, which only made her sister laugh even more.

'He must like you if he came all the way from Goxhill to bring you these,' Ruby said, more kindly.

'If you must know, he's asked me to go out for dinner with him.'

That stopped Iris's laughter. They both turned to stare at her, their mouths gaping and eyes wide.

'Why are you looking at me like that?' Florence asked. 'Is it such a shocking idea?'

'Well, yes,' Iris said. 'Since you in't been out with a man since before Armistice Day.'

'And I'm not going now, either,' Florence said.

Ruby and Iris looked at each other. 'And she wonders why she's not married!' Iris said, rolling her eyes.

'Why wouldn't you go?' Ruby asked.

'Because I'm too busy, for one thing.'

'Doing what? Your ARP duty?' Iris mocked her. 'Yes, I can see why sitting in a hut drinking tea with a load of old fogeys is a lot more fun than going out to dinner with a handsome Air Force officer.'

'I wouldn't expect you to understand anything about civic duty!' Florence snapped back. 'Anyway, he was only asking me to be polite,' she added.

'You mean to tell me he took the trouble to find out your home address and come all this way just to be polite?' Ruby said. 'He likes you, Florence. There's no two ways about it.'

Florence remembered the knowing looks the girls in the typing pool had given each other after Colonel Forrest visited the office. Could it be she was missing something? she wondered. Might it really be possible that someone was interested in her? It had been so long since she'd entertained the idea that it hadn't even occurred to her.

Before she had a chance to reply, the back door flew open and her mother bustled in, looking thoroughly disgruntled.

'I'll swing for Beattie Scuttle,' she muttered. 'Nearly an hour I stood outside the Co-op, and there wasn't a sniff of an onion—' She stopped when she saw all the food spread out on the kitchen table. 'What's all this?'

'Christmas has come early,' Iris grinned.

'Florence has an admirer,' Ruby put in.

Florence saw the look of disbelief on her mother's face, and the small flare of happiness inside her died away.

'He came all the way over from Goxhill to ask her out to dinner,' Ruby said.

'Well, I never.' Her mother barely spared Florence a glance as she put down her shopping basket and began to unpack it.

'But she says she won't go,' Ruby went on.

'Yes, well, I'm sure she knows her own mind. Here, put this away, would you?' May handed Ruby a jar of jam. 'I managed to get some bacon scraps, but nowhere near the full ration. They said they'd have more on Thursday.'

Florence stared at her mother. It was as if her news had barely registered with her. She couldn't have shown less interest if she'd tried.

'I've told you, it's my business,' she snapped.

As she flounced out, she heard Ruby say, 'Oh dear, I hope I didn't speak out of turn?'

'You never know with our Florence,' her mother sighed.

'I only said she should give this man a chance.'

'I agree,' Iris piped up. 'Besides, it'll probably be her last chance to find a man.'

'Iris!' her mother scolded, but Florence could hear the laughter in her voice.

It was a huge joke to them, she thought. She wished her mother would stand up for her for once, but deep down she knew May would never do that.

Was the idea of a man showing an interest in her really so amusing and ridiculous? In that moment, standing in the hall, she made up her mind she would find out.

Chapter 19

September 1942

'You don't have to go, you know,' said Joan.

'What else can I do? I can't leave Syb on her own.'

'Why not? She's the one who got herself into this mess.'

After nearly two weeks, it was still the talk of the Waafery. How that hussy Sybil Maguire had stolen Tom Davenport from poor Imogen Banks, and while she was in the sick bay with a bad case of flu, too. Talk about kicking someone while they were down, everyone said.

All the girls in the hut had sided with Imogen, of course, and now no one was speaking to Sybil. The atmosphere was so tense that it was almost a relief when Corporal Banks finally emerged from her sickbed and pulled some strings to have Sybil transferred to another hut.

And what else could Maudie do but go with her?

'I should go, anyway,' she said to Joan as she packed up her kitbag. 'I know I'm not welcome here.'

'That's not true.'

Maudie gazed around the hut. No one bothered to look her way. 'They've all been giving me the cold shoulder, too,' she whispered to Joan. 'They think I'm on Sybil's side.'

'Aren't you?'

'Of course not! I think what she did was awful. I've told her so, too. Not that she takes any notice of me,' she sighed.

They'd had several arguments about it. But as usual with Sybil, Maudie's words went in one ear and out of the other.

She did as she pleased, whatever anyone else thought about it.

'They can't believe I didn't know what Sybil was up to,' she said.

'I believe you,' Joan said loyally.

'Thanks,' Maudie smiled. 'You've been a good pal. I hope we can go on meeting up after I've moved to the new hut?'

'Of course,' Joan said. 'But it won't be the same, will it? No more cosy nights around the stove, chatting and laughing and telling stories.'

'I know.' She looked around at the other girls. They might not think much of her now, but she would miss them all dreadfully. 'I hope the WAAFs in our new hut are as nice as you lot.'

'I only hope your sister doesn't take a fancy to any of their boyfriends!' Joan said.

Maudie was all for packing up and leaving while the other girls were having their supper. But typically Sybil refused to go quietly.

'I still don't see why we're being driven out,' she said loudly, as she stuffed her belongings into her kitbag.

'Please, Syb, don't make a fuss,' Maudie begged. 'It's for the best if we move, honestly.'

She looked round at the faces of the other girls watching them. She could almost feel the hostility coming off them in waves. How could her sister be so oblivious to it?

'But I've done nothing wrong,' Sybil insisted.

'Syb! How can you say that?' Maudie lowered her voice. 'You stole Imogen's boyfriend and broke her heart!'

'I did nothing of the sort! Do you really think I could have stolen him if he'd been happy with her? I mean, look at you and Mitch. I wouldn't stand a chance of taking him away from you, would I? He's besotted with you.'

'Do you ... do you really think so?' Maudie forgot to be angry for a moment.

'Of course. Anyone can see that. But Tom was already bored with Imogen Banks long before I came along. All I did was give him the excuse he needed to leave her.'

'Shh! Don't let Imogen hear you saying that!'

'Why not? It's the truth. It's her own fault for being so clingy.'

Maudie sighed. 'I just wish you'd stayed away from him and saved us both a lot of trouble.'

Sybil grinned. 'You know I couldn't do that, Maud. What is it Granny May always used to say? Trouble's my middle name!'

'Don't I know it?' Maudie smiled back reluctantly. Sybil didn't make life easy for either of them, but it was certainly never dull, either. 'Well, it's done now, anyway,' she said. 'I just hope Tom Davenport is worth it.'

'He'll do for now,' Sybil shrugged.

Maudie looked at her sister. She had a worrying feeling that the real reason Sybil had set her sights on Tom Davenport was because he belonged to someone else. She wondered if Syb was more interested in getting one over on poor Imogen than she was in having him as a boyfriend.

And now she had, it wouldn't be long before she got bored and discarded him like all her other boyfriends.

She thought about what Mitch had said when he found out about Sybil and Tom.

'I don't have much time for him, and neither does anyone else,' he'd said. 'Except Ackroyd, of course, and that's because they're both cut from the same cloth.'

'Why don't you like him?' Maudie had wanted to know.

'He's charming enough, when he wants to be. But he doesn't have many real friends because he gets bored too easily. And he's reckless, too. He likes to take risks, even when he's flying. I just hope your sister doesn't end up getting hurt.'

'There's no chance of that,' Maudie had told him. 'If anyone does any hurting, it's usually Syb!'

Chapter 20

Florence was already convinced William Forrest was not going to show up for their date. She was so sure of it she planned to meet him in town, so no one in Jubilee Row would witness her humiliation. But her mother wouldn't hear of it.

'It's the done thing that he should come here to pick you up,' she said. 'Besides, your father wants to get a look at him, make sure he's all right.'

You mean you want to get a look at him, Florence thought. Her mother had never been a stickler for etiquette before.

'Don't you think I'm a bit old for Pop to be guarding my virtue?' she said.

'That's what I said,' Pop muttered from where he sat cleaning his boots on the back doorstep.

'I know what's right and what's wrong,' Big May insisted stubbornly. 'Unless you don't want him to meet us?' Her eyes narrowed. 'Happen you've got something to hide?'

Only you, Florence thought. While she refused to think for one moment of William Forrest as a potential suitor, she didn't want her mother scaring him off.

Just to make matters worse, the rest of the family decided they wanted to come and have a look, too. Ruby was there, of course; she had practically moved in since Sybil and Maudie left home. But then Iris decided to pay a visit with her children, and even Florence's younger brother Jack had unexpectedly dropped round with his wife Edie.

'We've come to borrow some flour,' Edie said, not meeting Florence's eye.

'Both of you?' Florence turned to her brother.

'Don't look at me,' Jack shrugged. 'Edie only dragged me here because she wanted to be nosey.'

'I did not!' Edie dug him in the ribs, but her blushing face gave her away.

'You can't blame us for being interested,' Iris said. 'It in't often you get a new boyfriend, is it?'

'He's not my boyfriend!' Florence denied heatedly. 'I told you, I'm just showing him round the city, that's all. Councillor Willis says we've got to extend the hand of friendship to our American allies.'

'As long as that's all you extend him!' Jack grinned.

They all laughed. Florence felt the heat rising in her face as she stared round at them all.

'If you're going to make fun then I'm going up to my room!' she snapped.

The sound of their raucous laughter followed Florence as she stomped upstairs.

'Take no notice of her,' she heard her mother saying. 'You know our Florence can't take a joke!'

She went into her room and closed the door behind her, relieved to be alone. The house could seem so claustrophobic sometimes, especially when the whole family was crammed inside its four narrow walls. And the more people there were around her, the more Florence felt at odds with them all.

But the main reason she wanted to be by herself was because she was almost certain William Forrest was going to stand her up, and she didn't want her family to see her humiliation. She needed time to prepare her mask of indifference before she had to face them again.

It was the only preparation she allowed herself. She refused to put on make-up, or to do her hair, or change into anything more fancy than her usual office outfit of skirt and blouse. The next few hours were going to be hard enough to face, without her being trussed up like a Christmas turkey.

As the time crept nearer, Florence became more nervous. Try as she might, she couldn't stop her gaze straying constantly to the alarm clock on her bedside table.

She was just composing herself in front of the mirror and wondering if she should risk the slightest dab of lipstick when Ruby yelled up the stairs, 'Florence! He's here.'

Is he? Oh God! Florence shot to her feet. She ran around her room, tripped over the trailing corner of her bedspread and nearly went flying in her haste to get to the door. And all the time her mind was racing.

He's here. He actually came.

He was in the parlour, sitting at the table, surrounded on all sides by her family. The children were staring at him agog, as were Iris and Edie.

It was all Florence could do not to smile. She could see the astonishment on their faces as plain as day. And no wonder. They were clearly not expecting Florence of all people to bring home a movie star.

She had almost forgotten how handsome he was. Even sitting down, he seemed to tower above everyone else, tall and broad-shouldered, like a god in his USAAF uniform, the silver eagle on his epaulettes.

She turned her head, caught sight of herself reflected in the mirror, and her triumph vanished at the sight of the drab, middle-aged woman who stared back at her.

No wonder her sisters were so surprised. It was certainly not the face of a woman who could charm a handsome American colonel.

'Here she is,' Ruby said.

Everyone turned round to face her, and Colonel Forrest rose to his feet, scattering the children who clustered around him.

'Miss Maguire.' He smiled at her.

'Colonel Forrest.' Florence smiled shyly back.

'Listen to them!' Jack laughed. 'That's a bit formal, in't it? Considering you're courting.'

'Jack!' Florence felt herself turning crimson. 'No one's courting anyone.'

'So where are you taking her?' Iris wanted to know.

'I'm not sure. I guess that's up to Miss Maguire . . .'

'Listen to him! Not even on first-name terms yet. Blimey, you really in't courting, are you?' Jack said.

Colonel Forrest hardly seemed to notice her brother's comment as he offered Florence his arm. 'Are you ready to go?' he said.

Florence took it gratefully. 'More than ready,' she muttered.

*   *   *

'Well, what do you think?' Ruby hardly waited until the front door had closed before she turned to the others.

'He seems like a nice enough lad,' Pop said.

'For a Yank!' Jack put in.

'He's very handsome,' Edie said.

'Oh, aye?' Jack turned to his wife, his brows raised.

'Not as handsome as you, of course.' Edie patted his arm.

'I should think not.' Jack pretended to look offended.

Big May listened to her family talking but for once she did not offer her opinion. She stood at the front window, watching her daughter walk down the street. It seemed so strange to see Florence on a man's arm after all these years. The last time had been with young Donald Davis, just before he went off to war.

'You never know, happen she's met the man of her dreams at last?' Ruby said.

'As long as she doesn't mess it up!' Iris muttered.

'Iris!'

'That's a bit unfair.' Edie looked reproachful.

'I'm sure I in't the only one thinking it,' Iris defended herself. 'You all know what our Florence is like. She's as prickly as a pincushion. You mark my words, it won't be long before she's scared him off. In't that right, Ma?'

'There's nowt wrong with knowing your own mind,' Pop put in, when May didn't reply. 'Florence is no fool and she won't put up with any nonsense, and that's a good thing in my book.' He looked round at the others, daring them to disagree. No one spoke, not even Iris.

Big May turned back to the window. Florence was at the top of the terrace now, turning the corner into Hessle Road. Pop might reckon she knew her own mind, but there was nothing self-assured about her pinched, nervous face as they had left the house.

She looked so stiff and awkward; May's heart went out to her. She had to remind herself that Florence was a forty-two-year-old woman and she certainly did not need her mother's compassion. She didn't need anything from her.

That was what Big May struggled with. She was used to being at the heart of the family, the centre of her children's lives. Grown up as they were, they still all came to her for help and advice, and she was glad to give it.

All except Florence. Even as a child, she had stood alone, apart from the rest of the family. She was so self-possessed, so bright and clever, she didn't seem to need her mother as much as her brothers and sister. And as she grew older, she only grew more distant.

Sometimes May felt as if she looked down on the rest of them, as if they weren't enough for her.

Chapter 21

Florence practically marched Colonel Forrest up Jubilee Row. She could feel all the neighbours watching them from behind their curtains as they passed by. She could imagine what they were saying, too.

Well, I never. Florence Maguire has got herself a fancy man. Wonders will never cease.

At the end of the road, Beattie Scuttle was standing on her doorstep, openly gawping as they hurried past. Florence kept her eyes firmly fixed ahead as she marched Colonel Forrest past her house.

'Hey, hey,' he protested. 'What's the hurry?'

'I'm sorry.' Florence slowed her footsteps as they turned into Hessle Road.

'Anyone would think you didn't want to be seen with me?'

'It's not that.' She looked back over her shoulder. 'I don't want everyone knowing my business, that's all.'

Colonel Forrest smiled. 'I guess that must be hard, coming from such a big family?'

'You can't imagine!' Florence groaned. 'I'm sorry about them all turning up to see you, by the way. It must have been quite an ordeal for you.'

'Oh, I didn't mind at all. They all seemed charming.'

Florence sent him a sideways look. 'You don't have to be polite.'

'I mean it. You're lucky to have such a close and loving family.' He smiled wistfully. 'I miss mine. Especially my boys.'

'Your boys?'

'My sons, Carl and William junior. They're around the same age as your nephews, I think. Seeing those boys really reminded me of them . . .'

But Florence wasn't listening. She stood rooted to the spot in the middle of the street.

'You're married?' she said.

'I'm a widower. My wife died five years ago.' He frowned. 'Do you really think I'd be here with you if I was married?'

'I don't know.' Florence slid her gaze away. 'You hear so many stories about the Americans . . .'

'Overpaid, oversexed and over here, you mean?' Colonel Forrest smiled wryly.

'I'm sorry, I didn't mean to be rude.'

'It's OK, you're right to be careful. I won't deny a lot of our men live up to their reputation. But in my case I can assure you, it isn't true. I'm just here to do my job and get home to my sons.'

'Who's looking after them while you're here?'

'They're at boarding school. But my mother and father are responsible for them while I'm away.'

Florence paused for a moment, looking up and down the broad, busy thoroughfare of Hessle Road.

'Where do you want to go, Colonel?' she asked.

'Please, call me William. Your brother was quite right, we can't go on being so formal with each other.'

'William.' She tested the name. It sounded strange on the tip of her tongue. He looked like a William, she thought, so tall and straight and proud. 'And you can call me Florence.'

'That's a pretty name.'

Florence looked away, flustered at the compliment. 'Is there anything in particular you'd like to see?'

'Wherever you like,' William said. 'Being new to this part of the world, I was hoping you might show me around?'

'There's not much left to see,' Florence said. 'The Luftwaffe have seen to that.' She looked around. 'Unless you want to look at the fish docks?'

'Why not?'

Florence laughed. 'Are you having me on?'

'I did say I wanted to get to know the area, didn't I?'

'All right. The fish docks it is, then. But I'm warning you, it's not a pretty sight.'

If this doesn't put him off, nothing will, Florence thought, as she led the way down to St Andrew's Dock. She pointed out where the trawlers had once come in before they all moved over to the west, and the lines of huts and warehouses that used to bustle with activity but now lay quiet.

She didn't know why she'd brought him to such a grim part of town. It would have been far nicer to take him into the city. Even though much of it had been devastated by bombing, it was still a better bet than down here on the lonely stretch of dockland in the thickening twilight, with a cold wind blowing off the Humber.

But perhaps that was the point, she thought. There was a part of her that wanted to put him off, to make him realise that he shouldn't be wasting his time on her. By showing him the worst of her city, she was showing him the worst of herself.

But if William Forrest was bored by her tour then he managed not to show it. If anything, he listened carefully, asked questions and seemed really interested in what she had to say.

She found herself opening up more, telling him about her family, and how generations of them had fished here, setting off in their trawlers across the North Sea. She explained how her brothers now ventured out on the same sea, this time after far more dangerous prey, their trawlers converted to minesweepers.

She pointed out Goxhill, across the steely expanse of the Humber.

'Home, sweet home,' William said grimly.

Florence sent him a sideways look. 'You don't like it there?'

'It's pretty much the same as every other base,' he shrugged. 'We've been moved around so much since we arrived here, I'm not sure which way is up at the moment.'

'That must be rather inconvenient for a pilot?'

He grinned. 'I guess so.'

Another gust of wind blew off the river, bringing the tang of factories and smoke with it. Florence shivered and wrapped her coat around herself.

'Shall we go get something to eat?' William said. 'Although I don't see any restaurants around here . . .'

'There's always fish and chips?' Florence said.

'I've heard of that. You eat it out of a newspaper, right?'

'It's the best way.'

To his credit, William didn't complain as they huddled together on a bench overlooking the river, eating their fish and chips.

'I've never eaten anything out of newspaper before,' he said.

'You don't like it?'

'It's . . . different.'

'I suppose you live on hamburgers and hot dogs where you come from?'

He shook his head. 'You really have got some ideas about us Americans, haven't you? You shouldn't believe everything about us, you know. We're really not that bad.' He grinned. 'And we've come to help you, don't forget!'

Florence bristled. 'We've managed perfectly well without you so far, thank you very much.'

'Oh really? From what I can see, things haven't been going so well for you guys.'

'At least we're still putting up a fight,' Florence snapped. 'Anyway, don't act as if you've come over here for our benefit when we all know perfectly well you wouldn't have got involved if it hadn't been for Pearl Harbour!'

William looked taken aback, and Florence immediately realised she had gone too far. This was it, she thought. This was where he walked away.

'Boy,' he said at last. 'You really speak your mind, don't you?'

'Is there something wrong with that?'

'No. No, not at all.' He smiled. 'I like it.'

Florence stared down at her chips, cooling in their newspaper wrapping. She didn't quite know what to make of his comment. Did that mean he liked her? Should she be flattered?

She didn't know what to make of any of it, really. It was so many years since she had been out with a man. And even when she was younger, she had never been very good at it. She was always much happier with her head in a book than flirting with the local lads.

'Florence?' She looked up with a start. William was smiling down at her. 'Shall we carry on with our walk?' he said.

Luckily, Florence didn't need to flirt with William Forrest. Instead, they talked as they walked the length of Hessle Road and back. He told her about his life before he joined the air force, his home in South Carolina, where he helped to manage his father's extensive tobacco plantation. It sounded a million miles from the bombed-out streets of Hull.

He also told her about his wife Alice, and how they had been high-school sweethearts, and how devastated he had been when she died, leaving him with two small boys to bring up.

'I don't know how I would have coped without my mother,' he said. 'She stepped in and took over everything.'

'She sounds like a wonderful woman.'

'Oh, she is. Very strong and forthright. She rules our family with a rod of iron.'

'She sounds like my mother,' Florence said.

'You must take after her?'

Florence shook her head. 'Believe me, I'm nothing like my mother!'

As they walked, Florence found herself telling him about Donald, and how he didn't come home from the war all those years ago.

'So you know what it's like to lose someone you love?' William said.

'We were very young.'

'But you've been mourning for him all these years.'

Florence looked away, to where the darkening sky met the iron-grey waters of the Humber. 'Shall we walk further?' she said, changing the subject.

It was a pleasant evening, and Florence was almost sorry when the time came for William to walk her back home. They parted company on the corner of Jubilee Row.

'I'm sure I can find my way to my own front door!' she joked, although the real reason was she didn't want him to come face to face with her family again.

'Thank you for the tour. It was very . . . enlightening.'

She looked at him, sensing sarcasm. But his smile was warm and genuine.

'Perhaps next time we could go into the city, maybe have a meal that doesn't come wrapped in newspaper?' he suggested.

Florence stared, taken aback. 'Next time?'

'I'd like to take you out again, if you wouldn't mind?'

'Why?' The word was out before she could stop herself.

His mouth curved. 'Because I like you, Florence. In spite of all your efforts to put me off.'

'I didn't . . .' Florence started to say, then stopped herself.

William had seen right through her. Instead of dressing up and presenting her best side, she had given him the un-varnished version of herself, sharp tongue and shabby clothes and all. Even the walk into the most down-at-heel part of town and the fish and chips had all been part of it.

And for some reason it hadn't been enough to discourage him.

'Look, if you really don't want to see me again then I'm not going to force you into it,' William said. 'Not that I'm sure anyone could force you into anything,' he added wryly. 'But if you would consent to seeing me again then I would like that very much. I find you intriguing, Florence.'

No one had ever called her intriguing before. Opinionated, yes. Stubborn, even tetchy. But never intriguing. She smiled, liking the sound of it.

'Well?' William prompted. 'Can I see you again?'

Florence pressed her lips together to stop another sharp comment escaping. *No*, was her first, panicky thought. *You're making a mistake, there are better women out there than me . . .*

'That would be very nice,' she answered instead.

Chapter 22

October 1942

'A commission? You?'

Sybil stared at her sister. Maudie was at the plotting table, her head down as she marked the latest readings on the chart.

'I was thinking about it,' she mumbled.

'But we've only been here five minutes. They'd never offer you a commission.'

Maudie blushed. 'Actually, it was the section officer who suggested it,' she said quietly.

'That makes sense. You've always been her favourite.'

Maudie sent her a quick look, then went back to her plotting. 'Yes, well, you haven't gone out of your way to impress her, have you?'

'I'm not a swot like you, if that's what you mean.'

But it still struck Sybil as unfair. It was just like being back at school, when Maudie was offered the chance to stay on and matriculate but Sybil wasn't.

'So when did you and the section officer have this little chat?' she wanted to know.

'Last week.'

'And you've only just decided to mention it?'

'I needed time to think.'

Sybil narrowed her eyes. This wasn't like Maudie. They usually discussed everything.

'What do you reckon?' Maudie asked.

'I don't know why you're bothering to ask me. It sounds as if you've already made up your mind.'

'I wouldn't be asking you if I had, would I?'

Sybil turned away to peep through the blackouts. It was nearly eight o'clock and pitch dark outside, but she knew the planes would be out there like lumbering grey beasts at their dispersal points, waiting for that night's ops.

'It's a lot of extra work,' she said.

'It wouldn't be that much. I'd have to do some studying, and have an interview – I might not even get through,' she said with a little laugh.

Of course she would get through, Sybil thought. Maudie was the one with her head screwed on, everyone said so. The section officer had spotted her potential, too.

No one had ever suggested Sybil might be good officer material. No one had ever suggested she might be good at anything.

Except once.

She thought shamefully of that day at Hammonds, when the supervisor had approached Sybil and asked if she would like to transfer to the accounts office.

'We've noticed you've got a good head for figures,' she had said. 'It's more money, and a chance for you to get on in the company.'

Sybil had been on the verge of saying yes when she remembered that she had borrowed Maudie's dress that morning.

Her worst fears were confirmed when the supervisor said, 'Look, I know what you're going to say. You don't want to leave your sister. But Sybil won't ever aspire to being anything but a shop girl. Not like you. We have high hopes for you, Maud. You mustn't let your sister hold you back.'

Anger had risen inside Sybil, and she was on the verge of blurting out exactly what she thought of the supervisor. But then she took a breath, and felt her rage settling, allowing her to think.

'I'm sorry,' she had said. 'I don't want to leave my sister.'

'But—'

'That's all I've got to say about it. Please don't ask me again.'

And that had been that. The supervisor had never raised the subject again, and Maudie had never known that the conversation took place.

Sybil told herself she had done it for her sister, that Maudie would have been miserable without her. But she still burned with guilt when she thought about it.

'Well? What do you think?' Maudie was watching her anxiously.

'I wonder why you'd want to be bothered with all that extra responsibility,' Sybil shrugged.

'I think I'd quite like it.'

'Having everyone bowing and scraping to you? I bet you would! Well, if you imagine I'm going to salute to you, you've got another thing coming!'

'You'd have to if I was an officer.'

'You'd have to make me!'

'A couple of days of jankers might change that!'

Maudie was laughing as she said it, but Sybil still felt a chill run through her. She could already see a difference in her sister since they had arrived at the station. Back in Jubilee Row, Sybil was the popular, outgoing one. But since all that business with Imogen Banks, the other WAAFs were wary around her. And she struggled with her duties, too. A lot of the work she did barely made sense to her. She wished she had bothered to apply herself during training, instead of going out dancing every night.

But Maudie seemed to be flourishing. She had become more confident, started making other friends. She was always getting praised by their superiors, too. Sybil didn't think she could bear it if they grew any further apart.

'Sounds like someone's having far too much fun in here?' Tom appeared in the doorway, already dressed for that night's ops in his thick cream polo-neck jumper and leather flying jacket. 'Care to share the joke?'

'Just my sister being fanciful,' Sybil said, feasting her eyes on Tom. He looked devilishly handsome, his dark hair flopping in his startling blue eyes. He even managed to make a regulation RAF haircut look dashing. 'Are you off?'

'Looks like it. Unless you can dream up a blanket of fog or something to stop us?' He looked hopefully at Maudie.

'No such luck, I'm afraid.'

'Then I suppose I'll be bidding you a fond farewell?' He swept Sybil into his arms and kissed her. Sybil kissed him back, not caring that the Met officer could come in at any moment.

'Sybil!' Maudie hissed anxiously. 'You'll get into trouble.'

'So what if I do?' Sybil replied carelessly. 'This could be the last time I see him.'

'Don't say that!'

'She's quite right,' Tom said. 'I very well might not come home.'

Maudie turned very pale. Sybil knew how much she hated thinking about all the boys that did not return. It affected them all, but Maudie took every loss to heart.

Tom clutched Sybil's hands in his, pressing them to his heart. 'Would you mourn me dreadfully, darling?' he asked in a dramatic whisper.

Sybil pretended to think about it. 'I expect so,' she said finally. 'For at least a week. Then I daresay I'd find someone else.'

'Sybil!' Maudie looked shocked, but Tom just laughed.

'That's the spirit! Well, goodbye, my fickle sweetheart.' He kissed her again. 'Watch out for me just before dawn, won't you?'

'If I'm not asleep,' Sybil said.

As soon as he'd gone, Maudie turned on her. 'How could you joke about it? What if he doesn't come home?'

'Of course he will.' Sybil lifted a corner of the blackout curtain to look down. She could just make out Tom's tall, lean figure as he strode across the road towards the Briefing Room, his leather jacket flapping. He was still laughing, she could tell.

She had no doubt that he would survive. She didn't know why, when so many other poor unfortunate souls did not, but somehow there was something invincible about Tom Davenport.

'You really like him, don't you?' Maudie's voice interrupted her thoughts.

Sybil shrugged. 'He's good fun.'

'He's more than that, I reckon. You've been together over a month now. That's longer than most of your other boyfriends have lasted.'

'Is it that long?' It didn't feel like it. Maudie was right; usually Sybil would be utterly bored by now. But there was something very special about Tom. He kept her guessing. She never quite knew where she was with him, and that piqued her interest. Even after so long, her stomach still did nervous somersaults when she saw him.

'Are you two serious?' Maudie asked.

Sybil laughed. 'Serious is not a word I'd associate with Tom Davenport! Or me, for that matter.'

And that was the way she liked it. She and Tom were of the same mind, that they should grab life and enjoy it as much as they could, because neither of them knew what was around the corner.

She turned away from the window. 'We're not love's young dream, like you and Mike Mitchell!'

Maudie turned pink. 'Stop it!'

'Where is he, by the way? I thought he'd be here to say goodbye.'

'He's not flying tonight, thank God.'

Maudie looked sick at the thought. Poor girl, Mitch was her first real boyfriend and she had fallen for him hard. Sybil was almost sorry she had helped bring them together because she knew how utterly heartbroken Maudie would be if anything happened to him.

She glanced back towards the blackouts. Outside, she could hear Tom's laughter as he strolled to the dispersal point with the rest of his crew. From the sound of them, anyone would think they were going off on a charabanc outing, not taking a bomber over enemy territory.

He had the right idea, Sybil thought. For the sake of one's heart, it was far better not to take life too seriously.

Chapter 23

It was Monday morning, and that meant another treat for the girls in the Corporation typing pool.

Every Sunday since he and Florence had started courting, William would come to visit Jubilee Row, bringing with him another box of treats from his base's BX stores.

Sometimes it was cosmetics, or stockings, or chocolates for the children. Other times it might be bacon and sugar and coffee for her mother. Whatever he brought would be divided up between Florence's family, and if there was anything left over – which there usually was – Florence would bring it in to work on Monday morning for the girls.

Florence was slightly embarrassed by his generosity.

'You don't have to bring me a present every time you visit,' she would say.

'How else can I buy my way into your affections?' he would reply with a grin.

He was certainly buying the affections of her sisters, not to mention the girls in the typing pool. They were always waiting for her when she arrived on a Monday morning, their eyes fixed greedily on the parcel, like salivating dogs.

Florence smiled to herself as she made them wait as usual, taking her time to hang her cardigan on the back of her chair, smooth back her hair and brush out the creases in her skirt. She had started to look forward to Monday mornings, almost as much as the girls.

Finally, she was ready. Ten pairs of eyes watched her avidly.

'All right,' she said. 'Come and have a look. But no pushing, mind,' she warned them.

They didn't need telling twice. They crowded around her desk, hands reaching into the box, sighing with pleasure as each new treasure was unearthed.

'Chocolate!'

'Lipstick!'

'Ooh, nylons! Can I have them, Miss Maguire? Please?' Dulcie begged, clutching them to her heart.

'Is it your turn?' Florence asked.

'No, it's mine,' said Hilda. 'She had them two weeks ago.'

'I did not!'

'Yes, you did! Give them here!'

Hilda went to snatch the stockings from Dulcie's hands and an unseemly tussle ensued.

'Stop it, both of you. There's more than enough for everyone.' Florence got between their clamouring hands. 'Dulcie, give the nylons to Hilda. I'll ask Colonel Forrest for some more for you.'

'Can I have some too, Miss?' Ivy Grey piped up.

'And me!' Mabel Burrows chimed in.

'I'll see what I can do,' Florence promised.

It was quite nice to be popular for once, she thought, as she watched the girls ransacking the box. Even her sister Iris had started to be a bit more pleasant to her since William had come along with his endless bounty.

Not that all the gifts impressed her mother, of course. Big May was very tight-lipped about William Forrest. Rude, even. William was always unfailingly polite and charming when he came to visit, but her mother refused to be won over. It was almost as if she couldn't bring herself to be pleased for Florence.

Gillian Munroe stood apart from the rest. She seemed loftily unimpressed as she watched them all dive in. Florence was surprised. Gillian was usually the first in there, elbows out, fighting the others off.

'Aren't you going to have a look, Gillian?' she asked.

'No thanks, I don't need them.'

'Gill's got her own Yank boyfriend now,' Hilda said.

'I've been seeing him for ages, for your information,' Gillian snapped.

'He was one of the lads fighting over her at Goxhill,' Dulcie said, through a mouth full of chocolate.

'Not the Italian one,' Hilda put in. 'The other one.'

'His name's Hank,' Deirdre said.

'Hank the Yank!' Dulcie laughed.

Gillian turned on her. 'Shut up, you! You're all just jealous.'

'Gill thinks she's going to marry him,' Hilda told Florence.

'I *am* going to marry him,' Gillian said.

'Has he asked you?'

Gillian shrugged.

'That means no,' Deirdre said.

'Give us a chance! We in't been courting that long.'

'I thought you just said you'd been going out for ages?' Hilda teased.

Florence allowed her thoughts to drift as she listened to them arguing.

She admired Gillian's optimism, and her determination. She certainly never imagined herself marrying William Forrest. In fact, whenever they met she prepared herself for the chance that it might be the last time she saw him.

She knew it wouldn't last. Their lives were too different. William had his life waiting back in America, for one thing. He was always telling her how much he missed his home and his family, and how he longed to see them again.

Florence wasn't surprised. When he described his father's estate, with its thousands of acres and the magnificent house, which had been in the Forrest family since before the Civil War, she imagined something out of *Gone With The Wind*.

'Miss Maguire?'

She swung round. Clement Saunders was standing in the doorway to his office.

'What's going on?' he demanded. 'Why aren't the girls at their desks?'

Florence opened her mouth to speak, but Ivy Grey got there first.

'It's Monday, sir. The day Miss Maguire brings in the box.'

'Oh. That.' His gaze fell on the package on Florence's desk and his face darkened. 'If you must show off, can't you do it in your own time? This is supposed to be a place of work, not a . . . a street bazaar!'

'Yes, of course. I'm sorry, Mr Saunders.' Florence started to gather up the bits and pieces left over and stuffed them back into the box. She did not look round until she heard Clement Saunders slam the door behind her.

'I wonder what's wrong with him?' Hilda said.

'I reckon I know,' Deirdre replied, with a sideways look at the other girls.

'Me too,' Gillian smirked.

'It's just a rumour,' Ivy said piously. 'We shouldn't repeat it.'

'What rumour? What are you talking about?' Hilda asked the question that Florence did not dare.

The other girls looked at each other and exchanged sly smiles.

'We shouldn't say anything,' Ivy warned them. 'We don't even know if it's true.'

'Hank reckons it is,' Gillian said. 'He says he's seen them. Up at the base together, bold as brass.'

Ivy looked at Clement Saunders' closed office door. 'No wonder poor Mr Saunders in't too fond of Americans at the moment,' she said in a low voice.

'Unlike his wife!' Gillian giggled.

'Shh! He'll hear you.'

'What?' Hilda gawped around at the others. 'You don't mean . . .?'

'She's at it again,' Deirdre said.

'With a Yank this time!' Gillian put in.

'That's enough,' Florence interrupted them. 'Mr Saunders is right – this is a place of work. Now, go back to your desks, girls. And we'll have no more gossiping either,' she warned, with a quick glance back at the manager's door.

The girls settled back to their work, but Florence could not stop thinking about what the girls had said.

Surely it couldn't be true? Clement Saunders was so devoted to his wife.

But was she devoted to him? Florence remembered Gwendoline Saunders at the air base dance, having the time of her life as she swooped around the floor in the arms of various American officers.

It certainly explained why Clement Saunders hadn't been his usual cheery self, she thought. Not for a few weeks, at least. He barely stopped to say good morning any more, let alone to shower everyone with compliments the way he used to.

She's at it again, Deirdre had said. Which meant she must have done it before. Florence thought about the framed photograph proudly displayed on Clement Saunders' desk. They looked like such a perfect couple.

It just went to show how deceptive appearances could be.

Chapter 24

November 1942

It was ops night, and Maudie was on her way down to the Flying Control building from the Waafery when her bicycle developed a puncture. She was crouched on the bank by the cinder track, trying to mend it when she heard the crunch of tyres behind her. The next moment, a truck moved slowly past and stopped just in front of her.

'Going our way, love?' A chirpy cockney voice came from the back of the truck. 'Climb in and we'll give you a lift.'

Sergeant Arthur Wallis, the wireless operator of D-Daisy aircraft, grinned out at her through the gap in the canvas flaps at the back of the truck. He was in his early twenties, a former East End barrow boy, stocky and barrel-chested, with slicked black hair and bright blue eyes.

'Yes, please.' Maudie quickly abandoned her bicycle, grabbed his extended hand and scrambled up.

'Someone's in a hurry?' Arthur grinned.

'I want to catch Mitch before he flies.'

'No rush, love. Got a while yet.' Arthur hoisted her up and over the tailgate of the truck. She tumbled into the back where the rest of the D-Daisy crew were already crammed in tightly together, dressed in their flying boots and thick roll-neck sweaters. In the gloom, Maudie picked out the thin, lugubrious face of the crew's mid gunner, Flight Officer George Smith, their navigator Peter Knowles and Sergeant

Mohand Singh, the shy, slightly built medical student who was now the craft's rear gunner.

The atmosphere seemed strangely tense, Maudie thought. Usually the crews tried to put up at least a pretence of laughing and joking before an op. But this time everyone was moodily silent. Even Arthur Wallis' cheeky banter seemed half-hearted.

Then Maudie realised something – or someone – else was missing.

'Where's Flight Lieutenant Cooper?' she asked.

'Good question,' George Smith muttered.

'I'll give you three guesses,' Peter Knowles said.

It didn't take her long to think about it. 'The sick bay?' she said.

'Right first time.' Jack Lawton, the bomb aimer, looked grim. He was a good friend of Mitch's, with grey-green eyes and a mop of brown curls that seemed to look unruly no matter how short he cut them. Like Mitch, he was the quiet one of the crew.

'What's wrong with him now?' John Cooper was always complaining about some imaginary ailment or another, much to the amusement and despair of the rest of the crew.

'Well, that's the funny thing,' Arthur Wallis said. 'He was moaning about having belly ache all last night and no one took any notice. But this morning he woke up in agony, so they whipped him off to the sick bay and it turns out he's got an inflamed appendix!'

'They're operating on him now,' Mohand Singh put in. 'He could have died.'

'And to think none of us believed the poor devil!' Arthur Wallis said.

Maudie looked from one to the other. 'So who's flying?'

The men exchanged wary looks. It was Peter Knowles who finally spoke. 'Squadron Leader Reade.'

'God help us!' Arthur Wallis groaned.

'Oh come on, he's not that bad,' said Singh. 'He's a very experienced officer.'

'A bit too experienced, if you ask me,' George Smith said grimly.

'Past it, you mean?'

'Watch it!' Patrick Eldridge, the crew's flight engineer, eyed them sternly. 'He's only a few years older than me.'

'Yes, but you're still flying,' George Smith pointed out. 'Reade's been stuck behind a desk for the past two years. I'll be surprised if he even remembers the way to the hangar, let alone how to fly the plane!'

'Don't you believe it,' said Eldridge. 'He could fly a Lanc in his sleep.'

'Blimey, let's hope he don't nod off at the controls!' Arthur Wallis replied.

The others laughed, except for Jack Lawton. Maudie glanced across at him. Even in the gloom of the back of the truck, she could see how pale and drawn he was. He looked as if he should be in the sick bay with Flight Lieutenant Cooper.

She leaned across. 'Are you all right?' she whispered.

He nodded. 'I just want tonight to be over.'

'Don't we all?' George Smith muttered.

They all fell silent for a moment. Maudie understood why they were so tense. Flight crews were a superstitious lot, and even the most minor changes were regarded as bad luck.

But it wasn't just that. She had taken the readings from the Stevenson screen herself earlier when she was on duty, and the dew point on the wet bulb thermometer was very low, which, combined with the high barometric pressure, meant the chance of fog.

She peered out of the crack in the canvas flaps, up at the canopy of low cloud. It was even worse now the wind had dropped. Maudie recalled the tense conversation earlier between the Met officer and the wing commander. Flight Lieutenant Ormerod had advised against flying, but apparently the mission was too important to delay.

She thought about the two planes they had lost the previous week, in similar weather conditions. Fourteen young men, their lives snuffed out in a matter of hours.

Please God, don't let it happen again, she prayed silently.

They reached the Flying Control building. Arthur Wallis jumped down first and helped Maudie down.

'There's your boyfriend over there,' he grinned. 'Looks like he's waiting for you.'

Maudie looked across to where Mitch was smoking a cigarette with the rest of P-Popeye's crew. He saw her and waved.

'Thanks for the lift,' Maudie said to Arthur.

'No trouble, love. We'll pick up your bicycle on the way back and drop it off at the Waafery for you, if you like?'

'Would you? That would be really kind.'

'It will be waiting for you in the morning.'

'Thanks.'

Maudie left them and started to walk towards Mitch. But just as she reached the spot where P-Popeye's crew was waiting, someone called her name. She turned to see Jack Lawton hurrying towards her.

'Would you do me a favour?' He reached into his pocket and pulled out a thin blue envelope. 'I forgot to post this letter to my fiancée. Do you think you could put it in the box for me?'

She looked down at the letter in his hand. 'The last post's already gone. You could do it yourself in the morning when you get back?'

146

'I'd rather you did it. If we're late back I might sleep late and miss the first collection. Please?' He proffered the letter again. He was still smiling, but there was a strange tension in his face that she did not quite understand.

'Of course.' She took it from him and slipped it into her pocket.

Lawton turned and walked away, and Maudie headed over to where Mitch and the other boys were standing.

'What did Lawton want?' he asked.

'He gave me a letter to post to his fiancée. I told him he could post it himself tomorrow, but he seemed very insistent about it.'

'Did he?' Mitch looked past her to where Lawton had now rejoined the rest of his crew. There was something about the look on his face that made her wary.

'What is it?' she asked. 'Is something wrong?'

The next moment his smile was back in place. 'No, nothing. Everyone's just a bit on edge, that's all. We've had a bit of a mishap.'

'What sort of mishap?'

'There was a problem with P-Popeye's engine. We're going up in Q-Queenie now.'

Maudie was dismayed. 'Will it be all right?'

'Of course it will,' Ackroyd answered for him. 'I could fly an orange crate if you stuck a set of wings on it!'

But Maudie could see the tension in the pilot's face as he puffed on his cigarette. And no wonder. What with P-Popeye's engine problems, and John Cooper's illness, there were too many bad omens around.

She wished the wing commander had listened to Flight Lieutenant Ormerod when he advised him to cancel ops.

Ackroyd tossed his cigarette butt to the ground and stamped it out with the heel of his flying boot. 'Come on,' he said. 'Can't put this off any longer.'

'Don't forget to kiss your girl for luck,' Owen Jones said.

'As if I would!' Mitch smiled as he took Maudie in his arms and planted a gentle kiss on her lips. It had become a ritual between them on ops night. Mitch called Maudie his good luck charm.

'If I kiss you before I go, it means I'll be coming home,' he said.

'Can I have a kiss for luck, too?' Wally Barnes asked with a cheeky wink.

'No,' Mitch growled back. 'Go and kiss your own girl.'

'I wish I could, mate, but she's been posted to Cambridge, remember?' Wally looked forlorn.

Maudie watched them go, trudging off towards the dispersal points with their helmets tucked under their arms.

'Good luck,' she called after them.

Stuart Ackroyd looked over his shoulder at her. 'What do they need luck for, when they've got the best ruddy pilot in the squadron?' he shouted back.

Chapter 25

Within an hour, the planes had taken off. Maudie was in the hut with the other girls after supper when they heard them revving up at their dispersal points, then taking off one by one, their bellies heavy with their bomb load, labouring to get their weight off the ground before they ran out of runway.

Not long after, they heard a tremendous roar over their heads, as the air filled with bombers from the neighbouring airfields.

'It's a big one tonight,' one of the other Met girls, Maggie, observed.

No wonder the wing commander had been so intent on the men of RAF Holme doing their bit. Maudie thought of Mitch and the rest of his crew. She could imagine them crammed into their seats in the tiny cockpit, all laughter and merriment forgotten, intent on doing their job and then getting home safely.

She suddenly felt very alone and bereft. She wished Sybil was with her, but her sister had gone off to Market Weighton with Tom and some of his friends.

Dot, another of the girls, pressed a cup of cocoa into her hands. 'Mitch will be all right,' she said. 'He'll come home safe.'

'I know.' Maudie tried to smile back at her, grateful for her reassurance.

The corrugated metal walls of the hut offered little protection from the damp evening chill. Inside, a couple of girls sat on their beds, wrapped in a cocoon of blankets to read or write letters, while most of the others huddled around the coke stove, their greatcoats slung over their pyjamas.

Maudie had some mending to do, but she was too worn down by worry to concentrate. Instead, her sewing lay untouched in her lap as she huddled in the warm fug of the stove and listened to the others talking. Tonight they were sharing ghost stories.

Maggie was telling the tale of when she was a parachute packer at RAF Lindholme, down near Doncaster. She and a friend had been waiting late at night for the last aircraft to return so they could collect their parachutes.

'We were just chatting away when we heard the heavy tread of flying boots on the concrete outside.' She looked around at them all, her face shadowy in the flickering light from the stove. 'We thought "oh good – they're back." Then we realised we hadn't heard the plane land.'

'What happened?' Dot whispered.

'Well, the footsteps got to the door and stopped. But no one came in. So we thought they must be mucking about. My friend went and opened the door, but there was no one there.'

'What do you mean, not there?' Claire, a slightly older and rather intimidating R/T operator, asked.

'Just what I said. There was no sign of them. And they didn't come home that night, either. Nor the next.'

'They were gone?' Dot whispered.

'You're making it up,' Claire accused.

'I swear it's true,' Maggie insisted. 'And I'll tell you something else, too. The message confirming them as lost came at exactly the same time as we'd heard them.'

'Don't!' Dot shuddered. 'You're giving me the creeps.'

They all went to bed shortly afterwards, but Maudie couldn't sleep. It had nothing to do with Maggie's ghost story. She couldn't stop thinking about the eight planes on ops somewhere over the North Sea. And judging by the restless stirrings around the hut, she guessed the other girls were having trouble settling, too.

She lay awake, listening. The wind, such as it was, was easterly, so they would probably have to pass over the WAAF huts on their way to the main runway. As the aircraft started to come back they would be right above them, touching down after they crossed the far hedge.

Just before midnight, she heard Sybil creeping into the hut, stumbling about in the dark as she got ready for bed.

'Any news?' she whispered to Maudie.

'Not yet.'

'It'll be all right.'

'I know.'

And then, after what seemed like hours and hours, the planes finally began to come home. Maudie lay in bed, listening to the heavy roar of their engines as they passed over, counting each one in turn.

Four planes. Then five, then six, then seven . . .

And then – nothing. Just an endless silence that seemed to stretch on for ever.

They all sat up in their beds and listened. Maudie could almost feel the other girls straining their ears, willing themselves to hear the telltale engine sound.

After what seemed like an eternity but was probably only a few minutes, they heard another aircraft approaching.

'It's here!' Maggie cried out in the darkness.

'Yes, but it doesn't sound right,' Claire said.

It was true, Maudie thought. The usual roar of four engines was muted. It sounded as if it was limping. Maudie held her breath as she listened to it trundle over the tin roof of the hut.

Almost home, almost home. Come on, you can do it . . .

Then there was one little 'pop' and silence.

As one, the girls all sprang out of bed and rushed outside in pyjamas, heedless of the bitter cold that seeped through their bare feet.

Across the field lay the aircraft, on fire from wingtip to wingtip, its tail section broken off and laying a few feet away. Everything was quiet except for the crackle of the flames. Red flames lit up the sky.

'Oh God,' Claire whispered. 'God, no.'

Sybil grabbed Maudie's hand in the darkness and squeezed it tight.

'Who is it? Can anyone see?' one of the other girls asked.

But Maudie already knew. She could already feel the cold, shrinking sensation in her stomach as she stared at the burning plane.

* * *

'I found this abandoned by the track. I think it's yours?'

Maudie looked at the bicycle, with its sad, flat tyre. 'It is,' she said. 'I left it there when I got a puncture. Arthur Wallis said he'd deliver it back . . .'

She stopped as the words stuck in her throat, nearly choking her. Poor Arthur hadn't been able to keep his promise.

The next moment, she was crying. Mitch let the bicycle fall to the ground and took her in his arms.

'I'm sorry,' she sobbed against his shoulder. 'I don't know why it's hit me so badly this time.'

'It's all right,' Mitch whispered, stroking her hair. 'It's hit us all, love.'

They had lost so many crews in the months Maudie had been at the station. So many young men who had not come home. But never like this. This time it had happened right before her eyes.

She didn't think she would ever forget the sight of that aircraft blazing, the flames lighting up the night sky. When she breathed in, the reek of burning fuel still filled her nostrils, and she could almost feel the heat against her skin.

'They were so close to home . . .' That was what seemed so cruel. That D-Daisy had limped all the way back to the station, only to stumble and fall at the last moment. 'Were they very frightened, do you think?'

'Don't.' Mitch held her closer. She could feel his heart thudding against hers. 'You can't think like that.'

'I can't help it. I couldn't get to sleep last night, wondering about it.'

She had lain awake, imagining what had been going on in D-Daisy's cockpit as they approached the runway.

They must have known where they were. They must have heard the R/T operator's voice, seen the runway and allowed themselves to hope that they were going to come home safe.

Everyone said it was a miracle the plane did not crash into the Waafery on its way down. Squadron Leader Reade must have made one last superhuman effort not to come down on their heads, even if it meant he couldn't manage those last few yards that would have brought them to the runway.

His decision had saved the lives of many WAAFs, but it had cost the crew dear. Did they know it? Maudie wondered. Did they understand they would have to give their own lives to save others?

'You've got to put it out of your head,' Mitch said. 'It will drive you mad if you keep thinking about it. You're safe, and that's all that matters.'

'Yes, but those boys—'

'They knew what they were taking on,' Mitch cut her off. 'They knew the risks. We all do.'

Maudie looked up at his grim face and a remark he had once made suddenly came back to her.

I'm on borrowed time.

A cold sickness rose up inside her. They had only been courting a few weeks, but she already knew that she couldn't bear to lose him. Was this what Sybil meant when she warned her not to get too attached? she wondered. If so, then it was too late.

'Do you know?' she asked him.

'Know what?'

'If you're not coming back?'

He was silent for a long time, and Maudie could tell he was weighing up how to answer her.

'They say you do,' he said finally.

'Do you think that's why Jack asked me to post that letter for him?'

'Yes.'

'You knew too, didn't you?'

Another silence. Mitch let out a long sigh. 'I've heard that some men write letters if they have a feeling they might not be coming home,' he said.

Maudie thought about the letter, still in her pocket. She imagined Jack's poor fiancée receiving it. Words of love from beyond the grave. Would she find them a comfort, or would they cause her more agony?

Either way, she hoped she would never have to open such a letter herself.

Chapter 26

It was a chilly November evening, and Florence was on ARP duty, patrolling the streets looking out for blackout violations.

It wasn't the most exciting way to spend an evening, but it made a welcome change from sitting in the ARP hut, drinking tea and playing whist for hours on end. It was a moonless night, and the darkness closed around her like a dense blanket. But after three years of nightly blackouts, Florence scarcely noticed it any more as she trudged along, her torch angled carefully towards the ground.

As she turned the corner into a tree-lined avenue just off Hedon Road, she suddenly saw a beacon of light piercing the darkness at the far end.

Honestly, how many times did people need to be told? she wondered, as she turned her feeble torch beam in the direction of the front gate.

She banged on the front door, but there was no answer. Florence looked up at the house. What if they'd gone out and left the light on? Thoughtless so-and-so's! She was almost looking forward to issuing them with a fine.

Not that it would trouble the kind of people who lived in a big house like that, she thought. The well-to-do were always the worst.

She bent down and pushed open the letter box to peer inside.

'Hello? Anyone in?'

Once again, there was no answer.

Florence peered into the darkened hallway. 'Hello? It's the ARP warden. Can you answer the door, please?'

She breathed in, and caught the distinct whiff of smoke. 'Hello?' She banged harder, her fist drumming against the door.

Still no reply.

She flicked her torch back on and ran round to the side of the house. The side alley was overgrown, and bare branches scratched at her face and arms as she fought her way through the gate and into the darkened garden.

Thankfully, the back door was unlocked. Florence opened it, and was nearly knocked off her feet by smoke billowing out.

Covering her face with her scarf, she groped her way into the kitchen. Even through the thick wool, she could taste the acrid smoke in her throat.

'What the—' She heard the sound of a man's voice through the smoke, and then, 'Jesus Christ! The pan!'

Everything happened very quickly after that. They both ran for the stove at once, the man went to grab the handle of the flaming pan and then snatched his hand away, cursing with pain. Florence quickly turned off the gas and then picked up a cloth, ran it quickly under the tap and threw it over the pan, dousing the flames.

The man slumped down at the kitchen table, his body sagging with relief. As the smoke cleared, Florence suddenly recognised him.

'Mr Saunders?'

He looked up. He was wearing a shrunken old brown dressing gown. Florence averted her gaze from his exposed chest.

He peered at her, bleary-eyed. 'Miss Maguire? What are you doing here?'

'I was doing my rounds and I saw you'd left a light on upstairs.'

'Did I? Sorry, I must have fallen asleep on the settee. I was dead to the world.'

Dead drunk, more like. Florence could smell the whisky fumes coming off him from the other side of the kitchen, even above the acrid tang of the smoke.

'You'd best go and turn it off now, before I issue you with a fine,' she said.

'A fine?' he laughed bitterly. 'That's the least of my worries.'

He dragged himself slowly to his feet and lumbered off up the hallway. Florence could see him weaving unsteadily towards the stairs, ricocheting off the walls.

She looked around the kitchen. It was an unholy mess, with dirty dishes piled up in the sink. The stove was thick with congealed grease. No wonder it had caught fire, Florence thought.

She had just put the kettle on when Clement returned, clutching a half-empty bottle of whisky.

'How's your hand?' she asked.

'My hand?'

'You burnt it when you picked up the pan?'

'Did I?' He stared at his hand blankly, as if he didn't quite recognise it. 'It seems all right.'

'All the same, you should run it under the tap.'

He ignored her and slumped back down at the kitchen table.

'I'm making you some coffee,' she said.

'No, thanks. I'm fine with this.' He waggled the bottle at her.

'That's a matter of opinion.' Florence watched him swigging from it, her mouth curling with distaste. 'Have you drunk all that?'

'Why? Do you want some?' He offered her the bottle.

'No, thank you.' Florence quivered with disgust.

'Why not? It might do you good to loosen your stays once in a while.'

She ignored the insult. 'I think yours are quite loose enough for both of us,' she said.

'A man's allowed to get drunk in his own home.'

'So drunk he nearly burns the house down with himself in it?'

Clement glanced at the remains of the pan, still smoulder-ing on the stove. 'So what if I do?' he muttered. 'No one cares what happens to me anyway.'

Then, to Florence's horror, he burst into tears.

She stared at him, mortified. She really wanted to run away, but she forced herself to stand rooted to the spot.

'I'm sorry,' Clement sniffed, wiping his face on the sleeve of his dressing gown. 'I don't know what you must think of me. I'm just finding it hard to manage at the moment . . .'

And then he started sobbing again. Florence watched him uneasily. This was all most inappropriate. She wanted to leave the whole sorry scene behind her, but she couldn't just leave him there, nursing a whisky bottle. Heaven only knew what state he would end up in.

'Gwendoline's gone.'

Oh lord, he was speaking again. Florence eyed the back door desperately and wondered if she could possibly just bolt through it.

'Oh?' she said, conveying as best she could that she didn't want to hear what was coming next.

'She's moved in with her sister in Hedon. When she's not out with her fancy man, that is.' He snatched up the bottle and took another gulp.

The kettle boiled and Florence set about making the coffee. It took a while for her to find the pot and some cups. The cupboards were empty, but she managed to retrieve them from the cold, greasy depths of the washing-up in the sink.

All the while, she kept wondering how soon she could decently leave. Even patrolling the chilly streets of Hull was better than this.

'Sorry about the mess,' Clement mumbled. 'I'm used to fending for myself, but I can't seem to be able to bring myself to do anything at the moment.'

Florence looked back at him, cradling his whisky bottle. He was a wretched sight, unkempt and unshaven, his eyes baggy and bloodshot. She suddenly longed for his chirpy good humour.

'She's gone off with a Yank,' he said dully.

Chapter 27

'Ah.' Didn't he know it was extraordinarily bad manners to spill such personal details, Florence thought. He was far too open for her liking especially as she had been trying so hard to ignore all the gossip flying around the office.

'She met him at that wretched dance. I knew it was going to happen,' Clement said. 'As soon as we got there, they were all round her like moths to a flame, flirting with her and asking her to dance. And of course she didn't say no to them. Gwendoline never says no.' His voice was bitter. 'She loves the attention, you see. Says it brings her alive. And it does, you only have to look at her to see it. She glows.' He tilted the bottle in his hands, staring at the amber liquid as it sloshed back and forth. 'I'd hoped nothing would come of it. Nothing serious, anyway. I thought it would fizzle out after a couple of weeks, the way it usually does. But no, not this time.'

She's at it again. Deirdre's words came into Florence's head. 'It's not the first time then?' she asked, in spite of herself.

'Oh no. But not for a while. The last time was when she went off with a Norwegian sailor a couple of years ago. I'd hoped she might have got it all out of her system after that, but apparently not.' He lifted his bleary gaze to meet hers. 'I suppose you think I'm a fool for putting up with it?'

'It's not for me to say, I'm sure.' Once again, Florence eyed the back door.

'Perhaps I am a fool. But I love her, you see. I've adored her ever since we were at school together. And when you're in love, you do foolish things.' His mouth twisted. 'Although I don't suppose you'd ever understand that, would you? I dare-say you've never done a foolish thing in your life?'

Not until I started this conversation. Florence was tight-lipped as she placed the cup of coffee down in front of him.

'Is there someone I can call?' she asked. 'A relative, perhaps, or a friend—'

'It's not all Gwendoline's fault,' Clement went on, ignoring the question. 'It's mine.' He stared down at his hands, his fingers knotted together so tightly his knuckles were white. 'I'm not the husband she deserves.'

Florence thought about Gwendoline Saunders, no doubt currently whooping it up with an American officer in some sordid hotel room. She wasn't sure she deserved any kind of husband.

'Here, drink your coffee.' She pushed the cup across the table towards him.

His mouth twisted bitterly. 'A cup of coffee won't make me feel better!'

'Neither will a bottle of whisky, but that didn't stop you.'

He sent her a long look, then reluctantly picked up his cup and took a sip.

'I've been such a disappointment to her,' he said. 'She gave me chance after chance, but all I ever did was let her down.' He took another gulp of his coffee, grimacing at the taste. 'Lord, this is awful.'

'Drink it,' Florence ordered. 'It will do you good.'

'Yes, Miss Maguire. At once, Miss Maguire.' His mouth twisted. 'You're very good at giving orders, aren't you? Far better than me. No wonder you think you could do my job.'

'I never said that—'

'You don't need to. It's written all over your face every day. And you're probably right,' he sighed. 'I know that job should have been yours. It would have been too, if Gwen's uncle hadn't stepped in and pulled some strings. Got me a nice, safe job at the Corporation. One even I couldn't mess up.' He smiled wryly. 'Except I do, don't I? Every day.'

Florence blushed. 'I don't know about that . . .'

'Oh, come on, Miss Maguire, we both know I'm hopeless. And I'll let you into a secret, shall I?' He leaned across the table towards her, his whisky breath making her reel. 'I don't even like the job. Oh, the girls are great fun. And you . . .' He waved his hand, his voice trailing off, lost for words. 'But all that wretched paperwork! All those endless reports, and invoices and ledgers to keep up to date. I don't see the point in it. It's all so deadly dull.'

Florence bristled. 'I like it,' she said.

'Yes,' he said, giving her a slightly pitying look. 'You would. You're a stickler for that sort of thing.' He made it sound like an insult.

'I wonder you stay in the job, then, if you dislike it so much?' she said.

'That's what I'm trying to tell you – I don't have any choice!' He brought his hand down on the table with a force that made her jump. 'It's my last chance, you see. My only opportunity to make something of myself and be the husband that Gwendoline wants me to be. Heaven knows I've been trying for the last ten years!'

'Ten years?' Florence frowned. 'I thought you said you were childhood sweethearts?'

'We were. But then the war happened and I was sent to France. By the time I came home, Gwendoline had found someone else. I didn't blame her. No one would want to be stuck with a cripple, eh?' He gazed dolefully at his shattered leg. 'Besides, she didn't even know if I was coming home, I spent so many months in that ghastly military hospital. And Alec was there and I wasn't, so—'

'Alec?'

'My cousin. The black sheep of the family, so to speak.' He shook his head. 'I could have told her he was a rogue. The mere fact that he somehow managed to avoid conscription should have told her there was something wrong about him. But he was such a charming devil, he rather swept her off her feet.'

Florence stared at him, intrigued in spite of herself. 'She married your cousin while you were in hospital?'

'Well, yes. Put it like that, it sounds dreadful, doesn't it? But it really wasn't,' he said quickly. 'I don't blame Gwen for anything.'

'I can see that,' Florence muttered.

'And I never stopped loving her,' he said. 'Fifteen years of pining for someone. Pathetic, isn't it? But I don't need to tell you what it's like. You never found another man to replace your boyfriend, did you?'

Florence reached for his coffee cup and refilled it, ignoring his protests.

'What happened to Alec?' she asked.

'Oh, he was an absolute beast to her. Her made her so unhappy. When he wasn't off with other women, he was gambling with his friends. Lost every penny they had. He was so awful, even his own father disowned him. My uncle left it all to me instead.' He looked around him. 'This was his house, as a matter of fact.'

'That must have been a shock for Alec?' Florence said.

'Oh, it was. He was furious. Blamed me, of course. But that was typical of him, always blaming someone else for his misfortune.' He picked up the teaspoon and stirred it around his half-empty cup. 'But at least it brought Gwen to her senses. She finally found the courage to leave him after fifteen years.' He smiled wistfully. 'Poor love. She was in such a terrible state after all those dreadful years. Thank God I was there, waiting for her. Although it took me a long time to persuade her to give me a chance.'

Florence looked around her at the large, comfortable kitchen, with its polished wooden floor and laundry rack hanging from the high ceiling.

I'll bet it did, she thought.

'All I ever wanted to do was make her happy,' he went on, his words slurring. 'I even gave up my career for her.'

'Your career?'

'I trained as a teacher when I came home from the war. I worked in a school out in Hedon for more than ten years, but Gwen said I should set my sights higher, really put my education to good use. And she was right, of course,' he said. 'The only trouble was, I wasn't very good at anything but teaching. I tried all kinds of other jobs, I even managed a paint factory up in Sculcoates for a while. But I couldn't settle to anything. Then her uncle found me the job at the Corporation. And you know how well that's gone ...' He sighed helplessly.

Florence thought of him at his desk, drowning in paperwork and flicking rubber bands at the portraits on the walls. 'Perhaps you should go back to teaching?' she suggested.

Clement shook his head. 'Oh no, I couldn't do that. Gwen said she doesn't want to be married to a penniless schoolmaster with leather patches on his coat and chalk dust on his trousers.' He looked rueful. 'It's a shame, though. I loved my work.'

Florence pictured Gwendoline's beautiful, brittle face. 'Yes, well, your wife's not here, is she?'

'Don't you think I know that? You don't have to remind me!' Clement flopped forward onto the table, his head resting on his arms. 'Oh God, what am I going to do?' he groaned.

Florence stared at him, still fighting the urge to walk away. It was none of her concern, she told herself. She had no business getting involved. And besides, overblown displays of emotion always made her feel uncomfortable. It was the part of her ARP work she disliked most, seeing people who had lost relatives or seen their homes destroyed, having to witness their terrible, heart-rending grief.

But she was never one to shy away from her duty, either. Or from taking charge of a situation.

She took a deep breath. 'The first thing you're going to do is get rid of this.' She snatched up the whisky bottle and carried it over to the sink.

Clement lifted his head, his springy brown hair absurdly ruffled. 'But that's a twenty-year-old single malt – what are you doing?'

'Pouring it away, what does it look like?'

'You can't do that ...' Clement protested feebly, but by then the bottle was already empty.

'Right,' Florence said, turning to face him. 'Now you're going to go upstairs and get a good night's sleep, and tomorrow morning you're going to have a wash and make yourself look respectable, and then you're going to come into work and do your job. And you're also going to tidy this place up,' she added, looking around.

'What's the point?' Clement sighed.

Florence looked at him, slumped at the kitchen table. 'What's the point? Goodness, what state would the world be in if we all thought like that? I daresay we'd all be living under the Nazi jackboot by now if we had that attitude.' She picked up a tea towel and flicked it at him. 'Besides, what would your wife say if she came home and saw you like this, living in a pigsty? She'd probably turn tail and run again, and I wouldn't blame her a bit.'

That seemed to do the trick. Clement looked up, his expression suddenly hopeful. 'Do you think she'll come home?'

Florence had no idea, and she secretly thought he'd be better off if she didn't. But Clement looked so pathetic she didn't dare say so.

'She's come back before, hasn't she?'

'Yes. Yes, she has. You're right, Miss Maguire.'

This seemed to cheer him up. He even found the energy to drain his coffee cup in one gulp.

Florence decided it was safe to leave him. 'I'd best get back on duty,' she said. 'Will you be all right?'

'I won't hit the bottle again, if that's what you mean. You've poured the last of the good stuff away, anyway.' His mouth twisted. 'Thank you for saving my life.' He looked towards the charred pan.

'I'm just doing my duty.'

'Is giving me a good talking-to part of your duty too?'

'Not usually.' She felt a smile twitching at the corners of her mouth and subdued it immediately. 'I'll see you in the office tomorrow morning?'

'Bright and early.'

As Florence headed for the back door, he said, 'Miss Maguire?'

'Yes?'

'Can I call you Florence, since we're friends now?'

Florence drew herself up to her full height. 'Friends? I can't think what gave you that idea,' she said, and left.

Chapter 28

December 1942

'Come on, you two. We haven't got all day!'

The LAC leaned on the horn, startling the occupants of the truck and the young couple locked in a passionate embrace in front of it. The couple separated, blinked for a moment at the irritable driver, then fell into each other's arms again.

Sybil moved to the front of the truck and leaned over the driver's shoulder to look out of the windscreen.

'It's ridiculous,' she muttered. 'They're only going to be apart for a couple of days.' She leaned over and pressed her weight on the horn again. 'Come on! Some of us want to get out of here, even if you don't!'

'Leave them be,' Tom said mildly from behind her. 'They're in love.'

Sybil looked back at him. 'Since when did you become such a romantic?' she said, as she took her seat on the bench beside him.

'Just because I'm immune to it myself doesn't mean I can't appreciate it in other people,' he shrugged.

Just then Maudie appeared at the back of the truck.

'At last!' Sybil reached down to help her sister up. 'I thought it was usually me that kept everyone waiting.'

'Sorry.' Maudie looked shamefaced. She was clutching a small package in her hand, Sybil noticed.

'What's that?' she asked.

'Mitch gave it to me. It's a Christmas present.'

'What's in it?'

'I don't know. He told me not to open it until Christmas Day.'

'Open it now,' Sybil urged.

'I promised I'd wait.'

'Not everyone's as impatient as you, sweetheart.' Tom put his arm around Sybil's shoulders.

They had travelled barely more than fifty yards when the truck lurched to a halt again, throwing them all out of their seats.

'What is it now?' Sybil wondered irritably.

There was a brief conversation between the LAC and someone that she couldn't make out. A moment later, a kitbag was tossed over the tailgate and landed with a thump at their feet.

'Room for one more?' a voice called out cheerily.

'The more the merrier.' Tom took his arm from around Sybil's shoulders to help the young woman up into the truck.

Edwina Jarvis, or Teddy, as everyone called her, was a WAAF section officer who had just been posted to Holme from Elvington. She was only a couple of years older than the twins, and all the WAAFs loved her because she was so kind and down-to-earth, not like an officer at all. The airmen loved her too because she looked like a pin-up girl, with her generous curves, honey blonde hair and sea-green eyes.

Maudie made a very efficient salute, while Sybil managed to unhook her cap and send it flying again.

'Oh, don't bother about that,' Teddy smiled, taking off her own cap. 'We're practically off duty, aren't we? I'm so pleased I caught you,' she went on, in her soft, lisping voice. 'If I don't get the last train to York, I'll be spending Christmas in the railway station!'

'We can't have that,' Tom smiled. He didn't try to put his arm around her again, Sybil noticed. Tom was always very careful about not showing too much affection when he was around other officers.

'No, indeed. My boyfriend would be most disappointed.' Teddy sat down on the bench beside Maudie and decorously pulled her skirt down over her knees. She was wearing silk stockings that showed off her shapely legs, Sybil noticed covetously. She had worn them herself until the malicious Corporal Banks had noticed and put her on yet another charge. Now she had to make do with the hateful, ugly lisle ones they were issued. And, to make matters worse, hers were more darn than stocking these days.

'Is he in Elvington, ma'am?' Maudie asked politely.

Teddy shook her head. 'No, he's stationed at Linton. He's with the Canadian Air Force.' She turned to Maudie. 'What about you? Are you going home for Christmas? Your family lives in Hull, don't they?'

Sybil looked at her in surprise. Officers barely remembered other ranks' names, let alone where they came from.

'Lucky you,' Teddy sighed. 'I've only got two days' leave, and that's not long enough to get home to the Cotswolds.'

'I'm the same,' Tom said. 'By the time I get home to London, I'll have to turn around and come back!'

'Are you spending Christmas together?' Teddy looked from Tom to Sybil and back again. So much for keeping their romance secret, Sybil thought with a smile.

'God, no!' Tom looked shocked at the idea. 'I'm meeting my brothers. They're both stationed in Lincolnshire, so Hull seemed the best place to meet up. So we can all be miserable and homesick together!' He pulled a mock-sorrowful face.

'I've already told you – you'd be more than welcome to spend Christmas with our family,' Sybil said quietly.

Tom shook his head. 'Don't want them to get the wrong idea, do we? They might think I have serious intentions towards you!'

He was grinning when he said it, and Sybil laughed too. But she could see Teddy watching them out of the corner of her eye, and embarrassment stabbed at her.

'What a mean thing to say,' Teddy said. 'I'd jump at the invitation if I were you. Who wouldn't want a lovely family Christmas? It sounds like a wonderful idea.'

She smiled warmly at Sybil, which only made her feel even more humiliated.

'You're right,' Tom said. 'Perhaps I will try to drop in, if I can?'

'Don't put yourself out on my account, will you?' Sybil replied haughtily, even though her heart leapt with hope inside her chest.

The truck reached Paragon Station, and the four of them tumbled out. As they hauled their kitbags out of the back, Sybil looked around.

'Where are your brothers? I'd like to meet them.'

'They're not here yet,' Tom mumbled. 'Their train doesn't get in for a while.'

There was something shifty about the way he said it. But before Sybil could say anything, Maudie suddenly cried, 'Look, it's Pop!'

Sybil turned around slowly, dread uncurling in the pit of her stomach. There, perched on top of his rully, was their grandfather, huddled in his old coat, his cap pulled down low over his eyes.

Teddy laughed. 'A horse and cart! How charming.'

Sybil glanced at Tom. From the look on his face, he didn't find it charming at all. Sybil suddenly saw it through his eyes, the battered cart and ancient horse, with a grizzled old man in tattered clothes driving it. How must it have seemed to a sophisticated doctor's son from London?

Maudie didn't seem to care as she dragged her kitbag across the road towards it, eager to get home. Sybil turned awkwardly to Tom.

'So I might see you on Christmas Day?' she said.

'We'll see.'

She waited for him to kiss her, but all he did was swoop in for a quick peck and then he was gone, walking away briskly. Teddy gave her a quick, sympathetic smile that cut her to the quick and then disappeared into the station.

'Are you coming or what?' Pop called across the road to her. 'Me and Bertha are nithered and we want our tea!'

Sybil hauled her kitbag over the road and dumped it into the back of the cart. As she scrambled up onto the seat beside Maudie, she saw Tom talking to two other tall, dark-haired young men in blue uniforms.

'Are those his brothers?' Maudie spoke up beside her. 'I thought he said they weren't coming until—'

'I don't know, do I?' Sybil snapped, cutting her off. 'Happen they decided to surprise him.'

Or happen he didn't want them to meet you. The thought tormented her all the way home.

Chapter 29

On the Saturday before Christmas, the Americans held a Christmas dance up at Goxhill.

It felt very different to Florence this time, walking in on the arm of Colonel William Forrest. This time she wasn't just a chaperone, a middle-aged wallflower of no interest to anyone. She was an officer's lady, no less, and she could feel the respectful way people looked at her as they entered. They treated her as if she was really someone important at last.

She felt herself walking with her head held high, for once not ashamed of her height, especially as William was still a head taller than her. She had borrowed another dress from Joyce for the occasion, this time in a royal blue colour that flattered her dark colouring and pale skin. She'd curled her hair around her face and, after a lot of pressure from her sister Iris, had even succumbed to face powder and a dab of pink lipstick.

Now, as they walked into the hangar, she was glad she'd made the effort. The dance was in full swing, with a seven-piece band playing, tables groaning with food and everyone laughing and dancing and having a good time under the colourful lights and Christmas decorations that festooned the hangar. There was even a giant Christmas tree twinkling to one side of the stage, something Florence had not seen in years.

Seeing it made her feel strangely bereft, reminding her of all the cheerless Christmases her family and neighbours had endured over the past few years, separated from their loved ones and living in fear.

'Honey, what's wrong?' William looked down at her with concern. 'You look sad.'

'It's nothing, really.' Florence managed a smile. 'I was just looking at all this, and thinking about how we've had to go without for so long. You don't know how lucky you are.'

'How lucky we are, you mean.' William squeezed her hand. 'I'm here to look after you, now. And I'm going to make sure you and your folks have a Christmas to remember. Especially since your mother was kind enough to invite me to spend it with you.'

He looked so pleased, Florence didn't want to tell him how half-hearted her mother's invitation had been.

It was actually Pop who had suggested that William should come to them for Christmas. They were discussing their plans for the usual family get-together, when he suddenly said, 'What about our Florence's boyfriend? We can't leave him out.'

'He's welcome to join us, of course,' Big May had said, but her face had told a different story.

And then, later, Florence had heard her in the kitchen, talking about it with Ruby.

'Don't you like William, Ma? Our Florence seems very fond of him.'

'He's nice enough, I suppose. But I wish she could have found herself a local man,' her mother had muttered.

Nothing she did was ever right, Florence thought. All these years she had made Florence feel like a failure for not having a man. And now she had found herself someone decent, he still wasn't good enough for her.

'Cooee! Miss Maguire!'

She turned round to see Gillian Munroe jitterbugging past her on the dance floor, looking very happy in the arms of her airman boyfriend. They made a lovely couple, she thought, and they certainly knew how to dance. Gillian matched the fast, complicated steps easily, although Florence was dismayed by the amount of leg the girl showed as her partner lifted her up and swooped her through the air. She made a mental note to have a word with Gillian on Monday morning.

The music slowed to a more sedate foxtrot, and a few of the younger couples left the floor. William turned to Florence. 'Shall we dance?' he asked.

'I'm warning you, I'm not much of a dancer,' Florence said, as he led her onto the floor.

Florence held herself stiffly at first as she shuffled around, trying to remember the steps. She was so concerned with not stepping on William's toes she could hardly move her feet at all.

But after a couple of minutes, the music took over and she started to relax.

'You see?' William said. 'You are a dancer, after all.'

'I don't know about that!' Florence muttered, embarrassed.

The band struck up another lively tune, and Florence went to leave, but William held onto her. He whirled her around and Florence laughed, surrendering to the music.

And then, as William spun her round, she suddenly came face to face with a sight that made her freeze where she stood.

On the other side of the dance floor, in the arms of a handsome American captain with sleek dark good looks, was Gwendoline Saunders.

'What is it?' William looked down at her curiously. 'Why have you stopped dancing?'

'I just saw someone I recognised.'

'Do you want to go and say hello?'

'No!' Florence looked away quickly, but not before she had caught Gwendoline's eye. 'No, let's keep dancing.'

William smiled as he swung her round, back into the dance. 'Not a friend of yours, then?'

'Definitely not,' Florence said.

She glanced back at Gwendoline. She looked even more ethereally beautiful in a gown of pewter-coloured satin that made her pale skin glow. She was looking back at Florence with a slight frown, as if she couldn't quite place her.

Florence managed to avoid her for the rest of the evening, although every so often she would hear her voice or pick out her tinkling laughter close by. Every time she heard it, she thought of Clement, sobbing and broken-hearted.

It's none of your business, she kept telling herself. But the image stayed in her mind.

Then, towards the end of the evening, Florence was in the cloakroom when Gwendoline came in.

Florence tried to ignore her as she went on washing her hands at the basin. But she could feel the other woman sending her sideways glances in the mirror.

Finally she said, 'It's Miss Maguire, isn't it?'

Florence's heart sank. 'That's right.'

'I'm Gwendoline Saunders. We met here last—'

'I know who you are,' Florence cut her off abruptly.

Gwendoline looked taken aback as she returned to powdering her nose. There was a pause, and then she spoke again.

'Things were a bit different then,' she said. 'You weren't on the arm of a handsome officer.'

'And you were with your husband.' The words were out before Florence had a chance to think about them.

Gwendoline's pale cheeks coloured. 'Looks like we've both come up in the world, doesn't it?' she said quietly.

Florence thought of poor Clement Saunders, slumped at his kitchen table, drowning his sorrows in whisky. He had clearly taken Florence's pep talk to heart and she could tell he was trying hard to make an effort in the office, at least. He turned up every morning looking quite presentable, and he kept a smile fixed on his face. But the heavy sorrow in his eyes was there for all to see.

And meanwhile here was his wife, without a care in the world, dancing and laughing and looking thoroughly pleased with herself. Florence had never met anyone so utterly heartless.

'That depends what you mean, doesn't it?' she said stiffly. 'If you think breaking your marriage vows is coming up in the world, then I suppose I would have to agree with you.'

Gwendoline stared at her. 'Clem always said you were a rigid old stick.'

'I'm sure there are worse things to be called.' Florence glared back.

Their eyes met and held for a moment. Then Gwendoline turned away to drop her powder compact into her bag. 'Anyway, you know nothing about my marriage.'

'I know your husband is heartbroken.'

Gwendoline's mouth twisted. 'I didn't realise you were so close? Perhaps I'm not the only one who's been breaking my marriage vows? I often wondered about the pair of you, and what you got up to in that office.'

'How dare you!'

'Keep your hair on, I'm only joking.' Gwendoline reached into her bag and took out her lipstick. 'I know Clem would never do that. He's far too dull, poor lamb.'

'Most people would appreciate a husband who's so loyal and devoted.'

'If I wanted devotion I'd get a dog!' Gwendoline applied lipstick to her pursed mouth. 'Anyway, as I said, you know nothing about it. Clem understands me. He knows I get bored, that I need a little adventure sometimes. And he knows I always come back to him in the end, so what's the harm in it?'

'And has it ever occurred to you that he might be hurt by your behaviour?' Florence said. 'I'm sure he seems to understand, because he loves you and he'd do anything to keep you. But that doesn't stop his heart breaking every time you leave.'

Gwendoline's brows lifted. 'My goodness, you have been having a good old chat, haven't you? Perhaps I really should be worried?'

Florence turned away in disgust. She had already said too much, far more than she had meant to say.

Then Gwendoline laughed and said, 'Of course not. You've got your handsome American. What would you want with poor Clem?' She looked away and carried on applying her lipstick. Florence watched her with utter distaste. 'Anyway, you needn't worry,' Gwendoline said. 'I'll be going back home soon enough. I won't have any choice, will I, once they all move down to Bassingbourn? What do they say? All good things must come to an end. Although I daresay you'll be more upset at losing your dashing colonel.'

Florence stared at her blankly. 'Bassingbourn?'

'Their new posting. In Cambridge?' Gwendoline looked at Florence out of the corner of her eye. 'Don't tell me he didn't tell you he was leaving?'

'No,' Florence said quietly. 'He didn't.'

Gwendoline smiled slowly. 'Well, well, well,' she said. 'What does that mean, I wonder?'

Chapter 30

It was nearly midnight but Big May was too wide awake to go to bed. She moved about the kitchen, saying she was tidying up but really just moving things around mindlessly. Every time she passed by the window, she would twitch the curtain aside a fraction to peer out into the darkness.

'Our Florence would have something to say about you showing a light!' Pop said. He was sitting by the dying fire, stirring the ashes with the poker to coax a bit more life out of the embers. Then he added, 'She'll be all right, you know. She's a grown woman. She knows how to take care of herself.'

'What makes you think I'm worried about our Florence?' Big May was indignant.

'Why else would you keep staring out of the window, if you in't waiting for her to come home?'

'I'm only wondering if there'll be another air raid tonight.'

'What on earth makes you think that? We in't had a raid for ages.'

Big May turned on her husband. 'Well, you've done it now, in't you? Them planes will probably be over tonight, now you've said that.'

Pop smiled knowingly. Big May turned away, ignoring his look. After so many years of marriage, he could read her like a book, worst luck.

'The bin lid's blowing around the yard again. I'll just go and put it back,' she said, heading for the back door.

'Here, let me do it.' Pop rose from his armchair.

'No, it's all right. I'll go. I could do with some fresh air.'

Outside, May closed the back door behind her quickly to stop the light from the kitchen spilling out. She stood for a moment, waiting until her eyes got used to the dense darkness. The December night air was so bitterly cold it took her breath away. She only hoped Florence had remembered to take a coat with her . . .

She stopped herself. Of course Florence would have taken a coat. She never forgot anything. She even still carried her gas mask, slung over her shoulder in its battered leather case, even though everyone else had long since given up. Big May had never had to chase after her for anything, even when she was a bain. While May would be trying to get the others ready for school, shouting herself hoarse as they skittered about searching for a lost this or that, Florence would be waiting calmly by the back door, pigtails neatly plaited, shoes polished and schoolbooks in her arms.

Big May had never had to remind her of anything. Florence took care of herself, and always had. Sometimes May felt as if Florence had never really needed her at all.

But that didn't stop her worrying. Not that she would ever let on to Florence. She knew what kind of answer she would get. Florence would give her that slightly superior look, and make some clever, prickly remark. She certainly wouldn't expect a welcoming cup of tea waiting for her like Iris always did. And she would never dream of curling up in the armchair by the fire and telling her mother all about her evening.

Big May knew better than to ask Florence anything because she knew the kind of sharp response she would get. She would certainly never let on how she fretted, how she would lay awake on the nights her daughter did her ARP duty, only relaxing when she heard Florence creeping in through the back door at dawn.

She heard footsteps in the dark, coming down towards the back gate and hurried back inside, tripping over the back step in her rush.

The kitchen was empty. Pop must have turned in for the night, she thought. May was clattering around the kitchen, trying to look busy, as the back door opened and Florence came in.

Big May was struck by how pretty she looked with her dark hair loose around her face and her cheeks flushed from the cold night air.

Florence stopped when she saw her mother. 'Oh! I thought you'd be in bed.'

'I was . . . just making myself some cocoa.' May snatched an empty pan from the draining board. 'Do you want some?'

Florence looked surprised, then shook her head. 'No, thank you. Were you in the yard just now?'

'No. Why?'

'I thought I heard the back door banging shut.'

'Must have been one of the neighbours.' May turned away so her daughter wouldn't see the guilty look in her eyes. 'You know what next door's like when he comes home from his shift.'

'Funny – I didn't see him in the alley.'

Florence shrugged off her coat. She was wearing a beautiful dress in deep blue that really flattered her slender figure. May could have remarked on how well it suited her, but she didn't think Florence would appreciate it. She always shrugged off compliments, especially from her mother.

'Did you have a nice time?' she asked instead.

'Yes, thank you.'

There was something about the way she said it that made May look over her shoulder at her as she poured milk into the pan. While Florence's expression gave nothing away, her mouth was pursed as it always was when she was thoughtful or distracted about something.

May pressed her own lips together to stop her probing too far. She knew how private Florence was, and how she didn't appreciate anyone prying into her business.

Instead she turned her attention to the brown paper parcel Florence had dumped on the table. 'What's that?'

'Leftovers from the dance. There's some cake, and a pork pie I thought Pop might like.'

'More food? We've got more than we know what to do with these days!'

As soon as she'd said the words, May knew she'd made a mistake. For heaven's sake, why couldn't she just thank her daughter, or say something nice?

Florence bristled. 'I can always stop bringing it if you don't want it!' she snapped.

May opened her mouth, wanting to put right her mistake. But pride made the words stick in her throat. Instead she shrugged and said, 'I'm sure your father will appreciate it.' She turned away back to the stove before she could see her daughter's expression. 'Are you sure you don't want a cup of cocoa?' she offered, trying to be conciliatory.

Florence was silent. When May glanced back at her, she saw a strange, almost wistful look in her daughter's face. For a moment it felt as if they were both sharing a vision of how things could be between them. Sitting by the fire, talking about her evening, listening to her daughter's woes. Because there was something on Florence's mind, May was certain of it.

But the next moment, Florence's guard was up again, like a gate clanging shut.

'No thanks,' she said. 'I'm going to bed.'

'Suit yourself.' Once again, May could have bitten off her tongue.

But by the time she had turned around again, Florence had already gone.

Chapter 31

It was nearly six o'clock in the evening on Christmas Eve, and snow had started to fall outside the windows of the Corporation office. Florence could hear the flurries pattering like fingertips against the windows on the other side of the blackout curtains as she sat overlooking the rows of empty desks.

All the other girls in the typing pool had gone home an hour ago. They had been so giddy all afternoon, it was nearly impossible for Florence to keep them to their work.

It had been a relief when they went home, still chattering like starlings about their Christmas plans. Now she was enjoying the blissful solitude as she caught up with her paperwork.

But it wasn't long before her thoughts started straying to William again, just as they had been all day.

She had seen him once since the dance at Goxhill, and he still hadn't mentioned his posting to Cambridge. Florence was waiting for him to tell her, but so far he had said nothing about it.

Perhaps Gwendoline Saunders had got it wrong, she thought. Or perhaps she had made it up, just to be malicious? Florence had no idea. But worry was gnawing away at her all the same.

It just showed how much she meant to him that he hadn't seen fit to tell her. Did she really mean so little to him? She had convinced herself that he might really have feelings for her, but she knew now she was wrong.

'Good lord, Miss Maguire. Are you still here?'

She looked up, startled, to where Clement Saunders stood in the doorway. He was dressed in a heavy overcoat, and he had a small parcel tucked under his arm.

'I thought everyone had gone home?' he said.

'I had some work to finish.'

'On Christmas Eve?'

'Christmas or not, it's got to be done.'

'I'm sure it can wait, whatever it is. You'll be wanting to get home to your family?'

Florence smiled at the thought of the festive chaos that would be waiting for her back at Jubilee Row. Her mother and Ruby would be fussing around trying to get everything ready, falling over each other in the kitchen and sniping at each other.

'I'd only be in the way,' she said.

They were both silent for a moment. Then Clement said, 'Actually, I'm glad you're still here. I've got something for you.'

'For me?'

He handed her the package he was carrying. 'I was going to leave it on your desk for you. But since you're here, you might as well open it.'

He looked shy, Florence noticed, as she unwrapped the gift. In spite of his lanky height, he reminded her of a small, bashful boy.

She unwrapped the brown paper, and took out a book.

'*The Moving Finger*,' she read the title on the cover.

'I know you like reading, since you're always scurrying off to the library. And it struck me you were the sort to enjoy a good mystery?'

'I do,' Florence said. 'And Agatha Christie is one of my favourites.'

'I thought she might be.'

Florence put the book down. 'Thank you,' she said. 'But I haven't bought you anything . . .'

'You've already given me more than you know.'

She frowned. 'I don't understand . . .'

'You saved my life,' Clement said simply. 'And I don't just mean the fire,' he added, as Florence opened her mouth to speak. 'You could have just walked away after that, but you took the trouble to stay and try to talk some sense into me. That meant a great deal to me. And I know how much extra work and responsibility you've been taking on here, in the office.'

'The work had to be done,' Florence said stiffly.

'Yes, but you could have used it to your advantage. If you'd gone to the councillors and told them I hadn't been pulling my weight I might have got into trouble. I might even have lost my job.'

Florence stared at him, shocked. 'I would never do that!'

'I know you wouldn't,' Clement smiled. 'You're a very kind woman, Miss Maguire. Even if you don't want to admit it!'

Florence looked down at the book in her hands. It was a very thoughtful gift. She hadn't realised Clement Saunders took such an interest in her reading habits.

'Anyway,' Clement said brightly, 'with any luck you won't have to cover for me any more. Things are looking up for me at last.'

'Oh?'

'Gwendoline is coming home.'

'Ah.'

'She just turned up last night with her suitcase. She wants to give it another go, she says.'

'And you said yes?'

'Of course. What else would I do?'

Florence looked at him. There was so much she wanted to say, but he was so bright and optimistic she couldn't bring herself to ruin it for him.

'I'm very glad for you,' she said.

He beamed. 'You know, I really wasn't looking forward to Christmas. But this is the best gift I could have had. Next year will be a lot better, I think.'

Florence suddenly thought about William leaving for Cambridge. Would he ever tell her, she wondered, or would he just disappear for ever from her life one day?

'I'm sure it will,' she said.

'Anyway, I'd better get home, or Gwen will think I've walked out on *her* this time!' Clement grinned sheepishly.

Clem would never do that. He's far too dull, poor lamb. Gwendoline's cruel, mocking words came back to her.

'Perhaps you should,' she murmured.

Clement frowned. 'What did you say?'

'I said, perhaps you should get home? We can't have Gwendoline worrying, can we?'

'I should say not!' He grinned at her. 'Well, I'll be on my way. Merry Christmas, Miss Maguire.'

'Mr Saunders?'

He turned at the door. 'Yes?'

There was so much she wanted to say, so much she needed to tell him, but she couldn't bring herself to say the words. She couldn't be the one to crush his spirit. It was a long time since she'd seen him smile, and she didn't want to be the one to take it away.

'Merry Christmas,' she said.

Chapter 32

The Maguires hadn't known a Christmas like it in years.

Since the war had started, Big May had always done her best to work around the rationing and shortages to make sure her family didn't go without too much. But even with her best efforts, their festive feast was hardly the same: the Christmas cake was filled with prunes and iced with soya flour, the Christmas pudding was sweetened with carrots and there were mountains of potatoes and vegetables to make the meagre roast chicken go further.

But this year all that had changed, thanks to Florence's boyfriend. He had arrived that morning with a huge box filled with all kinds of treats, including tinned ham and turkey, butter, bacon, sugar and biscuits, and, of course, lots of chocolate.

'Just to show my appreciation for you having me as a guest in your home, ma'am,' he had said to May.

Beattie Scuttle was certainly impressed with the spread.

'You're so lucky,' she said, as she stood at the stove, stirring the gravy. She and her family always joined the Maguires for Christmas dinner, and she and May shared the cooking every year. 'You'll never want for anything while he's around, will you?'

'My family has never wanted for anything!' Big May prickled defensively.

'You say that, but when was the last time you saw an orange?'

May had to admit that was true. The whole family had been wide-eyed when William produced oranges for each of the children that morning. They now took pride of place in the fruit bowl on the sideboard.

'Your Florence has done well for herself, I reckon,' Beattie went on. 'She's found a good 'un. Mind, she took long enough about it!' she chuckled.

'Hmm.' Big May lifted a big tin of roast potatoes out of the oven and set it down on the draining board.

Beattie looked over her shoulder at her. 'You don't sound too sure about it?' she said. 'Don't you like him?'

'He's nice enough, I suppose.'

'Nice? He's a cracker!' Beattie said. 'Good-looking, generous, charming . . . What more could you want?'

'I don't know.' May carefully heaped the golden roast potatoes onto the serving dish, arranging them around the chicken. 'There's just something about him. He in't like us, is he?'

Every time William Forrest opened his mouth, May was reminded of how different he was. That deep, drawling accent, the way he talked about his mother's charity work and his father's thousands of acres of land. May was shocked to learn he had never even seen the sea before he arrived in England, let alone set foot on a fishing boat.

And it wasn't just oranges, chocolate and tinned ham that William had brought with him. He had also brought change into their lives, and May had seen too many changes in her family over the past few years.

'Give the lad a chance, May,' Beattie said. 'He's doing his best to fit in.'

'I know.'

He had been so good, chatting to everyone all day, and joining in with the boys' games. He had complimented May on everything from her cooking to the tattered paper chains festooned across the parlour ceiling, even though they had seen better days. He had even gone out with Pop to feed and water his horse Bertha that morning, which was above and beyond as far as May was concerned.

'He obviously thinks a lot of your Florence,' Beattie went on. 'And she seems happier than I've seen her in a long time.' She nudged May. 'Here, what if she went and married him?'

'Don't be daft!'

'Why not? They seem fond of each other.'

May turned on her. 'Will you stop talking nonsense? Why would he want to marry our Florence? It's just a friendship, that's all. He'll soon move on and forget all about her.'

She stopped, suddenly aware that her friend was staring towards the door. Looking over her shoulder, she saw Florence standing in the doorway, a tray of dirty glasses in her hands.

'Don't stop on my account, will you?' she said, dumping the tray on the kitchen table. Then she turned on her heel and left, slamming the door behind her.

Beattie turned to May. 'Now you've done it.'

'I have, haven't I?' May sighed.

*　　*　　*

Florence was still stewing over her mother's words after dinner when William asked her to go for a walk.

She had hardly been able to eat her dinner for thinking about it. It didn't help that William was being so wonderful to everyone, charming all the women and laughing and joking with the men. Even Beattie Scuttle was giggling like a schoolgirl by the end of it. Everyone else was laughing and joking, except for Florence, who was too angry to join in.

It wasn't fair, she thought. She should have been enjoying her last Christmas with William, but her mother had ruined it.

He'll soon move on and forget all about her. Her dismissive comment played over and over again in Florence's mind, kindling her rage.

Deep down she knew it was true. And she didn't even mind that much about it, if she was honest. She'd had a wonderful few months with William, but she was sensible enough to know it couldn't last for ever. Now it was over and she was almost looking forward to going back to her old life. With all the gadding about she had done, she had started to miss her steady old routine of work and ARP duty and helping Pop with his newspaper crossword every evening.

But her mother's words still rankled. Did she really have such a low opinion of Florence, that she thought she was so forgettable?

'OK, sweetheart?' Florence came back to the present to see William looking down at her, frowning with concern.

'Fine, thank you.' She tried to smile back, but her muscles were so tense she could hardly move her mouth.

They walked in silence down to the fish docks. The streets were deserted, and the weather was bitterly cold. Neither of them spoke for a long time, and the silence felt like a heavy weight, waiting to fall.

'This is where we came on our first date,' William said suddenly. 'Do you remember?'

'How could I forget?'

She looked up at his profile as he stared out across the grey expanse of water. He looked troubled, she thought. Probably wondering how he was going to tell her it was all over without breaking her heart.

Finally, he said, 'Look, Florence, I've got something to say—'

'Is it about you being posted to Cambridge?' Tension made her blurt out the words.

He looked sharply at her. 'How did you know about that?'

'Someone told me, at the Christmas dance.' She flushed, thinking of Gwendoline's malicious smile.

'I'm sorry, I should have been the one to tell you. I don't know what you must think of me, keeping it from you.'

He looked so downcast, Florence smiled at him. 'It really doesn't matter. We both knew it wasn't going to be for ever, didn't we?'

'Did we?'

She gazed out across the river. 'I suppose it's quite poetic, isn't it? This was where we had our first and our last date. But all good things must come to an end, as they say.' She winced as she parroted the words Gwendoline had spoken that night at the Christmas dance.

'Does it really have to be the end?'

She smiled. 'We're both old enough to know how these things work, William. I'm sure we'll write to each other for a while. But you'll forget about me soon enough.'

Her mother's words rose up in her mind again. She wasn't sure she could bear May's smug expression when she found out it was all over.

'I don't want to forget you, Florence. In fact, I don't think I could if I tried.'

She turned to face him, and realised with a shock that he had dropped to one knee on the cobbles beside her. 'What are you doing—?' she started to say. Then she saw the tiny leather box he had pulled out of his pocket. 'Is . . . is that?'

'Your Christmas present, if you'll have it. Or should I say, if you'll have me?' He flicked open the box and held it out to her. 'Florence Maguire, will you do me the honour of becoming my wife?'

Chapter 33

'Married! You?'

It was Iris who spoke for all of them. The rest of the family just stood there, crowded into the Maguires' tiny parlour, staring open-mouthed at Florence.

'Don't sound so surprised. It's not such a ridiculous idea, is it?' Florence looked from one to the other of them. No one replied.

Big May could only stare too. It was rare that she was lost for words, but her eldest daughter's sudden announcement had caught her completely off guard.

And yet, at the same time, it hadn't been a surprise at all. Big May had been shifting furniture in the parlour in readiness for the party that night when she had seen Florence and William coming up the street hand in hand. There was something about the way Florence was smiling that sent a warning prickle up her spine.

Now here she was, standing next to William, showing off a sparkling engagement ring.

They made a handsome couple, May thought, William's fair hair and blue eyes were a perfect contrast to Florence's dark colouring. She had never seen her daughter looking so radiant.

And then, suddenly, everyone was hugging Florence and shaking William's hand. Ruby and Edie were weeping, her sons were laughing and everyone was talking over each other at once.

'So how did this come about?' Jack asked.

'I'm being posted down to Cambridge,' William explained. 'And as soon as I was told I had to go, I realised I couldn't leave this woman behind.'

May caught her daughter's eye, and wondered if she imagined the glint of triumph there.

So much for nothing more than a friendship, her expression seemed to say.

'And he proposed at the fish docks?' Iris was saying. 'Very romantic, I'm sure.'

'It was where we had our first date,' William said earnestly. 'I could have taken her out to dinner, but I wanted everything to be just right.'

'He asked my permission this morning,' Pop said. 'While we were mucking out Bertha.'

'I wondered why you were so keen to help!' Jack said to William.

'I knew he hadn't offered to help me out of the goodness of his heart,' Pop said. 'Mind, I made him take all the mucky straw out before I gave him my answer!'

Everyone laughed. May stared at her husband, silently furious. Why hadn't he said anything to her? He knew full well she didn't like to be caught unawares.

'So when's the big day?' Ruby asked, when the laughter had died down.

Florence opened her mouth, but William got in first.

'I'll get the application started as soon as I get to Bassing-bourn,' he said. 'From my experience, it will take a long time to get permission, so we need to start straight away.'

'Permission?' Ruby said. 'Who from?'

'My commanding officer. Then there'll be interviews, and Florence will need to supply character references . . .'

'Character references! The lass wants to get married, not join the bloody air force!' Pop said.

William looked rueful. 'It's all part of USAAF protocol, I'm afraid. They try to make it as hard as they can for the men to marry while they're here. You have to be really determined to make it through.'

May looked at her daughter the whole time William was speaking. She was looking dazed, as if she couldn't quite believe what was happening. May understood just how she felt. Her own world seemed to be shifting around her.

'I daresay our Florence will be determined,' Iris muttered beside her. 'Now she's found a man, she in't going to let him get away!'

She said it quietly, but not so quietly that it escaped Florence's attention. May caught her daughter's sharply accusing look. Why was she staring at her? The words had come out of Iris's mouth, not hers.

'Just think, another wedding!' Ruby broke the tense silence. 'We'll have to get everything organised, won't we, Ma?'

'I don't want a big fuss,' Florence said quietly.

'I don't think your mother knows what that means!' Pop laughed. 'Any excuse for a party. In't that right, May?'

'Talking of parties, we've got half the street arriving in a minute, and we in't nearly ready,' May replied, glad to change the subject.

'And we've really got something to celebrate tonight, eh?' Pop winked at Florence.

'No one will be celebrating anything if we don't get this furniture shifted.' May nodded to Jack. 'Push back the settee, will you? And shift the piano into the middle a bit.'

'I'll help.' William stepped forward, already rolling up his sleeves.

'It's all right, you're a guest.'

'No, let him help out. He'll be family soon,' Jack reminded her.

May eyed the tall, handsome American. She couldn't imagine him ever fitting into the Maguire clan. If anything, he would tear it apart.

'Do what you like,' she muttered. 'I've got the food to sort out. Ruby, come and give me a hand.'

'I'll help you,' Florence cut in.

They looked at each other, and May read the unspoken message in her daughter's eyes.

'As you like,' she said.

She could feel the weight of anticipation on her shoulders as Florence followed her down the narrow passageway into the kitchen. But her daughter remained silent as they started making the sandwiches.

May wondered if Florence was waiting for her to say something, but for once words eluded her. She was still struggling to come to terms with what had just happened.

Florence was getting married. It seemed such a strange idea, May could scarcely believe it.

She glanced out of the corner of her eye at her daughter, spreading potted meat on slices of bread with rapid, jerky movements. She seemed nervous, on edge, hardly like a radiant bride.

Or perhaps that was just her imagination? It was so hard to tell with Florence. She was like a book in a language May didn't understand.

They had always rubbed each other up the wrong way. May couldn't fathom her daughter's mind, so she was forever saying the wrong thing, earning herself another spiky retort.

She felt as if her daughter despised her sometimes. Florence acted as if she was so much better than the rest of them, with her good job and her independence. May knew Iris and Ruby and Edie felt it, too. Florence looked down on them all because they were nothing more than wives and mothers, with lives that barely extended beyond the narrow little terrace where they lived.

But May wished she could be as close to her daughter as she was to the other girls. Even Ruby and Edie, who were only family by marriage, felt more like her daughters than her own flesh and blood. She wished she could share her daughter's excitement at her engagement, instead of standing here in prickly silence, wondering what to say next.

From the far end of the passageway came the sound of a crash, followed by muffled laughter. May wondered what damage the men were causing in the parlour.

It wasn't until they had nearly finished preparing the food that Florence spoke up.

'Well?' she said in that sharp voice May knew so well.

'Well what?'

'What do you think about me and William getting married?' Florence turned to face her. 'You've said nothing about it since we told everyone.'

May looked down at the sandwich she was cutting. 'Happen I in't got anything to say.'

'That's not like you. You've always got something to say about everything.'

She was right. There was a lot May wanted to say, but the words wouldn't come.

She wanted to tell Florence how she would miss her clever comments and superior attitude, which made her smile as much as they irked her. Florence always gave as good as she got, and May secretly enjoyed their sparring.

Most of all, she wanted to tell Florence how proud she was of her. Contrary and wilful and independent as she was, she had accepted what fate had handed to her and made her own way in the world in a manner that May could never have done.

But underneath all that prickly independence, she was still May's little girl. And now she bitterly regretted that they were not close enough for her even now to speak up and tell her how much she cared.

'It's very sudden,' was all she could say.

'I'm forty-two,' Florence reminded her. 'Hardly a child bride.'

'All the same, you hardly know him.'

Florence put her knife down with a clatter that made May jump. 'I can't do anything right, can I? I thought you'd be pleased for me. You were happy enough when our Iris got wed,' she added, a bitter edge to her voice.

'Yes, well, we've known Sam for years.'

'What difference does that make?'

Sam was never going to take our Iris away from me. May pressed her lips together, to stop her fear loosening her tongue and making her say something foolish. The last thing she ever wanted to do was expose how afraid and vulnerable she felt.

'It's up to you, anyway,' she said, keeping her eyes fixed on her cutting. 'As you said, you're old enough to make your own decisions.'

'Yes. Yes, I am.' Florence sounded defiant. May didn't need to look at her to see the proud tilt of her chin and her blazing dark eyes. 'I thought you'd be happy for me,' she said. 'This is what you've always wanted, isn't it? For me to be married like the others?'

There was something about the choked emotion in her voice that made May turned round. But she was too late; Florence had already flounced out, slamming the kitchen door behind her.

Chapter 34

Sybil stood at the window of her grandparents' bedroom, staring out at the darkened street.

Downstairs, the party was still in full swing. Harry Pearce was at the piano in the parlour, thumping out 'You Made Me Love You', and everyone was singing along at the tops of their voices. The floor beneath Sybil's feet shook with the sound.

Sybil would usually be in the thick of it, laughing and singing and dancing with the rest of them. But she couldn't face it. She thought she would go mad if she had to pretend to be happy for a moment longer.

She looked back down at the street, even though she could see nothing in the blackness. There was no moon, not a star in the sky. She wouldn't be able to see Tom even if he did come.

But he wasn't coming. She knew that, had known it for a while. But she still couldn't seem to drag herself away from the window, to give up that last shred of hope.

He hadn't said he would come, she kept reminding herself. *We'll see*, was all he had said, maddeningly enigmatic as always.

But somehow Sybil had taken that as a promise, simply because she had never known a young man not to jump at the chance of spending time with her.

She had been so happy that morning, excited at the prospect of showing Tom off to her family. She had even told them he was coming.

'Well, I hope he in't expecting any dinner?' her grandmother had said. 'We're feeding the five thousand as it is!'

'Take no notice,' her mother had smiled. 'We can always find room for one more. I've never known Granny May turn anyone away hungry!'

'There's always a first time,' her grandmother had grumbled ominously.

But dinner had come and gone, and there had been no sign of Tom.

'He'll probably come later,' Sybil had said. 'I expect he's just lost track of time.'

'Sounds like you've got a lot in common!' her mother had replied.

Sybil had comforted herself, imagining how impressed they would all be when she showed Tom off to them. She hoped he would wear his RAF uniform because it made him look even more handsome. She pictured herself introducing him to her parents, basking in the admiration of her family. No doubt her aunties would all swoon over him, she thought. He was even better-looking than Auntie Florence's American colonel.

But the afternoon had worn on, and her confidence had faded with it.

'Where's this famous boyfriend of yours?' Uncle John had teased her. 'Stood you up, I reckon.'

'We didn't make any definite arrangements,' Sybil had said.

'That's not what you said earlier,' John had grinned. 'Happen he's forgotten about you?'

Then her Auntie Florence had come back from her walk with William with a ring on her finger and everyone had been in such a state of shock about it they had thankfully forgotten all about Tom.

But not Sybil. Even when it grew dark, she couldn't seem to stop herself going to the window and looking out. In the end, her mother had told her off for opening the blackouts, so she had sneaked upstairs to her grandparents' room to keep watch from there.

Granny May's bedroom had a faint scent of violets mingled with mothballs. As her eyes got used to the gloom, Sybil could make out the big, dark, heavy furniture that made the small room seem even more cramped. The big bed was covered with a silky eiderdown that had grown soft and worn with age.

There were footsteps coming up the stairs. Sybil hoped it would just be Auntie Florence going to her own room. But then she heard her sister's voice on the landing, calling out to her.

Maudie pushed the door open and stood in the open doorway, outlined in the light spilling from the landing. 'There you are. I was looking for you.'

'Close the door if you're coming in,' Sybil snapped irritably. 'You're letting the light in.'

The door closed, plunging the room into darkness again. Sybil heard her sister groping her way across the room, yelping in pain as she banged her shin on the carved wooden bedpost.

She came to sit beside Sybil on the bed. 'Still no sign of him?' she said.

Sybil stiffened at the sympathy in her voice. The last thing she wanted was her sister's pity.

'I wasn't looking for him,' she said. 'I only came upstairs to get some peace and quiet.'

Maudie said nothing, but Sybil knew she didn't believe her. It was hard to lie to your own twin, unfortunately.

'I'm sorry,' Maudie whispered in the darkness. 'I know you're disappointed.'

'Me? Disappointed?' Sybil shrugged. 'I in't disappointed. It wasn't even an arrangement, anyway. He only said he might come.'

She had just expected he would, because men usually rushed to do her bidding.

And that was what attracted her to Tom. He was the only man she had ever known who kept her guessing. She never knew where she was with him, which only made her fall for him even more.

And she had fallen for him. Being apart from him, even for a couple of days, had brought it home to her how much she cared.

She hadn't meant for it to happen. Tom was only ever supposed to be a bit of fun. If she was honest, the main reason she had pursued him was to spite Imogen Banks. But somehow, without her being aware of it, it had developed into something much more serious.

For her, anyway. She wasn't sure how Tom felt about her. And that, in itself, was enough to make her want him even more.

'Perhaps he didn't feel he could leave his brothers?' Maudie suggested.

Sybil had thought of that. She had even thought that Tom might bring them with him. They would all go dancing together and Sybil would flirt with them and drive Tom wild with jealousy so he finally realised how much he loved her.

'I told you, I'm not bothered,' she turned on her. 'I just wanted some peace and quiet. So if you're going to keep nattering I'd prefer it if you just left!'

'Sorry.' Maudie fell silent, but she didn't move. Sybil was secretly pleased her sister stayed with her. She had always hated being alone.

They sat quietly for a while. Outside in the street, Sybil caught the faint, wavering beam of a torch weaving down the street and her heart lifted, only to sink again when she realised it was only Mr Barnett from across the road, returning from his shift at the Smith & Nephew factory.

'What do you think about Auntie Florence getting married, then?' Maudie said, breaking the silence.

'I don't know why she's bothering,' Sybil said. 'She's too old to get married.'

'Syb!' Maudie was reproachful. 'I'm pleased for her,' she sighed. 'She's waited all these years, and now she's finally found love. I think it's romantic.'

'You would,' Sybil muttered. Maudie had started seeing everything through rose-tinted glasses since she began courting. It was hard to believe she used to be the sensible one.

'Colonel Forrest is such a nice man, don't you think?' Maudie went on. 'And so good-looking.'

'He's all right, I suppose. But he in't much fun.'

'What makes you say that?'

'Didn't you see his face when everyone was laughing and joking around the table? He wasn't really joining in. He was just staring round at everyone, as if he couldn't understand a word we were saying.'

'Happen he couldn't?' Maudie said.

Sybil shook her head. 'It in't that. He strikes me as a dry old stick. Not much of a sense of humour.'

'He and Auntie Florence should make a good couple, then.'

'Maudie Maguire!' Sybil turned on her, shocked. 'And I thought you were meant to be all sweetness and light? That's the sort of thing I'd say!'

'Happen you've rubbed off on—'

'Listen!' Sybil held up her hand. 'Did you hear that?'

Maudie cocked her head. 'I can't hear anything over that racket downstairs.'

The next minute, their father called up the stairs, 'Are you up there, girls? There's a young man in an RAF uniform looking lost in the street. I reckon he must be after one of you two?'

'Tom!'

Sybil jumped to her feet, tripping over her sister's feet in her mad dash to get out. She rushed downstairs and threw open the front door, ignoring everyone's cries of protest that she was letting the light in.

'You took your time—' she started to say, but as the young man approached, she realised it wasn't Tom.

'Syb?' Mitch stepped out of the darkness towards her. 'Thank God it's you. I forgot which number house Maudie told me she lived at. I've been walking up and down for ages.'

'You should have knocked on any door, lad,' Pop grinned. 'You'll find a Maguire behind most of 'em!'

'Mitch?' Maudie appeared at the foot of the stairs as the rest of the family crowded round to get a look at their visitor. 'What are you doing here?'

'I was given tonight as leave so I thought I'd hitch-hike over and see you.'

'You hitch-hiked all the way from Holme? It must have taken you ages.'

'It was worth it.' He grinned sheepishly. 'I missed you.'

They fell into each other's arms as the rest of the family looked on approvingly.

'Look at that,' their mother sighed. 'What a lovely thing to do.'

'That's love, that is,' Sybil heard her Auntie Iris reply.

'Well, don't just stand there letting all the light out!' Granny May broke the romantic moment. 'Bring the lad in. I daresay he'll be nithered after coming all that way.'

Sybil watched as Maudie shyly introduced Mitch to everyone, and he was quickly welcomed inside to join the party.

'Fancy coming all that way,' John murmured to her. 'And your boyfriend couldn't even catch a bus from the city centre!'

'Shut up, you!' Sybil turned on him sourly.

As they ushered Mitch into the parlour, Maudie turned to look over her shoulder at her. There it was again, that look of sympathy.

Sybil looked away sharply. She had never been the object of anyone's pity before, and she didn't like it one bit.

Chapter 35

It was a relief to get back to the office.

Looking out of the bus window, Clement had seen people shuffling dispiritedly through the grey December morning, their heads down, shoulders hunched against the miserably wet day. They seemed sad at the prospect of going back to work after celebrating Christmas with their friends and family.

But Clement couldn't wait to get out of the house.

It hadn't been the Christmas he had hoped for. Gwendoline had been quite dissatisfied, despite his best efforts. She did not like the Christmas tree he had gone to great trouble to find, and she laughed unkindly at the decorations he had put up.

But at least she had brightened up when she saw the necklace he'd bought her.

'I haven't got you anything,' she'd said, as she ripped off the paper wrapping eagerly.

'Having you home is the only present I need,' Clement had said, reaching for her. Gwendoline had then allowed him to hold her hand for at least a couple of minutes before slipping from his grasp, saying she needed a drink.

Her good mood hadn't lasted long. Over dinner, she had decided to tell him that she wanted to sell the house and move.

'I've always hated this place,' she had declared.

'I thought you liked it? You couldn't wait to move in after we married.'

'Yes, but it was Alec's home before it was ours. He grew up here.'

'That never seemed to bother you before?'

'Yes, well, it bothers me now.' She had glared at him across the table. 'If this marriage is going to work then we need to make a proper fresh start.'

Clement saw the glint in her eyes, daring him to argue, and he knew she was spoiling for a fight. He also knew there would be no pleasing her when she was in this mood.

'I'll talk to the estate agent,' he had said with a sigh.

But in the end, even that wasn't enough to keep her happy. Gwendoline had gone on pushing and provoking him until he had snapped back. That had been the excuse she needed to put on her hat and coat and announce she was spending the evening at her sister's.

'And you needn't think you're invited,' she had said.

It was almost a relief to have the house to himself again. It didn't seem empty, it seemed peaceful. Clement had decided to treat himself to a glass of whisky, then smiled as he remembered Florence Maguire had poured it all down the sink.

He had made himself a cup of tea instead and drank it sitting in the garden. He liked the cold, bracing weather in the gathering darkness, under the overhanging canopy of bare trees. He had climbed these same trees when he was a boy and his uncle had owned the house, falling and skinning his knees and spraining his limbs more times than he could count.

He had hoped that one day he would watch his own sons scrambling up into the branches, but it wasn't to be. Gwendoline disliked children, and she had made it clear from the start that she wasn't going to tie herself down with dribbling babies, as she put it.

Clement felt sad at the prospect of leaving the house. But it had to be done. Perhaps Gwendoline was right; perhaps there were too many memories of her first husband within its walls. After all, he had grown up there too.

Anyway, sacrifices must be made if he and Gwendoline were to have half a chance of salvaging their marriage.

Clement got off the bus and headed down Alfred Gelder Street, following the steady stream of office workers towards the Guildhall. Most were older men in suits, like himself, or very young girls who had not yet been called up. There were a few older women, too, wives and mothers who had taken the place of workers who had been conscripted.

Clement could hear a commotion coming from the typing pool as he was walking down the corridor. Laughter, and the sound of high-pitched voices, all talking at once. As he passed the legal department, Mr Gerrard, the manager, stuck his head out.

'Can you tell your lot to keep it down, Saunders?' he barked. 'We can scarcely hear ourselves think in here.'

'Yes, of course. Sorry.' No sooner had he said it than there was an excited squeal from beyond the typing-pool door. Clement headed towards it. This was most irregular, he thought. Miss Maguire usually kept impeccable order among the girls. She must be late or off sick, he decided.

But when he opened the door, there she was, right in the middle of a circle of excited, chattering girls.

'What's going on here?' He looked around at their smiling faces.

'You'll never guess what, Mr Saunders?' Ivy Grey turned to him. 'Miss Maguire has got engaged!'

'Good lord.' Clement looked at Florence Maguire. She smiled shyly back at him, as if she was embarrassed by her good fortune. She seemed to carry herself taller, no longer stooping to disguise her height, and her features looked softer, almost girlish. With her sparkling eyes and radiant complexion, she could have easily passed for one of the typing-pool girls.

Love had transformed her, he thought, and felt a stab of jealousy.

He realised everyone was staring at him, waiting for him to say something else.

'Congratulations,' he mumbled.

'She's going to live in America,' Mabel Burrows said.

Clement looked at Florence sharply. 'Are you?'

'Nothing's really been decided yet.'

'Right. Well. That's . . .' All kinds of thoughts and ideas were scrambling in his head at once, making it hard to get his words out. 'That's excellent news, I suppose.' He cleared his throat. 'It's nearly ten past nine,' he muttered, consulting his watch. 'Better get on with some work, I suppose.' Then he fled to his office, closing the door behind him.

He sat at his desk, staring at the portrait of a former mayor on the opposite wall. The pompous old face stared back at him, judging him as usual. He often liked to flick rubber bands at it, but today he couldn't seem to summon up the enthusiasm.

He should be happy for Florence, he told himself. After so many years, she had finally found someone who could give her all the love and happiness she deserved. She was going to make a wonderful new life for herself.

A new start, just like him and Gwendoline. Perhaps that was why he felt so sour inside, he thought. Perhaps he was jealous of the clean slate Florence had been offered, while he and Gwen could only struggle to rub out the messiness of their past.

But deep down he knew it was more than that. He and Florence Maguire might have clashed endlessly, but she had been his rock, one of the few certain things in his life. Even though he knew she disliked him, that she found him annoying, that she disapproved of almost everything he did, she was still there, a constant, unchanging presence in his day. She was calm and clear, and somehow the world made sense when she was there.

He even looked forward to their sparring, and the daily battle of wits between them. And even though Florence Maguire would never admit it, Clement had a feeling she would miss it too.

And now she was leaving him. Even if she didn't go to America by some miracle, he couldn't see her working in the typing pool once she was wed. Just the thought of it filled him with sorrow.

But he couldn't be selfish. Florence deserved to be happy, and that was all that needed to be said about it. His own messy feelings did not come into it.

He sprang out of his slump as the door opened and Florence came in, holding a sheaf of papers.

'Invoices for your signature,' she said briskly. 'I'll put them in your in-tray, shall I? If I can find it . . .' She cast a meaningful look over his cluttered desk.

'Here.' Clement scrabbled to uncover the in-tray from underneath a teetering pile of paper.

'I've already checked them, so there won't be any mistakes.'

'There never is, Miss Maguire.'

The smallest trace of a smile curved her lips.

As she went to leave, he said, 'Miss Maguire?'

She turned. 'Was there something else?'

'I am pleased for you. The engagement, I mean.'

'Thank you, Mr Saunders.'

'Although I suppose I'll have to look for a new typing-pool supervisor now.'

'I'm sure you'll find someone suitable.'

'I'll never find anyone like you.' He knew the words had come out wrong when he saw the colour rising in Florence's face. He was blushing too, he realised. He could feel his face burning.

'I'm not quite sure how to take that,' Florence said lightly. And then she was gone.

Clement lifted his eyes to meet the stern gaze of the old mayor.

'What are you staring at?' Clement snapped back at him. 'I can't help it if I'll miss her, can I?'

Chapter 36

January 1943

'Need a hand?'

Sybil heard Tom's voice and hurried to the window of the Met Office to see what was going on. For a moment, she thought he might be calling to her, but then she saw him a short distance away at the far end of the Flying Control building. He was standing on the track that skimmed the perimeter of the airfield, his hands on his hips, looking up at something just beyond her vision.

Sybil already knew what he would be looking at. Sure enough, as she craned her neck, she saw the figure of a pert little redhead carefully descending the metal ladder from the roof, a notebook tucked tightly under one arm. As she came closer, Tom grasped her by the waist and lifted her down.

For a moment before he set her on the ground, he held her so their faces were level. He must have whispered something to her because the little redhead threw back her head and laughed.

Jealousy shot through her. Philippa Townsend, or Pip, as she liked to be called, was one of the new intake of WAAFs who had arrived at Holme two days earlier. She was pretty, vivacious and full of fun, and she had already attracted the attention of several of the flying boys.

Including Tom, apparently.

'I see Tom Davenport is giving the new girls a warm welcome as usual?' Imogen Banks came up behind her and looked over her shoulder out of the window. 'Never a dull moment with him, is there?'

Sybil ignored the corporal's knowing smirk and headed for the door.

'That's right,' Imogen's taunting voice followed her, 'go and stake your claim. Much good it will do you,' she muttered under her breath.

Tom and Pip were still laughing together as she approached them. A stray lock of burnished copper hair had escaped from under Pip's cap, and she giggled as Tom reached forward and tucked it behind her ear.

He didn't even bother to snatch his hand away when he saw Sybil coming towards her.

'Hello, darling.' He greeted her with a lazy smile, his blue eyes squinting in the wintry sunshine.

Sybil forced her brightest grin in return. 'What are you up to? I hope you're not leading the new girl astray already?'

'Who, me? Never.' Tom looked innocent. 'I was giving Pip a hand.'

So it was Pip now, was it?

'I'm sure LACW Townsend can manage perfectly well without your help.' Sybil's smile didn't waver as she turned to her. 'You'll have to get used to this, I'm afraid. The flying boys make a point of standing at the bottom of this ladder to watch the Met girls come down.'

'You never know when you'll catch one,' Tom said.

'You certainly caught me, didn't you?' Sybil threaded her arm firmly through Tom's.

'Oh!' Pip looked from one to the other, blushing to the roots of her coppery hair. At least she'd got the message, Sybil thought.

As they walked back into the Flying Control building, Pip said, 'I'm sorry, I didn't realise you two were together. Tom didn't mention it . . .'

I'm not surprised, Sybil thought. She looked over her shoulder at him as he sauntered away without a backward glance.

It was proving to be quite exhausting, keeping tabs on Tom Davenport. Sybil had returned to the base after Christmas to find he had completely forgotten about their arrangement to meet.

'Sorry, sweetheart, did I really say I'd come round? I can't recall making any promises. And you know what it's like. My brothers and I hadn't seen each other for so long, once we got together we just lost track of time . . .'

'It's fine,' Sybil had said airily. 'I completely forgot you were supposed to be coming until Maudie reminded me, anyway.'

But then Teddy Jarvis had let slip that she had met up with Tom and his brothers after she missed the last train to York.

'They were my absolute saviours,' she had told Sybil in her soft, lisping voice. 'Honestly, I don't know what I would have done without them. They found me weeping on the platform and absolutely insisted that I should celebrate with them instead. We ended up having a fine old time.'

Sybil was certain it was all innocent, but there was still a part of her that wondered why Tom hadn't told her about it himself. She couldn't stop thinking about them sipping cocktails together while she waited patiently for him to arrive.

Not that she dared to question him about it. Tom had made it clear he resented her questioning him about his comings and goings.

He had become even more irritatingly vague in the weeks since then. Sybil simply didn't know where she was with him. Sometimes he was so offhand that she was convinced it was over between them. Then, just as she was plunging into despair, he would turn around completely and be the sweetest, most loving and considerate man she had ever met.

If any other young man had treated her so carelessly she would have thrown a fit and ditched him straight away. But the more carelessly Tom treated her, the more she seemed to cling to him. She couldn't even understand it herself.

'I have to tell you something,' Pip said, interrupting her thoughts. 'When we were talking, Tom told me about the dance at the Sergeants' Mess on Saturday.'

'What about it?'

Once again, the blush rose in the girl's face. 'He asked me if I wanted to go with him.'

Sybil stiffened. 'You must have been mistaken,' she said.

'I don't think so . . .'

'Look, he's my boyfriend!' Sybil turned on her. 'Why would he have asked you to go to a dance with him?'

'I don't know, but he definitely did.'

'Just stay away from him, all right?'

Sybil glared at her. The young girl faced her boldly, meeting her gaze.

'I think you should be telling him that, not me.'

Imogen looked up from her chart as they entered the Met Office. 'Is everything all right?' she asked, looking from one to the other.

'Fine,' Pip said shortly. 'I'd best get these figures through to HQ.'

She marched down to the other end of the long room. Imogen watched her go. 'I heard you talking,' she murmured, shaking her head. 'Looks like Tom's back to his old tricks.'

'Just because you couldn't keep hold of him, that doesn't mean I won't.'

Imogen turned to look at Sybil, that annoying smirk back in place. 'I look forward to seeing how you do it,' she said.

'I don't know what's she got to be so smug about,' Sybil said to Maudie in the hut later. 'At least Tom and I are still together. She couldn't keep him for more than five minutes!'

'I wish you wouldn't talk like that,' Maudie said in a low voice, glancing around the hut. There were only two others there, a pair of R/T girls called Evelyn and Dorothy. They were gathered around the coke stove, so close they were practically hugging it, their shoulders draped in thick blankets.

'She still hasn't forgiven me for taking him from her in the first place,' Sybil said.

'I don't see why,' Maudie replied, folding up her nightgown and putting it in her kitbag. 'From what I hear, she's blissfully happy with her new boyfriend.'

Ever since Christmas, Imogen had been bragging about her dashing Canadian navigator to anyone who would listen. It was quite sickening to hear, to avoid repetition of listen from previous sentence? her.

'That wouldn't stop her hating me.' Sybil looked at her sister. Maudie had no idea how complicated these things could be. She was utterly oblivious, blissfully in love with a man who was equally besotted with her. She had never had to fight anyone for Mitch's affections. They had been handed to her wholeheartedly on a plate.

Once Sybil would have thought it was too boring for words; now she envied her sister.

And now Maudie was going off on leave to meet Mitch's family for the first time. Sybil had never got as far as meeting any of her boyfriend's parents.

'You're surely not taking that with you?' she said, as Maudie picked up her gen-book and slipped it into her bag. 'I thought you were meant to be getting away from it all?'

'I need to keep studying,' Maudie said. 'I never know when I might be called before the board.'

Sybil pulled a face. In spite of all her cajoling, Maudie had decided to put in for her promotion after all. Sybil had come up with all kinds of arguments about why she shouldn't do it, but for once Maudie had stood her ground.

Sybil blamed Joan. They might be in different huts now, but she was still hanging around, whispering in Maudie's ear, putting all kinds of ideas in her head. The pair of them spent all their spare time together, swotting up on their gen-books. Sybil thought Joan was doing her best to make Maudie as boring as she was.

'I can't believe you're leaving me here on my own,' she said sulkily.

Maudie grinned. 'I can't very well take you with me, can I?'

'Yes, but what will I do when you're gone?'

'Try not to get into any mischief, I hope!'

'You know me. I can't make any promises about that!'

'We'll keep an eye on her, don't worry!' Evelyn said. She leaned down and fed a broken piece of broom handle into the coke stove. They had used up their ration several days earlier, and now they were reduced to using old bits of furniture or foraging in the frozen ground outside the window for old cinders that might still have a bit of heat left in them.

Sybil looked at Maudie's kitbag and felt a heavy dread in the pit of her stomach. 'It must be serious, if you're meeting his parents?' she said.

'I don't know about that,' Maudie replied, blushing. She looked so happy, Sybil thought. Her eyes were sparkling, and there was a flush in her cheeks.

'Just as long as you don't go off and elope?' she warned. 'You know we're supposed to be having a double wedding.'

'Since when?' Maudie laughed.

'We planned it when we were bains. Don't you remember?'

'So we did.' Maudie sounded rather half-hearted about it, Sybil thought.

'You'll have to get Tom to propose to you first!' Evelyn called out to her. Sybil did not like the sideways look she and Dorothy gave each other. She had started to notice too many knowing glances and comments lately. Even from girls she barely knew, like Evelyn and Dorothy.

'Take no notice of them,' Maudie whispered. 'They're just being daft.'

'They don't know anything about it,' Sybil muttered.

But the truth was, it was beginning to wear her down. She was used to being the girl everyone admired, not the one they laughed at. Now it was Maudie who had stepped into the limelight. And even though she was happy for her sister, Sybil really didn't like being the one in the shadow.

Chapter 37

Mrs Florence Forrest.

Florence stared down at the signature she had idly scribbled on her desk blotter. It didn't look right, seeing it written down like that. But it was bound to be strange, she told herself, getting used to a new name after living for forty-two years with her old one.

But she would have to get used to it, sooner or later. And it looked like being sooner, the way things were going.

After filling in endless forms and gathering all kinds of character references, not to mention travelling down to Cambridge for an interview with William's commanding officer, it finally looked as if they might be able to set a wedding date.

'My CO was very impressed with you,' William had told Florence on the telephone two days earlier. 'He said he had no hesitation in giving his permission for the marriage to go ahead. He said you'd make the perfect officer's wife,' he commented proudly.

'That's very kind of him,' Florence had said.

'He's going to pull some strings and get our paperwork done by the end of the month,' William went on. 'We'll be married by March. Isn't that wonderful news?'

'Wonderful,' Florence had agreed. 'But perhaps we shouldn't set a date yet?'

'Why not?'

'Oh, I don't know. It all just seems to be happening so fast, that's all.'

'The sooner the better, as far as I'm concerned,' William had said. 'I can't wait for you to move down to Cambridge. I miss you so much, sweetheart.'

'I miss you too.'

Someone cleared their throat, startling Florence out of her reverie. She looked up to see Gillian Munroe standing in front of her desk, holding a sheaf of papers.

'For you to check, miss,' she said.

'Put them in the tray.' Florence quickly covered the signature on her blotter with her hand. But Gillian didn't even look at her as she put the papers into the tray.

Florence watched the girl as she shuffled back to her desk, took another sheet of paper and fed it between the rollers of her typewriter. For once, Gillian didn't even glance at the girl next to her, let alone start chattering. It was most unlike her.

Come to think of it, she had been quiet for a few days now. Florence thought about asking her what was wrong, then thought better of it. As long as she got on with her work, it wasn't her business.

She picked up the document Gillian had just typed and started to read through it. But it wasn't long before her mind was wandering again, this time to a distant mansion, blazing white under the North Carolina sun.

William had shown her photographs of his home, a grand building with elegant pillars and a wide verandah that looked more like a palace than a house. He had told her about the land that surrounded it, hundreds of acres of fields and plantations. Florence worked out that it would have stretched the whole length of Hessle Road, and halfway across the Humber, too.

And one day it was going to be her home.

Florence felt the old familiar sickness rising up in her throat. She couldn't picture herself living in America. Every time she tried, her mind seemed to snag on the image.

She couldn't remember agreeing to go, but somehow William had just assumed that it would happen.

She recalled their conversation, just after he had proposed. They were discussing where and when they would marry. Florence had assumed they would go to the local register office and have done with it, but William was scandalised at the idea.

'I could never marry in a register office,' he had said in a shocked voice. 'My mother would never forgive me for it. No, it has to be a real marriage, in the eyes of God. Perhaps you could talk to your pastor about it?'

'My pastor?' Florence had laughed. 'I haven't been a regular churchgoer since Sunday School!'

'I guess that will change once we're living back at home,' William had said. 'No doubt my mother will have you volunteering with her at our local Baptist church in no time. I hope you like organising pot-luck suppers?'

But Florence was hardly listening. 'You expect me to move to America?' she had said.

'You surely don't expect me to stay here?' William had laughed.

'Why not?'

His smile had faded. 'My home and family are over there.'

'What about *my* family?'

'I'll be your family once we're married, remember?' He had reached for her, pulling her to him. 'Look, I know it's a lot to ask of you. But someone's got to run my family's estate, and my father's not getting any younger. And since I'm their only child, I guess it falls to me.'

Now, a month later, Florence was still trying to get used to the idea.

She didn't know why she was so uneasy at the thought of leaving Hull. After all, she was going to start a new life with the man she loved. She should be excited at the prospect. But every time she thought about it, a tight knot of apprehension formed in the pit of her stomach.

She was just being silly, she told herself. It made sense to move to America. Especially as William's sons were over there. It wouldn't be fair to uproot them from their home, especially when they'd already been through so much, losing their mother.

Poor lambs, she thought. She was nervous at the thought of being a mother to two sons, but William had done his best to reassure her.

'My mother will help you,' he had said. 'She's more or less brought them up since I lost my wife. And they're at boarding school most of the time now anyway.'

'Yes, but surely they won't have to go to boarding school any more once I'm there to take care of them?' Florence had reasoned. But William shook his head.

'It's a very good school, and they're settled there. My mother thinks it's the best place for them, and I agree.'

'Oh well, if your mother thinks it's the right decision . . .' Luckily William didn't notice the sarcasm creeping into her voice.

That was something else that worried her.

William had shown her photographs of his parents, and they had done nothing to soothe her nerves. Charles and Dorothea Forrest looked so formal, standing upright in front of their grand home with their son and two grandsons, posing for the camera with tight smiles. Dorothea had seemed particularly formidable, slender and elegant in her pearls, a broad-brimmed hat keeping off the Carolina sun. Florence had studied her future mother-in-law's expression, searching for a hint of warmth. But she could find nothing but steel in those shaded eyes.

This was the woman under whose roof she would be living.

Florence had mentioned to William that it would be nice to have a place of their own, but he wouldn't countenance.

'My mother wouldn't want that.' He had said. 'She likes to have her family around her.'

And what Dorothea Forrest wanted she usually got, from what Florence could gather. Perhaps she wasn't so different from Big May Maguire after all?

It was an unnerving thought.

Florence gave herself a mental shake and went back to checking Gillian's work. There were so many clumsy mistakes in the typewritten pages, Florence hardly knew where to start.

'Were you half asleep when you typed this letter?' she asked Gillian when she passed it back to her for correction.

'No, miss.'

Florence peered at her. She looked tired, dull-eyed and ashen. 'Are you ill?' she asked.

'No.'

'She is, miss,' Hilda Gornall spoke up for her.

'What's wrong with you?'

'Food poisoning,' Hilda answered for her again. 'She can't keep anything down.'

'I see.' Florence looked back at the girl's unhappy face. She was surprised she had come to work. Gillian was usually the first to skive off, if she had an excuse.

*   *   *

The rest of the day passed, until it was time for everyone to go home. The other girls immediately jumped up from their desks and began gathering up their belongings and putting on their coats. All except Gillian, who stayed at her typewriter, her head down.

'Hurry up,' Dulcie Allen said. 'We'll miss our bus.'

'You go on without me,' Gillian said. 'I've still got all this to finish.'

Florence was surprised. Gillian Munroe was usually the first to bolt out of the door, whether her work was finished or not. The poor girl really did look wretched, she thought.

'I'm sure those letters will wait until tomorrow,' Florence said. 'We've already missed tonight's post.'

'I'd still like to get them done, miss, if you don't mind?' Gillian said.

'As you wish.'

The other girls left, until only Florence and Gillian remained. Florence sat at her desk, reading through a sheaf of final demands that Deirdre Taylor had just dropped into her in-tray, half listening to the hesitant peck of Gillian's typewriter keys. Usually she was one of the fastest girls in the pool, clattering along at a lightning pace.

And then, gradually, the clacking keys slowed to a standstill. When Florence looked up, she saw Gillian sitting at her typewriter, her hands poised unmoving on the keyboard, staring blankly ahead of her.

Florence put down the report. 'Whatever is the matter?'

Gillian's head jerked up. 'Nothing, miss.'

'Are you sure?'

'Yes, miss.'

Florence went back to her work. But no sooner had she started reading than Gillian cleared her throat and said, 'Miss?'

Florence looked up. Gillian was staring at her, chewing her lip nervously. 'Yes? What is it?'

'Can I talk to you about something? It's personal.'

'Then I don't think—'

'Please, miss. I don't know who else to talk to . . .'

Florence felt a sudden surge of panic. She looked around the empty typing pool, half hoping someone would come in and rescue her.

'What is it?' she asked uneasily.

To her utter horror, Gillian burst into noisy tears. Florence looked at her in dismay. 'Good heavens, girl, whatever is the matter? Surely it can't be that bad?'

'I think I'm pregnant.'

'Oh, Gillian!'

'I in't been to the doctor yet. But my mum says I am.' She burst into tears again.

'Here.' Florence reluctantly came down from her dais and handed her a handkerchief.

'Thank you, miss.'

She watched Gillian mopping her eyes. As fast as she dried them, more tears seemed to flow.

'So your mother knows?' Florence asked.

'Yes.' Gillian blew her nose. 'But she says she wants nothing to do with me until I've got rid of it,' she said.

'I'm sure she doesn't mean that?'

'You don't know her, miss. She's always said she wouldn't have my sister or me in the house if we got ourselves in trouble.'

'What about your boyfriend?'

'I in't seen him since he went to Cambridge just after Christmas. I was going to write to him, but I was scared he wouldn't reply. My mum reckons he only wanted a bit of fun, and now he's had it he won't want to know.'

She started sobbing again. Florence reached out and patted her arm awkwardly. She felt hopelessly out of her depth. She

225

glanced at the door, half hoping Clement Saunders would walk in. He was much better with the girls than she was. But he had gone off to a meeting and was not due back for some time.

'Please tell me what to do, miss,' Gillian begged. 'You're so clever, you must be able to think of something.'

'Me?' Florence stared at her blankly. *This is none of your business*, a voice inside her head said firmly. *Don't get involved.* 'I know nothing about this sort of thing . . .' she started to say. But then she saw the trusting look in the girl's eyes. She had come to her for help, and Florence could not turn her back on her.

And she knew someone else who wouldn't turn her back, either.

She took a deep breath. 'Get your coat,' she said. 'You're coming with me.'

Chapter 38

To her credit, Big May Maguire did not bat an eyelid when Florence ushered a tearful Gillian in through the back door. She was in the kitchen, draping damp washing over the clothes horse around the fire.

'Trust it to start raining just as this lot was nearly dry,' she muttered. 'Now I'll have to start all over.' She looked over her shoulder to Gillian, then back to Florence. 'Who's this, then?'

'This is Gillian, from work,' Florence said. 'She's in a bit of trouble, so I said she could come home with me.'

She didn't have to say any more. Her mother abandoned the vest she had been folding and came over to greet them, drying her hands on her apron.

'Well, don't just stand there,' she said. 'Take your coat off and come and sit by the fire, lass. You must be nithered.' Her voice was brisk, but there was an underlying warmth there. 'Put the kettle on, Florence. I daresay your friend could do with a cup of tea, eh?'

Florence was silently grateful to her mother as she went to fill the kettle at the sink. She hadn't known what to say to the girl, but her mother chatted easily as she helped Gillian off with her coat and hung it up on the back of the door. Gillian could scarcely bring herself to speak at first, looking around nervously at her unfamiliar surroundings, Florence's handkerchief still crumpled in her hand.

But gradually she began to relax. By the time Florence put their tea in front of them, she even managed a faltering smile.

'Keep an eye on that pie in the oven, would you?' her mother said. 'And put some potatoes on to boil, too.'

Florence watched them as she rummaged for a pan under the sink. The way they leaned into each other, their heads close together as they talked in low voices. Gillian certainly seemed to be telling all her secrets, she thought.

Her mother had a way of drawing people out, of winning their confidence. Florence had no idea how she did it, but for some reason people seemed to trust her.

She was in the middle of peeling potatoes when Pop came in, all muddy boots and stinking of horses.

'Before you start, May, I'm telling you now I in't having a wash in that freezing back yard—' he started to say. Then he caught sight of his wife and the tearful young girl sitting by the fire and quickly shut up.

He tiptoed over to Florence, standing at the stove.

'Another waif and stray?' he whispered, his brows rising. Florence nodded.

'I had to bring her home with me,' she whispered. 'I didn't know what else to do . . .'

'Aye, well, I daresay your mother will know.' Pop sat down at the kitchen table and pulled off his boots. 'She generally does.'

'Yes, she does.' Florence surprised herself with the thought. Her mother was always helping out. Not just the family; there was not a single neighbour of Jubilee Row who hadn't turned to Big May Maguire at some time.

Pop was right about the waifs and the strays. For all her bluster, May had a big heart. She would never turn anyone away from her door.

And even though Florence resented her mother deeply at times, as soon as she had encountered trouble her first instinct had been to come to Big May.

Your mother will know what to do.

Her mother came over to her as she was lighting the gas under the potatoes.

'How is she?' Florence asked.

'Still heartbroken, poor lamb.'

'She doesn't know whether she's coming or going.'

Florence glanced back at Gillian, still sniffling by the fireside. 'I shouldn't have brought her here,' she said. 'I don't like to get involved in this sort of thing.'

'Nonsense, you did the right thing. You couldn't just stand aside and do nothing.'

But that's what I always do, Florence thought. She was nothing like her mother or her sisters. They were always wading into other people's business, getting involved in their messy lives. She had no idea why she had let her guard down this time. Perhaps meeting William had sent her soft?

'What should we do with her?' she asked.

'I'll take her home and have a word with her mother.'

'Do you think she'll listen?'

'If she knows what's good for her.'

Her mother's grim look filled Florence with foreboding. 'I'll come with you,' she said.

'I thought you didn't want to get involved?'

'I want to come. I might be able to help her see reason.'

May bristled. 'And I won't?'

'I know what you're like,' Florence said. 'You'll probably end up brawling in the middle of the street.'

Her mother's face clouded. 'I wonder you asked for my help, if you felt like that,' she muttered. But then she shrugged and said, 'All right, you can come. Since you don't trust me . . .'

*   *   *

Gillian lived to the north of the city, up by Pearson Park. As soon as Mrs Munroe answered the door, Florence knew she had made the right decision to come. Mrs Munroe looked every bit as belligerent as her own mother. It would surely be only a matter of time before the pair of them were scrapping in the street.

Mrs Munroe took one look at Gillian, cowering on the doorstep, then folded her arms and said, 'What's she done this time?'

Florence stepped in quickly. 'Hello, Mrs Munroe. I'm Florence Maguire. I work with Gillian at the Corporation . . .'

Mrs Munroe's eyes narrowed. 'She in't in any trouble, is she?'

'I think we all know the answer to that one,' May Maguire muttered.

Angry colour rose in Mrs Munroe's face and she turned on her daughter. 'Have you been telling the world our business?'

'She didn't know where else to turn,' Florence said.

'Yes, well, I don't know why she had to come crying to you. I've told her what's to be done, and that's an end to it. Now, if you don't mind—'

She went to shut the door in their faces, but Florence's mother put her hand out to stop it.

'The lass has got nowhere to go!' she said.

'She should have thought about that before she got herself in trouble, shouldn't she?' Mrs Munroe's gaze darted up and down the street.

'All the same, you don't turn your back on your own daughter.'

230

Florence watched as her mother squared up to Mrs Munroe. *Here she goes*, she thought, her heart sinking.

'I in't turned my back on her, for your information,' Gillian's mother said. 'She's welcome back under my roof once she's got rid of it.' She nodded to her daughter's belly. 'I've told her there's a woman on Sculcoates Lane who'll sort it out, but she won't go.'

'I-I'm too scared,' Gillian whispered, tears running down her pale cheeks.

'I'm not surprised,' May said. 'Do you know how dangerous that is? You hear about lasses being killed like that all the time.'

Mrs Munroe's lip curled. 'As I said, she should have thought about that before she got into trouble.'

She slammed the door on them before May could stop her.

The three of them stood for a moment on the doorstep. Gillian looked at them both with tear-filled eyes. 'What shall I do now?' she whispered.

'You're coming home with us, of course.' May took charge, putting her arm around Gillian's quivering shoulders. 'There's a roof over your head for as long as you need it, don't you worry about that. Happen your mother will come to her senses in time.'

She turned to go, but Florence didn't move. She stared at the closed front door, rage scorching through her veins.

'Florence?' she heard her mother say, but she ignored her. She launched herself at the door, pounding on the wood with her fist as if she could split the wood.

It flew open and Mrs Munroe stood there, furious. 'What? I've said all I want—'

'Then you listen to me!' Florence cut her off. 'You should be ashamed of yourself. Putting your own daughter out on the streets when she most needs you!'

Mrs Munroe's jaw jutted stubbornly. 'I in't having her bringing shame into my house.'

'So you'd rather she put herself under a butcher's knife than have the neighbours talking about you!' Anger was like a tide inside her, sweeping her away so she hardly knew what she was saying. 'Call yourself a mother? Look at her.' She pointed to Gillian, cowering under May's arm. 'That should be you putting your arms round her! She's alone, and she's terrified, and you're abandoning her just when she most needs you. What kind of mother does that, eh? Answer me that!'

'I don't have to answer to you!' Mrs Munroe slammed the front door in her face again.

'That's right, run away from the truth!' Florence bent down and shouted through the letter box. 'I hope the neighbours do start talking about you. I hope they're all saying what a terrible mother you are!'

'That's enough, Florence.'

The sound of her mother's voice was like a bucket of cold water, shocking her to her senses.

Florence looked around. May stood behind her, her arms around a weeping Gillian.

'You've said enough,' she said. 'Come away now.'

Florence looked back at the door. The fury that had consumed her like fire a moment earlier ebbed away, leaving her feeling dazed and weak. She turned and followed her mother and Gillian.

No one said anything as they made their way back to Jubilee Row. It wasn't until they got home and Gillian went upstairs to rest that her mother finally said, 'Well. And to think you were worried about *me* brawling in the street!'

Florence felt herself blushing. 'I don't know what came over me,' she said. 'I was just so angry . . .'

'And you were right to be, too. That woman has no right to call herself a mother.'

'But I lost my temper,' Florence said. Even now, thinking about it, she could scarcely believe what had happened. 'I was bellowing like a fishwife.'

'You spoke up like a true Maguire,' her mother said. 'You stood up for the lass, and I was proud of you.'

Their eyes met and held for a moment, and Florence caught her mother's rare smile of approval.

Chapter 39

'It's a sprain,' the doctor said. 'A bad one, by the look of it.'

Sybil flinched as he gently probed her ankle. She had missed her footing and slipped down the icy rungs of the ladder just after midnight. She had only fallen a few feet, but she had landed heavily, her foot twisting under her.

She had stumbled into bed when her shift was over, hoping it would get better after some rest. But she had woken up that morning to searing pain and an ankle that was so swollen she could barely pull on her lisle stocking.

The hut corporal had summoned the section officer, who took one look and sent her straight to the sick bay.

'We'll get it bandaged up to compress the swelling, but you'll be off your feet for the next few days,' the doctor said. 'No more climbing up and down ladders in the dark, young lady!' He wagged his finger at her.

But Sybil wasn't listening. 'But I'm supposed to be going dancing tonight!'

The doctor smiled. 'I don't think you'll be up to doing the foxtrot for a while. Complete rest is what you need.'

Panic filled her chest, making it hard for her to breathe. 'But you don't understand. I've got to be there . . .'

'No, LACW Maguire, I don't think *you* understand.' The doctor's genial smile disappeared. 'I'm ordering you to rest that ankle. And if you're not prepared to do that, I'm going to have to confine you to the sick bay.' He turned to the nurse beside him. 'Honestly, all these young women think about is having a good time!'

Sybil stared at him helplessly. This had nothing to do with having a good time, she thought. She didn't need to be at the dance to show off her footwork. She needed to be there to keep an eye on her boyfriend.

All the new WAAFs would be at the Sergeants' Mess dance. And Tom would be on his own, ripe for the taking.

She wished Maudie was there. Her sister could have watched him, made sure he wasn't getting up to anything. But Maudie was still away visiting Mitch's family, and not due to return until the following Tuesday.

Nor did she have any friends she could rely on to watch out for her. Sybil had never gone out of her way to make friends with the other girls the way Maudie had. She was too busy chasing boys to waste her time building friendships with girls. She had her twin sister and that was all she needed. Other girls might admire or envy Sybil, but Maudie was the one they really liked.

But for the first time, it began to dawn on her that she might have been wrong. If only she had taken the time to get to know the other girls, she might have someone she could turn to now.

She hadn't realised tears were running down her cheeks until the doctor said, 'Now then, there's no need to get so upset, my dear. I'm sure most WAAFs would enjoy a couple of days with their feet up and no duties!' But Sybil just went on crying until he turned to the nurse in despair and said, 'Just dress that ankle, will you? Good lord, anyone would think we'd told her she only had a week to live!'

The nurse was a motherly woman in her forties, with gentle hands and a soft, caring voice. Sybil found herself tearfully confiding in her as she bandaged her ankle.

'Well, he doesn't sound like much of a boyfriend to me, if you have to keep your eye on him all the time to make sure he behaves,' she said. 'If you ask me you'd be better off without him.'

'But I can't lose him,' Sybil wailed. She could just imagine what Imogen and all her cronies would say about that. They would have an absolute field day.

'It sounds like it wasn't meant to be, anyway. Do yourself a favour and find yourself a boyfriend you can trust. That's my advice.'

'But I love him.'

The nurse shook her head. 'You young girls are all the same. Losing your head over a man.'

That's just it, Sybil thought. She had never lost her head over anyone before. That's why it was so difficult.

She was still crying as the nurse helped her into bed and put a pillow under her ankle to support it. As she pulled the blankets over Sybil, she smiled and said, 'Don't look so worried, love. It will be all right in the end. You never know, he might surprise you and behave himself!'

There was only one other girl in the sick bay, a general duties WAAF Sybil had seen around and about at the station. She had 'flu so she was at the far end of the sick bay and slept much of the time. At first, Sybil was relieved not to have to make small talk with her. But as time wore on and her boredom grew, she found herself watching the girl and wishing they could chat, just to relieve the tedium.

She kept looking at the door, waiting for Tom to appear. Surely he must have heard what had happened to her by now? But as the hands on the clock crept towards midday with agonising slowness, he still didn't come. Perhaps he was in a briefing, Sybil thought. But she knew there were no ops due that night.

Meanwhile, the girl in the other bed had woken up to a steady stream of visitors. Girls had been dropping in and out all morning, bringing treats from the NAAFI, or sitting by her bed to gossip.

Sybil found herself watching them enviously, longing to join in.

Finally, someone arrived just before lunch to see her.

'I'm only here because the section officer sent me,' Joan announced bluntly. 'And because I know Maudie would have wanted me to come.'

'What's that?' Sybil nodded to the package in her hands.

'I've brought you some writing paper and a pen. And a book, in case you get bored.'

Sybil frowned. 'I would have preferred a movie magazine to a book.'

'Yes, well, beggars can't be choosers, can they? I can always take it away, if you don't want it?'

'No! Leave it here. I might have a look at it if I get bored enough.' Sybil picked up the leather-bound book and read the worn gold lettering on the spine. *Wuthering Heights*. It looked dreadful, like something the teachers tried to force them to read at school.

'Try it,' Joan said. 'It might be good for you to concentrate on something other than yourself for a while.'

She stayed long enough to ask her if there was anything else she needed, then went to leave.

'Joan?' Sybil called after her.

'What?'

Sybil hesitated. She wanted Joan to stay and chat for a while, but she was too embarrassed to say anything.

'Thank you,' she murmured instead.

'I told you, I did it for Maudie,' Joan said. But there was a slight smile at the corners of her mouth as she said it.

Chapter 40

When Joan had gone, Sybil picked up the book again and started to read, but she couldn't concentrate on it. She had never been much for reading, anyway, and it was hard to concentrate with the general duties WAAF and her friends shrieking with laughter at the other end of the sick bay. Even worse, they were discussing the dance that night – who was going, how they were going to do their hair, and who they had their eye on.

'Do you mind?' Sybil snapped at them finally. 'Some of us are trying to rest.'

'She's only got a sprained ankle, not scarlet fever!' she heard the general duties WAAF mutter to her friends, but at least it shut them up for a while.

Sybil picked up the writing paper and pen and started to write a letter to her mother instead. She was ashamed that she couldn't remember the last time she had put pen to paper herself – she usually left all that to Maudie. She was the dutiful correspondent, while Sybil dashed off the odd postcard when she remembered.

But once she started writing her letter she found she actually quite enjoyed it. She was on her third page when the door opened and Tom walked in, his arms full of flowers.

It was as if the sun had come out from behind a dark cloud. The other girls all stopped their chatter to stare at him as he made his way over to Sybil's bed.

'Hello, darling,' he leaned down to plant a kiss on her forehead. 'How are you?'

'All the better for seeing you.'

'I'm sorry I didn't come earlier, but I only just heard what happened. I was playing cards with the boys last night and I slept late.'

'It doesn't matter. You're here now.'

'So I am.'

But he didn't look too thrilled about it. Even as he sat at her bedside, he kept casting quick glances towards the door, as if he couldn't wait to get away.

Sybil didn't blame him. It was tedious to visit someone on their sickbed, she told herself. One never knew what to say to them.

They made desultory conversation for about ten minutes. Sybil did most of the talking. Tom lounged back in his chair, his eyes half closed, stifling a yawn with the back of his hand.

'Sorry, sweetheart,' he kept saying. 'I'm exhausted.'

Sybil smiled. 'Looks like we might both miss the dance?'

He snapped awake, looking at her intently. 'You're not coming to the dance?'

She pointed to her ankle. 'I can barely stand.'

'Oh no, poor you.' He looked sorrowful. 'Darling, I didn't think.'

'I know. I'm so disappointed ...' Tears pricked the backs of her eyes again, and she looked down so he wouldn't see them.

'Oh, Syb!' Tom reached for her hand. 'Buck up, darling. There will be other dances.'

Sybil summoned her bravest smile. 'You mustn't let it stop you, though. If you really want to go?'

He looked at her blankly, as if the idea simply hadn't occurred to him. 'Well, quite,' he said. 'No point in both of us missing out, is there? I mean, it's not as if it would make your ankle any better, would it?'

'No.' *But it would make me feel better*, Sybil thought. She desperately willed him to say he wouldn't go, to show some loyalty to her. She couldn't imagine Mitch going anywhere without Maudie.

'Anyway, it would be nice to have a bit of fun before I leave for Waddington,' Tom said.

Sybil frowned. 'Waddington?'

'Didn't I tell you? My crew's been sent down there for more training.'

'No,' said Sybil. 'No, you didn't mention it.'

'Are you sure? I could have sworn I mentioned it. Oh well, it must have slipped my mind.' He shrugged.

'How long will you be gone?'

'Only a week.'

'A week?' Disappointment swallowed her. He definitely hadn't mentioned it, she thought. How could he have forgotten to tell her?

'I'll be back before you know it. And by then you'll be on your feet again. Just think of that.'

'You'll have to take me out to make up for it,' Sybil said.

'Oh, I will.'

'Somewhere really fancy, mind.'

'Oh, absolutely. Nothing but the best for my girl.'

He kissed her again, on the mouth this time. Sybil surrendered herself to the feel of his lips on hers, dizzy with desire.

He left a few minutes later. 'Will I see you before you go to Waddington?' Sybil called after him, hating herself for the desperation in her voice.

'I'll try, but I can't promise anything. We'll probably be leaving first thing, and I don't want to disturb you.'

'I don't mind—' Sybil started to say, but Tom was already gone, blowing a careless kiss to her as he left. 'I love you,' she whispered to the door as it closed behind him.

*　　*　　*

The afternoon dragged on after lunch. Sybil tried not to think about the other girls getting ready for the dance, their excitement as they capered around the hut, doing each other's hair and swapping their meagre supplies of make-up.

She thought about Pip Townsend getting ready, pinning up that glorious burnished copper hair, and remembered her sinking feeling when she had seen the young WAAF with Tom's hands circling her waist. She had warned her off, but would it be enough?

Finally, she couldn't stand it any longer.

'Where are you going?' The girl in the other bed finally roused herself to speak to her as Sybil manoeuvred herself awkwardly off the bed.

'Dancing,' Sybil replied through gritted teeth.

She landed heavily on her foot and hissed with pain.

'You can't even stand up,' the girl said. 'I'm calling the nurse—'

'Don't you dare!' Sybil snapped, as the girl reached for the bell.

She was struggling to get her uniform on, balancing on one leg and trying not to topple over, when the door opened and a corporal strode in.

'What do you think you're doing?' Imogen Banks demanded.

'What does it look like?' Sybil muttered under her breath.

'She thinks she's going dancing, Corporal,' the other girl put in helpfully.

'Is she now? No prizes for guessing why, I suppose.' Imogen stood at the foot of her bed, her hands on the rails. 'Get back into bed immediately, Maguire.'

'But I'm fine—'

'Get back into bed. That's an order!'

Sybil faced her boldly. She thought about disobeying, but she could tell from Imogen's twitching face that she wanted nothing more than to put her on yet another charge.

She sank down on the bed defeated and trying not to cry. Come what may, she would not give the corporal that satisfaction.

'What are you doing here, anyway?' she mumbled.

'Believe me, it's not a social call. Your hut corporal's got leave tonight, so the section officer told me to come and check on you, to see how you were. Looks like I arrived at just the right time.' Imogen looked her up and down with a grim smile. 'You must be really desperate to go to that dance,' she said.

'I'm just bored, that's all.'

'Yes, it's no fun in here, is it?' Imogen looked around. 'I remember feeling terribly fed up when I was in here with 'flu a while back. But I suppose you remember that, don't you?' She looked hard at Sybil. 'It's dreadful, lying here when everyone else is having a good time. Imagining what they might be getting up to. And all the while you're stuck in here and there's nothing you can do about it ...' Her mouth twisted. 'Looks like history's repeating itself, doesn't it?'

She was enjoying this, Sybil thought, seeing the corporal's tight little smile. She had probably waited months to get her revenge. On top of all her worry about Tom, it was more than she could bear.

'Hardly,' she said.

'How do you work that out? I reckon you're in exactly the same boat I was that night you took him away from me.'

'Yes, but he wasn't engaged to you, was he?'

The words were out before she knew what she was saying. Sybil wasn't even sure she'd uttered them out loud until she saw the look of shock on Imogen's face.

'Engaged?' she said. 'When did this happen?'

'Last week.'

Her eyes narrowed. 'Where's your ring, then?'

'We haven't had a chance to get one yet.' Sybil was shocked at how easily the lies flowed out of her.

'Why haven't we heard about this before?'

'We wanted to keep it a secret until we'd had a chance to tell our families. You won't tell anyone, will you?' she begged Imogen.

The corporal stared back at her for a moment. 'My lips are sealed,' she said.

Liar, Sybil thought. She was probably already wondering who she could tell first.

Chapter 41

'You may kiss the bride.'

Hank Rosen didn't need telling twice. Taking Gillian in his arms, he swooped her in a low movie-star embrace and planted a long, lingering kiss on her lips.

Florence caught Clement Saunders' eye across the register office. He was laughing at the scene. Florence tried to send him a disapproving look, but she could feel her own mouth twitching upwards.

It was difficult not to smile around Gillian and Hank. The young couple were so happy and in love, it was almost infectious.

Beside her, William cleared his throat.

'That's enough, Rosen,' he warned. 'Save it for the wedding night.'

'It's a bit late for that!' Gillian grinned, her hand going to the bump now barely concealed under her pink silk dress.

If only her mother could see them, Florence thought. But none of Gillian's family were there. There were only Florence and Clement to act as witnesses, and William, who had travelled up from Bassingbourn with the young airman.

They emerged from the register office into the wintry sunshine, arm in arm and laughing happily.

A couple of elderly women were passing by and looked askance at Gillian's belly.

'Disgraceful,' one of them whispered to the other.

Florence glared after them until they caught her eye and hurried away, their heads down. She looked round to see Clement watching her with a smile. Florence turned away, feeling oddly embarrassed.

As they headed down the steps, he said, 'What about a picture to mark the happy event?'

Gillian looked crestfallen. 'Oh, I didn't think of that.'

'Lucky I did, isn't it?' With a flourish, Clement produced a Box Brownie camera from inside his jacket. 'Gather together, everyone!'

Florence immediately stepped to one side, but Gillian grabbed her arm and pulled her back in to the frame.

'No,' she said. 'You need to be in the picture too, Miss Maguire. After all, we wouldn't be wed if it wasn't for you.'

'Well, I don't know about that . . .'

'Say cheese, Miss Maguire!' Clement called out to her. Florence gritted her teeth and raised her eyebrows warningly at him as the shutter clicked.

Gillian turned to Florence and said, 'I meant what I said, miss. We owe everything to you. I don't know how I'll ever thank you.'

Florence felt herself blushing. 'I really didn't do anything,' she mumbled. 'It was Colonel Forrest who pulled all the strings.' She smiled up at William, who stood beside her.

To his credit, he had worked very hard to make the wedding happen quickly. He had pushed through the necessary paperwork, while Florence and Clement had helped Gillian with glowing references.

'You took me in when I had nowhere to go,' Gillian reached for her hand. 'You've been such a good friend, Miss Maguire.'

Florence stared down at the wedding band on the girl's left hand. It was only cheap, nothing special, but it clearly meant the whole world to Gillian.

Even Mrs Munroe had softened towards her daughter since she found out she was going to be made 'respectable'. Although Florence was very glad she hadn't come to the wedding, as she didn't know if she would be able to be civil towards her.

'Mind, I never thought I'd be getting wed before you, miss!' Gillian laughed.

'Yes, well, it was a bit more urgent for you, wasn't it?' Florence said.

'You can say that again!' Gillian pressed her hand on her swollen belly. She was glowing, Florence thought. It was lovely to see her so happy, she couldn't help smiling herself.

Once again, she caught Clement watching her with that intrigued look, and she glanced away, embarrassed.

'Gilly?' Hank called out to her. 'Come on, honey, we can't miss our train.'

'Coming!' Gillian turned back to Florence. 'Listen to him, giving me orders already!'

'You'll soon show him who's really boss, I'm sure.'

'You bet I will!' Gillian hesitated for a moment, then leaned in and planted a kiss on Florence's cheek. 'Goodbye, Miss Maguire. I'll see you when you get to Cambridge!'

And then she was off, hand in hand with her husband, running to catch their train and start their new life together.

'Good luck with the baby,' Florence called after them.

'Anyone would think you cared,' Clement said, coming up behind her.

'I'm just relieved it's all ended well, that's all.'

'If you say so,' Clement grinned. 'I won't tell anyone you have a heart, I promise. Your secret's safe with me.'

Before she could reply, William came over to join them. Florence saw Clement stiffen slightly as he approached.

Gwendoline might be safely home, but the sight of that American uniform clearly still bothered him.

'Mr Saunders.' William greeted him with a nod.

'Colonel.' Clement's smile was soon back in place, even if it was a bit forced. 'I suppose you two will be next?' he said.

'Well, that really depends, doesn't it?' William sent Florence a meaningful look.

'On what?' Clement asked.

'On when you decide you can do without Florence.' There was a hint of steel in William's voice.

'I explained to William that we're very short-staffed, especially now Gillian's gone,' Florence said quickly. 'And two of the girls left to join the ATS last week.'

'That's not your problem, honey,' William said. 'Besides, surely it can't be that tough to find someone to replace you?'

'I don't think I'll ever find another woman like Miss Maguire,' Clement said, sending her a long look.

'Well, I'm sure that's true.' William reached for Florence's hand, jolting her back to reality. 'But you can't keep her to yourself for ever, Mr Saunders. She belongs to me now.'

'I'm not sure I like the idea of belonging to anyone,' Florence said with a tight smile.

There was an awkward silence. Then Clement cleared his throat. 'Yes, well, speaking of work, I'd best get back to the office. Someone's got to make sure those invoices are typed up on time.'

There was an ironic twist to his mouth that only Florence understood. Clement had never delivered a single piece of paperwork on time, and had no inclination to do so, either.

'I'll come with you—' she started to say, but Clement shook his head.

'Take the rest of the afternoon off,' he said. 'I'm sure I can manage. Besides, I daresay you and the Colonel have wedding plans to make!'

He winked at her, and then he was gone.

'So much for you being indispensible!' William remarked, as they watched him sauntering down the street. He put his arm around her. 'You see?' he said. 'It wasn't so hard to speak to him, was it?'

'No,' Florence said. 'No, I suppose it wasn't.'

'He seems like a reasonable guy. I'm sure he understands the situation.'

Florence followed Clement with her gaze as he crossed the road. When he reached the opposite corner, he looked back at her and gave her a cheery wave. As if he knew she would be watching him.

Chapter 42

Sybil was allowed out of the sick bay two days later, by which time Tom was already in Waddington.

He hadn't come to see her before he left. Sybil had woken up before dawn and waited for him, but when the orderly had brought her breakfast, she told her that the pilots had already left two hours earlier.

'And a right shambles they were, too,' she had grumbled. 'You should have seen them, their uniforms all askew and reeking of drink. The LAC who drove them to the station reckoned they'd fallen straight out of the Sergeants' Mess after that dance. It's a disgrace. God knows what Waddington will make of them.'

But Sybil was barely listening. She was lost between disappointment that Tom hadn't bothered to call before he left, and relief that he had gone before rumours of their engagement started circulating around the station.

Just as she had feared, Imogen's lips didn't stay sealed for long. By the time Sybil was discharged back to her duties, it seemed as if everyone at Holme had heard the good news about her and Tom Davenport.

She was unpacking her belongings back at the hut when Maudie burst in, freshly returned from her leave, still in her greatcoat and hauling her kitbag behind her.

'Hello,' Sybil greeted her. 'Did you have a nice time? What were Mitch's parents like? Did his mother ask you if your intentions were honourable?'

'Never mind that! What's this I hear about you getting engaged?' Maudie demanded.

Sybil sighed. 'I suppose Imogen told you?'

'Actually, it was the LAC who gave me a lift from the gate. Everyone knows about it, apparently. Except me.'

'Not everyone.' Sybil sat down on the bed. 'Tom doesn't know, either.'

'What?' Maudie dumped her kitbag on the floor and sat down beside her. 'You'd best tell me what's going on,' she said.

And so Sybil told her. She kept her gaze fixed on the floor, trying to ignore the look of dawning dismay on her sister's face.

'Oh, Syb!' Maudie said when she'd finished. 'What have you done?'

'It was Imogen's fault,' Sybil protested. 'She was provoking me. I had to say something to shut her up. Anyway, I told her not to say anything.'

'You're the one who should have kept her mouth shut!' Maudie sighed. 'Honestly, I only went away for a few days, and you still managed to get into trouble. And Tom knows nothing about this, you say?'

Imogen shook her head. 'He's in Waddington until Sunday.'

'Then you're going to have to put this mess right before he comes back.'

'But how? What can I say?'

'I don't know, do I?' Maudie thought for a moment. 'You could tell everyone it was a joke?'

'I can't. I'd look such a fool.'

'You'll look an even bigger fool when Tom comes back and everyone finds out you've been lying!'

'It might not be like that,' Sybil said. 'I've been thinking, it might be just the nudge he needs.'

'To do what?'

'Propose to me.'

Maudie gawped at her. 'You can't be serious?'

'Why not?'

The more Sybil thought about it, the more she was certain she was right. She was sure Tom had feelings for her, but he was not the type to be tied down willingly. Giving up his freedom and committing to a girl was bound to be a big step for him. But if Sybil pushed him into it, it might be a different story?

'Oh, Syb.' Maudie shook her head despairingly. 'I just hope you know what you're doing, that's all,' she said.

* * *

By the time the weekend came, Sybil was completely immersed in her fantasy. She daydreamed about taking Tom home to Hull to meet her parents, of shopping for an engagement ring. She would make sure she got a diamond big enough to act as a warning to all those other WAAFs and stop them sniffing around.

Tom wasn't due back until Sunday, so she was surprised to see Peter Reckitt, the pilot of B-Bobby, emerging from the NAAFI on Saturday afternoon. He was with another pilot, a French Canadian called Claude Dumas.

'What are you doing here?' she asked them. 'I thought you lot weren't coming back until tomorrow morning?'

'They realised they couldn't teach us anything, so they sent us home a day early,' Peter grinned.

'They were sick of the sight of us,' Claude added. 'Some of us, anyway.'

'When did you get back?'

'About an hour ago.'

'Where's Tom?'

The two young men looked at each other. 'We dropped him off in the village on the way here,' Claude said.

'He said he fancied the walk,' Peter added.

Sybil frowned. 'It doesn't take an hour to walk from the village?'

'Perhaps he took the scenic route,' Peter said.

Once again, Sybil saw the look that passed between the two young men. But before she could ask any more, Peter said, 'Here he comes now. You can ask him about it.'

She looked over her shoulder to see Tom strolling up the track towards them.

'Tom!' she called out to him. His eyes met hers and she could have sworn his smile slipped a fraction.

'Hello, Syb,' he said.

'We were just talking about you,' Claude said.

'Oh yes?'

'Your girlfriend was wondering why you hadn't rushed straight to her arms?' Peter said.

'I said no such thing!' Sybil reached up to kiss him, but Tom jerked his head away.

'Not here,' he muttered. 'People are watching.'

Sybil frowned. Was this really the same daring young man who had swept her into his arms in front of the entire Met Office?

'I need to talk to you,' she said.

'I need to talk to you, too.'

Just then, Ackroyd emerged from the NAAFI, laughing and looking thoroughly pleased with himself. He saw Sybil and Tom and his eyes lit up.

'Well, if it isn't love's young dream!' he shouted.

Tom scowled. 'Shut up, Ackroyd.'

Sybil looked around. Suddenly there seemed to be an awful lot of people, watching and listening.

'Don't be like that, old man. I hear congratulations are in order?'

'What are you talking about?'

'Let's find somewhere to talk—' Sybil took his arm and started to move away, but Ackroyd got there first.

'Your secret engagement, of course,' he called after them.

Tom stopped in his tracks and turned around. 'Engagement?'

'And to think you kept quiet about it the whole time we were away! You really are a dark horse, aren't you?'

He was enjoying this, Sybil thought. The grin on his face was one of pure malice.

'Anyway, it's all out now. Sybil spilt the beans while you were away, and now it's the talk of the NAAFI!'

'Is it?' Tom stared at her coldly. Sybil felt a horrible, shrinking sensation in her stomach.

'I can explain,' she said. 'If we could just talk for a minute—'

Tom took his arm slowly and deliberately from hers. 'It sounds as if you've already done enough talking,' he said quietly.

Sybil looked at him. She scarcely recognised the hard, unsmiling face that stared back at her. She had never seen him so angry. His teeth were clenched so tightly.

Out of the corner of her eye, she saw Maudie approaching with Mitch.

'Is everything all right?' she asked, looking from one to the other.

Sybil ignored her, turning back to Tom. 'It was just a joke,' she whispered. She no longer cared about looking a fool in front of everyone else, as long as Tom forgave her. 'I only said it to shut Imogen up because she was trying to make me jealous.'

'You don't need anyone to make you jealous,' Tom said. 'You're already bad enough. I can't even look at another girl

253

without you storming in, warning her off as if I'm your personal property.'

'Happen if you didn't flirt with every girl in this station I wouldn't have to!' Sybil retaliated.

'Yes, well, you won't have to do it any more.'

An uncomfortable sensation prickled over her skin. 'What do you mean?'

'I mean it's over, Sybil. I don't want to be with you any more.'

She felt all the life drain out of her, every ounce of strength leaving her bones. She thought she would collapse, but Maudie was suddenly there, her arm around her, holding her up.

'You don't mean that,' Sybil whispered.

'I do mean it. I've been thinking about it for a while. I wanted to break it off with you before I left for Waddington, but then you ended up in the sick bay and I felt sorry for you.'

'Very big of you, I'm sure,' Maudie muttered. 'Don't do her any favours, will you?'

Sybil stared at him. It was all so unreal; she was sure any minute he would break into a grin and tell her it was another of his daft jokes.

But there was no hint of laughter in those cold eyes.

'But we've been together for such a long time,' she murmured.

'Yes, and it was fun while it lasted. But that's all it was ever meant to be – a bit of fun. I thought you understood that?'

'I . . .'

'She changed her mind,' Maudie spoke up for Sybil when words failed her. 'She really fell for you.'

'Well, I'm sorry about that.' There was a slight curl to his mouth as he said it. 'But I don't feel the same. How could I?'

Sybil felt Maudie stiffen beside her. 'What's that supposed to mean?'

'I mean I'm an officer.'

'You might be an officer, but you certainly in't a gentleman!' Maudie retorted.

'And your sister's no lady. Ask any of the boys here . . .'

'That's enough!' Mitch stepped in. 'You've already broken the girl's heart, you don't have to insult her as well.'

Tom turned on him. 'And what are you going to do about it, Flight Sergeant Mitchell?'

'Open your mouth again and you'll find out.'

'Lay a hand on me and I'll have you up on a charge.'

'It would be worth it to wipe that smirk off your face!'

The two men squared up to each other for a moment. Then Tom backed down.

'I'm not going to start brawling like a common thug,' he sneered. 'I've got more breeding than that.'

'That's a matter of opinion!' Maudie shouted after him as he strode away.

Seeing him go, Sybil felt all her strength go with him. Her knees buckled and she would have collapsed, but she felt her sister's arms tighten around her, holding her up.

'It's all right,' Maudie whispered. 'I'm here. I'll look after you.'

Chapter 43

February 1943

'What about this one?'

Florence looked at the dress her sister was holding up. 'It's a bit fancy.'

'It's a utility dress, Florence. There's barely a pleat or a button on it. Besides, this is your wedding dress we're talking about. You're meant to look a bit fancy!'

'It's just not me though, is it? None of this is.' She looked around her. The House of Mirelle on King Edward Street was one of the poshest dress shops in Hull, selling expensive couture dresses to the wealthiest women in the city. Florence had passed by its doors many times, but she would never have dreamed of going inside if Iris and Edie hadn't dragged her there.

Florence had never been shopping with her sisters before, and she wasn't sure she liked it. Meanwhile, Iris and Edie were in their element, oohing and aahing over all the gowns on the mannequins. They were enjoying the experience far more than Florence was.

At least they were happy, she thought. They usually ignored her, so it was nice to be the centre of attention for once.

And she was grateful to them for coming with her. She would have been completely lost without them. She would certainly never have made an appointment at a shop like this, with its glittering chandeliers and gilt chairs.

She wouldn't have been shopping for a wedding dress at all if William hadn't cajoled her into finally setting a date.

'I still don't know why I can't get Joyce Shelby to alter one of my old dresses,' she said.

'Oh, Florence! Where's your sense of romance?' Iris grinned. 'You're marrying the man of your dreams so you should have the dress of your dreams.'

'I suppose so. But it all seems like a lot of fuss and expense to me.'

'How about that one?' Iris ignored her, pointing to another dress. 'Surely that's plain enough for you?'

Florence frowned. Iris was right, the design was very simple. 'It's red,' she said. 'I can't wear a red dress to the office.'

She tried to picture Clement Saunders' face if she turned up to work in a daring red frock instead of her usual sober skirt and blouse, and found herself smiling.

'You won't be going to the office after you're married, will you?' Iris reminded her, shaking her out of her reverie.

Florence felt a pang. 'I suppose not,' she said quietly. For a moment, she thought of her desk overlooking the typing pool, and how she spent all her days listening to the clattering of typewriter keys. Sometimes she even heard them in her sleep.

Then she pictured herself, helping William's mother at one of her church fundraisers. How would a red dress fit in with her new life? she wondered.

'All the same, I'd like something I can wear again,' she said, gazing around her. None of the fine gowns on the mannequins struck her as remotely practical.

'Nonsense,' Iris dismissed. 'Don't you want William's face to light up when he sees you?'

'Leave her be,' Edie said. 'Why should she wear anything fancy if she doesn't feel right in it? It's Florence's day and she can wear what she likes.'

'Thank you,' Florence said. 'Anyway, William might not recognise me if I'm done up like a dog's dinner—'

'It's Miss Maguire, isn't it?'

Florence turned around and found herself looking into the smiling, feline face of Gwendoline Saunders. She was dressed in a stylish navy blue dress, her blonde hair swept up in an elegant chignon at the nape of her swanlike neck.

She suddenly remembered Clement once mentioning that his wife worked in a dress shop in the city. At the time, she had not paid much attention.

'I didn't expect to see you here.' Gwendoline Saunders wore a professional smile, but her green eyes were cold. 'Are you looking for something special?'

'She's come to find a wedding dress,' Iris answered for her.

'For you?' Gwendoline stared at Florence, incredulous.

'That's right.'

'Well, I never.' She looked her up and down, a smirk playing on her crimson painted lips. 'What sort of gown were you looking for? I'm sure we can find something to suit.'

'Nothing too fancy,' Edie pitched in helpfully.

'Of course not.' Gwendoline's green eyes glittered with malicious amusement. 'I can tell that's not really you, is it?'

Florence bristled. She was just about to respond when Iris got in first.

'Bring us the most expensive dress in your shop,' she said.

Gwendoline frowned in confusion. 'I don't think—'

'I'm not asking you to think,' Iris cut her off. 'My sister is the customer, and she deserves the best. And you're here to make sure she gets it. That's what you're paid for, in't it?'

Florence caught the light of battle in her sister's eye. Iris might never have met Gwendoline Saunders, but she already had the measure of her. And she clearly wasn't putting up with any of her nonsense.

'Yes, but—'

'I'm sorry, don't you understand?' Florence chimed in. 'It seems like a simple enough request to me. Perhaps I should get the manageress to explain it to you.'

'No! No, it's quite all right.' Gwendoline flushed deep crimson. 'I'll see what I can find,' she muttered, and hurried off.

'Well!' Edie said, as they watched her go. 'You've changed your tune.'

'Oh, she's not going to buy anything, are you?' Iris said.

Florence shook her head. 'I wouldn't dream of it.'

'We just wanted to bring her down a peg or two,' Iris went on. 'High-handed cow. How dare she look down her nose at my sister!'

Florence looked at her. She was so used to being the butt of Iris's jokes, it was nice to have her sticking up for her.

And it was even nicer to have Gwendoline dancing attendance on her. Florence stood in the fitting room as she fussed around her. And every time she fitted a dress on her, Florence dismissed it out of hand. Sometimes she didn't even bother looking at herself in the mirror before waving her hand and saying, 'No, this won't do. Take it away.'

She sensed Gwendoline growing more and more frustrated, but she didn't dare say anything. Florence felt a slight twinge of guilt at wasting the other woman's time, but then reminded herself how cruel Gwendoline had been, to her and to Clement.

As she was fastening the buttons on the tenth dress, a green taffeta number, Gwendoline suddenly said, 'Just so you know, I've left Clement.'

'What?' Florence twisted round to look at the top of her blonde head as she stood behind her.

'I walked out on him. I told him last night I'd finally had enough of him.'

Florence took a moment to compose herself in the mirror. 'I don't know why you're telling me,' she said.

'I thought you two were close?'

'You're quite wrong. I scarcely know him.'

'Clement seems to think the two of you are friends.' Gwendoline gave the dress a savage tug to tighten it.

'Do you mind? I can't breathe.'

'I can't help that, can I? You know what they say, you have to suffer to be beautiful. Anyway, we've parted and that's all there is to it,' she said.

'I'm sorry to hear that.'

'I should never have gone back to him in the first place. I only did it because I had nowhere else to go.' Gwendoline lifted her chin. 'I told him that, too,' she said with a malicious smile.

Florence watched Gwendoline's reflection in the mirror as she pulled at the dress, fastening up the buttons. *How could you*, she thought. What kind of a woman could break a man's heart, over and over again, and smile about it?

She looked back at herself, and suddenly all the fun seemed to go out of the day.

'Stop,' she said shortly. 'I've seen enough.'

Gwendoline looked around at the array of gowns hanging up around them. 'You've made a decision?'

'Yes,' Florence said. 'I've decided I don't want any of them.'

Gwendoline's face twitched. 'You mean to tell me I've wasted all this time?'

'It's your job, isn't it?' Florence shrugged. 'And you can take this off, too,' she said, indicating the taffeta dress. 'Green really isn't my colour.'

Gwendoline helped her out of the dress in sulky silence. As Florence was leaving the shop, she said, 'And when you see Clement, you can tell him I'm not going back to him, no matter how much he begs and pleads!'

Florence looked back over her shoulder at her.

'Tell him yourself,' she snapped. 'I'm not your messenger!'

Chapter 44

It was none of her business, Florence told herself as she rounded the corner into Hedon Road.

It was late on a Sunday night, she had been walking the dark, rain-washed streets for the best part of two hours, her feet ached inside her stout shoes and her dark blue greatcoat was soaked through to her skin. All she wanted to do was get back to the ARP post for a nice hot cup of tea and to dry off around the fire.

And yet somehow she found herself walking in the opposite direction, towards Clement Saunders' house.

She couldn't stop thinking about Clement, after what Gwendoline had told her in the dress shop the previous day. The last time she had left, he had tried to drink himself into oblivion and ended up nearly burning his house down. And Florence couldn't imagine he would take it any better this time around, especially as he'd had such high hopes for their reconciliation.

She was almost afraid to look as she approached his neat semi-detached house. The house was in darkness, which meant at least he had remembered to put up his blackouts. That must be a good sign, she thought.

Unless he was out. Or . . .

She ran up the path to knock on the door. There was no reply. He must be out, she thought. But where would Clement Saunders go on a wet Sunday night?

It's none of your business, she told herself as she knocked again. *He's entitled to his privacy. It's not even as if you know him that well.*

Florence turned to go, then, as an afterthought, she bent down and peered through the letter box.

From the depths of the house, she could hear the sound of music playing on a gramophone.

And the faint smell of burning.

Not again! Florence ran down the side alley to the back of the house, her feet slipping on the slick cobbles.

'Mr Saunders! Clement!' she yelled at the top of her voice as she threw herself against the back door, hammering on the wooden panel with the flat of her hand.

It opened straight away and Florence fell through it, just stopping herself from sprawling headlong at the slippered feet of Clement Saunders.

'Miss Maguire? Good gracious, what are you doing here?' He stood over her, looking mystified, a cup in one hand and a piece of blackened toast in the other.

Florence stood up, brushing herself down with as much dignity as she could muster. 'I knocked at the front door, but there was no answer . . . I smelt burning . . .'

'Oh yes, my toast caught under the grill.' He held up the charred slice. 'Sorry I didn't hear you. I must have had my music too loud. Here, hold on a minute . . .' He put down his cup and the toast and shuffled out of the kitchen. A moment later, the faint crackly sound of the gramophone stopped and he returned. 'There, that's better. I can hear myself think now.' He smiled at her. 'But where are my manners? You're soaked through. Here, take your coat off and come and sit by the fire. Would you like a cup of tea? It's just brewed.'

'Thank you.'

Florence watched him out of the corner of her eye as he helped her off with her coat and hung it up carefully to dry. He was humming tunelessly, and certainly didn't look like a man whose wife had just deserted him.

He set down the cup in front of her, smiling. 'Now,' he said. 'What can I do for you?'

She opened her mouth, then closed it again. Now she could see Clement was in one piece, she felt rather foolish.

'Don't tell me I've left another light showing? I've been so careful to keep the blackouts closed every night since the last time—'

'I saw Gwendoline,' Florence blurted out. 'When I went to buy a wedding dress.'

'Oh.' Clement's smile slowly faded. 'Oh, I see. And I suppose she told you—'

'Yes.'

He sipped his tea for a moment, taking it in. Then something seemed to strike him and he looked up sharply. 'Good lord, is that why you're here? You were worried I might do myself in?'

'You were very upset last time she left,' Florence said.

'And you thought I'd do the same again?' Clement put down his cup. 'What did Gwendoline tell you, exactly?' he asked.

'She said she had left you – for good, this time.'

'Did she now?' To her amazement, Clement burst out laughing. 'Typical Gwendoline! She always has to have the last word.'

Florence stared at him, mystified. 'I don't see what's so funny?'

'Gwendoline didn't leave me, Miss Maguire. I was the one who told her to go.'

'What? But I don't understand . . .'

'I know, I must say I surprised myself.'

She considered it for a moment. 'Was she – you know . . .'

'Up to her old tricks?' Clement finished for her. 'I don't think so. Not yet, anyway. Although knowing Gwendoline, it would only have been a matter of time,' he said grimly.

'Then why?'

'I just realised I'd had enough.' He stared down into his cup. 'I couldn't stand the thought of waking up every morning with that terrible feeling of dread, wondering what the day would bring. Whether I'd say or do something to upset Gwendoline and send her into one of her moods, whether I was going to let her down in some way. I couldn't stand another day of looking into her eyes and seeing the disappointment there.'

'I'm sorry,' Florence said.

'It was for the best, believe me. Gwendoline never really loved me. I'm just sorry it took me so long to realise it. All those years I wasted, trying to change myself, to be the man she wanted me to be. But in the end, I just had to admit this is who I am, and that's not good enough for Gwendoline.' He looked down at his shattered leg with genuine sorrow.

'You're good enough for any woman. And if Gwendoline doesn't realise that then she's even more of an idiot than I thought!' Florence blurted out the words without thinking.

Clement looked up at her, his brows lifting. 'Why, Miss Maguire, I do believe that's the first nice thing you've ever said to me.'

'Yes, well, don't get too used to it.' Florence dropped her gaze back to her teacup.

'Anyway, enough about my miserable life,' Clement said, brightening up. 'You've been shopping for a wedding dress, you say? Does this mean you've finally set a date?'

Florence nodded. 'Next month. The fourteenth.'

'Colonel Forrest must be relieved?'

'Yes.'

'And how about you?'

She looked at him sharply. He was smiling blandly, but there was a look in his eyes she did not like. As if he could see into her soul.

'I'm glad we've set a date at last,' she said.

'Then why have you been putting it off for so long?'

'I-I haven't . . .'

'Oh, come on, Miss Maguire! William Forrest might believe all that nonsense about us not being able to replace you, but we both know better.'

'It's not nonsense!' Florence defended herself stiffly. 'Someone has to keep the department running. And you certainly can't,' she added.

He ignored the remark as he met her gaze across the table. 'Be honest. Are you having doubts?'

'No! Good heavens, why would you ask such a thing?'

'Because you seem to be putting it off.'

'I'm not! There's just a lot to think about, to organise, that's all.' Florence could feel herself blushing as she looked away from his searching gaze. 'The wedding, and moving to Cambridge. You can't rush these things, you know.'

'Gillian Munroe managed it.'

'Yes, well, we can't all be as giddy as Gillian Munroe!'

Even though she wasn't looking at him, she could feel Clement's steady gaze on her, making her squirm.

'You don't know what you're talking about, anyway,' she snapped. 'William is a wonderful man, and I'm looking forward to marrying him. Why wouldn't I be?'

'Why indeed?' There was something about the way he said it that made her hackles rise.

Florence set down her cup with an angry clatter and blundered to her feet.

'I should go,' she muttered, reaching for her coat.

'But you haven't finished your tea?'

'I should get back – I'm needed on duty. They'll be wondering why I haven't reported back to the post . . .' The excuses spilled out, tumbling over each other. But all she could think was that she needed to get away from Clement Saunders and his searching gaze.

Before she said something she regretted.

Chapter 45

Clement watched Florence Maguire disappearing off into the night, her head down, the collar of her greatcoat turned up against the rain.

Whatever she said, she didn't look like a radiantly happy bride-to-be. She seemed as if she had the weight of the world on her shoulders.

Come to think of it, she hadn't been herself for the past few days. Once or twice, Clement had had to come out of his office and tell the girls to keep the noise down, only to find Florence sitting at her desk, her chin in her hands, apparently lost in reverie. He'd even noticed a few mistakes creeping into her work, which wasn't like her at all.

At the time, he'd put it down to her being preoccupied with her forthcoming wedding. But seeing the troubled look on her face tonight, Clement began to wonder if she had something else on her mind.

Either way, it's none of your business, he told himself. Florence Maguire had made that very clear.

He shuffled into the sitting room, wound up the gramophone and set the needle back on the moving record. The crackling sounds of Beethoven's Pastoral Symphony filled the air.

It was such a luxury to be able to play his favourite music again. Gwendoline always said classical music gave her a headache.

'Give me a tune I can dance to any day,' she would say.

Clement knew it wouldn't be long before she found some-one else to dance with. He waited for the old familiar stab of jealousy, but it didn't come. Instead there was nothing more than a little wistful sadness for what might have been.

He had tried so hard to make Gwendoline happy, but he had to admit now that he would never be the man she truly wanted. If he was, then she would never have run off and married his cousin Alec in the first place. But he'd clung on because he loved her, and because he was so afraid of what his life might be without her.

But now he had dragged the truth into the light and con-fronted it, he found the idea of being alone was not nearly as awful or as terrifying as he had always feared. It was certainly better than being with the wrong person for ever.

For some reason, an image of Florence Maguire filled his mind. He hoped she wasn't making the same mistake.

And what do you know about it? He laughed out loud at his own presumption. As if he was qualified to judge anyone else, given his own woeful history!

No wonder Florence had walked out the way she did. Although he had the distinct feeling that she had been on the verge of admitting something to him before she left so hastily.

Whatever it was, it was none of his business. He and Flor-ence Maguire were not friends, as she had so often made plain.

But, friend or not, he couldn't help caring about her. In fact, he was rather dismayed to find how important her hap-piness was to him, and how often his thoughts strayed to her.

Good lord, what was he thinking? He had just finished filling his head with one doomed romantic fantasy, he cer-tainly didn't need another. Especially when Florence had made it so clear she was happy to be marrying her square-jawed, handsome American . . .

He must have fallen asleep on the settee because the next moment a knock on the door jerked him awake. Clement glanced at the clock. Nearly ten o'clock. Who on earth would be calling at this time?

He opened the door to see Florence Maguire standing on his doorstep, her greatcoat soaked, rain dripping off her dark hair.

'Good lord, Miss Maguire,' Clement said. 'What happened? Did you fall in Barmston Drain?'

Florence ignored the question, meeting his gaze with those serious dark brown eyes of hers.

'I need to talk to you,' she said.

He stepped to one side. 'Then you'd best come in,' he said.

*   *   *

He put her greatcoat in front of the fire to dry. Florence declined his offer of a change of clothes and instead sat there on the settee, shivering in her damp ARP uniform.

Clement eyed her warily as he poured them both a drink. He wasn't sure how best to approach her. He had no idea why she had returned. But he could tell she had a lot going on in her mind as she stared into the fire's flames, lost in thought.

'Here.' He pressed a glass of brandy into her hand. 'This will help warm you up. I did have a nice bottle of whisky, but someone poured it down the sink.'

'Thank you.' Florence smiled faintly as she took it.

Clement sank down into the armchair opposite, still unsure of what to say.

'I owe you an apology,' he ventured finally.

That made her look up. 'What for?'

'I shouldn't have questioned you about your marriage plans. It was none of my business. I'm sure you're—'

'You were right.'

Clement stared at her profile as she gazed into the flames. Firelight flickered on her face, lighting up her eyes.

'I beg your pardon?'

'I've been putting off the wedding.'

'I see. So you are having doubts?'

'No! I don't know. Perhaps.' She looked down at the amber liquid swirling around in her glass. 'I don't know what's got into me,' she said. 'I should be looking forward to this, shouldn't I? It's the most exciting and wonderful thing that could ever have happened to me. Something I could never have imagined, even in my wildest dreams . . .'

The words sounded dull, almost as if she was reciting them from a book.

'Perhaps it's just pre-wedding nerves?' Clement suggested kindly.

'That's what I thought.' She turned to look at him. 'Do you think that might be it? It seems so silly at my age.'

Her face was so full of hope, it nearly broke his heart.

'I don't think age has anything to do with it. Your whole life is changing. You're getting married, moving to a foreign country. It would be very strange if you weren't apprehensive about it.'

'That's true.' Florence turned her head to stare back into the flames. 'I've been rather worried about how I'll manage. I mean, I've scarcely been further than Grimsby my whole life! There's so much to take in, to learn. It will be a whole new way of life for me, living in that big house, being a mother to his sons. And then there's the rest of his family to think about. His mother sounds like a very formidable woman. How will she take to me, I wonder?'

'I'm sure you'll be more than a match for her, Miss Maguire.'

Florence smiled, but she didn't look too convinced. Clement noticed the way her hands knotted nervously in her lap. He had never known Florence Maguire to lose her composure over anything.

'Have you spoken to Colonel Forrest about this?' he asked.

'Oh no,' Florence shook her head. 'I mean, I did mention how concerned I was, when we first got engaged. But he says he'll look after me, so I've got nothing to worry about. And he's so happy and excited about our future, I wouldn't want to let him down.'

And what about you? Clement thought. He wondered whether William had ever stopped to consider how his bride-to-be might really be feeling.

He was suddenly filled with a dark dislike for the handsome colonel.

'I just wish I could feel more excited about it all,' Florence went on. 'But I've never really been one for weddings and so on. All the other girls used to get terribly giddy, talking about boys and planning their wedding, but I didn't see the point. While they were dressing up as brides with lace curtains on their heads and pretending to keep house with their dolls, I had my nose stuck in a book.' She looked rueful. 'Perhaps I always knew it would never happen to me.'

'What about your boyfriend – the one who was killed in the war?'

'Donald?' Florence shook her head. 'It was never that serious between us. I think he only started courting me because he wanted someone to write to him while he was away. I don't think we would have ever got married.' She smiled wistfully. 'I was sad when he didn't come home, of course. Sad for him, and for his family. But I wasn't as heartbroken as all the other girls whose sweethearts were lost. And there were so many, weren't there? All those women, with not enough men left to marry.'

'I'm sure you could have found someone else eventually? Lots of women did.'

'You sound like my mother and my sisters!' Florence's mouth twisted. 'They couldn't fathom why I wasn't searching for a man like the rest of them. But I just assumed that was it for me. I was never going to find a man, so I might as well buckle down and learn to fend for myself.' She sipped her drink. 'So that's what I did. I went to night classes for shorthand and typing, got a job at the Corporation and worked my way up from there. And I enjoyed it.' There was a hint of defiance in her voice. Clement wondered how often she'd had to defend herself and her choices in the past. 'I was good at my job, and I liked being independent. And I couldn't imagine wanting to give it up for a man.'

'Until now?' Clement said.

Florence flashed him a quick, wary look. 'Until now,' she agreed.

They were both silent for a moment, staring into the fire's dancing flames. There was so much Clement wanted to say but he knew he had to tread carefully. Florence had briefly let down her defences, but it wouldn't take much for them to go up again.

'What if I can't do it?' Florence broke the silence suddenly. 'What if I'm too old to change my ways for anyone?'

'You won't have to change anything about yourself if you're marrying the right man.'

She laughed. 'That's absurd!'

'Is it? Look at me. I tried to change myself for Gwendoline and it was a disaster.'

'Yes, but that's different,' Florence dismissed. 'I'm talking about compromise. That's what marriage is about, isn't it?'

'I don't see Colonel Forrest compromising on anything,' Clement said. 'As far as I can see, you're changing your whole life for him. But what's he doing in return?'

Florence stared at him for a long moment. Clement could almost see the steel shutters clanging down behind her eyes.

'He's making me happy,' she said firmly. She set her drink down on the low table in front of her. 'I should go,' she said for the second time that evening.

'Please stay. I'm sorry if I overstepped the mark again . . .'

'No, really, I should go.' She stood up. 'I've already taken up far too much of your time.'

'I wasn't doing anything else. Besides, I like talking to you.'

'Yes, well . . .' He had embarrassed her, he could tell. Her voice was suddenly stilted. 'Thank you for your advice,' she said. 'Although I really can't think what made me knock on your door.'

'Because we're friends?' Clement suggested.

Florence smiled reluctantly. 'Perhaps we are,' she said.

Chapter 46

'Oh no, not again!'

Maudie heard Mitch groan a moment before she saw her sister storming down the path towards them. Sybil's expression was as threatening as the dark sky overhead.

'What is it this time, I wonder?' she murmured.

'As if we didn't know.'

There was only one thing Sybil had talked about in the month since Tom had finished with her. When she wasn't crying, she was plotting her revenge or trying to work out ways to win him back.

'Can't we just pretend we haven't seen her?' Mitch pleaded. But no sooner had he said it than Maudie heard Sybil calling out to her.

'Better see what she wants,' she said.

'If we must,' Mitch gave a long-suffering sigh. 'But I'm warning you, if she mentions Davenport's name more than three times . . .'

'Guess what I've just heard?' Sybil rushed up to them. 'Tom's got a new girlfriend. And you'll never guess who it is?'

'Who?' Maudie asked, with a sinking feeling of dread.

'Teddy Jarvis! It's all over the station, apparently. She's swanning around showing off and telling everyone he's her boyfriend. Can you believe it?' Sybil looked outraged.

Maudie sighed. She'd heard the rumour too, and she'd prayed Sybil would not find out. 'It was bound to happen sometime,' she said.

'Yes, but why her? Why pick a girl from the Met Office? It's so cruel.'

You didn't think that when you took him from poor Imogen, Maudie thought. But she said nothing.

'You don't seem very surprised?' Sybil said, her eyes narrowing.

'I'd heard a whisper,' she admitted.

'And you didn't think to tell me?'

'You were already so upset, I didn't want to make things worse . . .' She caught Mitch's eye as she said it. There was a lot she was not telling Sybil at the moment.

'As if anything could be worse than this.' Sybil looked furious. 'Teddy Jarvis, of all people! And to think, I actually liked her. I even felt sorry for her when she split up with her boyfriend. I didn't realise that all this time she was planning to steal mine!'

'It takes two, you know,' Mitch said in a low voice.

'It didn't take her long, either,' Sybil went on, ignoring him. 'She must have been sniffing around him the minute we broke up.'

Maudie sent Mitch another sidelong glance, willing him not to say anything. He had told her it was common knowledge among the flying crews that Tom Davenport had been chasing Teddy Jarvis for months. She wondered if it was any accident that they had ended up spending Christmas together.

Not that she dared say anything to Sybil. The poor girl was distraught enough without hearing more bad news.

'You're better off without him,' she said. She had been repeating the same words over and over for weeks, but they never seemed to sink in.

Sybil looked thoughtful for a moment, then she lifted her chin and said, 'You're right – I am better off without him.'

Maudie smiled with relief. 'That's the spirit.'

'And he just needs time to realise what he's missing.'

'If you say so.' Maudie glanced at Mitch, deflated. He raised his brows but said nothing.

'Anyway, I'm not doing myself any good, moping around here,' Sybil said. 'I should go out and enjoy my freedom, shouldn't I? Tell you what, why don't we go out for a drink to-night, just you and me? It's ages since we've been out together.'

'Well, I'm not sure ... Mitch might be on ops tonight.'

Sybil looked irritated. 'He's not taking you with him, though, is he?'

'No, but ...' She never liked to go far from the station when Mitch was flying. And she always had to be there to give him his good luck kiss, otherwise it simply didn't feel right.

'It's all right,' Mitch said. 'It looks like P-Popeye's going to be grounded with engine trouble anyway, so I probably won't be flying. You two can go off and have fun.'

'You see?' Sybil said, smiling brightly. 'That's settled then.'

'I still don't think—' Maudie started to say, but Sybil cut her off.

'I'm off duty at six,' she said. 'We'll go out at seven.'

She went off, looking a lot happier than when she had arrived.

'You didn't get a chance to tell her you've got a date for your board interview,' Mitch said.

'She wouldn't be interested.' Sybil made a point of never talking about Maudie's application if she could help it. The only time she mentioned it was to scold Maudie for spending too much time studying with Joan. 'Anyway, it didn't seem to be the right moment.'

'It never is, is it?' Mitch sighed. 'It seems to me there's a lot you're keeping from your sister.'

'I know.' Maudie dropped her gaze. 'I'm sorry. I will talk to her, honestly.'

'When?'

'When I can find the right time.'

'God knows when that will be,' Mitch muttered. 'There never seems to be a right time with Sybil, does there?'

He was right, Maudie thought. Sybil always seemed to be in the middle of some crisis or other. Whether it was the Met officer shouting at her over misplaced figures, the hut corporal putting her on report for not cleaning the bathroom floor properly, or Tom deliberately snubbing her, anything was enough to trigger more floods of tears and angry tantrums.

'I don't want to upset her.'

'Surely she'll be pleased for you?'

'You don't know Sybil.'

'I know she's the most self-centred creature I've ever met.'

'Mitch!'

'It's true,' Mitch said. 'She never shows the slightest interest or concern for you. It's always about herself.'

He was right about that too, Maudie thought. But it had been that way for so long she had almost stopped noticing.

'I will talk to her tonight, I promise,' she said.

'And you'll tell her everything?'

'I will.' Although she couldn't say she was looking forward to it.

* * *

But as usual it was hard to get a word in edgeways. The only time her sister stopped talking was when she was at the bar buying drinks. And even then she started again as soon as she returned.

'I think it's because she's an officer,' she declared, as she put Maudie's port and lemon down on the table in front of her. 'That's the only reason I can think why he'd go out with her. I mean, it's a lot easier for him, in't it? It was always so difficult for us to be seen together because of this silly rule about officers and other ranks not mixing.'

Maudie sipped her drink and said nothing. The rule didn't seem to trouble Tom or any other officer when they felt like breaking it. Maudie suspected he used it as an excuse.

'Can we talk about something else?' she pleaded.

So much for taking her sister's mind off it, she thought. Sybil had done nothing but talk about Tom in the hour they had been there.

'If you want.' Sybil fell silent for a moment, her gaze shifting to the door. Then she said, 'Do you think he's doing it to get back at me?'

'What?'

'Going out with Teddy Jarvis. It makes sense, doesn't it? I mean, why else would he choose a Met girl?'

'Because he likes her?' Maudie said, but Sybil wasn't listening.

'That must be it,' she continued. 'He's doing it on purpose just to upset me. That means he must have feelings for me, doesn't it?'

'Syb—'

'I mean, you don't try to provoke someone if you don't care about them, do you?'

'Sybil, please—'

'The question is, what should I do about it? Should I pretend not to notice, or should I show him I care?'

'I think you should just try to forget about Tom altogether,' Maudie said wearily. 'I'm sure he's already forgotten about you!'

Sybil stared at her, her brown eyes turning liquid with tears. 'How can you say that?'

'Because it's true. Look, he doesn't deserve you,' Maudie said. 'Remember the way he humiliated you, all those cruel things he said? You don't say things like that if you really care about someone.' She reached across the table to grasp her sister's hand. 'Forget about him, Syb. Please? Find someone who really loves you.'

'Like you, you mean?'

Maudie met Sybil's watery gaze across the table. *Tell her*, a small voice inside her head whispered. *This is your chance.*

She took a deep breath. 'Syb, listen. I've got something to tell you,' she began.

'Oh yes?' Sybil said absently, her gaze fixed on the door.

'While I was away meeting Mitch's parents, he ... Syb, are you listening to me?'

'What? Yes, of course.'

'Why do you keep looking at the door? Are you expecting someone?'

'No!'

No sooner had the word left her mouth than the door opened and the crew of N-Nancy had just walked in, along with a few WAAFs. Tom was with them, his arm firmly around the waist of Teddy Jarvis.

'Sybil, no!' Maudie turned on her sister. 'You knew they were coming, didn't you?'

'I didn't, honestly,' Sybil protested, but her guilty colour gave her away.

'Why, Syb? Why would you want to put yourself through more humiliation?'

'I told you, I want to show him what he's missing.' She raised her glass tauntingly in Tom's direction. His expression hardened and he immediately veered off in the other direction, the others following.

Maudie shook her head. 'You don't understand, do you? He in't interested, Syb.' She put down her glass and reached for her bag. 'Come on,' she said.

'Where are you going?'

'Back to Holme, where do you think? I'm not sitting here all night, watching you make a fool of yourself.'

'She's coming over!'

Maudie looked up to see Teddy Jarvis approaching their table. Beside her, Sybil sat up a bit straighter in her seat, ready to do battle.

'What are you doing here?' Teddy asked.

'We've got as much right to be here as you do,' Sybil snapped back.

'I wasn't talking to you.' She turned to Maudie. 'I thought you'd be at the station tonight, to see your boyfriend off?'

'Mitch isn't flying tonight. P-Popeye was grounded with engine trouble,' Maudie said. But something about the urgent way Teddy looked at her sent a cold trickle of fear down her spine.

'Oh lord, you didn't know? They were ordered to take J-Jericho up half an hour ago.' She looked genuinely concerned.

Maudie was already on her feet.

Teddy glanced at her watch. 'I'd say you've got ten minutes,' she said.

Chapter 47

It was a long walk back to Holme, and they ran all the way.

They were nearly at the gates when Sybil suddenly shouted, 'Stop!'

'I can't, I've got to get back!'

'Listen!'

Maudie stopped. To her right, she heard the roar of approaching engines. A moment later, the sky was filled with the sound as eight planes roared overhead.

She looked up into the night sky at the shapes passing low overhead, their bellies heavy with bombs.

'He's gone,' she whispered.

'It will be all right.' Sybil put her hand on her arm in the darkness.

'He's gone and I wasn't there.' It was all Maudie could think about. The words filled her mind, crowding out all other thoughts.

I wasn't there. She had a sudden vision of Mitch in his overalls and flying boots, pausing for a moment on the airstrip, looking around for her, waiting for his lucky charm . . .

Why did it have to be him? Why couldn't it have been another crew that got sent up in J-Jericho?

And why hadn't she been here to see him off, instead of sitting in a pub, listening to her sister droning on and on about Tom Davenport?

As soon as they reached Holme, Maudie headed straight for the Watch Office. Joan was on duty, sitting at a bench which ran down the centre of the room, wedged in between two other R/T operators, each of them frantically flicking switches between 'receive' and 'transmit' as they talked to the aircraft.

Joan looked briefly over her shoulder and caught Maudie's eye.

'You can't be here,' she said. 'If the flying officer catches you—'

'Is it true?' Maudie interrupted her. 'Mitch went up in J-Jericho?'

Joan whispered something to the girl next to her, then got up from her seat and went over to Maudie.

'You really should leave,' she said, 'before we both end up on a charge.'

'Where are they going?'

Joan looked reproachful. 'You know better than to ask that.'

'When are they due back?'

'Around zero four hundred.'

They were going a long way then, right into enemy territory.

'Try not to worry,' Joan said. 'He seemed in really good spirits before he left.'

'You saw him?'

Joan nodded. 'He gave me this to give you . . .'

Maudie felt the earth shift under her feet as Joan took the letter out of the pocket of her battledress and held it out to her.

'Don't you want it?' Joan asked.

Maudie said nothing. She could only stare dumbly at the thin blue envelope in her friend's hand.

I've heard that some men write letters if they have a feeling they might not be coming home.

At that moment, they heard footsteps coming up the stairs.

'That's the flying officer.' Joan hurriedly thrust the letter into Maudie's hands. 'You'd best go, before he catches you. Go through the side door, then he won't see you.' She gave Maudie a quick smile. 'I'll watch out for him,' she whispered.

Outside, the night air was cold and eerily still now the aircraft had all gone. Sybil turned right towards the perimeter track that led to the Waafery, but Maudie stayed rooted to the spot.

'In't you coming?' Sybil turned to look back at her.

Maudie shook her head. 'I'm going up on the roof to wait.'

'You heard what Joan said. They're not due back for hours. Why don't you come back to the hut and get some sleep?'

'How do you expect me to sleep?'

Sybil frowned. 'What's wrong with you? You're never usually like this when Mitch is on ops?'

That's because I've always been there before, she thought. She looked at the letter in her hand.

'Come on,' Sybil urged her. 'Get some rest. He'll be back before you know it.'

'You go. I want to wait.'

'We can't sit on the roof all night. We'll freeze to death.'

'You go,' Maudie repeated. 'I'd rather be on my own anyway.'

For a moment, they stared at each other. Then, without a word, Sybil turned and walked off up the track towards the WAAF huts.

*   *   *

Sybil went to bed, but she couldn't sleep. All she could think about was her sister, alone on the roof, waiting for Mitch to come home.

In the end, she got out of bed, put her greatcoat on over her pyjamas and crept out of the hut.

The night was dark and silent, and Sybil's footsteps crunched loudly on the cinder track as she made her way down to the Flying Control building. Inside, behind the blacked-out windows, she knew everyone would be busy. In the Signals Office the R/T operators would be at their machines, straining to hear the first faint signals from the crews, telling them they were on their way. Downstairs, the Met assistants would be preparing their charts and watching out for changes in the weather that might affect their return. And everyone else would be scanning the skies, waiting and hoping and praying that they would come home safely.

As she carefully climbed the rungs of the metal ladder that led up to the roof, Sybil could see her sister outlined in the darkness, illuminated by feeble torchlight, keeping her lonely vigil.

'Maudie?' Sybil whispered.

She climbed over the ledge onto the roof. Maudie didn't even register her presence, keeping her face turned up to the sky.

'Not long to wait now.' Sybil peered over the edge of the roof. Someone must have given word that the planes were on their way because the ground crews were starting to emerge on the other side of the airfield. She could hear the grating sound of the giant hangar doors being opened, and the sound of the emergency vehicle engines.

Please God they won't be needed tonight, she thought.

'Here, you must be freezing.' Sybil took off her greatcoat and draped it over her sister's shoulders. Once again, Maudie did not react. It was as if she was completely unaware of anything around her.

She was still clutching Mitch's letter in her hand, Sybil noticed.

She was about to ask her about it when she heard the faint rumble of a distant engine.

'They're coming home!' she cried.

Maudie tensed beside her, her whole body stiffening, all her senses suddenly on high alert.

And then, one by one, the aircraft began to return. Sybil counted them in her mind as they came in.

One . . . two . . . three . . .

More people began to spill out onto the peri-track below. A couple of the pilots climbed the ladder to the roof to get a better look.

Four . . . five . . .

Two more planes came home and the men on the roof and down below gave a half-hearted cheer, quickly quelled as they looked back up towards the sky.

'Three more to go,' Sybil said.

And then, from far away, came an ominous sputtering sound. The men on the roof exchanged worried looks. On the field, the ground crews shouted to each other as they rushed towards the emergency vehicles.

Meanwhile, the coughing sound grew louder as the plane limped towards the airfield, sinking lower and lower . . .

Please don't let it be his, Sybil prayed silently.

And then, suddenly, a dark shape swooped down, skimmed over their heads before landing with a shuddering bump just a few hundred yards from the Flying Control building. Sybil flinched and covered her face, remembering the awful night when D-Daisy had crash-landed and burst into flames right in front of their eyes.

'It's all right,' one of the men said. 'They're safe.'

Sybil risked a look between her fingers to see the crew clambering out of the badly damaged Lanc.

'How they got that back over the North Sea I have no idea,' one of the men murmured admiringly.

In all the fuss, no one noticed a seventh plane swooping in and landing on the airfield. Except Sybil, who leaned over the parapet, craning her neck to try to see who it was.

'T-Tommy.' Maudie's voice came out of the darkness, clear and quiet.

And then, nothing. The minutes crawled back, each one seeming like hours. Sybil kept her gaze fixed on the sky, willing the last plane to appear.

After a while, the two men gave up and climbed off the roof, leaving Sybil and Maudie alone. Sybil wanted to scream after them, to beg them not to give up hope.

'He'll be back,' she whispered. 'You'll see.'

Maudie ignored her, still staring up at the sky.

Dawn started to break, feathers of light streaking the sky, and Maudie still stood there, her face turned upwards. Sybil wanted to tell her to rest, but she didn't dare. She hunched down below the parapet, still in her pyjamas, her muscles stiff with cold.

Below them, the rest of the station was waking up, going about their business, the night watch going off duty.

'He might have landed somewhere else?' Sybil suggested. 'You know, if there was an emergency . . .'

She broke off, hearing the metallic clang of feet climbing up the ladder rungs. A moment later, Joan's head appeared above the parapet. She looked weary, her face grey after a long night on the transmitter.

'Any news?' Sybil asked.

Joan shook her head. 'I'm sorry.'

'I was just saying to Maudie, he might have made an emergency landing somewhere?' She stared at Joan, silently pleading with her.

'It's possible.' Joan turned to Maudie. 'Have you been up here all night? You need to get some rest.'

'I want to stay here.'

'Joan's right,' Sybil started to say. 'Come back to the hut—'

'I told you, I want to stay here!' Maudie looked at her for the first time, anger flaring in her eyes.

'Leave her be,' Joan said quietly. 'She's better off by herself.'

Sybil hesitated, still looking at Maudie.

She's better off by herself.

But we're twins, she wanted to say. *We're not supposed to be by ourselves . . .*

Sybil followed Joan down the ladder. As they trudged back towards the Waafery, she looked back at the lonely figure standing on the roof, still scanning the dawn sky, expecting a miracle.

She had never felt more alone in her life.

Chapter 48

March 1943

'I can't believe he's gone.'

Maudie looked at Mitch's mother, sitting across from her on the other side of the fireside. The poor woman seemed to have aged at least twenty years since the last time Maudie saw her. Her neat clothes hung off her gaunt frame, and her raw grief was etched in the dark hollows of her face.

Maudie couldn't help but remember the first time she had been in this room. Was it really only a couple of months ago? It seemed like a lifetime now, so much had happened since then.

She remembered how she had sat on the same settee with Mitch, holding his hand. They had all been so happy then. His mother and father had been so warm, welcoming her into their family.

Sitting here now, by herself, she felt Mitch's absence even more painfully than ever. It was like looking at a jigsaw with a missing piece. A piece that would never, ever be found.

She hadn't wanted to come today. Not because she didn't want to see his parents, but because she didn't think she had the strength to face them. She had spent nearly two weeks putting on a brave face, going through her duties and forcing herself to smile even though her face ached. The thought of keeping up the charade for his mother and father was almost too much for her.

But it was what Mitch would have wanted, and so Maudie had pushed herself to do it for his sake.

She had waited a week until she read his letter. It had lain untouched in her bedside locker until she finally found the strength to open it. Even then she had borrowed a bicycle and left the station, pedalling far out into the countryside, until she found a place where she could sit by herself and allow herself to cry alone.

She had only managed to read it once, but she already had every line memorised by heart. His tender words of love, the only ones she would ever hear from him. His loving hopes that she would find happiness in her future, and his sorrow that he might not be there to share it with her. Every single word was almost too painful to read.

I'd be so grateful if you could find some time to visit Mum and Dad, if you could possibly bear it, he had written. *It would mean so much to them, and to me.*

Typical Mitch, she thought, always thinking of other people.

'I know what you mean,' she replied to Mrs Mitchell. 'Sometimes when I wake up in the morning, I forget for a minute that he's not here.'

The moment after she opened her eyes was the happiest in her day, just before realisation rushed in and hit her like a blow.

Not that she could let it show. Maudie forced herself to get up, to wash and dress and go to breakfast with the other girls, even though her limbs were so heavy all she wanted to do was hide under the blanket and sleep the day away.

It was what everyone expected. Heartbreak and loss and grief were nothing new at the station. Only two nights after Mitch didn't come home, the crew of T-Tommy crashed into the sea just off the Lincolnshire coast. Then, last night, another plane was shot down over Belgium. Sixteen more young lives ended in the blink of an eye. Everyone mourned for an hour or two, then they were forgotten, consigned to the past. It was harsh, but it was the only way anyone survived.

Only, Maudie knew she would never forget. She felt the pain of every boy that died now, as if their names were etched on her heart. And she would carry the pain around with her for ever, like a dark heaviness in the pit of her stomach.

'It isn't that.' Mitch's mother leaned forward, her face urgent. Her eyes protruded from her thin face. 'I don't believe he's dead. He's out there somewhere, I know he is.'

'Now then, Annie.' Mitch's father looked embarrassed. He was tall, lean and sandy-haired like his son. 'You can't go talking like that.'

'But I'm his mother. I'd know if anything had happened to him. I'd feel it, wouldn't I?' She turned to Maudie, her eyes filled with desperate hope.

'Stop it, love. You'll upset the girl.'

'It's all right,' Maudie smiled. If anything, she envied Annie Mitchell her optimism. She only wished she could share it, but she had seen too many young men lost to believe Mitch's fate might be different.

'I'm sorry, love,' his mother smiled sadly. 'You probably don't want to hear me going on about him.'

Maudie shook her head. 'I'm glad to have someone to talk to, honestly. There's no one else who really understands.'

Death was a fact of life at the bomber station, and dwelling on it too much was frowned upon. Girls were expected to just get on with it, to mop up their tears and carry on with their duties.

She couldn't even talk to Sybil about it. She knew her sister was doing her best to be understanding, but there was so much bitterness and resentment in Maudie's heart, she could hardly bring herself to speak to her, let alone confide in her.

If only Sybil hadn't been so selfish, she thought. If only she had shown any kind of interest or concern for her before Mitch died, perhaps Maudie wouldn't be feeling so wretched.

Mrs Mitchell smiled approvingly. 'You're such a nice girl, Maudie. I'm so glad Michael met you. He thought the world of you, you know. I only had to look at the pair of you to see how happy you made him. Isn't that right, George?' she turned to her husband.

'That's right,' he nodded. 'We would have been proud to call you our daughter-in-law.'

Maudie smiled. Mitch's parents were the only ones who knew they were engaged. Mitch had asked Maudie to marry him when they went to visit them. It had been such a wonderful weekend, making plans and dreaming about their future together.

'That reminds me ...' Mrs Mitchell leaned down and picked something out of her sewing box. 'Michael asked me to have this cleaned, ready to give you. He was supposed to come and collect it himself next time he was on leave ...' She pressed her lips together, and Maudie saw the tears glistening in her eyes.

Maudie stared down at the beautiful diamond solitaire sparkling in the palm of her hand. Its facets caught the spring sunlight streaming in through the window.

'It belonged to my mother – his grandmother,' Mrs Mitchell explained. 'She left it to Michael to pass on to the girl he was going to marry.'

'It's beautiful,' Maudie murmured. 'But I couldn't take it.'

She tried to hand it back, but Mitch's mother shook her head.

'It's only right you should have it,' she said. 'You were his fiancée, after all. Who else will wear it, if you don't . . .' Her voice trailed off, choked with tears. 'Anyway,' she said, more brightly, 'Michael will want to see you wearing it when he comes home.'

Maudie glanced at Mitch's father. He could only smile sadly back at her.

Chapter 49

Maudie returned to Holme just as Sybil was coming off duty. Her heart sank when she saw her sister coming out of the Flying Control building. Maudie slowed her steps so she wouldn't catch up with her, but Sybil must have seen her because she was waiting for her by the time Maudie reached the corner of the airfield where the track split off towards the Waafery.

'You're back,' Sybil said. 'I was worried about you.'

Maudie didn't reply.

'How were Mitch's parents?' Sybil asked.

'How do you think they were? They've lost their son.'

Sybil looked taken aback, but Maudie didn't care. She had spent far too long being concerned about her sister's feelings.

They trudged back to the hut in silence. Maudie hoped Sybil might take the hint and leave, but her sister stayed doggedly at her side. Inside the hut, she could feel Sybil watching her as she gathered up her washbag and headed for the bathroom.

She filled the tub up to the meagre four-inch line. She longed for the days when she could enjoy a lovely, deep soak, but with so many other WAAFs queuing to use the bathroom, and hot water in short supply, she knew she was lucky to get a bath at all.

She lingered in the tepid water, trying to avoid Sybil. It felt as if her sister had not stopped hanging around her since

Mitch's plane went missing. She knew she was trying to be sensitive, but having her around, pretending to care, made Maudie want to scream.

When she returned from the bathroom, Sybil was sitting on her bed, waiting for her. Maudie could feel her sister watching her as she quickly dressed.

Don't you dare, she thought. *Don't you dare try to talk to me.* She had so much pent-up resentment inside her she wasn't sure she could trust herself to be civil.

'What's this?' Sybil said.

Maudie turned. Her sister was holding Mitch's ring out to her.

'Don't touch that!' Maudie snatched it out of her hand. 'You have no right going through my things.'

'It was just lying there, on your bedside locker. You want to be careful, it looks valuable.'

'It is.' *More valuable than you could ever imagine*, she thought.

'Where did you get it?'

'It belonged to Mitch's grandmother.'

Sybil looked from the ring to her and back again. 'Is it an engagement ring?'

Maudie ignored her, slipping the ring onto her left hand. It looked so strange there, she wondered if she would ever get used to it.

'When did this happen?'

'Two months.'

'Oh, Maud,' Sybil said. 'Why didn't you tell me?'

Maudie looked at her sister's face, so full of concern. Concern that was just a bit too little, too late.

'We didn't get the chance,' she said tightly. 'You were too busy crying over Tom Davenport, remember?'

Sybil's face flushed. 'All the same, you should have told me. We're twins, we're supposed to share everything . . .'

'Don't you think I wanted to tell you?' Maudie turned on her harshly. 'I was so happy, I couldn't wait to share it with the world. But you put paid to all that, didn't you? You were upset, so no one else was allowed to be happy. You had to take over, to overshadow everything. Just like you always do.'

Sybil looked shaken. 'That's not true! I would have been happy for you.'

'Yes, well, we'll never know now, will we? There's not going to be an engagement or a wedding. It's all gone.' Hot tears pricked the backs of her eyes.

All she could think about was how she had let Mitch down. He had wanted to tell the world their good news, and she'd made him keep it a secret because of Sybil's feelings.

It was yet another regret that would forever fester in her soul.

'Oh, Maudie, I'm so sorry.' Sybil moved to put her arms around her, but Maudie shrugged her off.

'Leave me alone,' she snapped. 'Stop pretending you care. If it wasn't for you, Mitch might still be here!'

Sybil stared at her. 'What? How do you work that out?'

'I wasn't here,' Maudie muttered. 'I always used to see him off, and I wasn't here.'

Realisation dawned on her sister's face. 'Is that what this is about?' she said slowly. 'You blame me for what happened to Mitch?'

Maudie said nothing as she turned away to finish buttoning up her tunic.

'It in't my fault,' Sybil said. 'You being here that night wouldn't have stopped anything from happening. It wouldn't have stopped him going missing—'

'You don't know that! He's always come home safely before. But the night I wasn't here to see him off . . .' Maudie stopped, not trusting herself to say any more.

'Oh, Maudie. That in't the way it works. You couldn't make Mitch come home safely, any more than you can make the sun come out in the morning.' Sybil shook her head sadly. 'I wish you'd told me how you felt. I might have been able to help you.'

'Help me?' Maudie laughed harshly. 'You've never cared about anyone but yourself in your life!'

'I care about you,' Sybil said in a hurt voice.

'You care that I'm always around to look after you and pick up the pieces when you get into trouble.'

'We look after each other,' Sybil insisted. 'We're—'

'Don't say it,' Maudie warned. 'I don't want to be your twin any more. I'm sick of always tagging along behind you, looking out for you. "Maudie, keep an eye on your sister,"' she parroted her mother's words. 'It's all I've ever heard. But I'm fed up with being in your shadow, doing everything you say. I want to be on my own!'

'Maud—'

'Didn't you hear what I said? Leave me alone!'

There was a long silence, then she felt Sybil shift away from her.

'Fine,' she said, in a small, hurt voice. 'If that's really what you want.' She stood up, her footsteps crossing the hut towards the door. Maudie heard the door close, and then Sybil was gone.

Chapter 50

'What's this I hear about you giving up the corporal's course?'

Sybil looked round in surprise at the section officer standing in the doorway behind her. She was so surprised, she forgot to salute. 'What?'

Miss Leech frowned. 'Oh dear, I've got the wrong one again, haven't I? I'm always mixing the two of you up. Although your sister would always remember how to address an officer,' she added sternly.

'I'm sorry, ma'am.' Sybil quickly saluted, knocking her cap askew over one eye as she did.

The officer acknowledged the gesture, her mouth twisting. 'Tell your sister I'm sorry to hear her decision. She would have made an excellent corporal.'

She strode off, and Sybil watched her go. Maudie hadn't said anything to her about giving up the corporal's course.

But then, Maudie didn't seem to say anything to her any more.

It had been nearly a week since their argument, and they had hardly spoken to each other in that time. Sybil couldn't bear the silence. She could see the emptiness behind her sister's eyes, the way she seemed to move like an automaton, pushing herself through each day. It was as if her heart had somehow been taken out of her.

Sybil was desperately worried about her, but she didn't dare approach her. She missed the closeness between them, the whispered secrets, shared confidences and secret laughter. There was so much she wanted to say to her ...

Perhaps that's the trouble, she thought. Perhaps if she had said less and listened more, she and Maudie might still be close.

It hurt especially when she saw Maudie talking to Joan. She saw how the other girl listened and consoled her, and she was jealous.

It should be me, she thought. *I'm her twin sister, I should be the one she turns to, not a stranger.*

But perhaps they were not as close as she had thought? She could not forget her sister's harsh words, how she had said she was sick of being a twin.

Sybil couldn't understand it because she loved having a twin sister. It meant the world to her to have a best friend always by her side, someone she could turn to, rely on.

Now it had started to dawn on her that she had not been the friend she might have been to Maudie. Her sister was right: she had taken Maudie for granted and expected a lot of her. And she had not given much in return.

But it wasn't too late, she thought. She couldn't do anything about the past, but she could show an interest now, stop her making a terrible mistake.

Maudie was in the hut when Sybil returned to get ready for her night duty. She was sitting by the stove writing a letter. She barely looked up when Sybil came in.

Sybil looked around at the other girls in the hut. She would have preferred to have this conversation when they were alone, but that never seemed to happen these days.

'Is it true you're not doing the corporal's course?' she asked.

Maudie flashed her a quick look of surprise, then went back to her sewing.

'Why didn't you tell me?' Sybil said.

'I didn't know I had to ask your permission.'

Sybil blushed, aware that the other girls were watching them with interest now.

She took a deep breath. 'I think you're making a big mistake,' she said.

'Why do you care? You never wanted me to take the wretched exam anyway.'

'I did!'

'Is that why you tried to talk me out of it?'

'I'm sure I didn't . . .'

'You did!'

'All right, perhaps I did,' Sybil conceded. 'But only because I was worried it might be too much work for you.'

'That's a lie, and you know it. You just couldn't bear the thought that I might have something you didn't.'

'No!' Sybil could feel her face burning.

'You've always been the same,' Maudie said. 'I've never been allowed to have anything if you haven't got it too.'

Sybil thought guiltily about the job at Hammonds, and how she had stood in Maudie's way. There was more truth in Maudie's words than she wanted to admit.

'But it was different here,' Maudie went on. 'People didn't treat us as a pair, the way they usually do. They started to notice me for who I was – Maudie Maguire, not just Sybil's twin sister. I started to realise I could do things on my own, things you couldn't. I made my own friends, I went for promotion, I found someone who loved me . . .' She took a deep, steadying breath. 'And you didn't like it, did you? You were jealous because I had all those things and you didn't. Because people started to notice me first and not you.'

'That in't true! I was happy for you . . .'

Maudie's mouth twisted. 'Happy for me? Don't make me laugh!' She shook her head. 'As far as you're concerned, the only one whose happiness counts is yours!'

* * *

It was a relief to get away from everyone and go on night duty. Thankfully for Sybil, she was on duty with a Met officer who was not very talkative and there were no ops that night, so after an initial briefing, he retired off to the anteroom to sleep, leaving Sybil alone.

She had just finished taking the readings and she was filling in the chart when Joan appeared with a cup in her hand.

'I thought you might like some cocoa?' she offered.

Sybil regarded it suspiciously, then looked back up at her. 'You do realise I'm not Maudie?'

Joan smiled. 'I know.'

Sybil frowned, still suspicious. It wasn't like Joan to be kind to her. She pulled the cup across the bench towards herself. 'Thank you.'

She expected Joan to go, but she sat down at the bench beside her. For a long time, neither of them spoke. Sybil could tell Joan was waiting, choosing her words carefully.

'I heard about your argument,' she said finally.

Sybil grimaced. 'You and the rest of the station!' She stared down into her cup. 'I didn't realise my sister hated me so much.'

'She doesn't hate you. She's just upset, that's all.'

'She's wrong, you know. I would have been happy for her. I only ever wanted the best for her.'

'Is that why you tried to stop us being friends?'

Sybil opened her mouth to bite back, then closed it again. Joan wasn't looking for an argument, she realised. Her face was full of sympathy and understanding. And without Maudie, Sybil badly needed someone to talk to.

'I was afraid of losing her,' she said quietly. 'I know everyone thinks I'm the confident one, but the truth is I'm nothing without Maudie. She's the clever one. I need her, not the other way round.'

It was joining the WAAFs that had made them both realise the truth. While Maudie had blossomed, Sybil had found herself left behind.

'I didn't want to hold her back,' she said. 'But I was scared that she might not need me any more.'

'She'll always need you,' Joan said. 'You're her sister.'

'She hates me,' Sybil said. 'All she wants is to be free of me.'

'She wouldn't be here if that was true.'

'What do you mean?'

Joan gave her a long, quizzical look. 'You do know she had the chance to join the Wrens, didn't you?'

'You're wrong.' Sybil shook her head. 'We both got turned down.'

But then it dawned on Sybil that she had never seen her sister's letter. She remembered opening hers, and how utterly disappointed she had been. As usual, she had been so consumed by her own feelings she hadn't even noticed Maudie opening her own letter.

'She told me she hadn't got in either,' she said. 'But why would she say that?'

'Why do you think?'

Sybil looked down at her hands. 'Probably because she knew I'd get upset,' she muttered.

'Because she wanted to stay with you,' Joan said. 'I know she said some harsh things to you, but Maudie loves you. And she's just as lost without you as you are without her.'

'Do you really think so?'

Joan nodded. 'I know it might not seem like it now, but she'll come round soon enough.'

'I hope so.' Sybil sighed. 'I've not been a good sister to her, have I? I just wish I could make it up to her in some way.'

'Perhaps there is a way,' Joan said slowly. 'If you're really serious about helping her?'

'What is it?'

Joan looked at her. 'It won't be easy. And it's a big risk, too. It could land you in big trouble if you're ever caught?'

Sybil smiled. 'Since when did that ever stop me?' she said.

Chapter 51

By the time dawn crept over the rooftops on the morning of her wedding, Florence had already been awake for hours.

'I heard you up and about last night,' Pop commented to her as she put the kettle on, bleary-eyed.

'I couldn't sleep.'

Her father regarded her sympathetically. 'You sure you're all right, lass? You look a bit peaky to me.'

'I'm fine, Pop.'

Florence's mother shuffled into the room, already dressed in her old faded pinny and house dress, in spite of the early hour. When she was a bain, Florence had wondered if her mother ever took it off, or if she slept in it so she could be ready for action at any time.

She had certainly worked hard to get the house ready for the wedding, Florence thought. It was bedecked with bunting, there were barrels of beer outside the back door and the larder was full of food. Later on, all their friends and neighbours would cram into the tiny house for another party, and this time, for the first time in her life, Florence would be the centre of attention.

After breakfast, the rest of the family started to arrive. Edie and Ruby came, bringing more food, and little gifts for Florence. A pearl-encrusted clip for her hair, a lace-trimmed garter, a special necklace.

'You need something borrowed and something blue, to bring you luck,' they said. Florence was so touched by their kindness, it was all she could do to stop herself crying.

Then, later, Iris arrived to do her hair.

'You look awful,' were her blunt first words as she unpacked her rollers and hairbrush onto the kitchen table.

'Thank you very much,' Florence replied. 'I knew I could rely on you to lift my spirits.'

'It's your wedding day, you don't need me to lift your spirits for you. But you do need me to make you look like a blushing bride. So let's have a look at you.' She lifted Florence's chin, examining her with a critical eye. 'Look at those bloodshot eyes. And those dark circles!' She tutted bossily. 'Never mind, I'm sure I can do something about them. Lucky your William sent some extra supplies, eh?' She grinned as she tipped out the contents of her make-up bag onto the table. 'I hope you'll remember to keep sending lipsticks and powder our way when you've moved down to Cambridge.'

Cambridge. Florence's stomach lurched at the thought of it.

This time tomorrow she would be on her way down south to start a new life with her new husband.

She fell silent as Iris set to work on her hair. She pictured Cambridge, with its cobbled streets and spires and beautiful old buildings, and the picturesque river than ran through the city that was nothing like the flat, grey expanse of the Humber.

She would fit in there, she told herself. It would be an adventure. And besides, she wouldn't be alone. She would be at Bassingbourn, living as an officer's wife.

She suddenly thought of Monday morning, and all the girls in the typing pool arriving for work, and her not being there to greet them, or criticise their appearance. Deirdre

Taylor would turn up wearing nail varnish again, no doubt. And Mabel Burrows would have a hole in her stocking. They would be getting away with murder, and Clement Saunders probably wouldn't even notice . . .

'Stop frowning,' Iris warned. 'You'll give yourself lines.'

'Sorry.' Florence deliberately tried to turn her thoughts away, back to her big day. She was getting married, she reminded herself. This was a day she had never ever dreamed would happen. If anyone had told her this time last year that plain old spinster Florence Maguire would have met a dashing, handsome American Air Force officer, let alone married him, she would have thought they were mad. And yet, here she was, about to embark on the greatest adventure of her life . . .

'You're frowning again,' Iris said.

'Sorry.'

'What have you got to frown about, anyway?' Iris asked, as she pinned another roller into place.

'I was just thinking about Cambridge.'

'Ah.'

'It feels strange, the thought of living so far away.'

'Aye, it does.'

Iris fell silent for a moment. Florence twisted round to look at her sister. 'Are you crying?'

'No!' Iris turned away sharply to pick up another roller. But not before Florence saw the tears glistening in her sister's eyes.

'You *are* crying!'

'So what if I am?' Iris snapped back defiantly. 'I can't help it if I'm going to miss you, can I?'

'You? Miss me?' Florence laughed incredulously. 'Now I've heard everything!'

'What's so funny?' Iris demanded, her voice choked. 'Why shouldn't I miss you? You're my only sister.'

'You've got Edie and Ruby.'

'Yes, but they in't my real sisters. Not like you. You're my flesh and blood.'

Florence turned back in her seat. 'I just never imagined you cared that much. We've never been that close.'

'I s'pose not,' Iris admitted quietly. 'But I've always looked up to you.'

Before Florence could reply, her mother came into the kitchen.

'Are you going to be much longer?' she asked. 'Only I've got a trifle to make.'

'More food?' Iris said. 'We've already got enough to feed a regiment as it is.'

Big May sent them both a scowling glance and then shuffled off. As her footsteps retreated back down the passageway, Iris leaned over and whispered, 'Now there's someone who'll really miss you!'

Florence laughed. 'You're joking! Ma can't wait for me to leave.'

'Don't you believe it. You know what Ma's like, she don't like to give her feelings away. But she's heartbroken, believe me. You've always been her favourite.'

'Get away!'

'I mean it.'

'We argue all the time, in case you hadn't noticed?'

'Yes, but that's just her way. She fights with all of us. Don't you remember the rows I've had with her in the past?'

'Yes, but it's different with me,' Florence said quietly.

'You're right. You are different. She respects you. You're the only one who can make her back down in an argument, and I think she likes that, even though she'd never admit it. I've even been a bit jealous of you at times,' Iris admitted sheepishly.

Florence stared at her sister. 'I was jealous of you, too,' she said.

Now it was Iris's turn to laugh. 'Why would you ever be jealous of me?'

'Because you and Ma are so close.'

'You could be close to her too, if you weren't so bloody prickly all the time.'

'I'm not prickly!'

'No?' Iris raised an eyebrow at her reflection in the mirror.

'All right, perhaps I am,' Florence relented. 'But you and Ma are so alike. She approves of you. You got married, had a family, all the things you're meant to do. All the things I failed to do,' she murmured.

'How can you ever say you've failed?' Iris looked incredulous. 'Look at you, Florence! You're the only one of us who's made something of themselves. Ma's proud of you, even though she'd probably rather poke her own eyes out than admit it.' She reached for another curler. 'Anyway, you'll soon be married yourself. Then you'll be just like the rest of us, won't you?'

'Yes,' Florence lifted her chin at her reflection. 'Yes, I will.'

Chapter 52

When Iris had finished doing her hair and make-up, Florence went over to Joyce Shelby's shop to pick up the dress she had been altering for her.

'Are you sure I can't go and collect it for you?' Pop said. 'I'm passing that way to pick up the twins from the station. I can easily call in . . .'

'I'd rather go myself. The fresh air will do me good.'

'As long as you don't ruin your hair,' Iris said, peering out of the back window. 'It's just starting to rain.'

'I'll put a scarf on.'

'And stop frowning!' Iris called after her, as she left. 'You'll crack your make-up.'

Florence walked up to Anlaby Road, passing along what was left of Bean Street. Like the rest of the city, it had been ravaged during the Blitz. Many of the houses were reduced to piles of rubble. Florence averted her gaze as she passed by where the public shelter had once stood. She still couldn't bear to look at the place where so many people had sought shelter, thinking they were safe, only to lose their lives when it took a direct hit.

So many families had suffered so much tragedy over the years since the war began. But somehow they had weathered the storm, picked themselves up again and got on with their lives. Florence felt fiercely proud of her city for its resilience, its determination to carry on. She was proud of herself, too, for doing her bit to protect it, patrolling the streets and manning the shelters in her ARP uniform.

Hull had always been her home and it gave her a physical pang to think of leaving it.

She could always come home, she told herself. She had already made up her mind that she would come back to visit as often as she could.

But what about when you move to America? She wouldn't be able to come home then. She braced herself against the thought. Once she left, she would probably never see her family again.

She tried to picture herself on the plantation in North Carolina, living a different life, helping William's mother with her charity work and learning to make peach pie, which she had never heard of, but which was apparently William's favourite. She imagined sitting on the porch with her husband watching the sun go down and sipping on mint juleps, something else she had never heard of.

She couldn't imagine what she would do with herself all day. There would be no housework to do, as William's family had actual servants.

'Although my mother likes to keep an eye on them, to make sure they're not slacking,' William had told her. 'She's a stickler for having things done right, as I'm sure you will be, too.'

Florence wasn't sure she would take to ordering servants about while she sat idle. She wasn't sure how she would take to Dorothea Forrest, either.

'I hope your mother isn't a stickler with me,' she had said to William, but he'd just laughed.

'I imagine you'll give each other a run for your money,' he had said, which didn't sound too promising. Florence had an uncomfortable feeling that Dorothea might turn out to be an even steelier and more disapproving version of her own mother.

She thought of Clement's comment, the one that had been haunting her ever since he had asked it.

I don't see Colonel Forrest compromising on anything. As far as I can see, you're changing your whole life for him. But what's he doing in return?

She shook her head, as if she could somehow dislodge the thought from her mind. It wasn't fair to think like that. She and William had talked about it; she had agreed it was the most sensible thing to do. His life was over in America . . .

But what about her life?

She would never have imagined she had a life, but now, looking around her, she realised that she did. She even had the love of her family, if what Iris said was true.

Not if you ruin this, she thought. They wouldn't love her then. She could only imagine their terrible disappointment that somehow, in spite of everything, Florence had managed to fail again.

Are you having doubts, Miss Maguire?

Another of Clement's questions.

She told herself she was being ridiculous. A wonderful new life was within her grasp, and she would be a fool not to take it. There was no question that she was going to take it. She had to take it.

*   *   *

There was no one in the shop when Florence arrived, but there was laughter coming from the back room. At the sound of the bell tinkling over the door, Joyce emerged, patting her hair and looking slightly flustered.

'Oh, hello,' she said. 'You're early.'

'Is everything all right?' Florence frowned.

'Yes, everything's fine. Wonderful, in fact.' Joyce beamed at her.

Just then, Charlie came out of the back room. He grinned sheepishly at Florence.

'You can keep an eye on the shop while I help Florence with her dress, can't you?' Joyce said.

Charlie nodded. Florence saw the smile that passed between them.

'What's going on?' she asked, as she followed Joyce into the back room.

'Nothing. Why do you ask?'

'You both seem very giddy, that's all.'

'I can't think why,' Joyce mumbled. But her blushing face told a different story. 'You wait there, I'll fetch your dress.'

'Joyce Shelby!' Florence confronted her friend when she returned. 'I've known you long enough to know when you're hiding something. So go on, what is it?'

Joyce was quiet for a moment, then she broke into a wide smile.

'I didn't want to say anything just yet because it's your big day,' she said. 'But I'm so happy, I can't keep it a secret!'

'Keep what a secret?'

'Charlie and I are engaged!'

Florence stared at her, stunned. 'You and Charlie?'

Joyce's smile faltered. 'I suppose you think I'm daft, don't you?'

'No, I'm just surprised, that's all. I had no idea the two of you . . .' she broke off, lost for words.

'I didn't know either,' Joyce confessed. 'It just crept up on us. He's been such a good friend to me all these years. He was at my side all through the nasty business with Reg, and ever since then he's been such a help to me. I wouldn't have been able to manage without him. But then I started to realise he meant more to me than that. I knew I had feelings for him. But I tried to ignore it because I thought he'd never feel the same way about me. But it turns out he did.' She smiled, a faraway look in her eyes.

'Oh Joyce,' Florence laughed. 'Anyone could have told you that!'

Joyce looked at her blankly. 'Really?'

'Why else would he have stayed here and put up with Reg Shelby for so many years?' Charlie Scuttle had always adored Joyce, right from when they were young and at school to-gether. But, like so many people, the war had come between them. By the time Charlie returned a broken shell of a man, Joyce had already married Reg.

But even then, Charlie had not given up. He'd gone to work for the Shelbys and put up with years of taunting and cruelty from Reg, just so he could watch over Joyce.

He might not have a voice, but Florence was pleased he had finally made his feelings for her clear in his own way.

'I wish I'd realised sooner,' Joyce said. 'I sound like a silly young girl, don't I? I know everyone's going to say I'm being daft, at my age.'

'Then I must be daft too,' Florence reminded her.

Joyce smiled. 'Charlie's not exactly like your handsome colonel though, is he? I daresay there will be those who wonder what I see in him. But I honestly can't imagine my life without him.' Embarrassed colour rose in her cheeks. 'Now I really do sound daft! But that's how love feels, isn't it? I'm sure I don't need to tell you that.'

Florence did not reply, but Joyce hardly seemed to notice. She chatted away happily as she helped Florence into her dress. Once again, Joyce had come to the rescue, lending her something from her own wardrobe when Florence had given up on her search for a wedding dress.

'I suppose it's mayhem at your house, isn't it? I bet your mother's up to her eyeballs in sausage rolls and bunting!'

'She is.' Florence thought about how she had woken up before dawn to the sound of May Maguire bustling about downstairs, preparing for the wedding. Florence wondered if she had even gone to sleep the previous night. 'You know how Ma likes a party.'

'This isn't just any party though, is it?' Joyce looked at Florence in the mirror. 'This is her daughter's wedding. I expect she's been planning it for years.'

'I daresay she gave up hope long ago!' Florence said. 'Anyway, it's not like I'm the first. She's already seen Iris and my two brothers married. And Iris and Jack have both wed twice.'

'Yes, but you're different,' Joyce said.

'Because she never expected it to happen?'

Joyce smiled. 'It will be special for her, you mark my words.'

As she fussed about with her dress, Florence stared blankly at her reflection in the looking glass. She could barely take in the woman in the cream flowery dress who stood before her.

Joyce finished doing up Florence's buttons and stepped back. 'Right, let's have a look at this dress, shall we? What do you think?'

'It's lovely,' Florence said.

'It's a shame you didn't go for a traditional white dress. You would have looked lovely in it.'

'I would have looked a fool,' Florence said. 'White dresses are for young girls, not an ugly old spinster like me.'

'Don't you dare say that about yourself, Florence Maguire! You're a beautiful woman, and you're marrying the man of your dreams.' Joyce sighed happily. 'We're so lucky, aren't we? Not everyone gets a second chance at happiness like us.'

'No,' Florence said, staring back at her reflection. 'No, they don't.'

Chapter 53

On the morning when she should have been sitting her board interview, Maudie went home for Aunt Florence's wedding.

She couldn't have done it, she told herself. Her mind was too foggy to even think about picking up her books. And every time she tried, she was filled with a deep hopelessness. What was the point, anyway? Promotion might have seemed so important once, but now it didn't matter at all.

But she still felt a twinge of regret as she sat on the bus looking out at the passing scenery. She knew how much Mitch had wanted her to pass the board interview, how proud he would have been if she'd made it to corporal.

Joan was disappointed, too. Maudie had offered to help her with her studying, but Joan insisted she was happy to carry on without her. Maudie wondered if her friend was angry with her for not seeing it through.

She looked down at her bare left hand. She had decided to leave her engagement ring off so she wouldn't have to answer questions from her mother, but now she was upset at herself for not wearing it.

She closed her eyes. She always seemed to be angry at herself one way or another these days.

The bus rumbled into the city. It still shocked Maudie to see the ugly, devastated streets that had once bustled with life. Even now, more than a year later, workmen still toiled to clear the piles of rubble and broken masonry where shops and buildings had once stood.

The bus passed down West Street and Maudie turned her head to see shoppers going in and out of the new Hammonds store. After the old premises had been flattened, a new store had been set up hastily in what had once been some old storerooms around the corner. Maudie and Sybil had both worked there for a few months before they were called up, and she remembered the chaos of trying to sell hats from makeshift counters, duckboards under their feet because it flooded so often.

She turned to Sybil to say something about it, then remembered her sister wasn't there. Two days earlier, Sybil had announced her leave had been cancelled and she had to stay behind at Holme.

At first, Maudie had been quite relieved. Things were still very strained between them, and she wasn't looking forward to having to pretend all was well at the wedding. But now it felt strange to be going home without her. Maudie couldn't remember a time when they had been apart for more than a few hours. Even though they were barely speaking, she was still always aware of Sybil's presence close by.

In a last-ditch attempt to make peace, Maudie had gone to look for Sybil before she left Holme, just to say goodbye. But she was nowhere to be found.

Maudie knew Sybil was hurt by what she had said. She regretted lashing out at her, and allowing years of resentment and bitterness to spill out. But that didn't stop her being angry. And she knew Sybil was angry too. Maudie even wondered if she had given up her own leave so that she wouldn't have to spend time with her.

Perhaps some time apart would do them both good, she thought. She was desperate to get home. The past month had been a real strain on her, pushing herself through each day, trying to keep up a pretence that her life was going on, even though she felt dead inside.

As she got off the bus, Pop was there waiting for her. Maudie nearly cried at the sight of him, perched on top of his rully, his cap pulled down low over his grizzled face.

'You didn't have to come,' she said, as she threw her bag into the back of the cart.

'I couldn't let you walk all the way to Hessle Road in the rain, could I? And, to be honest, I was glad of an excuse to get out of the house. It's pandemonium there, everyone running round like headless chickens.' He looked around. 'Where's your sister?'

'She in't coming. Her leave got cancelled at the last minute.'

'That's a shame. Our Sybil always loves a party.'

'Yes,' Maudie said. Pop had a point, she thought. Sybil would never have cancelled her own leave. She was far too selfish to miss out on anything.

She clambered up onto the bench seat beside Pop. Even that felt strange, not being crammed in beside her sister.

'How's Auntie Florence?' she asked, as she put up the umbrella he handed her.

'Very quiet,' Pop said. 'I think she's letting it all wash over her. But you know your aunt, she's never been much for a fuss.'

'She's in the wrong family, then!'

'Aye,' he grimaced.

Maudie glanced at her grandfather's pensive face. 'What do you think about her marrying an American?'

'If she's happy, I'm happy.' Pop's shoulders shifted under his old coat. 'But I'll miss her, I'll tell you that. She's always been my little girl.' He gave a sad smile. 'Still, she's a grown woman now. She can make up her own mind what she wants.'

They rode on for a while, the only sound the jingling of the leather reins and the slow, steady clop of Bertha's hooves. Maudie thought she could have probably walked home faster than the old horse moved.

Finally Pop said, 'I was sorry to hear about your young man. I know we only met him once but we were right fond of him.' He shook his head. 'It's a terrible shame, it really is. Life can be very cruel at times.'

Maudie curled her left hand to hide her bare engagement finger. She wished she had worn her ring. She owed that much to Mitch, at least.

'Still, at least you've got your sister with you,' Pop went on. 'She must be a comfort to you.'

'Hardly!' Maudie muttered.

Pop sent her a sideways look. 'You in't had a falling out?'

'You could say that.'

He sighed. 'Aye, well, you two were always scrapping, even when you were bains. You'll make it up in the end. You always do.'

'Not this time.'

His bushy brows rose. 'How's that, then?'

Maudie dropped her gaze. 'I don't want to talk about it.'

'Please yourself, love. I in't one to pry.' He turned back to watch the road in front of them. Then he said, 'But I wonder what that young man of yours would make of it all?'

Maudie fell silent, taking it in. Pop was right, Mitch wouldn't have wanted them to fall out. He was an only child himself, and he always used to say how lucky Maudie was to have a twin sister to share everything with.

'It's a cruel world, all right,' Pop mused out loud. 'But it strikes me that blaming each other in't going to make it any easier.'

Maudie glanced at her grandfather. Pop was a man of few words, but he was very wise.

She was still musing on what he had said when they reached Jubilee Row. As they turned the corner, Pop let out a groan.

'Now what's happened?' he said.

Maudie looked up to see front doors open all the way down the street. All the neighbours were out, milling about in the rain, talking amongst themselves.

Her grandmother came bustling up the street towards them, her hair still in curlers. Pop drew the cart to a halt and looked down at her.

'What's going on here?' he said.

'You might well ask.' Granny May looked grim. 'Have you seen our Florence?'

'Not since I left.' Pop frowned. 'I thought she was going to Joyce's to collect her dress?'

'Yes, well, she should have been back by now.'

The rest of the family had started to gather around the rully. Maudie's mother, Ruby, was there, looking worried, as were Uncle Jack and his wife Edie.

'I've asked all the neighbours,' Edie said. 'No one's seen her.'

'It's a mystery,' Ruby said, shaking her head.

'Do you think she's forgotten something?' Edie suggested.

'Aye. Forgotten to turn up to her own wedding!' Jack grinned. Edie nudged him in the ribs.

Just then, Auntie Iris came running down the street behind them, looking breathless. 'I've been down to the shop,' she said. 'Joyce doesn't know where she is. She said she went upstairs to fetch some pins, and when she came back, our Florence had gone.'

'And when was this?' Pop asked.

'About half an hour ago, Joyce said.'

'It don't take half an hour to get back from Anlaby Road,' Edie said.

Maudie's mother looked anxious. 'I hope she in't had an accident,' she said.

Pop shook his head. 'We've just come that way. We would have noticed if something was up.'

They all looked at each other, and Maudie could tell they were all thinking the same thing.

It was her mother who spoke up. 'You don't think . . .'

'I reckon so!' Jack laughed. 'It looks like our Florence has done a runner!'

Chapter 54

William looked shocked when he opened the door of his hotel room and saw Florence there.

'Sweetheart, what are you doing here? Is everything OK?' he asked.

Florence's heart lurched at the sight of him, with his fair hair rumpled and his shirt half unbuttoned.

She dragged her gaze back to his face. 'I need to talk to you,' she said.

'Can't it wait? We're getting married in an hour.'

She shook her head. 'We need to talk now.'

He stared at her for a moment, then nodded. 'OK. I'll meet you downstairs in five minutes,' he said.

Florence sat in the hotel foyer, her hands bunched in her lap, fingernails biting into the soft flesh of her palms. The hem of her beautiful dress was splashed with mud, and she could only imagine what the rain had done to her carefully styled curls under her headscarf.

People went past her, back and forth, going about their daily business. They didn't even spare a glance at the slightly bedraggled middle-aged woman. And why should they? They didn't know she was a bride on her wedding day. Or that she was about to make a decision that might change her life for ever.

But was it the right decision? Even now, Florence wasn't sure. All she knew was that, one way or another, nothing was going to be the same.

She looked up to see William walking towards her, looking impeccable in his Air Force uniform. A couple of women turned to watch him admiringly as he passed by.

He smiled uneasily as he sat down. 'You do realise it's bad luck for the bride to see the groom on their wedding day, don't you?'

'I know.'

'So what's so important that you had to break with tradition?'

Florence forced herself to meet his gaze, despite the nerves fluttering in her chest. 'I want to ask you a question,' she said.

'What's that?' He was smiling, intrigued.

'Will you live here with me?'

His brows locked in a frown. 'I don't understand.'

'I don't want to go to America. I want to stay here.'

'Honey, we talked about this—'

'No, we didn't. You just told me what was going to happen and assumed I'd be all right with it.'

William looked pained. 'But my family is in the States.'

'And my family is over here.'

'I didn't realise they meant so much to you.' His voice was cold. 'I got the feeling you couldn't wait to get away from them?'

That was before I realised that I might mean something to them. 'I know. But I've realised now I don't want to leave them. Ma and Pop aren't getting any younger. I'd hate to think I'd never see any of them again ...' Even just thinking about it brought a lump to her throat. 'They're important to me,' she said.

'More important than me?'

'I could ask you the same question about your family.'

They faced each other, and Florence could feel her heart hammering in her chest as William weighed up her words.

'And what would you have me do?' he said at last. 'Work on the trawlers with your brothers?'

'Why not?'

'It's hardly me!'

'And helping your mother with her charity work isn't me, either.'

'So you'd rather work in that typing pool of yours?'

She bristled at the sneer in his voice. 'I enjoy my work.'

'I know.' His tone softened. 'But I'm offering you a wonderful life, sweetheart. You must see that?'

'Yes, but it's not *my* life, is it?' Florence wanted to look away from the hurt and confusion in his eyes, but she forced herself to face him. 'You want me to step into your wife's shoes, to be her and do everything she would have done. But that's just not me.'

'No,' he said quietly. 'No, I suppose not.' He was silent for a long time, considering. 'How about if we didn't live with my folks?' he said at last. 'We could find a place of our own? How about that?'

'It's still a long way from my family.'

'Then I guess you leave me no choice, do you? If I want us to be together then I'll have to move here.'

Florence stared at him, lost for words. 'You'd do that – for me?' she managed at last.

'I'd do anything for you, Florence.' William's mouth curved into a knowing smile. 'But that's not what you want either, is it?'

'I . . . don't understand what you mean . . .'

'Sweetheart, I know we haven't been together for very long, but I reckon I understand you better than you think.' He reached for her hands. 'You don't really want to marry me, Florence. I'm not sure you ever did.'

324

'That's not true! Of course I want to marry you. Why else would I have said yes when you proposed?'

'I don't know. I've been trying to figure that out myself. Maybe my proposal caught you off guard, or maybe you really did think it was what you wanted. But whatever it is, I know you've been cooling off the idea ever since we got engaged.'

'I haven't!' Even as she said the words, she knew it was a lie. And William knew it too, she could see it in his eyes.

'Honey, please. Why not just be honest with yourself? You were more excited about that girl Gillian getting married than you were about your own wedding!' He smiled. 'Come on, admit it. You didn't come here to persuade me to come and live here with you. You were hoping I'd say no and give you a reason to call the wedding off.'

Florence faltered, her gaze dropping. If she was honest with herself, she had been wondering what she would do if William agreed to stay in England. Now, seeing the understanding on his face, she felt thoroughly ashamed of herself.

'I'm sorry,' she murmured. 'I thought this was what I wanted . . .'

'But it isn't, is it?'

'No.'

She slid the ring off her finger and looked down at it in her hand. Seeing the band of gold gleaming in her palm, for the first time she felt a moment's hesitation.

What was wrong with her? Why couldn't she be like other women? She couldn't imagine anyone else giving up the chance of a new life with a wonderful man like William Forrest.

'You can still change your mind?' William said softly.

It would be so easy. To slip that ring back on her finger, go through with the wedding. It would be easier than facing up to the consequences of what she was doing now.

But Florence had never taken the easy way out of anything.

'No.' She took a deep breath and handed the ring back to him. 'You take it. I hope one day you find someone who truly deserves it.'

'So do I.' William looked down at the ring in his hand, his face full of sorrow. 'I'm just so tired of being on my own,' he sighed. 'When my wife died, it near broke my heart. She was everything I'd ever wanted. I guess I've been looking for someone like her ever since.'

'And you'll find her one day, I'm sure.'

'I thought I had?'

Florence shook her head. 'I'm no Southern belle, William. I'm just a trawlerman's daughter from Hull.'

'That's more than enough for any man.'

They gazed at each other, and Florence felt the treacherous tug on her heart again.

'So what happens now?' William spoke, breaking the spell.

'I suppose I'd better go home. My family will be wondering what's happened to me. Although I can't say I'm looking forward to telling them,' she said ruefully.

'Do you want me to come with you?' William offered.

'No, thank you. I'd best do it myself.'

'Independent as always!'

Florence gave him a sad smile. 'I don't know how else to be.'

He walked her to the door, holding it open for her like the gentleman he was.

Florence peered out at the rain. 'Not such a nice day for a wedding,' she said grimly.

'I'd still marry you if it was a snowstorm.'

'Don't, William,' she pleaded.

'You're right. I'm sorry. Do you want to take shelter here while I find you a taxi?'

'I'd rather walk.'

William looked as if he might argue, then changed his mind. 'As you wish. So I guess this is where we say goodbye?' he said.

'I suppose so.'

He moved to kiss her, but Florence stuck out her hand to shake instead.

'Goodbye, William. I hope you find your Southern belle,' she said.

'And I hope you find the man you're looking for, too.'

She laughed. 'I haven't met him in forty-odd years, so I don't hold out much hope!'

'But you never know.'

'No,' she said, with a wistful smile. 'You never know.'

Chapter 55

The whole family was up in arms, running around in increasingly desperate circles.

'Where is she, do you think?'

'It in't like our Florence to flounce off and not tell anyone.'

'You don't think she's done anything daft, do you?'

'Get on with you. Since when did Florence do anything daft?'

Big May watched them all dashing about, knocking on doors and searching the streets, and said nothing. She knew exactly what was happening. It was all unfolding just as she had expected.

The rest of the family was so busy trying to find Florence, they didn't notice their mother's silence. Except for Pop, of course, who missed nothing after forty-five years of marriage.

'You're very quiet, May?' he commented when they were alone in the kitchen together. May was putting damp tea towels over the sandwiches and stacking them back in the larder. 'Do you know something we don't?'

'I don't know any more than you do,' she said. But she had her instincts. And they had seldom played her wrong.

Sure enough, half an hour later, Florence came in through the back door, looking very sorry for herself, her dress soaked through and her carefully coiffed hair blown into a bird's nest.

Of course, that led to even more uproar as the whole family gathered to find out what was going on.

'Thank God!' Pop cried. 'Jack and I were about to set off in the rully to look for you.'

'Look at your lovely dress!' Ruby said. 'It's ruined.'

'Never mind that. What about her hair?' Iris looked furious. 'It took me ages to set those curls. And if you think I've got the time to do it all again . . .'

'There's no need,' Florence said quietly. She looked very pale under her smudged make-up, May noticed.

'Oh, so you're going to walk down the aisle like that, are you?' Iris said. 'That'll be a treat for William . . .'

'Your sister's not walking down any aisle today,' May spoke up. Everyone turned to face her.

'What are you talking about, Ma?' Ruby asked.

May looked at Florence, staring into the dark eyes that were so like her own.

'There's not going to be a wedding,' she said. 'In't that right, Florence?'

Florence nodded slowly, her eyes never leaving her mother's face. 'That's right.'

That started them up again, all clamouring to talk at once.

'What's she talking about, Florence?'

'What's happened?'

'Have you got cold feet?'

'Don't talk soft, our Florence wouldn't get cold feet. More like the other way round!'

'Has he jilted you, Florence? Is that what's happened?' Ruby asked.

'If he has, I'll find him and take Bertha's whip to him!' Pop threatened.

'She's messed it up again, hasn't she?' Iris said. 'I might have known she'd end up ruining everything—'

'Leave her be, all of you!' May roared, silencing them. 'She's told you all you need to know, now stop mithering the lass.'

'Yes, but she can't leave it like this,' Iris protested. 'One minute there's going to be a wedding, and the next—'

'You heard your mother,' Pop joined in. 'Our Florence will tell us what's going on when she's ready.'

May took charge, handing out her orders to the rest of the family. 'Jack, take down all this bunting,' she said. 'And you girls get all this food put away in the larder.'

'There won't be enough room for it all,' Iris grumbled.

'Then take it out into the street and give it to the neighbours! I'm sure Beattie Scuttle can make use of a few sandwiches. But tell her not to bother coming up here snooping because she'll get nowt out of any of us. Is that understood?'

'Everyone's bound to ask questions—'

'Then send them to me!' May snapped. 'I'll soon let them know what's what!' She pushed up her sleeves as if squaring up for a fight.

The rest of the family headed off, and May turned to Florence, still standing in the back doorway, looking like a wet rag.

'Come on,' she said. 'Let's go upstairs and get you out of that dress, before you catch your death of cold.' She nodded to Pop. 'Put some pans on to boil, will you? She could do with a nice bath to warm her up.'

For once, Florence did not argue. She followed her mother upstairs to her bedroom and stood still while May undressed her like a child, unfastening the buttons down the back of her dress.

For a long time, neither of them spoke. May did not usually care for silences, but she understood this was one time when she should hold her tongue.

Finally Florence said, 'You don't seem very surprised.'

'I'm not. I could tell for a while you've been having doubts.'

330

'Could you?' Florence twisted round to look at her. Unguarded, her face looked young and vulnerable, framed by damp corkscrews of dark hair. 'Why didn't you say anything?'

'And have you accusing me of trying to ruin your big day?' May said. 'Anyway, knowing you, you would have probably married him just to prove me wrong.'

The shadow of a smile crossed Florence's face. 'Probably,' she murmured.

May helped her out of her dress and fetched her dressing gown from the hook on the door. She half expected Florence to shrug off her efforts to help her, but she succumbed meekly, like a child.

'I suppose they'll all be downstairs, having a good laugh at my expense,' she said bitterly.

'Never mind them.'

'I can just hear our Iris now. "Poor, pathetic Florence, letting a decent man slip through her fingers,"' she mimicked her sister's broad Hull accent.

'No one will say anything.' *Not while I'm around*, May thought.

'Yes, they will, and you know it! I've always been the butt of everyone's jokes.'

'Take no notice.'

'I don't,' Florence said. 'But it's hard sometimes, always feeling like the odd one out.' She looked down at her bare left hand.

May looked at her in surprise. 'Why on earth would you ever think that?'

'It's true, isn't it?' Florence's mouth twisted. 'It's always been you and the other girls, all pals together, going off shopping or cooking or running errands for each other. I've never been part of all that.'

'I never thought you wanted to be.'

331

'Didn't I?'

Florence looked at her, and for the first time, May saw the hurt she had always kept so well hidden behind that mask of indifference.

'You always seemed to look down on us,' May said.

'Yes, well, what was I supposed to do? You have to grow a thick skin, don't you?'

Looking at her daughter, May wondered how she had ever missed the loneliness behind that tough, defiant front she put up. If only she had known, things might have been very different for them all.

'I didn't think you needed me,' she said quietly. 'You were always so independent, even as a bain. And happen I did treat you differently because of that. But that doesn't mean I thought any less of you. You're still my daughter, and I'd defend you to my last breath. I hope you know that?'

They faced each other across the room for a moment, before May quickly bent down to gather up Florence's wet dress and shoes from the floor. She wasn't one for talking about her feelings, and she sensed Florence was uncomfortable with it, too.

Perhaps they were more alike than either of them imagined, she thought.

'I should go downstairs and face the music,' Florence said. 'I daresay they'll all have something to say about it!' She looked pale and sick at the prospect.

'You leave everyone to me,' May said. 'No one will say anything to you while I'm around. Besides, we're all on your side, don't forget. We're your family, Florence. And families stick together, come what may.'

Impulsively, she reached out and patted her daughter's hand. They were both still for a moment, looking down at their hands touching. Then May pulled her fingers away.

'I'll go and see if Pop's drawn that bath yet,' she said.

'Thank you.' There was a warmth in her daughter's voice that May had seldom heard before.

'Whatever for?'

'For looking after me.'

'You're my little girl. What else would I do?'

As she reached the door, Florence said, 'Are you sure you don't mind that I'm not going to America?'

'Well, I would've been glad of the extra room ...' May started to say, then stopped herself. 'But I would have missed you,' she added.

Florence smiled. 'I would have missed you too, Ma.'

Chapter 56

Maudie returned to RAF Holme in a state of high excitement.

She couldn't quite believe what had happened the previous day. Imagine, staid old Auntie Florence running away from her own wedding! And to think Pop had said that she wasn't one for making a fuss. She had certainly set the cat among the pigeons yesterday. It had been the talk of Jubilee Row, at least until Granny May stepped in and put a stop to the gossip.

'I'll not have anyone talking about our Florence, is that understood?' she had warned the family. 'And if any of the neighbours have got anything to say about it, they can speak to me.'

There was the glint of battle in her eyes as she said it. Maudie knew it would have to be a very brave or foolish person who spoke out of turn to Big May Maguire.

Sybil would have been so disappointed to have missed all the drama, Maudie thought. Even when it was all unfolding around her, her first thought was that her sister should have been there to share it with her. And she certainly wouldn't have let Granny May's threats stop her gossiping about it, either.

It made Maudie realise how much she missed her sister. Nothing was as much fun without Sybil.

Pop was right, she thought. Blaming her sister for her pain certainly didn't make it go away. And she knew she was blaming Sybil unfairly. Mitch's death had wrenched her heart out. She needed to focus all her pain and rage on someone, so she had chosen her sister. But it wasn't Sybil's fault.

She just hoped her sister would forgive her, and that they could mend the rift between them. Pop had said that they never stayed angry with each other for long. Perhaps he would be right about that, too?

The hut was empty when she arrived. Sybil must still be on duty, Maudie thought. She was unpacking when two Signals girls, Polly and Kate, walked in.

'You're back,' Polly grinned. 'How did you get on?'

'Was it awful?' Kate said.

Maudie frowned. Surely they couldn't be talking about the wedding? 'Well . . .'

'You wouldn't catch me doing it, that's for sure,' Polly said.

'Me neither,' Kate agreed. 'Although I suppose it might be worth it, if it meant we didn't have to take any more orders from Corporal Kent . . .'

'That's true,' Polly said. 'D'you know, she confiscated my flask the other day? I'd hidden it so carefully in my kitbag, too. She must have gone through it like a bloodhound. And it took me ages to scrounge it off the flying boys, too . . .'

Maudie stared from one to the other, completely mystified. 'What are you talking about?' she asked.

'Your board interview?' Polly said. 'That's where you've been, isn't it?'

Maudie shook her head. 'You're mistaken,' she said. 'I haven't—'

Before she could finish her sentence, the door to the hut opened and Miss Leech, the section officer, strode in. Maudie and the other girls immediately straightened up and saluted.

'At ease, girls.' Miss Leech smiled at them all, then turned to Maudie. 'You've returned at the right time, Maguire. I've just received a telephone call from the Commission Board.'

Maudie stared at her. Why was everyone speaking in riddles all of a sudden?

'Don't look so worried, girl. You passed with flying colours.' The section officer smiled. 'Although I wouldn't have expected anything less from you.'

Behind her, Polly and Kate both gave a little cheer, which quickly ended when the section officer raised her eyebrows at them.

'I'm so glad you changed your mind and decided to go ahead with your application,' Miss Leech said to Maudie with a smile. 'I knew you could do it.'

'But I don't understand. How—'

At that moment, the door burst open and Sybil flew in.

'Maudie! Thank heavens you're back. Look, there's something you need to—' She saw the section officer and screeched to a halt, her mouth slammed shut.

Miss Leech sighed. 'One day, Maguire, you will remember to salute when you see me,' she said.

'Yes, ma'am. Sorry, ma'am.' Sybil snapped her right hand up, dislodging her cap and sending it sliding down her nose as usual.

The section officer shook her head. 'If only you could be more like your sister,' she said.

'Yes, ma'am.' Sybil straightened her cap and lowered her gaze.

Maudie watched tensely as the section officer looked her sister up and down, inspecting her from head to toe.

'Well,' she said finally. 'That makes a change, doesn't it? For once, your appearance doesn't disappoint. Perhaps you are starting to take after your sister, after all? Who knows, if you buck your ideas up, you might even end up a corporal like her?'

'Yes, ma'am. Thank you, ma'am.'

She left, and Polly and Kate followed her, leaving the two of them alone together.

Sybil grinned. 'Did I hear that right? You're Corporal Maguire now?'

Maudie turned to her. 'Would you mind telling me what's going on?'

A blush rose in Sybil's face. 'Before you start, it wasn't all my idea.' She was gabbling, a sure sign she was guilty of something. 'But Joan and I talked about it, and we agreed you'd already lost so much, we just couldn't bear the idea of you losing your commission, too. Especially when you'd worked so hard for it . . .'

'I still don't understand. What did you—' And then, suddenly, it dawned on her. 'Oh, Sybil, you didn't?'

'It wasn't that difficult to fool them, honestly.' She was off again, gabbling nineteen to the dozen. 'It helped that you were off on leave anyway. All I had to do was persuade the general duties WAAF that she'd got us mixed up, and that Sybil was the one on leave and I was the one doing the board interview.'

'But I cancelled the interview.'

'And I un-cancelled it.' Sybil smiled brightly. 'As I said, it wasn't that difficult to persuade them they'd made a mistake. Those general duties WAAFs in't all that bright, as it turns out.' She looked at Maudie. 'What's the matter? I thought you'd be pleased?'

'Pleased? Do you know what a terrible risk you took? We could have both been up on a serious charge if you'd been found out. We might even have been thrown out altogether.' She shook her head. 'Of all the stupid, irresponsible things to do . . .'

'Well, I think she was very brave.'

Maudie looked up. She hadn't heard Joan come into the hut. She stood in the doorway now, watching them both.

'Of course she knew she could get into trouble,' she said. 'But she took the risk anyway because she cares about you and she was so desperate to help you.'

Maudie glanced at Sybil. She looked close to tears.

'You have no idea how hard she worked,' Joan went on. 'She's been studying every spare minute to get through this interview. It wasn't easy for her, but she did it for you.'

'And I passed,' Sybil said quietly.

Joan turned to her, smiling. 'Did you? Well done! You see, I told you you could do it.'

'Thanks to you,' Sybil said. 'If you hadn't helped me, I would have been lost.'

Joan shook her head. 'You were the one that put the hard work in. You should be proud of yourself.'

'Thank you.'

Maudie looked at her sister. Sybil seemed to be standing straighter, her chin held high.

'I can't believe you did it for me,' she murmured.

'I had to do something, after everything you've done for me over the years.'

Maudie lowered her gaze. 'I'm sorry,' she said. 'I shouldn't have lashed out at you like that. I was just upset—'

'You had every right to be,' Sybil interrupted her. 'I know I've been selfish and thoughtless over the years. And you're right – I have taken you for granted. Joan told me about you giving up your chance to join the Wrens,' she said.

'It wouldn't have been any fun without you.'

They smiled at each other hesitantly. 'Does this mean I'm forgiven?' Sybil said.

'If you'll forgive me?'

'There's nowt to forgive.'

Joan looked from one to the other. 'Right, now you two have finally made up, perhaps we should go and celebrate getting our commissions?' she said. 'If you don't mind me tagging along with you two, that is?' she said to Sybil.

'Don't be like that!' Sybil looked abashed. 'Any friend of Maudie's is a friend of mine.'

Maudie hesitated. 'I'm not sure it's right if I come,' she said. 'After all, I wasn't the one that passed the board interview. You earned that commission, Syb, not me.'

'Yes, but I did it for you,' Sybil said. 'And you put in just as much work as I did. You know you would have passed it yourself. Anyway,' she added with a grin, 'can you honestly imagine me as a corporal?'

'Why not?' Joan said. 'You've proved you could do it.'

'She's right,' Maudie said. 'You're just as good as anyone else.'

Sybil looked shyly pleased with herself. 'Happen I in't so stupid after all,' she mumbled.

'There's nothing stupid about you, Sybil Maguire,' Maudie said. 'You might act a bit daft at times, but you certainly in't stupid!'

Sybil grinned. 'You're stuck with me, though.'

'And I wouldn't have it any other way,' Maudie said.

Chapter 57

June 1943

Sybil was late again.

Maudie stood shivering outside the railway station, stamping her feet to bring some life into them. Any promise of summer had been dampened by three days of solid rain. It dripped off the peak of her cap and trickled down in icy rivulets inside her collar.

Typical Syb! She cursed her sister under her breath. She had probably lost track of time again and completely forgotten they were supposed to meet. One of these days she would learn to look at her watch, Maudie thought irritably.

She had just made up her mind to go without her when suddenly, out of nowhere, an RAF truck swerved round the corner and sped up Ferensway towards her. Maudie just had time to jump out of the way before it screeched to a halt in front of her, sending up a spray of muddy water that narrowly missed her shoes.

Maudie looked up, ready to give the driver a mouthful, and was astonished to see her twin sister grinning at her from behind the wheel.

'Bet you weren't expecting that, were you?' Sybil called cheerfully as she clambered out.

Maudie stared at her in astonishment. 'When did you learn to drive?'

'Malcolm's teaching me. I haven't got the hang of braking yet, though. Have I, Malcolm?' She gave him a cheery wave.

Maudie looked at the ashen face of the young LAC as he clambered into the driving seat. He looked as if his nerves couldn't take another driving lesson.

'Shall we go?' Sybil said, threading her arm through Maudie's. 'We don't want to be late, do we?'

'I thought you'd abandoned me?'

'As if I would! Sorry I was late. Q-Queenie had a problem with her bomb bay doors that needed fixing.'

'Did you manage it?'

'Of course – it just needed a few new rivets put in.'

Maudie shook her head. 'I still can't believe you're a mechanic now!'

'I know!' Sybil smiled. 'Who'd have thought it, eh? Me, going from selling hats to fixing planes!'

One day, out of the blue, Sybil had suddenly announced that she wanted to retrain as a mechanic. It sounded like one of her whims and no one ever imagined she would get through the training, least of all Maudie. But Sybil had surprised them all with her hard work, her dedication and her willingness to get her hands dirty.

'You know me,' she said. 'I was never really cut out for office work.'

'So you don't miss the Met Office, then?'

'No more than they miss me!' Sybil grimaced. 'I think Flight Lieutenant Ormerod did a little dance the day I left!'

Maudie looked at her sister's stripes. 'I'm so glad you decided to do the board interview,' she said. 'You deserved that promotion.'

'I thought I might as well, since I'd already done the work the first time round,' Sybil shrugged. 'Besides, I've got to keep up with you, in't I? We are twins, after all. Even if I never get to see you these days.'

Parting had been really hard. When Maudie got the news that she was being posted to RAF Church Fenton, she had expected Sybil to put in for a transfer too. But, to her surprise, her sister had decided to stay put.

'I've only just started retraining,' she had said. 'Besides, it might do us good to have some time apart.'

Maudie had agreed at the time. But she was finding the separation a lot harder than Sybil. While her sister was flourishing in her new role and making friends among the boys in the ground crews, Maudie was struggling to find her feet.

There was a lot to be said for her new posting. Church Fenton was a fighter station, which came as a welcome change from all the bombing missions. There were lots of foreign crews there, which was interesting, and Maudie had made some friends among the other WAAFs.

And being away from Holme meant she was not constantly surrounded by memories. But even though there were no physical reminders, that didn't stop her missing Mitch. She carried his loss with her like a scar on her heart.

And, of course, she missed Sybil, far more than she ever imagined she would. She missed her sister's antics, her mishaps, her sense of adventure. Maudie had always prided herself on being the sensible one, but she was beginning to realise how much laughter and fun Sybil brought into her life.

As they headed down Hessle Road, they discussed the wedding they had returned home to attend.

'I hope the bride doesn't do a runner this time!' Maudie said.

'I hope she does.' Sybil was furious to have missed all the excitement of Auntie Florence's non-existent wedding. She had made Maudie describe every excruciating detail to her.

'I was surprised when I found out Joyce Shelby was getting married, weren't you?' Maudie said.

Sybil nodded. 'I never imagined she'd do it, especially after what she went through with Reg.'

'And marrying Charlie Scuttle, of all people,' Maudie said. 'I mean, I like him. But I wonder what she sees in him . . .'

'Yes, well, you can't always choose who you fall in love with.'

Maudie looked sideways at her sister. 'You sound as if you're speaking from experience?' she said.

'Me? Don't be daft!' But Sybil's blushing face gave her away.

'Go on, who is he? And don't you lie to me, Sybil Maguire, because Joan's already told me in her last letter that you've got a new man.'

'Joan talks too much,' Sybil muttered, hiding a smile. 'Anyway, he's no one special.'

But she didn't meet her eye as she said it, and Maudie knew she was lying.

She also knew why.

'It's all right, you can talk about him,' she said. 'I won't get upset, I promise.'

Sybil hesitated, eyeing her warily. 'His name's Eric,' she said at last. 'He's a mechanic.'

Maudie grinned. 'Don't tell me. He's tall, dark and handsome?'

'Actually, he's short and stocky and his hair's sort of mousey brown. I don't even know why I like him.' Sybil looked so puzzled about it, Maudie had to laugh.

'It must be love!' she said.

'Don't talk soft!' Sybil's colour deepened. 'I just like being with him, that's all. He makes me laugh.'

Maudie squeezed her sister's linked arm. 'I'm happy for you, I really am,' she said.

Sybil sent her a sideways look. 'I wasn't sure whether to tell you about him,' she said. 'It didn't seem right, after . . .'

'I know,' Maudie said. 'And I appreciate it. But you not being happy in't going to bring Mitch back, is it?'

'I suppose not.' Sybil looked sombre.

* * *

It was good to be home again.

They found their mother in the kitchen as usual, her hair in curlers and an apron over her best dress, putting the finishing touches to the wedding feast. The kitchen table was covered in plates of sandwiches and fancy cakes, all covered in damp tea towels to keep them from drying out.

She looked over her shoulder at them as they came in through the back door, dragging their kitbags behind them.

'There you are,' she scolded. 'I was beginning to think you weren't coming.'

'Sorry, Mum. Sybil had to stop and fix a plane,' Maudie said.

Their mother looked nonplussed for a moment, as if she couldn't quite believe what she was hearing. Then she turned back to the bread she was buttering. 'Hurry up and get dressed – you don't have much time,' she said. 'The wedding starts in half an hour.'

'If it happens,' Sybil said, winking at Maudie.

'Don't say that! It took us three days to eat all the sandwiches after last time.'

'I'm here this time. I'll make sure nothing goes to waste.' Sybil sneaked her hand under the tea towel to help herself to a sandwich, but her mother batted her hand away.

'Go and get dressed!' she said. Then, as they turned to go, she added, 'I nearly forgot. There's a letter for you on the hallstand, Maudie.'

Maudie frowned. 'Who'd be writing to me here?'

'I don't know. It looks as if they wrote to you at Holme and it got forwarded on here. I was going to send it to Church Fenton, but I thought I might as well leave it, seeing as you were coming home anyway.'

As they headed into the hall, Sybil whispered, 'Did I tell you Teddy Jarvis has been posted down to Uxbridge? And she broke it off with Tom Davenport before she left, too. He's utterly devastated, so I hear. Serves him right, I say. Now he knows what it feels like to — Maudie? What is it? What's wrong?'

Maudie couldn't answer her. She was too busy staring at the letter propped on the hallstand. The original address had been scrawled out, but she recognised the handwriting.

'It's from Mitch's mother,' she said quietly. She had been meaning to write to her with her Church Fenton address, but in the three weeks she had been there, she hadn't got around to it.

'What's she got to say, I wonder?' Sybil said.

'I-I don't know.' But she did know. That was the reason her skin crawled with fear and she couldn't bring herself to pick it up.

There was only one reason why Mrs Mitchell would be writing to her. To tell her that Mitch had been confirmed dead.

'In't you going to open it?' Sybil asked.

'I-I can't . . .'

'Here, let me.' Before she could stop her, Sybil had snatched up the envelope and was ripping it open. Maudie watched her, helpless with fear.

'What does it say?' she whispered. 'No, don't tell me, I don't want to know.' She watched the colour drain from her sister's face as she scanned the letter. 'Oh God, he's dead, in't he?' she groaned. 'I knew it. That's why I didn't want to—'

'He's alive.'

Maudie stared at her, too frightened to believe what she was hearing. 'What?'

'They've just had official word that he was taken prisoner. He's in a POW camp in Italy.'

For a moment, they stared at each other. Maudie was too numb to speak.

She remembered Annie Mitchell's words. *I'm his mother. I'd know if anything had happened to him. I'd feel it, wouldn't I?*

All this time, Maudie had thought she was clinging to false hope. But it turned out she was right all along.

'Are you two still not getting ready—' Their mother appeared in the doorway. Her face dropped when she saw Maudie. 'What's happened?'

Maudie opened her mouth to speak, but no sound came out.

'Mitch is alive,' Sybil spoke up for her.

Their mother's face lit up. 'Is he coming home?'

Maudie looked back at the letter Sybil had handed her. 'I-I don't think so,' she said. 'He's still a prisoner . . .' The reality hit her like a blow.

'But he's alive,' Sybil reminded her. 'That means he'll come home to you one day.'

I'll always find a way home to you.

Maudie stared down at the letter. 'Yes,' she said. 'Yes, he will.' And she didn't care how long it took, because she would be there waiting for him.

Chapter 58

'Talk about always the bridesmaid, never the bride!'

John grinned at his own joke, but for once the rest of the family weren't amused. They pounced on him straight away.

'That's enough, John!' his mother snapped at him.

'You in't funny,' Iris joined in.

'It's all right,' Florence said. 'I don't mind our John having a laugh at my expense.'

But she was grateful to her family for their support. Her mother had been as good as her word. Florence didn't know what had been said, but her sisters and sisters-in-law had all rallied round her, shielding her from gossip. No one asked any questions or passed comment on Florence's failed wedding while they were around.

But John, typically, had returned home from sea the day before and blundered straight in.

'Sorry, sis,' he mumbled. 'I was only larking about.'

'I know, John.' Florence smiled at him. It was impossible to be angry with him, whatever he said.

'You look very nice, by the way.'

'Thank you. Iris showed me how to do my hair and make-up.' Florence smiled sheepishly at her sister. Iris and Edie had taken her in hand over the past couple of months, showing her which hairstyles suited her and how to put make-up on properly. Florence had never known there was

347

so much to dabbing on a bit of powder and lipstick. 'I only hope I do Joyce proud,' she said.

'From what I can tell, Joyce is so over the moon with happiness, she wouldn't notice if you turned up dressed in a flour sack with Pop's old cap on your head!' Iris laughed.

She was right, too. Joyce was utterly radiant with joy when Florence went round to Shelby's shop with Pop on the rully to pick her up. Her father Horace travelled with them so he could give his daughter away.

'Will I do?' Joyce asked shyly, doing a little twirl in front of her.

'You look beautiful,' Florence replied. She meant it, too, and not just because of the elegant cream two-piece she wore. Love had transformed Joyce Shelby. Her face was flushed and youthful, and her eyes sparkled with happiness. Seeing her friend look so full of joy convinced Florence even more that she had made the right decision not to marry William. In all the time they had been together, she had never radiated the same love and happiness that Joyce did. 'Charlie's a lucky man.'

Joyce blushed. 'We're both lucky,' she said quietly.

Charlie had scrubbed up well, too. Florence scarcely recognised the tall, handsome man in a smart suit who stood beside his brother Sam in the register office. Charlie no longer shambled with his head down, but walked with confidence and pride, holding himself straight.

And, to everyone's surprise, he even managed to say his vows. He stuttered painfully over every word, and Florence could see the sheer effort on his face as he stumbled through the lines. But he was determined to do it for Joyce's sake, and by the end of the service, Florence noticed even her tough older brothers surreptitiously wiping away tears on their jacket sleeves.

Afterwards, they all gathered at Beattie Scuttle's house for the celebration.

'It should be the bride's family that organises it all by rights, but we all know Constance Huggins would never do anything like that for her daughter,' Beattie said, her lips pursed disapprovingly. 'She's far too house-proud to let anyone through her front door!'

'At least you haven't had to do it for once, Granny May,' Sybil said.

'Who do you think made that meat and potato pie?' May grumbled. 'Beattie Scuttle's always had a very heavy hand with pastry.'

All the while they were talking, Florence kept glancing around her. Harry Pearce had wasted no time in sitting down at the piano, and people were beginning to sing and dance.

'Are you looking for someone?' John asked.

'I did invite someone,' Florence mumbled, embarrassed. 'But I only mentioned it in passing. He probably won't even remember . . .'

'He?' John's brows rose questioningly. 'Have you got another man, Florence Maguire?'

Florence felt herself blushing. 'Stop it, John, it's nothing like that . . .'

'I don't know,' John shook his head. 'You'll get a reputation, you will, chopping and changing your boyfriends. You're worse than our Sybil!'

'Two boyfriends in twenty-five years hardly makes me a heartbreaker, does it?'

'So you admit he's your boyfriend?'

'No! That's not what I meant and you know it!'

John laughed. 'I'm only teasing you.' He lowered his voice. 'And between you and me, I'm glad you didn't marry that Yank.'

'I thought you liked him?'

'I did. But I didn't like the idea of you going to live in America.' He leaned closer. 'Don't tell anyone,' he said in a low voice, 'but you're actually my favourite sister.'

'I'll let our Iris know that, shall I?'

'If you tell her, I'll say you made it up.' John looked past her towards the door. 'Don't look now, but someone's just walked in, and he's looking a bit lost. Tall, skinny man, untidy-looking, walks with a limp. That wouldn't be your friend, would it?'

'That's him!' Florence swung round to wave at Clement, who stood in the doorway. He waved back and started to make his way over to her.

'I can tell by the way your face just lit up,' John said wryly.

'Shut up, John, and fetch me another drink!' Florence pushed him away just as Clement approached them.

She could already feel herself blushing.

'Hello,' she said. 'I wasn't sure if you would come . . .'

'Yes, well, my social diary is rather full at the moment, but I managed to squeeze you in.'

'I can well imagine.'

'Seriously, it was very kind of you to invite me. It certainly beats sitting at home staring at four walls.'

'That doesn't say much, does it?'

'I'm sorry,' he said. 'I'm rather out of practice at this sort of thing. Gwendoline was always the social butterfly. Rather too social at times,' he added ruefully.

At least he could smile about it now, Florence thought. He had done his best to stay cheerful, but she knew the last three months had been very difficult for him. Gwendoline had quickly realised that living life alone wasn't as appealing as she had thought and had made a few efforts at a reconciliation. But for once Clement had stood firm.

He looked her up and down. 'I like your dress,' he said.

'Thank you.' She looked back at him. His tie was slightly askew and his shirt collar was slightly frayed.

Before Clement could say any more, John came barging over, a drink in each hand.

'Hello,' he said. 'I'm John, Florence's youngest and most favourite brother.'

'Clement Saunders. Her least favourite Administration Manager.'

He held out his hand and John stuck a glass of beer in it.

'I don't know about least favourite,' he said. 'She seemed very anxious for you to arrive.'

'I was not!' Florence protested.

'She was practically climbing the walls,' John went on, ignoring her. 'I swear she was pining.'

'Was she, indeed?' Clement raised his brows. 'I can't really imagine Miss Maguire pining.'

'Certainly not!' Florence snapped.

'Miss Maguire?' John snorted with laughter. 'Oh dear, that's not a good sign, is it?'

'She won't let me call her anything else.'

'I'm sure she would, if you asked her nicely . . .'

'John!' Florence turned on him, exasperated. 'Can't you go and annoy someone else?'

'I'm sure she'd dance with you too, if you asked her?'

'Mr Saunders doesn't dance, and neither do I.'

'Oh, I don't know. I'm game to try if you are?' Clement winked at her.

'Are you sure? I thought you couldn't . . .' She looked down at his leg.

'I can still shuffle around a bit. Gwendoline always refused to dance with me because she said I made her look foolish.'

Florence had had no intention of taking to the dance floor, but something about his downcast expression changed her mind.

'Well, I'm sure I shall look foolish anyway, so it makes no difference to me,' she said.

'In that case, shall we make fools of ourselves together?' He held out his hands to her.

'That's the spirit!' John encouraged.

'All right,' Florence said. 'But only to get away from you!' she glared at her brother.

There wasn't a lot of room to dance in Beattie Scuttle's tiny front parlour. Clement and Florence found themselves pressed awkwardly close together as they turned in a small circle together.

'I'm sorry,' Clement said. 'I'm not very good at this, am I?'

'Neither am I.'

Florence thought about all those nights dancing with William, how he would spin and swing her around like an expert. And yet somehow her heart had never raced the way it did dancing in Clement Saunders' arms.

It must be the heat in the room, she thought. Perhaps someone should open a window?

Clement must have felt it too, because after a minute or two, he said, 'How about we stop before we break each other's toes?'

'Good idea.'

They walked off the dance floor, Clement leading her by the hand. As he went to fetch them both a drink, Florence caught her mother watching her from the other side of the room.

'Here you are.' Clement was back, handing her a port and lemon. He held a glass of beer in his other hand. 'By the way, I haven't told you my news, have I?'

'What's that?' Florence asked, her gaze still fixed on her mother.

'I'm leaving the Corporation.'

Florence swung round to face him. 'What? When? Where are you going?'

'So many questions!' Clement laughed. 'I'm going back to school. I applied for a post as a schoolmaster in Hedon and I received a letter this morning to say I'd been appointed. I shall be handing in my resignation on Monday morning, but I thought I'd let you know first.'

'That's wonderful news. I'm so pleased.'

'I thought you'd say that,' he smiled. 'Just think, you'll never have to shudder at my messy desk ever again.'

'I mean I'm pleased for you,' Florence said. 'I know how much you loved being a teacher.'

'Yes, I did. And now Gwendoline's gone, it finally dawned on me that I didn't have to spend any more time trying to fit into a job I was so clearly ill-suited for. Of course, I'll be recommending that you're appointed manager in my place,' he went on.

'Well, I don't know about that . . .'

'Don't be modest. We both know you're the only one who could do that job. Lord knows, you've been all but running the place since I got there!' he grinned. 'Honestly, I couldn't think of anyone who would deserve it more.'

Florence turned away, embarrassed by the warmth of his gaze, and found herself looking back at her mother across the room. Big May Maguire was still watching her with a look of intrigue on her face.

'I'll miss you,' Clement said suddenly.

'Oh.' Florence froze, not quite sure what to say.

'I was wondering,' he went on, 'if perhaps we might meet sometime? Now you're not having to scold me about my work, I thought perhaps we could be friends? Of course, I quite understand if that would be out of the question . . .'

Florence opened her mouth to speak, then caught her mother's eye across the room. As if she knew what was being said, she gave her daughter an encouraging nod.

'I'd like that,' she said.

'Would you? Would you really?' His face brightened. 'Oh well, in that case,' he held up his glass, 'here's to new beginnings, Miss Maguire.'

She lifted her glass to meet his. 'Please,' she said. 'Call me Florence.'

Acknowledgements

My thanks to Rhea Kurien for stepping into the breach at the last moment and for all her helpful advice. Also to Sanah Ahmed for steering the book so deftly through the production process. I'd also like to thank my agent Caroline Sheldon and my family for their endless patience, as always

Credits

Orion Fiction would like to thank everyone at Orion who worked on the publication of *A Daughter's Hope* in the UK.

Editorial
Rhea Kurien
Sanah Ahmed

Copyeditor
Clare Wallis

Proofreader
Jade Craddock

Audio
Paul Stark
Jake Alderson

Production
Ruth Sharvell

Editorial Management
Charlie Panayiotou
Jane Hughes
Bartley Shaw
Tamara Morriss

Contracts
Anne Goddard
Humayra Ahmed
Ellie Bowker

Design
Debbie Holmes
Joanna Ridley
Nick May

Sales
Jen Wilson
Esther Waters
Victoria Laws
Rachael Hum
Anna Egelstaff
Frances Doyle
Georgina Cutler

Operations
Jo Jacobs
Sharon Willis

If you enjoyed *A Daughter's Hope*, don't miss the
first book in the sweeping saga from *Sunday Times*
bestseller Donna Douglas . . .

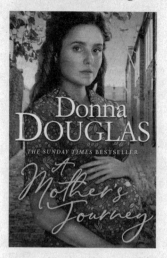

**Yorkshire, 1940. Edie Copeland has just arrived on Jubilee Row,
carrying a suitcase and a secret.**

She left York and her job at the Rowntrees Factory after tragedy
struck to make a fresh start, but she's a stranger to this street, and her
fellow tenant doesn't hesitate to remind her of this, widow or no.

Luckily, the neighbours are a little more welcoming and Edie is soon
made to feel at home by the Maguires and the Scuttles. As air raids
sound, and the war feels closer than ever, the community has to stick
together.

**But Edie is hiding something, and she doesn't know how much
longer she can keep it up. Is the past going to catch up with her?
And will Edie still be able to call Jubilee Row home when the truth
comes out?**

And follow up with the second book in the Yorkshire Blitz Trilogy . . .

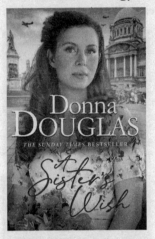

Spring, 1941. The families of Jubilee Row are still reeling from the loss of one of their own, and as the Blitz on Hull intensifies, it seems as if there will be more tragedies to come.

As the street braces itself, Iris Fletcher returns home from the hospital, where she has been recovering after the death of her best friend and youngest child. But Iris has no time to mourn - devastated by the loss of their little sister, Archie and Kitty desperately need their mother.

Meanwhile, Edie Copeland is besotted with her infant son. Being a single mother is hard, but Edie finds support in the form of Jack Maguire who, like Edie, is raising his boys alone. As the pair grow closer, Edie begins to wonder whether they could ever be anything more than friends.

Capable mum, Ruby Maguire takes charge as usual, bolstering spirits and lending a hand, as well as trying to keep her flighty sister Pearl on the straight and narrow. But the unexpected appearance of a face from her past threatens Ruby's future far more than Hitler's bombs.